Eternal Fire

Eternal Fire

A Novel
by

Michel Fattah

ROUNDTABLE PUBLISHING, INC.
Santa Monica   California

Fic

ROUNDTABLE PUBLISHING, INC.
933 Pico Boulevard
Santa Monica, CA 90405

447p.

First Printing, 1987

Library of Congress Catalog Card Number—83—063202

PRINTED IN THE UNITED STATES OF AMERICA

Contents

Prologue—1903

PART I
ASHES—1904-1906

PART II
EMBERS—1907-1913

PART III
SPARKS—1913-1917

PART IV
FLAMES—1917-1921

Epilogue—1926

To Shirley

Eternal Fire

Prologue—1903

It was one of those childhood events that would not fade into uncertain memory, but would linger as fresh and clear as the day it happened, molding and shaping and influencing the rest of life's events. Gregor had been only ten years old at the time, but even then he sensed there was something very special about the experience.

It had been a splendid day for an outing—a Sunday in May, with the early morning sky nearly cloudless. Most days a heavy black haze hovered over the city of Baku, but this morning it had been swept out to sea by a fresh breeze. The city, with its one tall mosque that dated back to the eleventh century and its broad boulevard by the sea, looked almost beautiful. The water in the harbor was a dark blue-gray, and the sunlight danced on the tips of small breakers. Beyond, the Caspian seemed to stretch forever.

Gregor hoped someday to be able to board one of the large steamers that were always in the harbor of Baku and travel to far-off places—cities with magical sounding names—Enzeli, Tehran, Paris, Moscow, London. He realized, of course, that it was impractical for a boy to dream of such things, but he had already had experiences that most of his friends in the neighborhood had not. For one thing, he attended school, not the Moslem school that taught only the Koran, but the Christian school that taught things like mathematics, history, and geography. It was at his school that he had learned these places with the magical sounding names existed, and the simple knowledge of such things made them seem attainable.

It had been Gregor's insatiable desire for knowledge that had prompted his father to plan that particular day's outing. He had recollections of his mother's parents, who had died only a few years before, but he knew nothing about his father's family, only that he had an Uncle Vladimir who lived in Baku, an uncle he had never met. After hearing his parents argue about his uncle, Gregor had begun to ask questions of his father, learning that

Alexei Mehdovi had not grown up in Baku, as Mama had, but in the country, and that his parents had died when he was very young. There had been some dispute, which Papa would not talk about, between him and his older brother, Vladimir.

At first, Papa had been annoyed by the questions. However, once he had begun talking about his youth, he seemed to enjoy recalling his memories with his son and daughter. This had prompted him to plan a picnic at the place where he had spent his boyhood.

Papa had borrowed a horse and wagon; Mama had prepared baskets of food and had dressed the children in their best clothes, admonishing them that they must be careful not to soil them. Then they set out in the wagon at sunrise, Gregor in the front beside Papa, and Tatiana, his older sister, in the back with Mama. Traveling the cobblestone streets of the city had, been a bumpy ride, which delighted Gregor and Tatiana, but Mama complained of the discomfort.

Outside the city, on the dirt road leading up the steep hill southwest of Baku, the ride became smoother. The higher they climbed, the slower the horse moved, straining to pull the wagon and its passengers.

When they reached a level area, Papa stopped the wagon and said, "Gregor, you and I will walk for a while. We still have some distance to travel, and we do not want to tire this old horse too soon."

As they set out on foot, with Papa leading the horse, Gregor looked behind him. What he saw thrilled him beyond anything he had experienced in his ten years. He stood transfixed, staring down at the expansive vista of sea and city and mountains. He had never known such a scene was possible, for he had never left the confines of his neighborhood. To him his home was an ugly place—grim and gray and oppressively confined—but from this distance Baku did not look quite so dirty.

Directly below them was the city of Baku itself: a jumble of houses amid a maze of narrow streets. Beyond was a dark swath of smaller buildings, including Black Town, his home and home to poor refinery workers. Towering over Black Town were the circular oil tanks and the dozens of refinery smokestacks that created the heavy cloud that gave the area its name. Beyond Black Town was White Town, a section of gleaming white homes that belonged to the wealthy families of Baku; the princes of the merchant class and the oil industry. In one of those houses, Gregor knew, his Uncle Vladimir lived. Beyond that were hills and mountains in varying shades of gray, blue, and purple.

To his right was a vast expanse of pure and sparkling blue water, which met the city in a long stone quay where hundreds of boats were berthed.

Gazing at the scene, Gregor realized how truly small his world was compared to the rest of the world.

"Gregor!" his father's voice called from behind him. "Don't tarry! We'll never get there if you lag behind."

With one last look at the beautiful view, Gregor hurried to catch up with the wagon. As they traveled on, there were other sights to enchant him—fields of oranges and grapes, green valleys and mountains that seemed to stretch forever in unimaginable grandeur. Looking at the distant mountains to the south, Gregor asked, "Papa, is that Persia?"

Alexei looked down at his son and smiled. "The most distant mountains may be in Persia," he said, "but I'm not really sure." He fell silent for a moment, then added, "At one time, many years ago, this land—all the land around—was part of Persia. That was before the Czar came and took it and made it Russian."

"The Czar must be very powerful," Gregor said, "to take so much land."

"Yes," Alexei acknowledged. "But he is not so powerful that he can take the hearts of the people of Azerbaijan. In our hearts we will always be Persian."

"Alexei!' Maria Mehdovi cried out sharply from behind them. "You must not speak of such things to the boy! If he should repeat your words at school, there would be trouble. Remember what happened last year, when the governor closed the schools!"

"I say nothing that is not the truth," Alexei told his wife firmly, but he did not talk further of politics.

Traveling across a wide valley, they missed the cooling sea breezes, for the sun in the cloudless sky beat down on them hotly. When they complained of thirst, Papa bought grapes from a farmer. It was almost midday before they reached their destination. On the way, they had passed through lush green farmland, with fields of ripening fruits and freshly planted grain. Gregor and Tatiana had seen the multitude of farm animals they had been promised—the chickens, sheep, and goats. But as they approached their father's boyhood home, the scenery had begun to change. Large wooden oil derricks broke the landscape, and all around them the earth was blackened. There was very little vegetation remaining.

With the change in the landscape, Gregor noticed an alteration in his father's manner. Alexei became silent. A sadness clouded his eyes. They had been traveling among the ugly dark derricks for some time before he spoke to Gregor again. "At one time, all this land here—off to our left—

belonged to my family, the Mehdovis," he said. "For many generations, as long as anyone can recall, it was ours. But this is no more. Now it belongs to an oil company, to foreigners who might never as much as cast their eyes upon it."

"Does it belong to the Czar?" Gregor asked.

"No," his father replied. "It does not even belong to a Russian. Your Uncle Vladimir sold it to a Swede—a man named Nobel."

"Why did Uncle Vladimir sell it?" Gregor asked.

Papa sighed. "That is a long story," he said. "But it all comes down to one thing—greed. Money is much more important to Vladimir than his heritage or his family."

"Hush, Alexei," Mama said sternly. "Do not spoil the day by opening old wounds. Gregor is only a child. He will not understand what you say."

"I want to understand, Mama," Gregor said. "I want to know. Why, Papa? Wasn't it as much your land as his?"

"No," Alexei replied sadly. "I was only a second son. My brother was the elder, and by rights of inheritance, the land was his to sell if he chose. It was merely family tradition that said it should stay in the family." Abruptly he changed the subject. "We are almost there. Look for a bend in the road, with a large juniper tree on the right. It was the first tree I ever climbed. I don't know if our house will still be there, but it used to stand on a little slope just past the turn."

The children kept their eyes on the road ahead, with Tatiana standing up in the wagon to peer over Gregor's shoulder.

"I see it," Tatiana cried suddenly. "There's a turn in the road."

"That can't be it," Gregor said disdainfully. "There's no large juniper tree."

Alexei pulled on the horse's reins to stop the wagon, gazing sadly at the blackened skeleton of a large stump that had once been a living thing, lush with green foliage. "That was the tree," he said. "I thought surely it would have survived. It was always what I remembered when I thought of happy times."

Suddenly he slapped the reins against the horse's flanks and moved on, past the bend in the road. On a little slope to the left were the ruins of a farmhouse. Only the sun-baked brick walls still stood; the roof was gone, and the doors and windows were merely gaping holes.

They looked for a clean, shady spot to picnic, but there was no suitable place, for the ugly film of oil was everywhere. So they sat in silent discomfort in the wagon to eat the food that Maria Mehdovi served. She said nothing. She had been against the outing from the beginning, but had submitted obediently to her husband's wishes.

Alexei had pulled the horse and wagon to the shaded side of the ghostly farmhouse, but even that provided little respite from the midday sun. The food they chewed silently gave them little pleasure, for it had now been seasoned with disappointment.

"I know what we should do," Alexei said with sudden eagerness. "There is one place that will not have changed, at least not greatly. It was where I always went when I wanted to be alone."

Maria frowned, a wariness entering her eyes. "What place is that?" she asked.

"The Parsee shrine," Alexei replied. "I've told you about it. It is thousands of years old, and an important part of my people's heritage."

"When we were married, " Maria reminded, "you agreed that the children would be brought up as Christians, the religion of my family. You promised to do nothing to influence them to the ways of your people."

Gregor listened carefully. He had heard his parents disagree many times, but this was a subject he had not heard them discuss.

"Visiting the shrine will do nothing to harm the children," Alexei told her placatingly. "It is now simply an interesting place to look at. As a religion, the Parsee hardly exists at all, except as the fountain of all religions, including your own Christianity."

The journey to the Parsee shrine was not a long one, but it was slow. The road they followed up a mountainside was hardly more than a narrow winding goat-trail, rocky and rutted. Finally it ended completely, and they had to leave the wagon to climb the rest of the way on foot, descending now and again into the small valley.

The shrine, built of the native stone, was small, square, and hardly distinguishable from the outcroppings of rock that surrounded it. It was so crudely built and so time-weathered that it might not have been recognized as man-made if it had not been for the arched doorway.

"Is that it?" Gregor asked, as they approached the small structure. "I thought it would be like a church."

Noting the disappointment in his son's voice, Alexei replied, "It is not the building that is important here. It is what is inside the *atashk adeh*— the eternal flame that is holy to the Parsee."

As they drew near, Gregor could see that there was a faint red glow emanating from the doorway of the shrine. Suddenly, a thin, high-pitched voice called out from behind them, saying, "The peace of Ahura Mazda be with you."

They all turned to see a small, thin man with white hair and beard hurrying toward them. His feet were bare, and he wore only a loincloth and a ragged shawl. His skin was leathery, wrinkled with age, but his dark eyes seemed bright and alive, filled with wisdom and kindness.

"Peace be with you," Alexei replied automatically. Then he paused, studying the old man with amazement. "Is it you, Rama?" he asked incredulously. "Can it be that you are still here?"

"Alexei," the old man beamed. "Alexei Mehdovi! The little boy is now a mature man with children of his own!" He encompassed Maria and the children in his welcoming gaze.

Alexei was still staring at the priest in disbelief. "I truly expected to find the " shrine abandoned and unattended," he said.

The old man shook his head sadly. "It may have to be abandoned soon. When I am gone, there may be no one to replace me. There are so few of the faithful left. You are the first pilgrims I have seen in many months. The only faces I see these days are the men in their oil trucks."

"We are not true pilgrims," Alexei said apologetically. "I am not faithful to any religion, and my wife and children are Christians. I have brought them here to show them a place that once had much meaning for me." He hesitated, then asked, "Would it be possible for us to see the sacred flame?"

"Of course," the guardian said. "There are so few wor shippers left, I don't think it will matter. Come inside."

He led them into the small stone building. Anticipation had led Gregor to expect something truly impressive. He was disappointed to see nothing more than a small fire, no larger than the one in their hearth at home, leaping up from a formation of rock in the middle of the earthen floor. It gave the stone-walled interior a warm red glow and cast dancing shadows of the figures who stood around it, but there was nothing in its appearance to marvel at. Certainly it seemed nothing to worship.

The Parsee's penetrating eyes seemed to perceive what Gregor was thinking. "Once there were other shrines more impressive than this one, but over the centuries they have been extinguished by those who wish to destroy our belief. Most of the shrines were north of here, in the Caucasus; this one has so far been over looked. It does not matter that it does not look so grand; what matters is that it be preserved. The flame has burned continuously for over two thousand years—some say since the flood—and if it is guarded, it will burn until the end of the world."

Gregor was awed. "Where do you find the wood to keep it burning so long?" he asked.

The Parsee smiled. "We do not have to feed the flame. It comes up from under the rocks naturally, like water from a spring."

"It is because of the oil," Alexei explained. "Where there is oil, there is also natural gas. Sometimes the gas seeps up from underground and catches fire."

"And this flame has burned for over two thousand years?" Gregor asked.

"Yes," the old man said, "and it will continue eternally. That is why we consider it holy. Men may come and go, kings and czars and tyrants, but the fire continues to burn."

"You do not worship God then?" Gregor asked. "You worship the fire?"

"That is not quite true," the Parsee said patiently. "Some call us fire worshippers, but to us the fire is only one of the elements of purification that is an expression of God in Nature, one of his blessed gifts. It is the light against darkness, the warmth against cold, the truth against deceit, the good against evil. The fire is the reminder to God's chosen people, the Persians, to serve goodness and truth."

Maria Mehdovi was visibly disturbed by this. "Alexei," she whispered in an irritable voice. "Remember your promise. They are Christian."

The old Parsee heard her whisper, but he did not take offense. "It is all right," he said. "I will not try to convert your son and daughter. Unlike more recent religions, we do not try to persuade others to our belief. In fact, one cannot be Parsee except by birth."

"But Parsee means Persian, doesn't it?" Gregor asked, then rushed on. "I'm half-Parsee, because my father is Persian."

The old man's smile appeared to be on the verge of laughter. "I do not know if it is possible to be half-Parsee," he said kindly. "One is or one is not. One believes or does not. It is impossible to change a person's spirit as one would change a suit of clothes."

What Gregor felt at that moment was indescribable. He felt he understood what the old Parsee was saying. A thrill of excitement and recognition ran through him. He stared into the flame and suddenly felt as one with it. The sensation lasted only for a moment, but its effect lingered, and would return to him at times throughout his life.

It was not something that he would talk about with anyone, not even with his father, for no one else would understand. He was a part of an ancient heritage, something greater than himself, something good and kind and loving that would last for all time.

PART I

ASHES—1904 to 1906

Chapter 1

After giving the large wheel several full turns, shutting off the valves of the pump mechanism, Alexei Mehdovi climbed down the ladder and—following the routine of months that had grown into years—locked the door, delivered the key to the clerk in the office, punched his timecard in the machine below the clock, and walked out of the refinery gates into the rapidly advancing evening. He was always the first to come in and the last to leave. That was expected of the foreman at the refinery; he set the example for the other workers.

In the beginning, that had been difficult for him. To obtain the work that would provide him the income to feed and house and care for his family, it had been necessary for him to quell many of his native instincts, hopes, and beliefs. For ten to twelve hours every day, Alexei the man did not exist; he became nothing more than a part of the vast machinery that produced and refined the oil of Baku. It gave him some satisfaction that he was an important part, but it did nothing to fulfill the yearnings his soul had known in his youth.

Once the pattern had become routine, it became easy. In the evenings, he was too tired to think of anything except going home and resting, enjoying an hour or so with his wife and children. In the mornings, his only concern was to get to work early and get a good start on the day.

But in the past few months it had been increasingly difficult to submerge the aspirations of his youth. It was all because of Gregor, he knew. His son reminded him so much of himself at that age. Though Alexei was dark and Gregor was fair, there was a physical resemblance. It was perhaps the dark eyes. And all those questions the boy asked about his own childhood; they reminded him of the things he had been forced to give up in order to be a good husband and father.

Then, last spring, they had made the trip to his old home. Since that unhappy return, he had had the unsettling sensation that his entire life had been a failure. He would do nothing to change his life; he could not. But he recognized that he was not happy.

On this evening, as he passed through the refinery gates, he said his customary good evening to the night guards and set off toward home, as usual. One thing, however, was different from most evenings. There were two men standing next to the fence, and they were waiting for him.

"Are you Alexei Mehdovi?" the short one asked, approaching him.

There was something about the question that sent a surge of apprehension, almost of fear, through him. "Yes,"he replied cautiously. "Why do you want to know?"

"We are from the Committee of Transcaucasian Workers," he explained. "My name is Koba."

Something about the man's manner made Alexei suspect that was not his true name. It was clear that he was Russian, probably Georgian, from his swarthy, heavy-browed appearance.

"Joseph Koba," the man added, extending his hand. "My companion is Nikolai Karenkov."

Alexei shook their hands, but not warmly. He knew something of the activities of the Committee of Transcaucasian Workers, and it was dangerous even to be seen talking to its members. It was one of the many revolutionist groups that had been springing up all over Russia, stirring up trouble between the workers or peasants and the government, industry, and landlords. Sometimes the trouble had been only public speeches or mass marches on government buildings; other times they had caused riots, or even planted bombs at industrial sites, destroying property and causing deaths.

"Why do you want to talk to me?" Alexei asked stiffly.

The men clearly understood his reticence. "We know you are on your way home," Joseph said. "We will walk with you and explain." He nodded toward the night guard at the gate, who was watching them curiously.

Alexei knew that he should refuse to speak with them, but he did not want to cause a scene. He set off again toward home, in the company of the two men. "I am no revolutionist," he told them guardedly. "I have a family, and I cannot afford to help stir up trouble here."

"We know all about you," Joseph said smoothly. "Much more than you might think. It would have been a great risk for us if we had approached you without knowing what kind of man you are."

Alexei stopped suddenly and gave Koba a hard, almost angry look. "What do you mean?" he demanded.

"Do not be upset." Joseph smiled. "Come, let us continue our walk." Alexei did as he asked, but he did not let down his guard. Joseph continued: "What I mean to say is that we know you are an honest conscientious man. We know that you are a good worker and that the other workers have much respect for you. We also know that you care about the men who work under your supervision."

The man called Nikolai, who walked at Alexei's left, joined in to speak for the first time. He was tall and thin and slightly older than Joseph, who Alexei guessed to be in his mid-twenties. "We merely want to warn you of something that will soon happen at your plant, something that will be extremely harmful to the workers."

For the first time since he had met these men, a deep fear gripped Alexei. He understood where they were leading him; he had already heard the rumors; and he knew his own feelings, fearing how easily he might be led to go along with them.

"The refinery management has a plan to bring in a new group of workers from Tiflitz, men who will work for ten kopecks less a day than your men. When they do, your men will be let go."

"That is only rumor," Alexei protested. "The managers would be foolish to do such a thing. My men are skilled workers. I am sure the managers intend only to hire day laborers to do the unskilled work in another division."

"It is more than rumor," Nikolai insisted. "We have it confirmed by one who knows. Management has decided that, for the money they will save, they can afford to have you train the new men for the jobs."

Intuitively, Alexei knew that what these men were saying was true. That was exactly how management would think. He felt himself being swept along by what he was hearing, all the time knowing where it was leading. The streets of Black Town, rapidly fading in the dusk, were strangely quiet, so quiet Alexei could hear his heart beating, out of time with the sounds of the footsteps against the paving stones. He was aware of the bleak gray cottages that lined the streets, cottages owned by the oil companies and occupied by the workers, who struggled to give their families a decent life, rarely achieving it.

Alexei knew that Joseph and Nikolai were going to try to persuade him to do something to help these people, and he knew how his heart would respond to their plea. He knew, but he had to endeavor to fight it. He had to think about Maria first—and about Gregor and Tatiana.

"If you think I can do something to stop this plan," he said, "you are mistaken. I have no more power than other workers, even though I am a foreman."

"We realize that," Joseph said, his black brows furrowing over his dark eyes. "We want you to know what we have planned, and we want to ask you to help us."

"There is no way I can help you," Alexei protested. "I am not Russian. I am Persian."

"That does not matter," Nikolai said encouragingly. "What matters is that you are a worker, someone the other workers respect and listen to. And when the workers strike, we want you to . . . "

"Strike!" Alexei exclaimed. "Here? At the refineries?"

"Surely you do not expect the workers to accept this without a fight?" Joseph asked. "There have been several meetings, and most of the men have already agreed. If you will join us, we believe that every worker can be persuaded to walk out."

Alexei was flattered, but embarrassed. "You overestimate my influence," he said. "Most workers do not even know me."

Joseph Koba smiled. "You underestimate yourself," he said. "Every worker in Baku has heard the name Alexei Mehdovi. They talk among themselves, and they say that Alexei Mehdovi is the best foreman in Baku. Not only does he know his job, they say he also listens to their complaints and does everything he can to take their grievances to management. They say he is both fair and wise."

By this time, the group had reached the block where Alexei lived. They had stopped to stand beneath the streetlight across from his cottage. Dusk had faded into darkness, and the grimy gas lamp above them cast lonely shadows. Despite himself, Alexei was moved by Joseph's words. The man had a smooth tongue, and although he was surely exaggerating, hoping to flatter Alexei, to feed his vanity, it was possible there was also some truth in his words. If there were not, the men would not have bothered to waste their time with him; they would not have made this kind of effort for an ordinary worker.

If he were not married, if he did not have children to think of, Alexei would have readily agreed to their request. He believed as they did, that the workers suffered much injustice, but a man had to think first of his own concerns, and his concerns were Maria and Gregor and Tatiana.

He thought guiltily of Maria; she would have expected him home by now. He wondered if she had looked out the window, if she had seen him talking to these men. Would she question him about them? Would she suspect what kind of men they were? Somehow he felt he was betraying her merely by talking to them, listening to their entreaties. She had given up things to marry him. That was what happened when people of different backgrounds married. She was a Russian Christian, he a Persian, practicing no religion faithfully.

Maria's father had been a merchant seaman, working the boats that traveled the Caspian. Originally, the family had come from Kiev, and that was where Maria had been born. Alexei had not really meant to fall in love with her. Maria's blond hair and blue eyes had warned him to keep his distance, but once he had gotten to know her, his love had been inevitable. Her friends and her family had not approved of him, just as his brother had not approved. Family and friends were important for a woman. Who could she turn to now, if something should happen to him?

"I am sympathetic to what you say," Alexei told the men finally. "But I cannot do as you ask. I am sorry, but it is simply not possible."

"Don't decide right now," Joseph said. "Give it some time. Think it over for a few days, and we will talk again."

Alexei did not want to leave the matter unconcluded; he did not want to think about it. He was afraid to ponder too deeply their proposal, but neither did he wish to press his refusal too strongly.

They parted amicably, and he turned to cross the street to his small cottage, a heaviness descending on him, as if a great burden had been placed on his shoulders.

* * * * *

Maria sensed trouble as soon as she saw Alexei standing across the street talking to the two men. At the time, she did not understand why, but later, on reflection, she realized it was because he had not invited them into the house. It was not like Alexei to be impolite, even to strangers. He was such a generous, warm-hearted man, he would offer hospitality to anyone. To stand and talk to them on the street meant only one thing—he did not want her to know the subject of their conversation.

From their appearance, she knew the men were foreigners, probably Russians. They were respectably dressed, in suits and ties, but they wore them with a slightly careless manner. The trousers were not neatly pressed, and there was an overall disheveled look to them. Maria was sure they were the organizers of the strike the other women had been telling her about.

The strike had been the main subject of discussion at the public bath for the past few weeks. Most of the women approved of the action, urging their husbands to participate, but Maria had expressed no opinion. She approved of the strike's purpose, but she was fearful of the action itself, praying silently to herself that Alexei would not be tempted to join. As long as he said nothing to her about it, she was certain that he was not involved, and for that reason she did not bring up the subject herself. Since he was a foreman, she had hoped he might not even hear about it. Alexei was a good husband; he did nothing that would seriously affect his family without first discussing it with his wife. Once discussed, however, he would follow his conscience.

And Maria knew Alexei's conscience. It was one of the things that had attracted her to him as a young girl, and still made her love him, despite her better judgment. It was a part of his goodness, and that gave her much pride among the women, for her husband was greatly respected in the Black Town, though he himself was unaware of the fact.

He cared deeply about others, and he had a profound sense of justice. However, in the past few years, he had kept those qualities carefully restrained, and Maria understood his reason. She did not like being the cause of his restraint, but she was as concerned as he was about the future of their family.

She was waiting to greet him when he walked through the door, as was their custom, to take his coat and inquire about his day. She dared not mention that she had seen him talking to the two men, and she could see from his manner that he was trying very hard to be cheerful, pretending that there was nothing disturbing him.

That, in itself, was not a good sign. She waited to see if he would mention the conversation that had taken place outside.

"How was your day?" he asked her with a smile. "Have the children behaved themselves?" He glanced over at the hearth, where Gregor sat reading to Tatiana by the light from the fire.

"They have been very good," Maria replied. "But Gregor tore his tunic on the way home from school." Then, trying to match his cheerfulness to hide her own thoughts, she asked, "Is there anything new at the refinery?"

"No," he said, not looking at her. "It was just an ordinary day, like any other."

As Maria put away Alexei's coat and hat, he moved to the hearth to greet the children. "Is it your lesson you're reading, Gregor?" he asked.

His son looked up at him and smiled, "Yes, Papa. It is geography, about a place called North America, which has many large cities and a river called the Mississippi."

Alexei was very proud of Gregor; the reports from his school were that he was the brightest boy in his class. He hoped that meant he might also have a bright future. Tatiana, already twelve years old, also attended the school, though he had mixed feelings about that. According to his tradition, daughters did not need formal education, but the school was run by the church his wife and children attended. As an extension of the Christian upbringing he had agreed to, he could not object strongly.

As was his custom, Alexei sat in his chair near the children and listened to Gregor's lesson. Maria went to the samovar to get him his customary cup of tea. Her husband was trying to pretend that nothing was out of the ordinary, so she, too, must carry on the pretense. If he wanted to discuss what was on his mind, he would choose his own time. The waiting would have been difficult if she did not have cooking to occupy her attention.

She went out to the kitchen at the back of the house, to check the rice to make sure it was not burning, and stirred the lamb stew. It was almost ready. When she returned to the house, there was no sound except the soft crackling of the fire in the hearth and Gregor's voice reading softly, monotonously. Alexei appeared to be listening to his son's lesson, but Maria was sure he did not really hear the words; she could feel the weight of her husband's thoughts all the way across the room.

Alexei did not speak of his thoughts until they were seated at the table for dinner, and then he tried to make it sound as if it were nothing of importance.

"There have been rumors at the refinery that some of the men are to be fired," he said. "I hope there is no truth in it."

"Oh?" Maria replied, trying to sound disinterested. "Do they say how many men might be affected?"

"You know how rumors are," he told her. "They are saying all of my men will be replaced by unskilled workers from Tiflitz. There are many who want to stage a strike."

"Would that do any good?" Maria asked. "Would it make the company managers change their minds?"

"I don't know," Alexei replied, and Maria could feel his anguish. "But I don't think it would do any harm. If the company fired the men, they would not only be without jobs, they would also be forced to leave their homes."

Maria knew now what her husband intended to do, and she realized there was no use in arguing with him. If their friends and neighbors, his fellow workers, were to be cast out of their homes in the cold of winter, he could not bear the shame of having his own family warm and secure.

"I saw you from the window, talking to two men," she said. "Was it the strike you were talking about?"

"Yes," he said. "They were trying to persuade me to join it." He looked at her then, and his eyes were filled with pain. "I did not say that I would. My job is not in danger. Not now, at least. The company will need me to train the new workers."

"But you will say yes, won't you?" she asked.

His eyes darted away from her to study the bowl of rice and stew in front of him. "The only way a strike might succeed," he said softly, "would be for all of the workers to join, including the foremen."

"Alexei, you are a good husband," she said lovingly. "Whatever happens, I know that you will provide for us. If you should lose your job, I know that you will find another. And if it is not quite so good as this one, I can take in sewing as I used to do. I am still the best seamstress in Baku."

* * * * *

It was two evenings later when Alexei found Josef and Nikolai again waiting for him as he left the refinery. This time he invited the men into his modest home to have tea while they talked. He had made a few inquiries, confirming the rumor of the intended firings and also learning a few facts about Josef and Nikolai. They were—as he had suspected—socialists, and they were from Baku, but had come there from the north to organize strikes and demonstrations. In addition to the refinery workers, they were also organizing the tram workers and the dock workers.

Their objective was to achieve a general strike throughout all of Baku, uniting the workers of every industry. There were also rumors, which Alexei had been unable to confirm, that they had been trying to rekindle the ancient racial and religious hatred between the Armenian Christians and the Tatar Moslems. That rumor had made no sense to Alexei at the time; he assumed it was a misunderstanding of the class conflict they espoused. For the most part, the working class was made up of Tatars, and the wealthy ruling class—those who were not Russian, English, or Swedish—was predominantly Armenian.

Alexei did not entirely trust the two men, but he was sympathetic with their cause, and he agreed to join them. However, he promised himself—and Maria—that he would be careful.

Josef Koba and Nikolai had obviously foreseen what Alexei's decision would be, for this time they had brought leaflets and pamphlets, which they hoped he would help to distribute among the workers.

"I will read them first," Alexei told them as he took the packets, bound in string, and set them on the lamp table beside the front window. "Please come in. Sit down and have some tea." He turned to his wife. "Maria, I hope the samovar is full. We have visitors. This is Josef and Nikolai." He turned to his guests. "This is my wife, Maria—and my children over by the fire are Gregor and Tatiana."

The men nodded a greeting that was polite but disinterested. Alexei noticed that Gregor was staring at the men with a great deal of curiosity. He hoped the boy would not embarrass him by asking questions.

To distract him, Alexei said, "Gregor, help your mother with the hats and coats." By his quiet obedience, his son indicated that he would keep a respectful distance with these guests. Tatiana got up and went to help her mother.

After they had been seated near the fire and given tea, Josef spoke more bluntly than he had before. "Whether you distribute the pamphlets or not is immaterial," he said. "The main thing we want you to do is far more important. In two weeks, there is to be a meeting in Petrovsk Square. We hope to have all of the workers there, and we want you to speak to them."

"Me?" Alexei was truly astonished. "I am no orator. I would not even know what to say."

"We will help you prepare your speech," Nikolai told him. "We feel you can do it, and we know the workers will listen to you."

"No, I couldn't possibly," Alexei insisted. "If I stood up in front of a crowd, I'm sure I would be struck dumb."

"With our help you can do it," Koba said, reassuringly. "Don't refuse until you give us a chance to prepare you. If, in a week, you still do not have the confidence, we can get someone else."

"But why me?" Alexei asked.

"Because you are neither Tatar nor Armenian," Koba said. "And we have yet to find a worker who does not respect you."

Despite himself, Alexei was flattered.

Chapter 2

Gregor marked the change in his family life from the visit of the two Russians. After that evening, nothing would ever be the same. It was not that he blamed them for what happened afterward—in fact, there was much that he was proud of in his father's actions—but the men possessed an aura of dispassionate coldness that he would forever associate with violence.

The face of Josef Koba became etched into his memory, and it would appear in the nightmares he was to experience for the rest of his life—the dark, daggerlike eyes beneath the black brows that did not acquire warmth even when the man smiled; the strong jaw and the smooth manner; the assurance that he was in control of any situation.

Gregor did not understand his father's association with these men until several days had passed; indeed, he did not understand the full implications of what happened until many years later. Papa was to speak at a great gathering of people in the square outside the palace in Baku; that much Mama explained to him. Alexei was somehow being singled out as special in their community. All their friends and neighbors would be going to hear him talk, along with more people who were strangers to them—merchants and tram workers and dock workers and oil field workers.

Mama had promised to take Tatiana and Gregor to the meeting so they could see and hear their father on this important occasion.

Gregor looked forward to the day with great expectations. He told his friends and his teachers at school about it, and they were much impressed. The priests at the school spoke of the meeting with something akin to reverence, and they praised Alexei for his courage in accepting a position of leadership. Father Constantine, the headmaster, called Gregor into his office one day to tell him, "Please convey to your father that we support him with our prayers, and that we will be at the meeting to support him with our presence as well."

By that time, Gregor was not surprised at the words, but he was surprised by the passion with which they were spoken. He did not know precisely what the connection was; he sensed that it had something to do with the closing of the school the previous year by the authorities.

This passion seemed to grip all of the adults who spoke of the meeting. It seemed to affect the entire working class, and some of the merchants as well—Moslems, Christians, and Jews alike, Armenians as well as Tatars. They were united against an injustice they all blamed on the foreigners—Russians, British, and Swedes—who controlled the industry of Baku.

The passion increased as the day of the meeting approached. And so did the apprehension and fear that Gregor sensed in his mother.

Maria never voiced an objection to Alexei's plans, but neither did she speak with enthusiasm for them. When the men Josef and Nikolai were meeting with Papa, Mama kept her silence as she went about her work. And when Papa was not at home, she had gone about the house picking up the pamphlets and leaflets the men had left, muttering angrily to herself. Once, Gregor had thought she might burn the materials; she had stood with them, hesitating, before the fire for a long time before putting them away in Papa's clothes chest.

On the day of the meeting, a Sunday, Mama dressed Gregor and Tatiana in their best clothes and admonished them repeatedly to be on their best behavior. To Papa, she said, "You will do well, Alexei; I know you will."

Papa left early, having arranged for Mama to take the children with some of the neighbors. They rode the tram from Black Town into the heart of Baku, to the great square surrounding the ancient palace of the Persian rulers, which was now a museum. Gregor had been there once before, on a school outing.

By the time they arrived, the square was already crowded with restless, excited people. "You must not let go of my hands," Mama warned Tatiana and Gregor. "If we were to be separated, I might never find you again, in the middle of so many people."

The frown on Mama's face was unusually severe. Gregor sensed that she feared something more than simply being separated in the crowd, but the impression did not linger with him. He was enjoying the sights and sounds all about him. There were people of all sorts in the crowd. Some of the men wore western suits and appeared to be European; others wore suits and a bright red fez. There were Tatars in Moslem robes and turbans, and others were in uniforms that ranged from those of tram conductors to those of Russian cossacks. And there were priests in cassocks.

Most of the women were covered by the Moslem chador, but there were also quite a number in the simple dresses traditional to the Armenians. A few wore the more stylish walking suits and hats of Russia and Europe. A great many women had brought their children along, some of them merely infants.

It was a sunny, clear afternoon, surprisingly warm for the time of year, almost like spring. There was a slight breeze from the sea, but it was more invigorating than chilling.

The speeches were to be made from the steps of the palace. After considerable maneuvering through the crowd, Maria managed to find a place near the front, where Gregor and Tatiana would be able to see and hear their father. They had not been there long when a group of men made its way through the crowd and climbed the palace steps. Alexei was in the group, but neither Koba nor Nikolai were there.

"There's Papa!" Tatiana cried out excitedly. "I see him!"

As if he had heard and recognized his daughter's voice, Alexei looked in their direction and smiled. Gregor and Tatiana both waved proudly.

"Be still," Mama said sternly. "Do not attract attention to yourselves."

Gregor did not understand how waving to Papa would attract attention, for many others in the crowd were both waving and shouting. He suspected her words were merely another expression of her unspoken fears.

Two men spoke before Alexei did, one a Tatar with an unruly beard and fierce eyes under dark brows, the other a young Armenian student. The Tatar's words were angry; Gregor knew just enough of the language to understand that. He shouted out what he had to say, and many of the listeners shouted back in response to his words. The young Armenian had clearly rehearsed his speech, for he let his voice rise and fall dramatically as a practiced orator. The crowd cheered him enthusiastically when he was finished.

But the most enthusiastic response was to Alexei's speech. He began haltingly, almost too softly to be heard by the crowd, but gradually his words grew more confident. The listeners were silent, attentive. Gregor sensed that everyone was impressed by what his father was saying.

"We are of different backgrounds," Alexei said emotionally. "Armenians, Tatars, Persians, Moslems, Christians, Jews. But we must forget those things that divide us. We must join as one for the common good. For our Russian masters and their English and Swedish collaborators wish to use our differences to keep us subjugated. We must not let them do this any longer.

"If we join for the common good—if we all strike as one people—we can force the government and the industrialists to hear us."

There was a cheer from the crowd. It came up with a deafening roar, sending a chill through Gregor. Neither of the other speakers had prompted such a response from the listeners. It made Gregor proud of his father.

"We must no longer allow ourselves to be oppressed. This is our land. Despite our differences, all our peoples have been here for hundreds of years, far longer than any of these foreigners. We may not be able to drive them out from our land, but we can prevent them from making us their slaves."

Again there was a roar of approval from the people. Alexei waited for it to subside before continuing to speak. But suddenly, as if a wave had swept over the people assembled, the mood of the crowd changed. The cheering became a rumble of fear. People began to look around them, speaking to their neighbors in consternation. One word was passed along from person to person—"cossacks."

"What is it, Mama?" Gregor asked. "What's wrong?" He strained to look around, but could not see over the heads of the people congregated behind him.

"It is what we all feared the most," Maria said, her voice trembling. "The authorities have sent the cossacks." She clutched her children tightly to her sides.

Then, abruptly, Alexei began to shout, trying to be heard above the crowd. "Please, be silent," he cried out. "Let me have your attention! We are peacefully assembled! If you will all listen and be calm, there will be no trouble!"

The crowd hushed. "We must stand together, and there will be no harm. If we separate, if even one of us panics, we are all lost. We will hear their commander, and we will either obey his request or we will not. But we will act together, as one!"

There was fear within the crowd. Gregor could feel it, but everyone obeyed Alexei. They were poised silently, waiting, giving their consent to his leadership.

Alexei's eyes scanned the distant perimeter of the square. Then he spoke, strongly, firmly, confidently. "Cossacks, I cannot see your leader, but I address my words to him! We are assembled peaceably! We have that right! We intend no violence! We know that, if you choose, you can attack us and kill or injure many! But you cannot kill every one of us! There are women and children here. I am sure you know that any violence you provoke will simply strengthen our resistance. You do not want martyrs, and neither do we! If you will speak to us and state your purpose, we will hear!"

There was a moment of silence, while everyone waited tensely. Then, softly, a rumble of whispers swept through the crowd, and people began to move slightly, adjusting their space.

"What's happening, Mama?" Gregor asked.

"Hush, child," she replied. "You will see very soon. The commander of the cossacks is riding through the crowd with some of his men."

It was only a matter of moments before Gregor saw the group of splendidly uniformed men riding horseback straight for the front steps of the palace and Alexei. They were moving slowly, their sabers sheathed, their guns at their sides, and the crowd was parting to let them through. Gregor was entranced by what was happening. There was a beauty and a magnificence about the cossacks, but it was also frightening. He would not be able to understand that incongruity until he was much older, but the conflicting feelings were impressed upon him at that moment, and he did intuitively realize that what he was seeing was a display of power, and that what his father displayed in response was courage.

When the cossack leader reached the palace steps, he did not dismount, but rode his horse up them to halt alongside Alexei, then turned to face the crowd. His guards stopped their horses at the foot of the steps.

"We are here to preserve the peace," he announced sternly. "This is an unlawful assembly, and we demand that you disperse immediately and quietly! No one will be harmed if you do so! If you do not, it will be necessary to use force!"

There was a restless murmur through the crowd, but no one made a move to obey.

The officer turned to face Alexei. "Will you instruct them to do as I say?"

Alexei hesitated, a look of uncertainty on his face. Then he spoke quietly to the cossack in tones that could not be heard by the people. After an exchange that seemed to last an eternity, but was probably no longer than two minutes, Alexei stepped forward decisively and again addressed the crowd.

"I have assured this officer that our intention is peaceful. I know that there are some here who would wish to resist their display of force and to insist upon our right to assemble. However, I ask that you all recall my comments about acting as one. This is not a time to risk the lives of our women and children. For now, I ask that everyone return to their homes. The purpose of our meeting has been served. We will meet again, and we will achieve our goals."

There was only a momentary delay between his final word and the obedience of the crowd. The people turned, almost as one, and began to walk slowly away from the palace toward the city streets at the edge of the square. The mounted cossacks silently let them pass into the dusky late afternoon.

Maria sighed with relief, murmuring in a trembling voice, "God be praised for Alexei's wisdom." Clutching her children's hands tightly, she guided them to follow the crowd. "And God protect him now," she muttered.

The people around them talked about what had happened, as they moved off, some criticizing or complaining about Alexei's decision, others praising it. "I don't like this," one Tatar said strongly. "We should stand up to them. Show them we are not afraid of them."

"You may talk like that, Johanjir," an associate replied. "You don't have a family to be concerned about. I think this Alexei Mehdovi made the right decision. We can fight another day. I want my wife and children to be safe at home."

They were halfway to the street when Gregor asked, "Mama, don't you think we should wait for Papa?"

"No, child," Maria replied. "It is better that we wait for him at home."

"Will he be home soon?" Tatiana asked.

"I don't know," Maria said. Gregor looked at her and saw that she was weeping quietly. Then he turned to look back to the palace steps to see what his father was doing.

The cossack guards had dismounted and joined their leader at the top of the steps, completely surrounding Alexei and the small group of men who had addressed the crowd.

* * * * *

It had been difficult for Alexei to maintain an appearance of calm. In truth, he was frightened by the arrival of the cossacks, not for himself, but for the safety of Maria and the children. He did not know what the cossacks would do to him, but he was certain they would not allow him to walk away unpunished. The most he could hope for was to be arrested and imprisoned. It would require all his wits to survive with his life.

As the people in the square began to disperse, the cossack leader and his guards dismounted and surrounded the group of speakers.

"You were wise to handle this as you did," the commander told him imperiously. "I'm sure the magistrate will consider that in your favor."

"We have done nothing wrong," Alexei said. "This was a peaceful assembly. We have proven that."

"That will be for the court to decide," the commander replied. "Where is your leader?"

"What do you mean?" Alexei asked. "We have no leaders. We were all gathered here to talk about our mutual problems."

"Where is Josef Koba?" the commander asked. "Where is Nikolai Karenkov?"

Alexei hesitated. "I don't know who you're talking about," he said cautiously.

"Don't lie!" the commander snapped harshly, his dark eyes narrowing. "The magistrate will not look kindly on lies! We know about the activities of Koba and Karenkov. They have been watched since they arrived in Baku. They are socialists, and they were sent here to stir up unrest. We know when and where they met with each of you. We know where they came from, and we know why."

"Then you know more than we know," Ahmed the Tatar said belligerently. "Why do you need us?"

"We do not know where they have gone," the commander said. "They were in Baku yesterday, but last night they disappeared. They are the ones we want. If you will help us, the magistrate will be lenient on you."

Alexei wasn't sure if the cossack's promise was reliable. Swiftly, he attempted to assess the situation. He knew that outright defiance, which was Ahmed's approach, would provoke severe punishment from the authorities. They would be made examples for the rest of the people. But complete capitulation would be far worse. Not only would it destroy the chances for a successful strike, but it would also be an admission of wrong-doing, taken by the authorities as a confession to be used against others. Somehow they must appear to cooperate without giving in completely. It was their only chance.

"You keep speaking of the magistrate," he said. "As far as I know, we have broken no laws. You have not even informed us that we are under arrest. If we are, I would like to know the charges against us."

"I should think the charges would be quite obvious," the commander said stiffly. "Koba and Karenkov are socialist revolutionaries, working to overthrow the Czar. You are to be charged with conspiring to civil insurrection."

There was an audible gasp of shock from Danilo, the Armenian. "But we are not revolutionaries," he said, his voice trembling with fear. "We are attempting only to get better treatment for the workers of Baku."

The commander turned to face the young student, whom he had so far ignored. Alexei knew that he would attempt to take every possible advantage of this sign of weakness, unless he could somehow distract the cossack until Danilo had regained his courage.

"What he says is true," Alexei said strongly. "We know nothing of the other activities of Koba and Karenkov, and we have no idea where they have gone."

"But I do know," Danilo offered hastily, his voice trembling. "They are still in Baku. They are staying in a house below the cliffs near Baladjari."

Hope drained from Alexei. There was little chance of salvation now. Koba and Karenkov had not made him privy to any information such as this, but the authorities would surely not believe it. If the socialists had trusted the weak-willed young student, it would be reasonable to suspect that Alexei and Ahmed would have been trusted with even more information. They would be tortured until they confessed.

"I will take you to them," Danilo offered too eagerly, "but you must believe I knew nothing of any revolt against the Czar."

"At least one of you has the wisdom to cooperate," the commander said grimly. Turning to his guards, he instructed, "Sergeant Litvinov, you and your men will take these two back to headquarters and hold them. Bind them to make sure they do not escape. I will take the rest of the troops and follow the Armenian to arrest Koba and Karenkov."

Silently Alexei bore the humiliation of having his hands bound behind his back and having a rope placed around his neck. When they did the same to Ahmed, he protested, but his resistance merely resulted in a severe beating. Then the two prisoners were led off through the darkening streets of Baku toward the Russian military headquarters. If either of them lagged behind the mounted cossacks, the nooses would tighten around their necks, so they were forced to trot at a swift pace.

Ahmed continued to resist, but Alexei realized this was not the time to try to prove his courage. The cossacks delighted in their prisoners' suffering, laughing when Ahmed gagged and cried out with pain and rage.

"Don't resist," Alexei called to him, breathing heavily from the exertion of running on the cobbled streets. "It will gain us nothing. Save your strength for later."

But Ahmed refused to heed his words. If anything, his defiance increased. The tighter the noose around his neck, the more the Tatar struggled. His face had turned purple; the veins in his temples seemed on the point of bursting; his eyes were rolled back, and his tongue protruded from his open mouth.

Alexei was sure that his companion could not endure much more without strangling. "Stop," he called to the cossacks. "Loosen his rope! You're killing him!" But the cossacks merely laughed.

"No, infidel," one of them shouted back. "He's doing it to himself!"

Night was falling rapidly, and the streetlamps were not yet lit. It was becoming increasingly difficult to see more than a few feet ahead. It would take only one false step on the rough cobbles for either Alexei or Ahmed to stumble and fall. Once that happened, it would be certain death.

They were making a turn into a narrow street leading uphill to the military base, when Ahmed stumbled. The Tatar screamed as he fell. Then there was only a faint gurgling as the body jerked helplessly alongside Alexei, like a rag doll, bumping against his ankles and making each step even more uncertain for him.

"You sadistic swine!" he screamed at the cossacks. "He's dead now! Cut the rope! Don't mutilate his body like this!"

"What do you care?" the sergeant called back. "You're still alive!"

"You're a fool!" Alexei shouted. "Don't you know what your commander will say when he learns you have created a martyr for the mob?"

"Halt!" the sergeant ordered, reining his horse. He turned to one of the men. "Pick up the body and throw it over the back of your horse."

Grateful for even a momentary pause, Alexei gasped for air. He wished that he could fall to his knees and rest his trembling legs, but he did not dare. The cossacks might suddenly start off up the hill again, and he would never get back to his feet.

Two of the cossacks dismounted, one rolling up the rope and the other untying it from Ahmed's neck. Alexei watched while they lifted Ahmed's limp body onto the horse, wondering if they would soon be doing the same for him. Then he turned his eyes to the sergeant to see if he could read the answer in his face.

It was then that he noticed a figure moving toward them down the hill. It was the district lamplighter, an elderly man wearing a fez and an ill-fitting suit and carrying the tall torch that was the instrument of his trade. Not far from them, he stopped at a lamp post to start the small gas flame at the top.

There was something about the old man that seemed odd or incongruous, but Alexei was so preoccupied with his own plight that he did not dwell upon the matter. Only later did he realize what it was—the man was too short to have been a lamplighter. He was straining on tiptoes to reach the lamp with his torch.

The sergeant noticed the lamplighter's struggle, but he was even less perceptive than Alexei. "Here, old man," he said, guiding his horse forward. "Let me do that for you. I'm higher than you are."

The lamplighter hesitated for a moment, then moved to meet the sergeant, extending his torch. The sergeant reached out with both hands to grasp the cumbersome instrument, leaning out of the saddle. What followed happened so quickly that Alexei was unable to comprehend it immediately.

The moment the sergeant clutched at the torch, the lamplighter pulled, bringing the cossack to the ground. Then, swiftly, all the guards were surrounded by a mob of people swinging sticks and ropes as makeshift weapons. Someone grasped Alexei by the arm, pulled a knife, and cut the rope that tethered him to the sergeant's horse. "Run," the man ordered him. "Come with me! This way!"

Alexei obeyed. His legs were aching, and he could not move fast with his hands still bound, but he ran as well and as quickly as he could, following a man he did not know, to an undetermined destination. Others were running into the dark streets as well; whether they were his rescuers or cossacks Alexei did not know, though he assumed they were friends. He heard no sounds of galloping horses, only the scuffle of human feet.

He had run for many blocks, uphill and down, when he could finally go no further. He collapsed against the wall of a brick building, gasping for air. "I'm sorry," he said to the young Tatar who was leading him. "Go on . . . without me. I have to rest."

"I'll wait," the young man said. "It's not much further, and I think we're safe now." He pulled his knife from his robes. "It will help if I cut the ropes from your wrists." And he proceeded to free Alexei's hands.

When Alexei had regained his strength, they set out again, walking the rest of the way. Their destination proved to be a small but comfortable house not far from Black Town. To his surprise, Alexei found Koba and Karenkov waiting for him there, along with several other men he had met in the past few weeks.

When he saw the socialist leaders, Alexei exclaimed in astonishment, "But what are you doing here? The cossacks have gone looking for you near Baladjari."

Koba smiled. "We did not think Danilo could be trusted fully," he explained. "It served our purpose to let him think that was where we were staying. Conveniently, the cossacks are now miles away from this place."

Alexei nodded in understanding. "But they will return," he said, "and I am now a fugitive. They will not rest until they find me. They will go to my home; they will persecute my family. I am grateful to be rescued, but do you think it was wise?"

Again Koba smiled. "Sit down and rest yourself, Alexei Mehdovi," he said, gesturing to a comfortable chair beside the fire. "Have some vodka and restore your strength. We have thought of everything. Your family is already aboard the train for Sabunchi. Your neighbors are packing your furniture and belongings on a wagon to follow. When the cossacks arrive at your home, they will find it empty, and your neighbors will know nothing about your disappearance."

Alexei sat down and accepted a glass of vodka from Nikolai Karenkov. Suddenly he realized how naive and trusting he had been. The possibility of trouble had occurred to him from the very beginning, but he had considered it merely a possibility. These men had expected it and had planned for it. But all Alexei could think about at this moment was his family. Maria and the children were fugitives, just as he was. They were suffering for what he had done.

But what had he done really? He had merely stood up and spoken to the people—voiced his opinions, urged them to stand as one against injustice and oppression.

"What will my family do in Sabunchi?" he asked Koba. "Won't the cossacks find them there? I would rather give myself up than have them suffer."

"I know," Koba said, his black brows furrowing, his dark eyes surprisingly sympathetic. "But they no longer bear the name Mehdovi. Nor do you, for you will be joining them very soon. Your name is now Alexei Baranov. We took the liberty of adopting your wife's maiden name. You and your family are Russians. Alexei Mehdovi and his family have completely disappeared. In three days, Alexei Baranov will appear in Sabunchi." He paused, then added apologetically, "Unfortunately, you will not be able to start work in the oil fields at Balakhani until after the strike is over. And I'm sorry it is not as good a job as the one you had in the refinery, but it is the best we could do."

Alexei stared at Koba in astonishment. "But why are you doing all this?" he asked.

Koba smiled, and for the first time Alexei saw genuine warmth in the man's eyes. "Perhaps you do not realize how eloquently you spoke or how deeply your listeners were moved. You have become a hero to the people of Baku. It will serve our cause to have you live but disappear. Stories will be spread about your whereabouts, and how you are serving the cause. Of course, none of them will be true, but the people will believe, and that is what is important."

"What about Ahmed?" Alexei asked. "Will his death serve the cause as well?"

A cloud drifted across Koba's eyes. "I don't know," he said. "That was unfortunate and unexpected. It presents us with a serious problem, especially since the people already know that 2-nilo betrayed the cause. We wanted to avoid racial and religious strife. But I fear that what all the people will remember about this day is the fact that Danilo is an Armenian and a Christian and Ahmed was a Tatar and a Moslem. That is all the more reason for us to have the people venerate you as a hero, for you spoke to them of unity and solidarity."

As the full meaning of Koba's words registered, a heavy pall fell over Alexei. Until that moment, he had not realized how fully he and the people were being manipulated. He was an idealist, acting from the heart, from his concerns about the daily lives of his family and neighbors and friends. These socialists were far more than that. They were idealogues, coldly calculating, attempting to change history, to alter nations. Alexei and others like him were merely pawns in their game.

This did not alter Alexei's commitment, but it did convince him that he must be cautious. Before every move, he realized, he must now analyze and question.

Chapter 3

The weeks that followed were difficult ones for Alexei. It was not that settling his family into a new home was so bad. After the cramped cottage in Black Town, the rental house in Sabunchi seemed nice and spacious. Though the town itself was an industrial one, it was small compared to Baku, and it had the atmosphere of the country, with the same kind of neighborliness that Alexei had grown up with.

It was in other ways that Alexei felt uprooted. He was cut off from the life he had begun to build for himself. He was not to start his work at the oil fields immediately. In fact, Koba had explained, he would not have a job until after the general strike was over. It hurt him not to be able to participate in the strike he had worked so hard to bring about.

The workers in Sabunchi participated in the strike, but there were so few that their efforts were hardly noticed. Most of the men who lived there worked two miles away in the oil fields at Balakhani, and they were striking, but Alexei had been warned not to show his face at the oilfields until he was to start work.

The reports that came from Baku made Alexei wish he could have been there. The industry of the city was virtually shut down. Everything came to a standstill. Fifty thousand workers stayed out on picket lines or at home—dock workers, railway workers, tram workers, refinery workers, cannery workers. Even the caviar plant had been shut down. Few crossed the picket lines and reported for their jobs. At the refinery where Alexei had worked, the manager attempted to bring in the workers from Tiflitz, but when these workers learned what was happening, most of them refused to cross the picket lines.

There had been a few isolated cases of violence, and those were caused largely by overzealous cossacks. The police, on the other hand, remained neutral, secretly sympathetic with the workers. There had been no deaths, and the injuries were few. The employers and the authorities had been forced to compromise. They did not give in to all of the workers' demands, but they gave in enough so that it was considered a victory for the workers.

The opinions expressed by the people in Sabunchi implied that the violence at the public meetings before the strike had served to unify the people of Baku as nothing had ever done before. People talked of Ahmed's death, of a railroad worker killed at another public meeting—and they talked about Alexei Mehdovi and his mysterious disappearance. As Koba had predicted, Alexei had become a kind of hero to the workers, his greatness embroidered with each passing day.

Alexei listened to these stories as if they were about a man he did not know. He felt, if he should confess to being Alexei Mehdovi, people would merely laugh at him.

When he started to work at the oil fields, he was looked upon with a degree of suspicion by the other workers. He had a Russian name, and his family was clearly Christian. The majority of the other workers on his level were Tatars, though there were quite a few Armenians. Generally the Russians and the Armenians had better jobs.

Alexei was assigned the most menial manual labor, lifting and carrying timber for the derricks and pipe for the drilling. He spent hours with a pick and shovel, clearing sites for the wells, moving the dirt with a wheelbarrow. The pay for this back-breaking labor was far less than what he had earned at his responsible position at the refinery.

Maria had begun to take in sewing again—as she had done in the early years of their marriage—and Gregor had been unable to continue his schooling, instead taking a job at the market, unpacking fruit and running errands.

The first friend Alexei acquired on the job was an Armenian named Vassily, who was a few years younger than Alexei. Vassily had been married less than a year, and his wife was expecting their first child. He had lost his job at the caviar cannery in Baku a few weeks before the strike because of his active support for the workers' movement. For that reason, the Tatar workers accepted him somewhat more than they did other Armenians.

It was Vassily who told Alexei about the latest trouble in Baku. They were working with picks and shovels, leveling the site for a new drilling rig. None of the Tatar workers were nearby.

"The authorities in Baku have taken a new approach against the workers," Vassily said cautiously. "They're trying to defeat us by dividing us, calling on old racial hatreds, pitting the Tatars against the Armenians."

"How do you know this?" Alexei asked. "What has happened?"

"It is nothing I can prove," Vassily told him. "It is only what the talk is, and I have put things together. Do you remember at one of the early meetings to enlist workers for the strike, there were three speakers?"

Alexei tensed, catching his breath. "Yes," he said tentatively, "I recall."

"The word has been spread among the Tatars that Danilo the Armenian was working with the authorities all along," Vassily explained. "They are saying that the Armenians are not true supporters of the movement. As proof, they point to the fact that Danilo was released the next day."

One of the Tatar workers returned with his empty wheelbarrow for another load of dirt, so Alexei and Vassily ceased their conversation. When the Tatar had gone off again, Alexei commented, "Surely the Tatars do not believe this. Surely they can see what the authorities are trying to do."

Vassily shook his head sadly. "It is working. There has been violence between the Tatars and the Armenians in Baku. Two weeks ago, Danilo was murdered. He was found in an alley with his throat cut. The Armenians say it was done by the Tatars, claiming a man named Lalaeff did it. Last week, a mob set upon Lalaeff outside his home and beat him to death.

"And the trouble quickly spread to the merchant class. That same day, Babaeff, the richest Tatar in Baku, the leader of an old respected family, was shot in Molohansky Square. They say it was done by an Armenian, but I am not so sure."

Alexei was deeply saddened. He paused in his digging and leaned on his shovel. There were questions he wanted to ask, but he noticed a group of workmen arriving with a wagonload of timber, and he and Vassily had to stop to help them unload.

When the two were again able to talk, Alexei asked, "Have the people already forgotten the words of Alexei Mehdovi? Don't they realize that they won their victory in the strike because they were united?"

"Mehdovi is now only a memory," Vassily said. "And even that has been tarnished by the talk."

"What talk?" Alexei asked anxiously.

"They are saying that he and his family were slaughtered by the Armenians and their bodies dumped into the Caspian."

Alexei could not hide his astonishment. "But why?" he gasped. "That makes no sense at all."

Vassily shrugged. "That is one reason I feel it is the authorities who are stirring up the trouble. Racial hatred doesn't have to make sense. It calls on passion without reason. The Russians can make the Tatars believe the Armenians want to drive them out along with all the other foreigners, to try to regain their homeland. They can make the Armenians believe the Tatars are jealous of the wealth and status they have achieved under the Russians. It is the old rule: divide and conquer."

Alexei was angered by what he had heard. He knew that what Vassily told him was true. He felt that he ought to be able to do something to put a stop to these troubles. The people had listened to him before. If he confessed his identity, would they listen to him again? Would they even believe that he was Alexei Mehdovi?

If they did, would he not be asking for even more trouble and suffering for his family?

It was inevitable that the racial fear and hatred demonstrated in Baku would infect the people of Sabunchi and Balakhani as well. There had been no violence in the oil field towns, but both Tatars and Armenians had begun to carry weapons with them to work and to walk in the streets. There was a silent wariness in everyone's eyes wherever they went, as if expecting trouble at any moment.

Alexei and the other workers sensed that the oil fields were a powder keg waiting to explode.

Finally, Maria forced Alexei to talk to her about the trouble, revealing that she had been aware of his anxious thoughts.

The children had been sent to bed, the dinner dishes washed and put away. Alexei was sitting beside the fire, staring silently into the flames, and Maria was sitting beside a kerosene lamp, working on some sewing for the wife of an English oil man. She came to the point indirectly.

"Until things calm down," she said, her eyes intent upon the tiny stitches she was making with needle and thread. "I think Gregor should stay home from his work. We can do without the money he brings in."

"You are right," Alexei said. "I will go and tell Mr. Assad not to expect him for a day or two. I'm sure he will understand."

"You are not to blame yourself for what has happened," Maria said suddenly. "After all that has happened, I believe you were right to do what you did. Alexei Mehdovi was a wise man. The people could use a wise man like him right now."

Alexei stared at her in astonishment. Sometimes he wondered if his wife could read his thoughts.

"Oh, Alexei Baranov is a fine man, too," she continued. "A good husband and a kind father. But Alexei Mehdovi was also a good neighbor and friend to others. He had a way with words. He knew how to make people think with their heads as well as their hearts."

Maria looked up from her sewing, and Alexei smiled warmly at her. "Perhaps," he said gently, "but Alexei Mehdovi's words brought harm to his family."

Maria set aside her sewing, got up, and came to kneel before Alexei's chair. As she looked up at him, he saw that there were tears streaming down her cheeks. To Alexei, his wife was still the most beautiful woman in the world, even after all these years, though her blonde hair was streaked with gray, and beneath her blue eyes, little lines had begun to form.

"Compared to the harm that others have suffered these past few weeks," Maria said, "what we have endured is nothing. I know what is in your heart, Alexei. You are not a man to hide away in silence when there is something you can do."

"What if the cossacks should come and take me away?" Alexei asked. "What would you do?"

"Right now," Maria said softly, "the cossacks are to be less feared than the mob. They have far better things to do with their time than to look for Alexei Mehdovi."

Alexei rose and pulled Maria to her feet, embracing her warmly and kissing her lovingly on the lips. "You are a good and understanding woman, Maria," he said. "If something should happen to me, I pray that God will take care of you and the children. Either your god or mine."

The next day, Alexei shared his secret with Vassily. It was when they broke for their midday meal. They went to their usual place, under a few blackened trees, where they sat atop some oil drums and unpacked the food their wives had prepared for them. Since they were the only two men working this well who were not Tatars, they were left alone. The Tatars gathered on benches alongside a storage shed, a good distance away from them.

While they were eating, Alexei said abruptly, "Vassily, I have something to tell you. Baranov is not my real name."

Vassily grunted disinterestedly and nodded his head. "I did not think you were really a Russian," he said. "But in these times, a man minds his own business. I felt you had been hiding something."

"I have," Alexei admitted. "My real name is Alexei Mehdovi."

Vassily stopped eating and stared at him, his mouth open. "I should have known," he said finally. "I was there that day. I heard you speak. But you have grown a beard since then. I never even suspected. But why are you here? And why do you keep this secret from the other workers?"

"For the sake of my family," he said with an embarrassed shrug. "But

I intend to tell the truth now. I fear that the riots may spread here from Baku, and I want to try to help prevent that."

Vassily nodded in understanding. "It may be too late, though," he said.

"I know," Alexei said, "but I must try."

"What do you intend to do?" Vassily asked.

"There is one man among the Tatars I think I can trust," Alexei told him. "Hassan. He is a wise man and very shrewd. The others listen to him. I understand he was their leader during the strike. I intend to talk to him, to try to gain his help. I cannot let everyone know that I am not who I appear to be, but I think I can share the fact with him."

*   *   *   *   *

Alexei approached the Tatar leader at the end of the day, asking if he might walk with him on the way home. Hassan lived in Balakhani, but his house was on the way to Sabunchi.

"If you wish," Hassan told him, but it was clear that he was suspicious of Alexei's motives. The two men had spoken very little to each other.

The darkening sky was a deep purple, and the tall derricks that lined the road the workers followed had become shadowed, taking on the look of a thick forest. The dirt and the soot and the ugly machinery could no longer be seen, though their smell lingered in the nostrils. Here and there lanterns and flares were being lit for the night shift, the small group of men who kept the wells pumping and watched for trouble until the daytime crews returned at sunrise.

"I want to talk to you about some things that are worrying me," Alexei told the Tatar.

Hassan grunted acknowledgment, but his dark eyes studied Alexei warily from beneath his heavy brows. Hassan was considerably older and heavier than Alexei, and he had spent most of his working years in the oil fields. He had seen many workers come and go, and Alexei was of no special interest to him.

"Why me?" he asked.

"The workers listen to you," Alexei said. "I think if we talk, we can prevent racial trouble here."

"What's that to you?" Hassan asked. "You are new here. You are a Russian."

"No, I'm not," Alexei said. "I was born near Khoja Hasan. My true name is Alexei Mehdovi."

Hassan stopped and turned to stare at Alexei. "You are lying," he challenged, almost angrily. "Alexei Mehdovi is dead."

"That is the rumor," Alexei said, "but it is untrue."

"Can you prove it?" Hassan asked.

"No," Alexei admitted. "Except for my family, there are only two men who can verify my identity—Josef Koba and Nikolai Karenkov. It was Koba who arranged my job here."

For the first time, Hassan smiled. "I know," he said. "I was the one he arranged it with, but he did not tell me you were Mehdovi."

"At the time, it was best no one knew," Alexei said. "It is perhaps still wise for me not to share this information with too many others."

Hassan grunted and began walking again. "So, Alexei Mehdovi," he said, "what is it you wish to talk to me about?"

Alexei explained the view that he and Vassily shared about the Baku riots, and Hassan listened intently. When they reached the commercial district of Balakhani, he invited Alexei to come into a teahouse for a drink. "Some friends of mine will be there," he added. "We will talk with them."

* * * * *

For a time, the efforts of Alexei, Hassan, and Vassily seemed to make a difference. No matter how horrifying the stories from Baku, everything remained calm at Sabunchi and Balakhani. People talked about their common interests, telling each other that Azerbaijan belonged to Tatar and Armenian alike. It did not matter who had occupied the land longer; both had been there for generations. It did not matter even that they worshipped different gods. What mattered was that this was the land where all had been born, would live out their lives, and die. Their common enemies were the foreigners who were there only temporarily to take the riches of Azerbaijan back to their own lands, without paying fairly for them.

But nothing could keep the peace once the Baku refugees began streaming into Sabunchi and Balakhani.

The last train from Baku before the violence completely halted the service brought five of the most powerful of the Tatar chieftains to Sabunchi. They were enraged that men of their race should try to live in peace and harmony with the Armenians. In a teahouse in Petrovsky Square that night, they gathered the local members of their tribes and chided them.

The eldest of their chieftains, Ali Hosseini, spoke in outrage. "Cowards!" he called them. "Does the honor of our people mean nothing to you? More than a thousand have died at the hands of these swine! They must be avenged! Allah demands it! As long as there remains one Armenian left alive, we cannot hold up our heads!"

Hassan was at the meeting, and he argued for reason. "It is true that our people have died at the hands of Armenians, but that is all they have been—the hands, the weapons. They have been controlled by other minds— Russian minds! These foreigners are our true enemies, not the Armenians!"

But Hassan was shouted down. "Traitor!" Ali bellowed. "You do not deserve to be called a Tatar! You are no better than an Armenian yourself!"

During the next few days, violence broke out between the Tatars and the Armenians in Sabunchi and Balakhani. Led by Ali and the other chieftains from Baku, groups of Tatars climbed aboard wagons and carriages and rode through the Armenian sections, shouting curses and firing guns at random.

After a few were killed, the Armenians felt compelled to retaliate. Violence bred more violence, with each death leading to others.

Tatars and Armenians both reported for work in the oil fields the following morning, but there was tension in the atmosphere. It was a bright, clear morning, with an unblemished blue sky, and a gentle breeze that seemed to clear the air of some of the noxious fumes of gas and oil. The great forest of derricks welcomed the workers silently; they seemed like giant black sentries, keeping guard over the men below them who might break into violence at any time.

Alexei arrived for his duty in the Mantascheff fields as quietly apprehensive as all of the other men, wondering if both sides would lay down their disputes and grievances during the working hours. If they did, there was a slight chance that reason might yet be restored.

The first few hours passed without incident. The two groups avoided each other as much as possible.

The sun had not yet reached the midheaven when, suddenly—for no apparent reason—the bell at Balakhani Church began to toll, slowly, mournfully.

Everyone, Tatar and Armenian alike, stopped in their work and began to murmur to each other. "What is it?" Alexei heard one Tatar ask another. "What does this mean?"

"It must be some kind of signal," the other replied. "We must be wary. They may be preparing to attack us."

"Something must have happened," a young Armenian driller said fearfully to Vassily and Alexei. "They must be trying to warn of something the

Tatars have planned."

Rumors and conjectures spread in hushed tones through all the oil fields. No one worked in the Mantascheff fields. The Tatars gathered near the oil storage tanks; the Armenians by the tool sheds. It was not long before Mantascheff's manager, an Armenian, came riding through the fields, shouting, "Get back to work! You are on company time! Don't stand around doing nothing!"

"What has happened?" an Armenian called out to him. "I have heard the Bishop is dead, killed by a Tatar."

"Nothing has happened," the manager cried. "Some fool has just slipped into the church to play mischief."

"You lie!" one of the Tatars called to him. "It is a signal for Armenian treachery."

"It is nothing, I tell you," the manager said strongly. "Now, get back to work! All of you!" Then he started to ride off to the next field.

"It's a trick," the Tatar shouted. "And he's part of it!" He stepped out in front of the group, drawing a pistol from his robe and brandishing it as he addressed his friends. "Armenians are cowards! They will not meet us face to face! They will attack us when our backs are turned! We should act now! Kill them and get it over with!"

The manager whirled his horse about and spurred it rapidly toward the man. "Get out!" he yelled angrily. "We want no trouble here! You're fired! Collect your pay at the office and don't come back!"

"Armenian swine!" the Tatar cried, lowering his pistol, aiming it at the manager's head, and firing.

There was a moment of shocked silence as workers of both groups watched the manager's horse rear back, throwing the lifeless body of its rider to the ground before dashing away in fright.

Then, as if that were the signal the two sides had been waiting for, the workmen scurried for shelter and drew their guns, firing at each other across the body of the manager. The Tatars sought protection fom the oil barrels and tanks, the Armenians positioned themselves inside and behind the tool shed.

Alexei and Vassily were both unarmed. They had been so determined to preserve the peace, they had not even prepared themselves for self-protection. They sought safety behind the tool shed and tried to determine what to do. Both acknowledged that there was no longer any hope for reason.

"Now they will listen only to force," Vassily said, shouting to be heard over the sound of gunfire. "It is up to the police and the cossacks."

"One of us must try to reach the company office," Alexei suggested. "The police will not come unless Mantascheff himself asks for their help."

Alexei looked out across the oil fields. Other workers were being drawn by the excitement on their field. Some were rushing toward them to join the fighting; others were merely finding secure positions from which to watch. To reach the ofice, which was some distance from this field, they would have to run across a large open space, before reaching the next shelter. The Tatars would surely fire at them as soon as they started running."

"I don't know," Alexei said. "Perhaps one should try to make it. If he doesn't succeed, then the other will try."

"Two targets are better than one," Vassily said with a wry smile. "More of a chance to make it through."

"All right," Alexei said. "We'll try to get to the pumping shed of the number nineteen well. Once there, I think we're safe. Are you ready?"

Vassily nodded.

He went first, and Alexei followed close behind. Shots whistled through the air around them, stirring up the dust beneath their running feet. Halfway across the open field, Alexei saw Vassily fall, a wound in his shoulder. Swiftly he passed him, but then turned back just before reaching safety.

Vassily was still alive. "Keep going!" he cried out. "I'll be all right!"

But Alexei refused to leave his friend lying in the open. As swiftly as he could, he lifted Vassily to his shoulders and ran to the pumping shed, dodging gunfire. Once there, he laid him on the ground and looked at the wound. There were several other men there, all Armenians, and they began to crowd around, asking, "What happened? How did it start?" But Alexei ignored them; he was concerned only about his friend's condition.

"It's only a small wound," Vassily told him weakly. "Go on! I'll be safe here."

Reluctantly, Alexei obeyed. He set out across the fields of derricks toward the Mantascheff offices, running as fast as he could. Excited crowds were gathering now, shouting angrily, and he had to dodge his way through workers.

Suddenly a voice cried out, "It's Baranov! The traitor! Get him!" Alexei did not see the man, but he recognized the voice. It was the old man from the meeting at Vassily's house. Hands began to clutch at him as he ran, other voices shouting, "The coward! He's running away from the fight!"

With fierce impact, a stone caught Alexei on the head, and he fell to the ground. He struggled to get up and keep going, but men surrounded him, kicking him angrily and crying, "Kill him!"

He was helpless under the onslaught. Then, abruptly, there was a loud explosion, diverting the attention of the crowd. "It's the oil drums!" he heard someone cry. "The Tatars are trapped!"

Alexei scrambled to his feet, looking back at the scene of the battle. A huge black cloud was rising into the air, pushed upward by fierce red flames. Tatars were running to escape the inferno, their robes blazing, voices screaming in agony. He did not want to see more, but ran while he had the chance, blood flowing from his temple, a terrible pain in his side.

By the time he reached the Mantascheff offices, the people there were already aware of the trouble in the fields, but they did not know what kind of trouble it was or how it had started. Alexei was permitted to speak to Mantascheff himself, a fat, arrogant man who listened with little appearance of sympathy. "You must call in the police," Alexei pleaded. "It is the only chance to stop what is taking place."

"No," Mantascheff said finally. "I'll get the cossacks. I can't rely on the police for something like this."

The men in the office wanted to take Alexei to the oil producers' hospital in Sabunchi, but now that his mission had been accomplished, all Alexei could think of was going back to help Vassily. His friend needed medical attention more than he did. He thanked the men, but set out again, moving towad the billowing cloud of black smoke.

This time, his progress was more difficult. Fighting had broken out throughout the oil fields. All around him was chaos as he ran. Men fought hand to hand with sticks and knives. The sounds of gunfire rang out from all sides. Not far from the office were the barracks where many of the unmarried Armenian workers lived. Apparently some had sought safety there, but it was surrounded by Tatars who were dousing the walls with kerosene. Shortly after Alexei passed it, he heard the rushing sound of sudden flames as the building was set fire to.

He was not far from the scene of the original fight when suddenly, straight ahead of him, there was another thunderous explosion, and he saw—in the midst of the cloud of black smoke that was rising—one of the oil derricks crumbling into the flames. It was only then that he realized the ultimate horror that was rapidly becoming inevitable. The oil derricks were so close together that the flames would spread from one well to another. Once started, there would be no stopping them until the vast fields of Balakhani—perhaps even those of Sabunchi as well—would become one huge inferno.

If the flames reached Sabunchi, there was a possibility that the residential section of the town might be also be affected. Ultimately, Maria and the children could be in danger. He must get Vassily to the hospital and then attempt to reach his family.

Men were rushing toward him, their clothes afire. Bodies littered the ground beneath his feet, but Alexei pressed forward, into the oppressive heat. Well nineteen was still standing, though the flames were near it, and it might go at any moment. Through the smoke, Alexei could not be sure that Vassily was still beside the pumping shed.

"Vassily!" he cried out, but he knew that his voice could not be heard over the roar of the fire and the screams of the dying. Near the shed, the smoke was so thick Alexei could barely breathe. Coughing and gasping for air, he called out again, "Vassily!"

"Alexei?" a voice called back weakly, hoarsely.

His friend was still alive, but he was now suffering more from a lack of oxygen than from his wound. Alexei again lifted Vassily's body onto his shoulders and hurriedly tried to escape the engulfing smoke and intense heat.

They had barely reached the open air when number nineteen exploded, creating more thick smoke and fresh flames.

"Alexei," Vassily said faintly, "you can't make it with me on your back. You must leave me and save yourself."

"No," Alexei said. "Don't worry. We will make it together."

He spoke with confidence, but very soon his assurance was shattered. Suddenly, Alexei found he had more to contend with than fire and fighting workmen and other fleeing men. Rushing toward them were hundreds of mounted men, firing indiscriminately at Tatars and Armenians alike—cossacks! Alexei was knocked from his feet by the first sweeping phalanx. He had barely regained his footing before the second rank rushed by.

The soldiers were doing nothing to remedy the horrible situation. They were merely adding to the chaos.

It was with the third phalanx that Alexei received his wound—a bullet in his right leg. But still, he struggled to try to stand.

"You can't possibly carry me any further," Vassily told him. "If you can walk, save yourself."

"If we make it," Alexei said, "we will make it together. Can you get to your feet? Do you have the strength?"

"I don't know," Vassily said. "I'll do my best."

As they attempted to move forward, another fleeing Armenian stopped to assist. "Here," he said, "hold onto my shoulder. I'll help you as far as the tunnel. Our people are gathering there for safety."

It seemed a sensible thing to do. The tunnel had been dug for a railway spur to run from Sabunchi station, beneath the town of Sabunchi, to the Balakhani oil fields. From the other end of the tunnel, it was only a few blocks to the hospital.

Just before they entered the tunnel, Alexei turned back to look at the oil fields from which they had fled. The afternoon sky had become as black as night from the thick billowing smoke, yet beneath the darkness, bright red flames spread as far as the eye could see. The entire forest of wooden derricks was burning, one by one crumbling into ashes.

To Alexei, it seemed that the end of the world was at hand. This was a conflagration so vast, it might never be quelled. It had been set by human hands—foolish humans—but it was nature unleashed, burning the oil and gas that had been stored underground for centuries. It was the eternal flame of his ancestors magnified a million times.

No, that was not true. The fire of his ancestors was good. It represented truth and light. The flames that raged before him were horrible and evil, the beginning signal of a time of darkness and fear.

Unable to control himself, Alexei began to weep.

"Gregor," he whispered. "Tatiana. God forgive me, I did not want to leave you a world like this."

Chapter 4

Maria had no way of knowing how the violence had begun. In fact, she did not know precisely what was happening. She could hear the sounds of the explosions like far-of thunder. From two miles away, they shook the walls of the small house at Sabunchi. Outside in the streets, people were running about, shouting and calling to each other excitedly, but as Alexei had requested, she remained locked inside with the children.

Then the pall of black smoke drifted over the town, seeping through the cracks in the windows and doors.

She began to regret the promise she had made to her husband. Sitting inside the locked house, silently listening to the noises from outside, hour after hour, was unbearable, far more frightening than it would have been outside in the midst of the crisis. With the children, at first, she tried to pretend that nothing was wrong, but it did no good. She could see the fear in their eyes.

It was Tatiana who finally asked the question, "What's happening, Mama?" Dear Tatiana was so trusting, so innocent, she seemed younger than her years. Her fair skin, her blue eyes, and her blond hair gave her an air of fragility.

"'I don't know," Maria replied simply. "Your father will tell us, when he comes home." Silently, to herself, she added, "if he comes home."

She had to consider the possibility that Alexei might not return. Whatever was happening, it appeared to be far worse than anything anyone had imagined. She had no idea what she would do if he were killed. There was very little she could do. Certainly there was no one she could turn to for help.

Gradually the smoke inside the house became so thick it made breathing difficult. The children began to cough, and painful tears were filling their trusting eyes. But still, Maria was determined not to leave. She went to the cupboard, took out some clean towels, dipped them in water, and gave them to Gregor and Tatiana.

"Lie down on the floor," she instructed, "and hold them over your faces. I will lie down with you and tell you stories."

She did this, periodically refreshing the water on the towels, until her voice grew hoarse and the children drifted into sleep.

Night came, and still Alexei did not return. Maria had to decide whether or not to light a lamp; she deliberated about it a long time before placing a single, dim kerosene lantern in the front window. Not long after that, her neighbor across the street, Mrs. Arounian, knocked at the door, calling out, "Mrs. Baranov! Are you there? Are you all right?"

Grateful for some contact from the outside, Maria opened the door and invited her neighbor in. Mrs. Arounian was a large woman in her fifties; her husband worked in the Balakhani fields with Alexei. She had six children to take care of, but her elderly mother lived with them and helped out with the work.

"I didn't see you all day," Mrs. Arounian said, stepping inside the Baranov house. "I thought you might have left town, like so many others have done. Then I saw your light. Are you and the children all right?"

"Yes," Maria replied. "We're just worried and frightened. Tell me, what is happening?"

"You haven't heard?" Mrs. Arounian asked, surprised.

"No," Maria admitted. "Alexei instructed us to stay inside until he returned."

"And you've talked to no one?" the neighbor asked incredulously.

They sat down beside the fire, and Mrs. Arounian told what she knew of the day's events. "My husband came home a few hours ago, but he went back," she said. "The trouble started in the field where he and your Alexei work. It was all the fault of those terrible Tatars; they killed the Mantascheff manager and then attacked our people. They have set fire to the oil fields, and now all of Balakhani is ablaze."

Maria questioned the objectivity of her neighbor's account, realizing she was hearing only the Armenian side of the story, but she tactfully said nothing. She was eager for news, so she listened sympathetically, as the older woman recounted terrible atrocities. But finally she could restrain herself no longer.

"And Alexei?" she asked. "Did your husband say anything about him? Has he seen him?"

"Oh, I'm sorry," Mrs. Arounian said, flustered. "I should have told you sooner. Your Alexei is all right. He has been wounded, shot in the leg I think, and he is safely with many of our people, inside the railway tunnel."

"He is injured?" Maria asked, fear gripping her. "I must go to him."

"No, my dear," Mrs. Arounian said. "Obey your husband. Stay here and look after the children."

"There is something you aren't telling me," Maria gasped, her voice shrill. "What is it?"

The neighbor hesitated, then answered. "The Tatars have our people trapped inside the tunnel. They have blocked off both entrances. That is where most of the fighting is taking place tonight. My husband has gone back to join those who are trying to rescue them."

Maria responded to this news with mixed emotions. At least Alexei was still alive, and she now knew why he had not come home. But at the same time, the fear and dread were almost unbearable. She wished that she could go to him, could at least look after his wound. However, she was a good wife, and she would obey him, even unto death.

Mrs. Arounian suggested that Maria and the children spend the night at her house; Maria thanked her, but refused; and the neighbor departed, promising to look in on her again the next day.

Maria slept very little that night. She lay on the floor beside the children, listening to the sounds of the fighting, trying to picture in her mind what was heppening. Occasionally, from exhaustion, she would drift into sleep, but within moments, her eyes would be open again, her ears intent on the distant sounds.

It was just before sunrise when the sounds of explosions began again, and this time they were nearer. Instinctively, Maria knew what they were. The fires had reached the oil fields of Sabunchi. Within a short time, the smoke, which had abated somewhat in the night, began to fill the house again.

Cautiously, she pulled back the curtain and looked out the window. On the street, many of the neighbors were beginning to fill wagons with furniture and possessions, preparing to flee the city. The sky was dark with smoke, and in the distance, beyond the houses, there was a red glow from the fires.

Somehow Maria knew then that she would never see her husband again, but she forced herself to believe that there was still hope, that he might yet return. She waited patiently for two more days, each day receiving reports from Mrs. Arounian. The Armenians inside the tunnel were still safe; however, the Tatars remained firmly at the two entrances, continuing to lay siege to it. Every effort made by the Armenians outside had failed to turn the Tatars away.

Then, late in the night of the third day, Maria was startled by a knocking at the front of the house. She was with the children, helping them get ready for bed. Apprehensively, she went to the door and asked, "Who is it?" Silently, Gregor and Tatiana followed her into the front room.

"It's Anya Arounian," the familiar voice said. "And my husband is with me."

Clutching her woolen shawl over her nightdress, Maria opened the door. One look at the faces of her neighbors told her they had come with the bad news.

"Come in," she said, her heart beating fearfully. "I'll put some coal on the fire."

"Don't trouble yourself," Mrs. Arounian said. "We'll be here only a moment."

"Sit down, please," Maria said.

They accepted her invitation and sat stiffly, uncomfortably. Maria could see that Mr. Arounian was struggling to find a way to give her the news. Sympathetically, she said gently, "It's Alexei, isn't it? You've come to tell me he's dead."

"Yes," Mr. Arounian nodded sadly. "All of our people who were in the railway tunnel have been killed."

Maria did not weep, but controlled her grief, though she did gather the children into her arms. "How did it happen?"

Mr. Arounian hesitated. "The Tatars poured oil into the tunnel, and then set fire to it."

The horror of what he had said did not register with her immediately. When it did, she could no longer control herself. Tears welled up in her eyes, and she broke into sobs, clutching Gregor and Tatiana to her breast. Tatiana wept, overcome by the loss. Gregor silently accepted grief as a heavy burden, not giving in to tears. He realized that he was now the man of the house, and the man was responsible for providing for the family. He was not really old enough to do the kind of work that would support a mother and a sister, and that disturbed him. It was a concern that he did not talk about, but kept inside.

The violence did not stop, but continued for days afterward, gradually subsiding, as death and grief became more a preoccupation than hatred.

Gregor insisted upon going back to work at Mr. Akopeff's shop in the market, so that he could earn a few coins each day. There was very little left of the once large and bountiful marketplace. Some shops had been burned, others destroyed by looters. Only a few of the merchants remained, and they had to spend much of their time trying to salvage what was left of their wares.

Mr. Akopeff had been lucky. He had been running low on fruits, and was awaiting a new shipment. Virtually his entire stock had been destroyed, but that hadn't been a big loss. The new shipment arrived the day Gregor started back to work.

That meant there was plenty of work for Gregor to do, stacking fruits, carrying packages for customers, and helping Mr. Akopeff repair the damage to his shop and stalls.

* * * * *

Tatiana felt the loss of her father severely. With the new burden on the family, she felt useless. Mama sought extra sewing work. Gregor, though he was two years younger than Tatiana, was able to go back to his job in the market. There was nothing Tatiana could do except help in the kitchen and occasionally go out to pick up or deliver Mama's sewing. And Mama would allow her to do that only when she was sure it would be safe.

Tatiana was a sensitive child, and she had been greatly affected by the changes that had taken place in the family—first the sudden move and change of name, then the violence in their new neighborhood and finally the death of her father. She did not talk about what she was feeling, but she thought about these things all the time.

It was almost a week later, after things had barely settled into a new routine, when there was another disruption, this one even more severe than the others.

Mama was in the house sewing, and Tatiana was out back in the cook-house preparing dinner so it would be ready when Gregor got home. It would not be a very big dinner, since there was no money to buy meat, but Tatiana was concentrating to make it the best it could be. There was rice, and some vegetables, and two melons Mr. Akopeff had given Gregor after work the day before.

Suddenly, she was startled by loud crashing sounds from inside the house. Then she heard her mother crying out, "Stop this! What are you doing? What do you want here?"

Rushing inside, she found soldiers storming through every room, over-turning furniture and emptying drawers, as if looking for something. Her mother was running about after one of them, one who seemed to be in charge, trying to make him stop.

Tatiana stood terrified in the doorway, unable to move.

To her horror, the soldier who seemed to be in charge turned on her mother, shoving her suddenly against a wall, and thrusting the barrel of his gun under her chin. "You are Maria Baranov?" he demanded.

"Yes," Mama replied, her voice quivering as much from anger as fear. "Why do you want to know?"

"You are the widow of Alexei Baranov?"

"I have told you I am Maria Baranov," she replied. "What do you want from me?"

"We have orders to search your house for subversive literature," he said. "You can save us the trouble by telling us where it is."

"I don't know what you're talking about," she said. "I am an honest, hard-working woman. I know nothing of politics. I keep house, take care of my children, and do sewing. I have no time for anything else."

Then one of the soldiers came into the room from her parents' room, waving some pamphlets in the air, saying, "I've found them. They were in a trunk."

Tatiana was astonished that this should be what they had been looking for. She remembered when the Russian men had given them to her father. He had treated them as unimportant; as far as she knew, he had never even bothered to read them. They were merely paper with words printed on them. The only pictures were ugly drawings of suffering people made with harsh black lines. It was incredible to her that these men could be so violent in their desire to have them.

But what followed was even more unbelievable to her. The soldiers grabbed her mother and roughly bound her hands with rope, telling her that she was being arrested as an enemy of the Czar.

Then Maria began to weep, crying out hysterically, "But my children! What will become of my children?" Tatiana recognized terror in her mother's eyes, and she, too, was frightened.

"They are no concern of ours," the leader told her curtly. "They can go to your family."

"But we have no family," Maria cried. "They have no one but me." Her voice was trembling. "Please, sir, have pity!"

"All right," he said. "The girl can go with you, at least for the moment. The magistrate will find a place for her."

"But my other child . . . ," Maria begged. "My son is not home yet! Please wait for him!"

"We have no time to wait," the officer replied, and he shoved her toward the front door.

"Tatiana!" Maria cried. "Go to Mrs. Arounian! Tell her what happened! Tell her to get Gregor!"

Tatiana was suddenly terrified that her mother would be taken and she left behind. She ran to Maria and clutched at her arm. "Don't leave me, Mama!" she cried. "Take me with you!"

Mama was weeping uncontrollably. "All right, my dearest. Come with me, but you must listen to me and do whatever I say. Will you promise me that?"

"I promise," Tatiana said. "Anything, as long as you don't leave me here."

* * * * *

Gregor hurried, trying to get home before sunset. Already the streets of Sabunchi were dim and shadowy, because of the heavy cloud of smoke and ash that had hung over the town for almost two weeks. Parts of the oil fields were still burning, and from time to time new fires had been set in the residential and commercial sections.

Gregor had been warned to be careful on the streets, by Mr. Akopeff as well as by his mother. But the only time he was frightened was when he had to go home after dark, and that was because of the recent violence.

The riots had changed everything. The worst seemed to take place at night, when it was impossible to see what was happening. There were only the sounds—gunshots and shouting, screaming, and far-off explosions— and he had only his imagination to tell him what was happening. Gregor had heard enough to know that the violence was horrible.

Gregor carried his first week's earnings in his pocket, and he was looking forward to handing it over to his mother, along with the small bag of oranges Mr. Akopeff had given him as a bonus. It made him feel proud, like a man, like his father, who had regularly given over a part of his pay for the food and household expenses.

When Gregor turned the corner onto the street where he lived, his fears were eased. He was on familiar territory, and felt almost happy. He knew, at least by name, almost every family living in the brick houses that lined both sides of the narrow street. In this neighborhood, no one would wish him harm.

The closer he was to his own front door, the happier he felt. Perhaps this would be a good evening. When he got home, Mama would be at her sewing. He would give her his pay, and she would give him a thank-you kiss on the cheek. Tatiana would be out in the cook-house, and he would go and greet her and find out what was for dinner. He knew it would not be much, but he would say a few kind words to make his sister feel good.

It would be a quiet, warm, cosy evening, the way their evenings used to be. Only without Papa.

Gregor burst excitedly through the front door, closing it carefully behind him as he had been taught to do, then looked expectantly for his mother.

She wasn't there.

He moved into the room, calling out, "Mama!" Fear began to creep stealthily back into his soul. Something was wrong. The room was not as it should be. The furniture was out of place. Papers and clothes and books were strewn about the floor. "Mama!" he cried out again. "Mama, what's happened?"

There was no answer.

The fear gripped him hard now. He ran to the back door, opened it, and looked out into the small backyard. "Mama!" he called. "Tatiana!" He ran the short distance to the cook-house. They were not there.

He ran back into the house, searching first the small room he shared with his sister. It was in disarray, just as the front room had been. He then rushed into his mother's room, and it was even more disturbed. The folding mattress had been ripped apart, and feathers from it were everywhere. Papa's trunk had been turned upside down and all of its contents spilled over the floor. And Mama's mirror had been broken.

Gregor stared at his frightened reflection, distorted by the cracks that looked like frozen ripples in a pool of water. Only then did he panic. "Mama!" he screamed in terror. "Tatiana! Where are you?" And the tears of terror welled up in his eyes.

He fled into the street, screaming hysterically for his mother and sister. He stood helplessly in the darkness, crying over and over, "Mama! Tatiana!" From lighted windows, neighbors peered out at him, but then fearfully closed their curtains and retreated inside. There had been so much trouble in Sabunchi and Balakhani the last two weeks no one wanted to step forward and share his misfortune.

When he had no more strength to yell, Gregor sat down on the front doorstep, resting his arms and head on his knees, and wept. He had no idea how long he had sat there before two figures moved out of the darkness to stand beside him. Hands reached down and touched his shoulder, and a gentle voice said, "You mustn't stay outside. You'll catch a chill."

Gregor looked up and saw Mr. and Mrs. Arounian standing over him. "Where is my mother?" he asked hoarsely. "Do you know what has happened to her and Tatiana?"

Mrs. Arounian hesitated. "The cossacks were here this afternoon," she said reluctantly. "They took your mother and sister away."

"Why?" Gregor asked. "Why should they do that?"

Before Mrs. Arounian could reply, her husband whispered curtly, "Don't say anything out here. Take the boy into the house and tell him."

Gregor allowed himself to be coaxed inside. There the neighbors explained that the cossacks had come to search for socialist literature. When they found what they were seeking, they took Maria and Tatiana with them. "The government has to have someone to blame the riots on," Mr. Arounian told him. "The socialists make easy scapegoats. Your papa was in the oil fields when the fighting started, so they came here trying to see if there was something that might incriminate him."

"But Papa was trying to prevent the riots," Gregor protested.

"I know that," Mr. Arounian said sympathetically. "But in a situation like this, the government doesn't care about the truth."

Angry tears welled up in Gregor's eyes. He knew which papers Mr. Arounian was referring to. They were the leaflets and pamphlets that had been given to Papa by the man named Koba back in Baku.

"When will they let my mother come home?" Gregor asked, trying to bear up manfully under the sorrow.

"I don't know," Mrs. Arounian told him gently. "It's possible they might keep her a very long time."

"What about Tatiana?" he asked. "Will they keep her, too?"

"You must not concern yourself with that," Mrs. Arounian told him. "You can do nothing about such things. Right now, you must have something to eat. Then you will come home with us to spend the night. In the morning, we will decide what is to be done with you. You stay right here, and I will go to the cook-house to see if there is any food for you."

Gregor obeyed. There was, after all, no place he could go. Mr. Arounian did not stay behind with him, but followed his wife out the back of the house. While he sat waiting for their return, Gregor could hear the muffled voices coming from outside.

"We cannot take the boy in," Mr. Arounian said sternly. "We must not become involved in this or we might get into trouble as well."

"Have you no heart?" Mrs. Arounian challenged. "He's just a child! He's helpless and frightened. First his father is killed, then is mother is taken from him."

"That is not our concern," Mr. Arounian replied strongly. "He is not our family. He is not even Armenian."

"I will not argue with you, husband," Mrs. Arounian said firmly. "Tonight, he is coming home with us. Tomorrow, we may know better what can be done with him."

A few moments later, the couple returned to Gregor. Mrs. Arounian was smiling and carrying a bowl of rice and vegetables. Mr. Arounian followed her, glowering silently. "Here now, you will feel much better after you have eaten," the woman said brightly. "Your mother left you some dinner, and you must not let it go to waste."

She set it down before Gregor, and he ate obediently. His mind, however, was not on the food. He was thinking about what he would do. He was grateful for Mrs. Arounian's kindness, but he could not go home with them, knowing how Mr. Arounian felt about it. He would have to refuse the invitation without insulting them. Whatever was to be done for him to go on with his life, he would have to do it himself. His trouble was his own, and it was to be shared with no one.

While Gregor ate, Mrs. Arounian set about straightening the room, as her husband watched her silently, occasionally picking up some miscellaneous piece of litter she had missed, staring at it contemplatively before handing it to her. When Gregor was finished, she took the bowl from him, announcing as she started to the cook-house with it, "Now you go and get the clothes you need for tonight, and you can sleep at our house."

"No," Gregor said. "Thank you, but I think I should stay here." Mrs. Arounian stopped at the door, turned, and looked back at him in surprise. She exchanged a glance with her husband, and started to insist. But Gregor explained. "If the cossacks were to let my mother come home tonight, she would be upset if I weren't here. I think I should stay home, just in case. You are very kind to want to help, but I'll be all right."

"Are you sure?" Mrs. Arounian asked.

Gregor nodded manfully. Inside, he wasn't at all sure of anything.

Chapter 5

Tatiana kept the promise she had made her mother. She remained silently and obediently beside Maria throughout the long ordeal. They spent the first night in a large, empty warehouse near the railroad station in Sabunchi, along with a great many other prisoners, having only bread and water for their evening meal. In the morning, all the prisoners were herded into wagons that were closed in on the sides, open only to the sky above, and they began the journey to Baku.

As the wagons rumbled along, the prisoners spoke very little, and when they did it was in hardly more than a whisper. Their thoughts were best left unexpressed, for if spoken, they might make the fear even greater. Tatiana was worried about what had happened to her brother. He had surely returned home to find them gone. What had he done? Would he try to find them? Would he even have any idea where to search for them?

Looking into her mother's eyes, Tatiana knew that she, too, was worried about Gregor. Once, with her eyes closed, Maria muttered a soft prayer, in which Tatiana heard her speak her brother's name.

Tatiana did not understand the reasons for what was happening to them. She huddled silently against her mother, terrified of the fierce-looking cossacks who stood guard over them with ugly black rifles. Her mother had tried to soothe her, but Tatiana was aware that she, too, was afraid. Since the afternoon of the previous day, what they had experienced had been like a living nightmare, horribly real but at the same time unreal, like nothing she had ever experienced.

That evening, as the wagon jostled along the cobblestone streets of Baku, nearing the prison that was their destination, Maria turned to her daughter and whispered, "If we are separated, and I fear that we will be, you must promise me one thing. When they ask you questions, say nothing. As long as you do not answer their questions, you will be safe. Do you understand?"

"Yes, Mama," Tatiana whispered back. "I understand. But I want to stay with you. Won't you let me stay with you?"

"Of course, my dearest," Maria said, kissing her gently on the forehead. "But they may not permit it." And there was something in her mother's manner that told Tatiana that this was what she should expect.

As the wagons pulled inside the walls of the military garrison and the gates were closed behind them, Tatiana felt the tension of the prisoners. No one spoke, but helplessness and fear could be read in the eyes of each man and woman. When they stopped, one of the guards opened the rear gate of the wagon and commanded, "Everybody get out!"

The prisoners got to their feet slowly, as if unable to will their bodies to obey. Maria gripped Tatiana's hand tightly, waiting for those ahead of them to get out of the wagon.

"Move!" one of the cossacks barked. "Hurry up!"

Maria had to let go of Tatiana's hand in order to step down first, turning quickly to lift her daughter out. It was as she bent to set her feet on the ground that the guard grabbed Tatiana by the arm, pulling her violently from her mother's grasp.

"What are you doing?" Maria cried, reaching for the child. "She's my daughter!" But another guard pulled her away.

"She'll be taken care of," he said. "With the other children."

"No!" Tatiana screamed. "I want to go with my mother!" She struggled to break away, but the soldier was too strong. He pulled her, kicking and screaming, to the doorway of an ugly dark building, while her mother was pulled to a similar building across the large open yard. Tatiana was thrust roughly through the doorway into the building, where other hands grabbed her and shoved her into the recesses of a dimly lit room containing more than a dozen other frightened children, some crying and others sitting in the shadows, staring silently and fearfully at the military guards.

Tatiana found herself a space in the shadows and crouched on the floor weeping quietly. But her tears did not last long. Her feelings were hurt, but—except for being separated from her mother—she had not been harmed. She realized that the other children were in the same position she was, and therefore she was not alone in her fears. Some were much younger than she was. She looked around at them, wishing there was something she could do to help them.

But there was nothing. She had promised her mother that she would keep silent if they were separated. If she did not speak to anyone, her mother had told her, everything would be all right. So she simply kept silent and waited. Her parents had taught her proper behavior for a child, and she would adhere to it strictly.

* * * * *

Gregor slept fitfully that night, awakened frequently by nightmares. By morning, he knew what he had to do. He had to try to find his mother and sister, and he had to do it by himself, without asking help of any of the neighbors. He had no idea where the cossacks were headquartered, but he did know where the Sabunchi police station was. He would go there and ask for directions.

What he did next would depend upon what he learned from the police. He would take it step by step, not thinking about the future, for it might make him afraid to do anything at all. He realized that there was one thing that was of extreme importance, and that was money. He had his pay, but that was not very much. His mother, he knew, kept her household money in the large, old Bible in her room. He went to it to see if any had been left.

Luck was with him. The Bible had not been disturbed, and in it he found eight kopecks. He also found something else he knew was important—the birth and citizenship papers for his mother, his sister, and himself, all in their original names. He knew they were important for any dealings with the authorities, and he hesitated a moment before deciding to take them with him.

He did not hesitate again until he reached the Sabunchi police station. Then, suddenly, overwhelmingly, fear gripped him. For a long time, he stood outside, across the street, staring at the building, afraid to go in. Policemen came and went through the large front door; the sun rose higher in the sky, growing warmer, until beads of sweat broke out on Gregor's forehead.

He did not realize how noticeable he was, until one of the police officers came out the front door and walked directly across the street toward him.

He had the urge to turn and run away, but he had stood there so long, he felt unable to move.

The police officer stopped directly in front of Gregor, frowning. But when he spoke, his manner was not unkind. "What is it, boy?" he asked. "Are you lost?"

"No, sir," Gregor replied shakily.

"Then why have you been standing out here all morning?" the policeman asked.

"It's my mother, sir," Gregor confessed, tears welling up in his eyes. "My mother has been taken by the cossacks, and I'm trying to find her."

"Oh, I see," the policeman said, his voice suddenly acquiring a coldness it had not possessed before. "Well, they don't bring their prisoners here. The army has nothing to do with us."

The tears were suddenly released from Gregor's eyes, despite his efforts to contain them. They eased their way slowly down his cheeks. "I thought perhaps you might be able to tell me where they took her," he said meekly.

The officer's manner softened again. "That depends," he said. "When did this happen?"

"Yesterday afternoon."

The officer scowled in contemplation for a moment, then told him, "The military has no prison here in Sabunchi. I would imagine she has been taken to Baku for trial." He smiled sadly. "I'm sorry. But if you really want to find out, go to the train station. That's where the cossacks have set up their temporary headquarters."

Gregor was unable to learn more from the cossacks. If anything, they were even less helpful than the policeman had been. "We don't keep prisoners here," one of the soldiers told him. "Now, go away and don't bother us."

There seemed only one thing Gregor could do—go to Baku in the hope of finding her there. He did not know the distance, but he did know the way. His family had come from Baku to Sabunchi only a few months ago. Then they had taken the train. Now, because of the riots, the train was no longer running, but he could go on foot, following the rails. It could not be a great distance; as he recalled, the train ride had taken less than an hour.

Gregor purchased some fruit for a midday meal and set out along the railroad tracks, with the sun high overhead. He walked between the rails, and his progress was slow. Because there was no level ground along the tracks, he had to step from one crosstie to the next. He noticed that the dusty dirt road paralleled the railroad tracks. Several times, he considered descending to the road and walking there, but each time he considered doing so, the road veered away from the railroad and disappeared, only to rejoin it later. He was afraid the road might not be going to Baku, while he was certain that the railroad went there.

There were a great many travelers on the road, and he could easily ask for directions. But travelers might be curious as to why a small boy was traveling alone on foot such a great distance. Gregor decided to resolve his problems by himself, without help from anyone, and he was determined to stick by his decision.

However, by the time the sun had crossed halfway from the midheaven toward the western horizon, Gregor began to grow weary. The railroad tracks went up a steep hill, and by the time he reached the top, he was breathing heavily and the muscles in his legs were aching. He was forced to sit down and rest.

It was the first time he had paused to look back at the city behind him. He was a great distance away now, and the towns of Sabunchi and Balakhani were spread out behind him as far as the eye could see, with a dark cloud of smoke rising above them. Here and there, Gregor could see the dark frameworks of oil derricks that had managed to escape destruction in the violence of the last two weeks. But, in places, the red glow of flames still threatened what remained of the once thriving industry.

It was a dying city he was leaving; he could see that from this distance, a city of death.

Emotion began to well up inside Gregor, and he tried vainly to quell it. Looking back, it was impossible not to think of his father and what had happened to him. But he knew he had to be strong. He could look back at sorrow without grieving, for he could also look back at happiness and pride. He could do nothing about what had been; he had to accept it and move on to try to regain the happiness he knew was possible, because he had experienced it before in the loving warmth of his family.

His strength restored, he set off again in the direction of Baku, his single purpose being to find his mother and sister. At a turn in the tracks, he did not notice the man who had stopped his wagon to water his horse in the drainage ditch at the bottom of the railroad embankment.

He was startled by the voice calling out to him, "Hey! Hey, boy! What do you think you're doing up there?"

Gregor stopped and looked down at the man, obviously a Tatar. Fear gripped him, and he could not find voice to reply.

"Railroad tracks are no place for a boy to play," the Tatar admonished. "You might get hit by a train."

"It's all right," Gregor replied. "The trains aren't running."

"It's true they haven't been," the Tatar replied, "but you never know when they might start again."

Silently, Gregor acknowledged that the man was right, but he shrugged. "I'll watch out for them."

"Where are you going?" the Tatar asked, climbing the embankment toward him. "Is it far?"

"To Baku," Gregor said cautiously. "I'm sure it's not much further."

"It's far enough you won't get there by nightfall on foot," the man told him. "That's where I'm going, and you're welcome to ride with me in my wagon."

Gregor hesitated. He wasn't sure whether he could trust the man or not. Gregor did not have the dark looks of a Tatar; the man had to know—or at least suspect—he was of an enemy race, either Armenian or Russian. He studied the wagon indecisively. It was loaded with large sacks of grain or rice; it meant the man was probably a merchant or a farmer. Was he trustworthy?

"Thank you, sir," Gregor said. "But I think I can manage to make it on my own."

The Tatar studied him skeptically. "Whatever you wish," he said, and returned to looking after his horse.

Gregor set out again along the tracks. But his feet were aching, and he felt a blister growing on his heel. He began to limp. Only a short distance further on, he had to sit down and rub his foot to try to ease the pain.

"Boy!" he heard the Tatar's voice call out again. Gregor looked down at the roadway and saw him, riding on his wagon, having set on his way again. "Come on and ride! I won't harm you! I've got a boy at home your age. You can ride in back, on top of the rice."

Gregor hesitated, then got painfully to his feet. "Yes, sir," he said. "Thank you, sir."

As the bright afternoon sunlight began to fade into dusk, with the steady rhythmic swaying of the loaded wagon, Gregor felt himself growing drowsy. It had been a tiring day, and he fell asleep well before nightfall.

* * * * *

Tatiana spent a difficult night at the military garrison in Baku, but she endured, aided by the resolves she had made. She ate all of the thin soup and hard bread they gave her for dinner, though it was tasteless and stuck in her throat. She accepted the blanket they issued her for sleeping and curled up obediently on the floor as instructed. In the morning, she ate the rancid fruit that was breakfast, and patiently waited her turn to go to the toilet, though it was painful to hold it in so long.

At midmorning, however, her real difficulties began. It was then that she and the other children were shown the first bit of kindness they had experienced since arriving in the prison. Two people cme to take charge of the children—a man and a woman. Except for one man at the door, the military guards left, and the atmosphere in the room brightened immeasurably.

The man was quite old, with snow white hair and soft warm eyes. The woman was small and plump, with rosy cheeks and lips that seemed always on the verge of a smile.

"My name is Gogo," the man said, addressing the children, a few of whom giggled, prompting him to smile. "With that name, I know I ought to be a clown, but I'm not. The lady with me is Nurse Afsar. We are in charge of the Baku Children's Displacement Center. Some people call our place an orphanage, but that makes it sound like a very grim place, and it's not grim at all. You are all going to come and stay with us for a while, and we will do our best to take care of you and make you happy. But you must help us in every way you can. Everything we ask you to do will be for your own good. Do you understand that?"

He looked around the room. A few of the children nodded.

"The first thing we ask," he continued, "is that you form a line in front of this table. We will ask each of you in turn some questions. Your answers will help us to know how we can help you." Again he looked around the room to see if the children understood. "All right. Let's form a line now." And then he sat down in a chair behind the table.

Obediently, the children moved toward the center of the room, gradually forming a long line. Tatiana joined them, but cautiously took the position at the very end. This was the moment her mother had foreseen and warned her about. They would ask her questions, and she would have to remain silent.

She did not want to make this man and woman angry by being disobedient, but she had to keep her promise.

All of the other children were answering Gogo's questions, then moving on for Nurse Afsar to examine their throats and ears to see if they were in good health. The line grew shorter all too quickly. The nearer Tatiana got to the table where Gogo sat, the more apprehensive she became.

By the time her turn came, her legs were trembling with fear. She had heard the questions as they were asked of each of the others; they were simple ones that any child could answer, not like a test at school.

The first thing they asked of each child was a name, and that made it even more difficult for Tatiana. She had two names, one when she had lived in Baku and another in Sabunchi. She knew the lie had been necessary to protect the family against the authorities. Now the authorities knew both names.

The kindly old man smiled at her. "And what is your name, young lady?" he asked.

Tatiana clenched her jaw shut and stared straight at him, as if she did not understand.

"Can you tell me your name?" he prodded.

Tatiana felt the urge to nod her head in reply, but she quelled the urge and merely blinked her eyes.

"You don't have to be afraid of me," Gogo said. "I won't bite you."

Tatiana blinked again. She felt tears welling up in her eyes, and she did not want to cry.

Gogo frowned. "You can speak, can't you?" He paused. "Are you mute? Deaf and dumb?"

She could not control the tears. They began to pour from her eyes, and she broke into helpless sobs.

Nurse Afsar moved swiftly to console her. "Here, child," she said gently, "you mustn't cry. We're here to help you."

Tatiana buried her head in the woman's comforting embrace, accepting her kindness but unable to stop the tears.

"What should we do about her?" Gogo asked. "If she's a deaf-mute, we may not be able to take care of her."

"Don't worry about it," Afsar said. "She'll be no trouble at all."

"But we don't even have a name for her," Gogo protested. "We can't even keep a file on her."

"Are files so important?" Afsar asked. "We can make up a name. What's important is that she's a frightened child, and she needs love and care."

After the children were fed a meal of cheese and bread, they were told to get ready to leave the prison. The cossacks would deliver them there in one of the military wagons. Gogo and Afsar would go ahead of them in their own carriage.

Tatiana felt a dull ache in her heart when they departed and the military guards returned to watch over the children. The cossacks gruffly commanded them to form a line in front of the door, the one through which they had entered the night before. Once the children were lined up, the leader of the guards opened the door and ordered them to follow him, and to stay in line.

The bright sunlight outside was painful to Tatiana's eyes after the darkness of the prison room. It took a few moments for her to adjust and see what was around her. One by one, the children ahead of her were climbing into a wagon. On each side of them were two guards, keeping them in line.

Then Tatiana looked across the courtyard and saw her mother. She, too, was in a line, watched over by cossacks, but her line consisted entirely of adults, and they were being loaded into a railroad boxcar.

Maria Baranov stopped when her eyes saw her daughter.

Tatiana started to move toward her, slowly at first, then running desperately, knowing a guard would try to stop her.

"No, Tatiana!" Maria cried. "No!"

Suddenly, a soldier hit Maria on the shoulder with the butt of his rifle, and she fell to the ground. An instant later, another one grabbed Tatiana from behind, lifted her high into the air, and threw her into the wagon with the other children.

She lay there for a few moments, stunned, as the last of the children climbed in.

Then the rear gate was slammed shut and locked, and the wagon started rumbling off across the courtyard, through the prison gates, and out into the streets of Baku.

Chapter 6

Gregor had to dodge out of the way of the horse and wagon that was coming through the gate of the Cossack garrison. He paid no attention to the wagon, he was so intent on getting to the gate before the guards closed it, hoping they would allow him inside.

He rushed up to the rapidly narrowing opening, trying to squeeze through.

"Hey, boy," one of the guards said sternly, grasping him by the collar, "you can't come in here!"

"Please, sir," Gregor said meekly. "I have business here. I need to see the man in charge."

"Oh?" the guard questioned skeptically. "The colonel? And what do you need to see him about?"

"I'm trying to find my mother and sister," Gregor replied. "I think they've been brought here."

With a sudden shove, the guard thrust Gregor outside and shut the iron-barred gate between them. "If they're in here," he said curtly, "they're prisoners. And no one is allowed to see the prisoners."

Gregor had gone to a great deal of trouble to get this far. He had come all the way from Sabunchi; he had spent the night sleeping in an alleyway, cold and shivering; and it had taken most of the morning for him to find the cossack garrison and prison. "Please, sir," he begged. "Can't I at least find out if they are here?"

"I'm warning, you, boy," the man said grimly, "if you don't leave, we'll have to use force. Now, you wouldn't want to get yourself hurt, would you?"

Gregor did not cower at the threat, but he realized it meant he would get nowhere by pleading with the guard. He retreated a short distance from the gate to think about what he could do.

Wandering about, kicking a stone across the cobbled pavement, he noticed a train engine backing along tracks that led through another gate into the cossack compound. Curious to learn if he might be able to slip through this entrance more easily, he casually walked over and looked through the narrow opening between the railroad tracks and the high stone wall.

He peered inside, frighteningly close to the enormous steel wheels of the engine. There was a sudden loud sound of metal hitting metal, as the engine connected to a line of boxcars inside the garrison, followed by a burst of steam that completely covered Gregor, causing him to gasp for air.

He realized this was his opportunity. Swiftly, he darted through the gate, running blindly in the midst of the thick steam.

Abruptly, he was stopped when he collided with something— someone— just as the steam was clearing.

"Hey, what is this?" the startled soldier looked down at Gregor. "Where did you come from, young man?"

Gregor stared at him dumbly. The train, now attached to the boxcars, began pulling out of the garrison, the loud chugging of its engine and the whine of its wheels against the tracks making all other sounds inaudible. It gave Gregor some time to think of an answer.

When the sound had subsided, he told the guard, "I was sent with a message for the colonel, and I got lost."

The soldier frowned, looking at Gregor's shabby, dirty clothes. "What kind of message would a boy like you have for the colonel?" he asked.

"It's a private matter, sir," Gregor replied, his confidence growing.

"Private for you?" the soldier asked. "Or for the colonel?"

Gregor took a deep breath. "If you would just tell me where to find the colonel, sir, I would appreciate it."

"I think you're lying, boy," the man said, scowling. "And, if you are . . .," He hesitated a moment, then said decisively, "Come along; I'll take you, and we'll see."

Gregor felt elated, but apprehensive. He had bluffed his way this far, but he had no idea what kind of response he would get when he confronted the colonel. At least he would be given a chance. He hurried to keep up with the soldier's long strides, hoping it would be only a short time before he was reunited with his mother and sister, even if it meant he would be imprisoned along with them.

In the reception room outside the colonel's office, Gregor faced another obstacle. An adjutant, seated at a desk, guarded the door. When the soldier explained how he had found Gregor wandering about the compound, the adjutant looked skeptical.

"What is your name?" he asked. "And what is your business with the colonel?"

"My name is Gregor Baranov," Gregor told him. "And it's a private matter, concerning my mother."

"Your mother?" the adjutant asked, surprised, then exchanged a shrewd grin with the guard, who did his best to stifle a chuckle.

"I see," the adjutant said. "And it's not something you can tell me about?"

Gregor hesitated. He did not understand the exchange of glances between the two cossack officers, but luck had been with him so far. "No, sir," he replied. "It's not. It's private and personal."

The adjutant instructed Gregor to wait there with the man who had brought him. He went into the colonel's office, closing the door behind him, then returned a moment later, holding the door open for Gregor.

Gregor's heart was pounding fearfully, as he stepped into the large, impressive office and faced the colonel, who was seated behind an enormous mahogany desk. The colonel was a red-faced man with eyes as black as his waxed mustache, and he glared at Gregor with a furrowed brow.

"What is this about your mother, boy?" he demanded curtly, while the adjutant hovered behind Gregor at the door. "Just who is your mother?"

Gregor took a deep breath. This was his chance. He could not lose it. He answered swiftly and surely. "Her name is Maria Baranov, and I'm told she is a prisoner here. If she is, I would like very much to see her."

The colonel's red face turned a brilliant crimson. When he spoke, it was an angry explosion. "If this is one of your little jokes, Lieutenant Petrovsky," he bellowed at the adjutant, "I fail to see the humor in it! Get this boy out of here! And if I set eyes on him again, somebody will be in serious trouble! Do you understand me?"

Within a matter of moments, Gregor was once again standing on the street outside the front gate of the garrison. This time, he knew he had been utterly defeated. It would do him no good at all to get back inside the military compound; he had to give up on that approach, but he would not give up his effort to find his mother and sister.

For the next few hours, Gregor wandered about the streets of Baku, thinking, trying to decide what he should do. He gravitated naturally into Black Town, the part of the city that was most familiar to him. That was where he had spent most of his life; that was where he and his family had known happiness, before his world was turned upside down.

It was not a very attractive place, a jumble of narrow streets and small brick houses that had turned black from the oily soot emitted by the refineries. Ugly as it was, Gregor wished fervently that his family had never left it. While he walked, Gregor found himself remembering the friends he had had here, and the good times—for a while forgetting his principal objective for being in Baku.

He stopped outside the house that had once been his home, staring at it wistfully. It had hardly changed since they had left it, though it clearly housed new tenants. The flowers his mother had tried so hard to nurture in the front yard were all dead, and the front gate had either fallen or been removed from its hinges. He had a great urge to walk through that gate and on into the house, feeling perhaps he might find his family all inside as they had once been.

But no, he had no family now. He had to remember that. His father was dead, and for all he knew his mother and sister might be, too. It was the first time that had occurred to him, and he quickly rejected it. It was not possible that he could be the only member of his family alive.

It was then that he remembered his Uncle Vladimir. Even though Gregor had never seen him, Uncle Vladimir was still a part of his family. He knew very well that his father and his uncle had fought, but to Gregor, being family meant you loved each other even when you had differences. Uncle Vladimir would surely want to know what had happened to his brother. He might even be able to help.

There were so many things an adult could do that a child could not. Gregor was certain that the cossacks had not listened to him, mainly because he was a child. Surely Uncle Vladimir would find out what had happened to his mother and sister, if anyone could. Uncle Vladimir was a rich and important man in Baku.

Gregor had no idea how to find his uncle's house. He knew only that he lived in the White Town, the section of great stone and marble mansions where all of the rich and powerful people lived. It was only a short distance from Black Town, but to Gregor it might have been the end of the earth. During all the years he had lived in Baku, he had never dared venture further than the outer edges of the wealthy section. The splendor of the homes and the fine dress and manners of the people who lived in them had always seemed somehow frightening to him.

However, Gregor decided, it could be no worse than facing the cossacks, and he had already done that today. He would find Uncle Vladimir's house; he would meet him, and he would ask for his help.

It was late when he finally located the house, which was not as formidable as he had expected. Not small by any definition, consisting of two stories with a basement, it was somewhat less grand than the surrounding mansions.

The front of it was plain, light-colored stone, with only a trace of ornate decoration covering a small balcony on the second floor, directly above the front entrance. Six stone steps led up to the front doors, which were of highly polished wood, with brass fixtures. Other steps led down to the basement, which had a servants' or tradesman's entrance.

Gregor paused for a moment in front of the house, reflecting upon which door to approach. It would be less frightening to approach the servants first, but he was family. He was also growing more bold this day; he had stopped several of the well-dressed residents of White Town on the street to ask for directions, and they had not been unkind.

Gathering his courage, he marched up the front steps, grasped the heavy brass knocker, and tapped it briskly against its metal plate.

Then he waited. Several minutes passed, and he was just about to try knocking again when finally the door was opened and a thin, older man wearing Tatar robes and a turban looked down at him, with a suspicious but not entirely unpleasant expression. He had the dark skin, large nose, and black beard of an Arab, and Gregor had come to be wary of such men in recent weeks.

"What do you want, boy?" the man asked.

"I would like to see Vladimir Mehdovi," Gregor told him manfully.

The Arab frowned. "I doubt if he would want to see you," he said. "He doesn't like children. Why are you here?"

"My name is Gregor Mehdovi. I am his nephew."

The man's jaw dropped in astonishment, and he let out an exclamation of surprise. Then he smiled and shook his head woefully. "I don't think he likes people he's related to any more than he likes children," he said. "But I will tell him you are here."

Gregor was not invited to wait inside the door; instead the door was closed in his face. He was surprised, but he refused to be dismayed. A few moments later, the Arab opened the door again. He smiled sympathetically and said "Mr. Mehdovi instructed me to ask why you wish to see him? If it's money you want, he told me to send you away."

Gregor's immediate reaction was a stunned silence. Then he began to feel insulted. He had not quite known what sort of reaction to expect from his uncle, but he had certainly not expected this.

"I do not want any of his money," Gregor said hotly. "But I have come to ask for his help. My father has been killed, and my mother and sister have been taken away by the cossacks. I hoped Uncle Vladimir might be able to find out where they are, but perhaps it was a mistake to come to ask him for anything." He turned angrily and started down the steps.

"Wait," the Arab called out, following him, closing the front door behind him. Taking Gregor by the shoulder, he said, "Here, sit down on the steps with me and tell me about it. My name is Ali Jabbar. I have been with Mr. Mehdovi for many years as his servant, and I am the first to admit that he can be obstinate and difficult, but I know how to manage him. I may be able to help you."

Gregor looked at him skeptically. Deciding he had nothing to lose, he sat down beside the man, and proceeded to tell him the entire story.

When he finished, Ali Jabbar sat for a moment in pensive silence. Then he said, "I am not sure what Mr. Mehdovi's reaction will be, but I'm sure he can be persuaded in time. I will take you in to see him, but you must try not to lose your temper, no matter what he says. His bark is much worse than his bite."

He led Gregor into the house, which was dark, cold, and sparsely furnished, which surprised Gregor. Ali Jabbar—noticing his reaction—explained in a whisper, "Mr. Mehdovi doesn't like to spend money for anything that isn't absolutely essential."

The servant opened a large door that led from the main hall, and it creaked painfully on its hinges. It occurred to Gregor that his uncle should at least spend money on some oil to get rid of that annoying sound. Stepping inside the room, Ali Jabbar announced, "Mr. Mehdovi, this is your nephew Gregor. He has not come to ask for money."

Gregor stepped inside the room, and as he did so, his uncle growled. "Humph, whatever it is, I'm sure it will cost me something."

"Only your time," Ali Jabbar said. "I think you should listen to him."

"All right," Vladimir said wearily, removing a pair of rimless spectacles and rubbing his eyes. "What is it you want, boy?"

Gregor moved toward the large, untidy desk behind which his uncle sat. He recognized Vladimir's resemblance to his father instantly, though the differences were more startling. Vladimir was only a few years older than Alexei had been, but his hair and beard were completely white, and there were deep lines on his forehead and around his dark, intense eyes. As Gregor studied his uncle's face, Ali Jabbar slipped out of the room, closing the creaking door and leaving the two of them alone together.

There was no trace of kindness in Vladimir's face, only an impassive curiosity and a wariness. Despite the vague resemblance to his father, Gregor decided that he did not like his uncle.

He wished he had not come, but he could not change that. He told his uncle about what had happened to his family. Rather than creating sympathy, the revelation that Alexei was dead and Maria and Tatiana were imprisoned seemed to give Vladimir much pleasure.

The old man leaned back in his chair and smiled. "I warned your father that no good would come of marrying a Russian woman. Now that I've been proved right, I'm expected to get his family out of trouble. Well, I won't do it. My brother's family is none of my responsibility. You've wasted your time, boy, and mine as well." He looked around the desk for his eyeglasses, found them, and put them on. "Now, go away and leave me alone." He returned to the work in front of him.

Gregor fought back tears of frustration. He did not want to show weakness before this man, who was mean and rude. He turned swiftly and walked out of the room, into the hallway, and out the front door. He decided there was only one good thing about this visit: he had gained an understanding of why his father had hated his only brother.

Gregor scampered down the front steps, anxious to put this house behind him as quickly as he could. But, before he could get away, a voice called to him, "Wait, boy!"

Gregor stopped, turned, and looked back. It was Ali Jabbar, coming out of the basement entrance, beckoning to him. Reluctantly Gregor retraced his steps.

"I take it Mr. Mehdovi was not sympathetic to your request," Ali said. Gregor shook his head.

The servant shrugged. "He may yet change his mind. Perhaps tomorrow."

"I don't intend to come back tomorrow to find out," Gregor said bitterly.

"You mustn't be disheartened," Ali said kindly, putting his hand on Gregor's shoulder. "Do you have a place to stay?"

Gregor shook his head. "I'll manage. I slept in an alley last night, and it wasn't too bad."

"Well, you won't sleep in an alley tonight," the servant told him decisively. "You will sleep here, in this house."

"In my uncle's house?" Gregor asked. "No, I couldn't. I wouldn't if I could."

"He doesn't have to know," Ali said. "You can sleep in my room."

"No," Gregor protested. "If my uncle found out, it would get you in trouble. He might fire you."

"He wouldn't dare," Ali grinned. "He knows he couldn't get anybody to work as cheaply as I do. He's tried it before."

"Thank you for wanting to help," Gregor said. "But after seeing what my uncle is like, I think I would rather sleep anywhere but under his roof."

"You must be practical," Ali said. "Tomorrow Mr. Mehdovi may change his mind. Which is more important, your pride or finding your mother and sister?"

For a moment, Gregor still hesitated. When it was put that way, he could not refuse. "All right," he said. "But I will sleep in the kitchen and leave before he gets up."

* * * * *

Gregor was still sound asleep early the next morning, just before dawn, when Vladimir Mehdovi came downstairs to the kitchen for tea. As he had predicted, the uncle was angry to find him there, curled up on the floor under a blanket Ali had loaned him, so angry that he kicked Gregor roughly in the ribs to wake him.

"Ali! What is this boy doing here?" he screamed. "You have no right to let him stay in this house without my approval! I threw him out, and I do not want him here!"

Startled at being awakened so roughly, Gregor did not immediately realize where he was or what was happening. It was only after Ali came running in from his small room alongside the kitchen that Gregor remembered. He struggled to get to his feet and gain his composure.

"This boy is a thief!" Vladimir challenged.

"He is your nephew," Ali replied, "and he had no place to stay."

"Yes," Vladimir said, his voice trembling, as he tried to control his rage, "and I threw him out. Therefore, he is an intruder and a thief."

"I have taken nothing from you," Gregor spoke up defensively.

"You have taken a night's lodging," the uncle stated accusingly. "And I'll warrant you've had a meal as well."

"I have money," Gregor said. "I can pay you for my night's lodging and my dinner."

This seemed to suprise Vladimir, for he became considerably calmer. "Probably stolen," he grumbled. "Where else could a boy like you get money?"

"By working," Gregor said proudly. "I am strong and healthy and smart. I can even read and write."

Vladimir cast his eyes heavenward. "So now they're educating thieves."

"Master," Ali interjected suddenly. "Perhaps the boy could do some work to pay for his room and board. There is much that needs to be done around the house, and I do not have time to do it all. Also, I am not as strong or as limber as I once was."

Vladimir looked as his servant shrewdly, then at the boy. "The new supply of coal is still out in the backyard," he said pensively. "And the water in the reservoir needs changing."

"I can make a bed for him here in the kitchen," Ali suggested encouragingly. "You'll hardly even know he's here."

"What do you mean?" Vladimir scowled. "I didn't say he could keep staying here. I meant he could work to pay for last night."

"But it makes sense, doesn't it?" the servant said slyly. "You would be getting a bargain. A full day's work from the boy for only room and board."

Vladimir Mehdovi contemplated the idea with obvious approval. "Yes," he said finally, "it might be worth it. But the boy would have to stay out of my way."

"I would be willing to do that, sir, "Gregor said, "but only on one condition—that you inquire at the military garrison about my mother and sister."

Vladimir frowned at him. "Well," he said noncommitally, "we'll see about that."

Chapter 7

After the first few days, Tatiana found it was not difficult to go without speaking, especially when others did not expect her to speak. Although some of the children made fun of her, most of them gave her special treatment, and so did the staff. Afsar was particularly kind to her, frequently sitting beside her in the dining hall or taking her for walks in the yard of the children's displacement center. Because no one knew her name, they called her Sarah, and Tatiana quickly learned to respond to it.

The only problem she had with keeping silent was that she really wanted to know what had happened to her mother. Tatiana longed to ask questions. She had heard enough from the other children to know that they were all here waiting to be placed in homes. Some no longer had parents, and they were up for adoption; others were to stay at the displacement center until their parents were released from prison. Tatiana did not know what she could expect.

The worst times for Tatiana were at night, when all the lights were out and she was lying alone on her little cot in the big dormitory room, where all of the girls slept. Then she would lie awake, thinking about her mother, reliving the horror of the last day they had spent together, weeping silently so no one would know how frightened she was.

During the day, she could watch the other children and sometimes even join in their games, and then she was not so lonely. There were several hundred children, both boys and girls, at the displacement center, and they were of all different races and backgrounds. Some spoke languages that were completely strange to Tatiana.

But there were times when Tatiana was almost happy, the times when Afsar would ask her to come along on her rounds to help distribute clean linens and underclothes to the other children. Tatiana would be allowed to push the cart that held the nurse's supplies, and that made her feel important and useful. Occasionally, Afsar would pause in her rounds to examine a child who appeared flushed, or one with a runny nose, or another with a sore on the arm; at these times, Tatiana would watch with great interest. She was not repelled by illness; she was fascinated by the way Nurse Afsar would treat the problems.

Tatiana had been at the children's displacement center about a week when, one morning, the nurse came out to the playground to tell her that Mr. Gogoli wanted to see her in his office. She had learned that "Gogo" was only what the children called the director of the center; his real name was "Gogoli."

Although no one yet knew that Tatiana could speak, by this time, Afsar had learned that she could hear and understand. Afsar had learned that one day in the infirmary, when she had misplaced some bandages. She went about, muttering to herself, "Now where did I put them?" Without thinking, Tatiana suddenly went to the shelf where Afsar had put the bandages, picked them up, and handed them to her. To Nurse Afsar, this revealed two things about the child: she was intelligent and she must have been from a Persian background, for Afsar had spoken the words in that language.

Tatiana accompanied Afsar to Gogo's office, scampering to keep up with the nurse's long steps. Although, on several occasions since arriving, she had seen the kindly old man who ran the children's center, Tatiana had not been asked to his office before. Among the children, it was accepted that there were only two reasons to be called into Mr. Gogoli's office— either to be reprimanded for misbehavior or to be released to a family. Since Tatiana had not misbehaved, she hoped that she was about to be returned to her mother.

The offices were in a two-story brick building on the opposite side of the playground from the dormitories and infirmary. The director and his wife lived on the second floor. The ground floor had four offices, the largest and most comfortable of which was Mr. Gogoli's. As soon as they arrived, Afsar and Tatiana were ushered inside.

To Tatiana's dismay, her mother was not there. Instead there was only a tall well-dressed man.

"This is the child I was telling you about," Gogo said, getting up from his desk. "We call her Sarah, for want of her true name."

The man turned and looked down at Tatiana, then smiled warmly. "She is certainly lovely," he said.

Tatiana felt tears rising, and she tried to quell them. The man seemed to be very nice, and she did not want to insult him, but she was disappointed.

"Sarah," Mr. Gogoli said gently, "this is Mr. Boustani. He is from Rasht, in Persia."

Philip Boustani moved toward her, smiling. Tatiana assessed him as she did all adult males, by comparing him to her father, and there were some similarities. He was about the same height, and there was a warmth about his dark eyes that reminded her of Papa. But, except for a well-trimmed mustache, this man was clean-shaven, while her father had had a beard.

Suddenly she realized that he was studying her, just as she was studying him.

"She doesn't look Jewish," Boustani said to Gogo. "She's too fair."

"I didn't say she was definitely Jewish," Gogo protested genially. "I merely said she might be, and she is the only child in the place at the moment who could be Jewish. I have seen Jews with blond hair and blue eyes."

"Perhaps in Germany or Poland," Boustani said with a frown. "But not many in this part of the world."

Tatiana felt embarrassed being discussed this way. She dropped her gaze to the floor, blushing. She wondered why they were so interested in her background.

Mr. Gogoli came from behind his desk to stand beside her. "Well," he said with a sigh. "We know she cannot be an Arab. At first we thought she might be Armenian, but then we learned that she understands the Persian language. The only thing we could think of was that she might be a Persian Jew. That's why I thought of you."

"She seems a sweet and beautiful child," Boustani said pensively. "But I have the same problem you do. If, as you say, she cannot speak, I doubt if any of my people would want to take her in. I have plenty of Jewish families who want to adopt, but only healthy children."

Suddenly, Afsar spoke up. "But sir," she said, "this child is perfectly healthy. I think she can speak if she wants to. My opinion is that she is suffering from the shock of what she has been through. The soldiers do not always treat political prisoners well. The child may have seen her parents injured or even killed. We don't know what she's feeling inside. But she is a well-behaved, good child, and physically strong and healthy."

Boustani began to pace the room, shaking his head. "I just don't know," he said. "What if we should place her with a family, and later find she isn't Jewish at all?"

The center's director frowned. "What is more important—race and religion or caring for an innocent child who desperately needs love. I will put it to you frankly: if you do not take this child, I do not think we will ever find a home for her. We have more children than we can place. Every day we get more. The Arabs and Tatars take care of their own. I have you to take the Jewish children. The rest I have to place in orphanages. This one I would have to try to get the Armenian Church to take, and their orphanage is already full. What would they do with the child if she should turn out to be Jewish—turn her over to you? No, they would bring her up as a Christian. Why can't you or one of your people bring her up as a Jew?"

Philip Boustani heaved a weary sigh. "All right," he said decisively. "I'll take her. If I can't find a family for her, perhaps I can persuade my wife that our daughter needs a sister. There is something about her that makes my heart go out to her."

* * * * *

Tatiana was frightened about leaving the children's center. She had grown attached to Asfar and accustomed to the routine. After all she had been through, she was grateful to be somewhere away from the violence. She still missed her family. But if she could not be with them, the displacement center was not really a bad place to be. As nice as Philip Boustani seemed, he and the place he was taking her were unknowns, fearful and uncertain.

When Afsar embraced her to kiss her goodbye, Tatiana clung to her desperately, hoping if she showed all the love she felt, perhaps the nurse would not send her away. "Bless you, child," she said, separating herself from Tatiana's grasp. "I hope you may find a good and loving family."

This time Tatiana could not hold back the tears. She wept bitterly as Philip Boustani took her hand and led her out the front gate of the displacement center to a waiting carriage.

As he sat down in the seat beside her and signaled the driver to go ahead, he said, "We are going to be getting on a large boat today. Have you ever been on a boat?"

Tatiana blinked her eyes, but did not admit that she had never even been close to one.

"It will take us to Enzeli," he continued. "That is in Persia, and it will take us a whole day to get there. After that, we will travel on to a city called Rasht, where I and my family live."

To Tatiana, that seemed far away indeed. She wondered how far that might be from where the train had taken her mother.

At the docks, Philip Boustani found a boy to take care of his luggage, then took Tatiana down from the carriage. "We're going to do a bit of shopping before we get on the boat," he said. "I must buy presents for my wife and daughter. I always do when I travel away from home."

He explained that there was a large outdoor market area near the Baku docks, where imported goods from other parts of the world were sold. Although Tatiana had never been to this market before, she had frequently accompanied her mother shopping, so she welcomed the familiar activity, browsing among the stalls, looking at all the fine merchandise, dreaming of things she would like one day to own for herself.

Philip Boustani first selected a gift for his wife. After browsing awhile and considering several possibilities, he finally chose a beautiful lace shawl that had come from Spain. Then he set out to find something for his daughter. "Her name is Nadia," he told Tatiana, "and she is about your age. What do you think a girl your age might want?"

Tatiana stared at him silently, and blinked her eyes.

After a moment, he said, "I see something over there she might like." Tatiana did not see what he was pointing at until they had found their way to the stall.

It contained dolls—lots of them—and they were the most beautiful dolls Tatiana had ever seen. They were not like the one her mother had made for her. Oh, the bodies were made of cloth like hers had been, but the heads, hands, and feet were of brightly painted porcelain. And the dresses, in all colors, were made of fancy lace and frills and ribbons. Tatiana desperately wanted to reach out and touch them, but she watched her manners and held her hands clenched tightly behind her back, satisfying herself with gazing longingly at the wonderful objects.

"Now, which one do you think she might like?" Philip asked. "There are so many to choose from." Tatiana reached out her hand and pointed to one in a lovely pink dress, but then as she started to withdraw her hand she saw another that seemed even nicer, in a yellow dress with green bows and ribbons. Then her finger pointed to one in a white dress. Finally she withdrew her hand and shrugged.

Philip laughed. "Yes," he said, "they're all beautiful, aren't they?" He picked up the one in the white dress and studied it. Then he compared it to the one in pink. The first had painted light brown hair; the other had black hair.

He studied the dolls, then he studied Tatiana's expression. Finally, he said, "I think I should get these two. The one with dark hair will be for Nadia, and the one with light hair will be for you, Sarah."

Tatiana stared at him uncomprehendingly for a moment. Then her mouth dropped open in disbelief at what she thought he had said. Only when he handed her the lovely doll in the lacy white dress did she fully understand and believe. She took it in her hands gently and lovingly. She wanted to speak, to thank him for the gift, but she didn't dare break the spell she had created with her silence.

Instead, she threw her arms around his long legs and embraced him gratefully.

Philip Boustani carressed her hair and patted her on the back. "I understand," he said. "It is my pleasure to give it to you. Perhaps it will be company for you on the trip to Enzeli and Rasht."

The merchant wrapped the other doll carefully in tissue paper and tied it with string, but Tatiana was permitted to carry hers. She clutched it tightly, for fear of dropping it and breaking it; and, as they picked their way back through the market to the dock, she kept looking at the shiny delicate face, wondering at the little rosebud lips and the large, bright blue eyes.

She was still mesmerized by her gift as she stood at the boat's railing with Philip, watching the city of Baku recede, growing gradually smaller, until it looked like a little toy town, just the right size for her doll. Then it grew even smaller.

*   *   *   *   *

It was a long time before the boat reached Enzeli, and Tatiana slept in her seat alongside Philip Boustani, clutching her doll to her breast. The day on the boat had been an exhausting one, for everything had been so strange and different from what she had been accustomed to. They had spent the morning walking about the deck, watching the large waves created by the wake of the boat, gazing off at the distant, mountainous shore they were following, and looking at the other ships that plied the Caspian.

Then they had their midday meal in a large dining hall with lots of little tables covered in white linen, eating off gold-trimmed china with heavy ornate silverware. Each table had a little bowl of flowers, and a band played sweet Russian music on balalaika, accordion, and flute. The food itself was incredibly rich-tasting, seasoned with herbs and spices that Tatiana did not recognize. It concluded with a chocolate pudding that made Tatiana think perhaps she was in a dream. If it was, she did not want to wake up, and so she curled up in the seat beside Philip Boustani and fell asleep.

He awakened her to disembark, and she stumbled groggily down the gangplank and allowed Philip to lift her into a carriage. This began the second stage of the journey, overland to the nearby city of Rasht. Finally, they reached the Boustani home. By the time they were there, Tatiana was fully awake and alert.

The carriage stopped before a very grand building, which was three floors high, made of stone, with the kind of fancy decoration Tatiana associated with government buildings. She did not realize that this was the Boustani home, instead assuming it was a place he would be making a stop, so she prepared herself to wait in the carriage for him.

But he turned to her after he had descended and announced happily, "We're home. You will now meet my wife Judith and my daughter Nadia."

She looked at him and then at the house. It was only then that she realized that Philip Boustani must be a very rich and a very important man. Of course, only rich men could buy not one but two dolls such as the one she carried in her arms.

Inside, the house was even more marvellous than outside. They were let in the front door by a man Tatiana later learned was a servant. From a grand marble hall with gilt-framed mirrors, crystal chandeliers, and an elegant staircase, Philip led her into a beautiful, warmly inviting parlor.

In the parlor, sitting on a red plush sofa, was a little dark-haired girl about Tatiana's age. She was wearing a pink dress as lovely as the ones on the porcelain dolls, with lots of ruffles and pretty white trimming. As soon as they walked through the door, the girl leaped up and rushed to embrace Philip, crying excitedly, "Papa! Welcome home! What did you bring me this time?"

Philip laughed, then chided gently. "Is that the kind of welcome I get? What did I bring you? Don't I at least get a kiss first?" He bent down and offered his cheek.

The girl laughed and gave him a kiss. "Now," she said, "what did you bring me?"

"First I want you to meet the child I have brought with me this time." Philip said. "We don't know her true name, but she is called Sarah." He turned to Tatiana. "This is my daughter Nadia."

"Hello," Nadia said brightly, then her eyes fell on the doll Tatiana held. "Oh, what a lovely doll! May I hold it?"

Tatiana's immediate reaction was to clutch the precious toy more tightly, but then she realized she must not be ungenerous to the daughter of the man who had so generously given it to her. Slowly she extended the doll for Nadia to take.

The girl held it gently, admiring it. "It must have come from England," Nadia said. "Or from America. They make some nice China dolls."

Tatiana wanted to correct her, to tell her it had been purchased in Baku, but she did not speak.

"Now, if you will give Sarah back her doll," Philip said, "I will give you your present."

Nadia returned the doll and turned expectantly to her father, who promptly handed her the carefully wrapped package. When she had removed all of the tissue, Nadia squealed with delight. "Oh, it's just like Sarah's! How wonderful! They're alike but different! It's like they're sisters!" She turned to Tatiana. "We must play with them together and visit often so that the sisters can visit. What did you name yours?"

Tatiana stared at her silently, feeling tears of frustration beginning to rise. She blinked to try to hold them down.

"Are you shy?" Nadia asked, not unkindly.

"No," Philip explained. "She doesn't speak. That's why we don't know her real name."

"Oh," Nadia said, crestfallen, a look a pity coming over her face. "I'm sorry," she said to Tatiana.

"The people at the displacement center think that she can speak if she wants to," Philip told her. "They believe she is suffering from some sort of terrible experience. There has been much unrest in Baku, with many people killed and injured. We don't have any idea what Sarah has been through."

"Well, we shall be friends anyway," Nadia said, taking Tatiana by the hand and leading her to the plush sofa. "Come and sit down with me and let our dolls play with each other."

While they sat there, Philip Boustani left the room, coming back a short while later with his wife, Judith, introducing Tatiana to her. Judith Boustani was a beautiful and gracious woman, with the same dark hair and eyes that Philip and Nadia had. She smiled warmly at Tatiana, saying kindly, "You are welcome in our home, Sarah, until we have found a place for you. Before we have dinner, I think perhaps you should have a nice warm bath and some fresh clothes. Some of Nadia's should fit you very well. Our servant Nerianai well see to it."

* * * * *

To Tatiana's relief, Neriani was not the servant who had admitted them at the door. His name was Serash, and Neriani was his wife. They were elderly, and they lived on the top floor of the house. Neriani took care of the cooking and the laundry, and Serash did most of the cleaning and serving.

The dress that Nadia gave her to wear was prettier than any Tatiana had ever owned, though it was far from Nadia's best. It was in the western style, and was pale blue, with white trim on the collar and the sleeves. The Boustanis had a separate room for dining, and they ate their sumptuous meal at a highly polished mahogany table beneath a crystal chandelier. Tatiana quickly began to feel as if she were an enchanted princess in a fairy tale world.

That night she shared the large bed in Nadia's room, and even that was grand. The mattress was of soft down, and the coverlet was quilted satin; overhead was a canopy, and surrounding the bed were thin, delicate curtains. In such a place, it took Tatiana a long time to fall asleep, and when she did she tossed and turned fitfully.

The nightmares returned even stronger than before. First she was being pulled violently from her mother's arms and thrown through the air to Gogo, who handed her to Afsar. Before she had fully calmed, she was ripped away from Afsar and thrown to Philip, who transformed her magically into a porcelain doll and presented her to Nadia. To save Tatiana, Nadia placed her in a stall with other dolls, but the cossacks were scrambling through all of them searching to find which one was Tatiana so that they could take her away again.

"No!" Tatiana screamed. "No! Don't let them take me, Nadia! Don't let them take me!"

Suddenly she felt a gentle hand on her shoulder, shaking her, and a sweet voice saying, "Sarah, wake up. Sarah, you're only dreaming."

Tatiana opened he eyes and looked up at Nadia's face in the darkness, very close to her own. "I'm sorry," she sobbed. "I didn't mean to wake you up."

"That's all right," Nadia said. "But you spoke. You called my name. Did you realize that?"

"Oh, no," Tatiana said shakily. "I didn't mean to speak."

"Well, now that you have," Nadia said, sitting up in bed, "why don't you tell me about your bad dream. Tell me about everything that's troubling you. If you don't want me to say anything to anybody else, I won't. But you and I must be friends; we must share all our secrets."

With a welcome sense of release, Tatiana sat up in bed and told Nadia all that had happened to her. She talked about her nightmares and about her fears. When she was done, she felt much better; the fears no longer seemed so bad.

Nadia took her hand and held it comfortingly, saying, "Would you let me tell Mama and Papa about all this? You don't have to say yes if you don't want to. But if I can tell them, I think I can persuade them to let you stay here with us. I want to ask them to adopt you and make you my own sister. Would you like to be my sister, Tatiana?"

She thought for a moment before replying. "Yes," she said finally. "I would like being your sister." She hesitated. "But I do miss my mother, and I would like her back."

"I understand that," Nadia said with a smile. "But if that's impossible, we can share my mother. She's wonderful. As wonderful as Papa."

Chapter 8

Gregor quickly came to regret the agreement he had made with his Uncle Vladimir. He was put to work immediately and given little time to contemplate any other choices he might have had. The labors he was assigned were hard, requiring far more physical strength than he possessed at his young age, but he attacked them with determination.

To replenish the water supply in the basement cistern, Gregor had to make countless trips to the street with buckets of the old water, followed by even more numerous trips into the basement with buckets of fresh water. He spent many hours shoveling coal from a large heap in the backyard into the coal-bin, where it would be dry. And in between these heavier chores, he was sent on errands for Uncle Vladimir's business.

When there were moments free from these pressing tasks, he was put to work scrubbing floors and polishing brass.

In return for all of this, Gregor was given his meals and a place to sleep in an empty room that had only a carpet and nothing more. His uncle's attitude was that he should be grateful to have this—that he would otherwise be out on the street, struggling each day for survival.

The days passed swiftly, one into another, consisting of working, eating, and sleeping. Each morning, Gregor was awakened before dawn to light the lamps and provide coal for the fires in Uncle Vladimir's bedroom and office, and then to assist Ali Jabbar in the kitchen. From before dawn until after nightfall, he was kept running. After his evening meal, he was allowed to collapse in exhaustion on his pallet on the floor, grateful to be able to fall asleep.

During the early days at Uncle Vladimir's, Gregor had a purpose, in performing his work well. By proving his honesty and diligence, he hoped his uncle would give him the reward he sought, the reward that had been left as no more than a vague promise. Gregor waited patiently for word that Vladimir had gone to the military garrison to inquire about his mother and sister.

Two weeks passed without Vladimir even mentioning the matter. Finally, Gregor decided to remind him.

It was in the middle of the afternoon, and Gregor was on the main floor of the house, performing one of his less important tasks—polishing the brass fixtures on the doors. Vladimir was alone in his office, doing the paperwork that was a part of his financial manipulations. At the time, Gregor had no idea what that business was, the management of vast sums of money being far beyond his comprehension.

He had been warned that Vladimir was not to be disturbed at these times, and the warnings had instilled a degree of fear in Gregor. Later Gregor would learn that it was through this fear that his uncle managed to manipulate people.

As he rubbed ceaselessly at a doorknob with his rag, a task that required no thought but only patience and physical activity, Gregor was able contemplated his life and purpose. The more he thought about his situation, the more ashamed and angry he became. It had been selfish of him to accept food and shelter, while his mother and sister might be suffering.

Dropping his polishing rag and gathering his courage, Gregor marched up to his uncle's office door and knocked decisively.

There was a moment of silence, and then Vladimir's irritated voice called out, "What is it?"

Gregor opened the door and stepped inside the large untidy room. Vladimir glowered at him over his rimless spectacles. "You knew that I was not to be interrupted this afternoon?" he challenged. "This had better be important."

"It is," Gregor said, trying to hide the trembling in his knees. "I need to know when you intend to find out about my mother and sister."

Vladimir's face grew as red as the crimson in the tapestry that hung on the wall behind him, a tapestry that struck Gregor as out of place, for it was the only trace of elegance in the furnishings of the house. "How dare you come to me now with this matter!" he growled furiously. "I made no promises to you! Get out of here and get back to your work!"

Gregor stood there a moment, staring at his uncle. He wanted to argue with him, but he sensed that it would do no good. Miserably, he turned around and left the room, going back to polishing the brass, but tears flowed silently and uncontrollably down his cheeks.

It was three days later that Vladimir told him he had made inquiries about

Maria and Tatiana. Gregor had taken a tray of food up to his uncle's office, where the old man usually dined alone with his work, and was about to return to the kitchen. But Vladimir stopped him, calling out, "Just a moment, boy."

Gregor turned back apprehensively to face his uncle, fearing he was about to be chastised for some unknown transgression.

"I have some news for you," Vladimir said with smug satisfaction, "but it is not news that will please you. I have been to the military garrison. Your mother has been sent to Siberia as a political prisoner."

"Siberia?" Gregor responded, his mind racing to recall where it was on the map in his geography book, trying to decide whether he could reach the place. "In Russia?"

"Yes, but it is very far away," Vladimir told him. "Thousands of miles away, in the most northern and eastern part of Russia. Prisoners who go there do not usually return."

Gregor knew by the smug way in which his uncle divulged this information that his chances of finding his mother were slim. "And Tatiana?" he asked. "Is she in Siberia with my mother?"

"No," his uncle replied, somewhat less happily. "The colonel could not tell me where she is. They have no record of her. All I could learn was that the children of political prisoners are turned over to a man named Haydar Gogoli, who runs a center for displaced children."

"Perhaps this man knows where Tatiana is," Gregor suggested, brightening.

"I've spoken to him," Vladimir said. "He has no record of a Tatiana Baranov." He paused. "Or a Tatiana Mehdovi."

Despair descended on Gregor with a heaviness that was far greater than he had ever experienced before, for it was a despair completely devoid of any hope. "What could have happened to her?" he asked, expecting no answer from his uncle, for it was a question he asked more of himself.

"Dead perhaps," Vladimir said curtly. "Or possibly taken in by some poor family with too many mouths to feed already. You must put these concerns out of your mind, boy. There is nothing you can do but go on with your work." He looked down at the tray of food on his desk, lifting the lid from the soup turreen. "You may go now."

Gregor left the office and returned to the kitchen, too stricken with grief for selfish tears.

Gregor remained at his Uncle Vladimir's house. In despair, living without hope, he accepted his fate, considering himself fortunate compared to his mother and sister. He performed his work, was grateful for his keep, and endeavored to stay out of the way of the old man. The days became weeks, and weeks became months, and inevitably those months turned into years.

His only friend was Ali Jabbar. In their servitude, they shared a resentment of Vladimir, ridiculing the old man when they were out of his sight, and commiserating with each other for the injustices they endured.

They truly cared about each other. Gregor learned that Ali had been orphaned as a child, and that was why the servant had been drawn to him on the first day. He had been little more than a boy, himself, when he had started working for Vladimir. In their common misfortune, they established what would serve as a family for each, with Ali becoming like a father to Gregor.

As such, Ali began to intercede with Vladimir on matters that were important. One matter that concerned the servant greatly was that of Gregor's future. With acceptance of his despair, Gregor had given up on any ambitions he had possessed, but Ali was impressed with the fact that the boy had been given several years of schooling, could read and write and speak four languages. These were advantages he did not want Gregor to forsake, and he tried to find some way to persuade Vladimir to finance a continuation of the boy's education.

But he knew his master well enough to realize he would accept no suggestion from him or anyone.

Opportunity arose quite by chance. Vladimir Mehdovi's eyesight had been growing gradually worse for a number of years. He spent most of his hours in his office reading or adding up figures in the dim light of a single lamp, too cheap to spend the money for added illumination. He could not read without his glasses, which were the thickest and most powerful available. True to his miserly character, he owned only one pair.

One morning, Ali came to Vladimir's office to report on the food budget, and discovered his master extremely upset. "This is terrible," Vladimir moaned. "I have broken my glasses. I dropped them on the floor, and while trying to find them I stepped on them and crushed them. I don't know what to do."

"I'm sorry," Ali said sympathetically. "I suppose you must get another pair."

"Of course I have to get another pair," Vladimir snapped angrily. "But you don't understand. I have some oil leases I must sign this morning. It will take several days to get new glasses."

"Well," Ali suggested helpfully, "you don't need to see to sign your name, do you?"

"Fool!" Vladimir barked. "I have to read the leases first! I would have to be insane to sign something without knowing what it says!"

Ali suddenly realized this was Gregor's opportunity. "Gregor can read," he announced.

"But he's just a boy," Vladimir grumbled. "He wouldn't understand what he's reading." Then it dawned on him. "Oh, you mean he could read them to me aloud. Of course." The old man brightened. "Send him up to me! Immediately!"

Gregor was in the basement cleaning out the coal bin when Ali came to him excitedly to tell him that Vladimir needed his help. Gregor was covered with fine black coal dust from head to toe. "I must have a bath first," he said. "I can't go into his office like this."

"No," Ali protested. "He wants you right now. Just wash your hands. Without his glasses, he won't be able to see what you look like."

Gregor read the documents well, stumbling on only a few of the more complex legal terms, but he was able to sound out those sufficiently for Vladimir to recognize them. After he finished, the old man was delighted. To Gregor's astonishment, his uncle thanked him profusely; it was the first display of kindness he had received from Vladimir. "Your eyes have saved me from making a grave mistake,' he told Gregor. "If I had signed these, I would have lost a great deal of money."

For the next few days, while Vladimir's new glasses were being made, Gregor became his uncle's eyes, spending most of his days and part of his evenings reading for him. Not once during that time did the old man yell at Gregor or treat him unkindly. Gregor understood the reason—Vladimir needed him.

Though Gregor did not realize it, Vladimir was making the same discovery, and for him it was a painful one. He had never needed anyone in his entire life, and therefore he had alienated everyone who might have been close to him. He was growing older now; his failing eyesight was proving that to him. What would he do if his vision left him entirely? He would have to depend on someone else, someone such as this boy.

He continued to ponder this, even after he had obtained new glasses. The boy was bright, that was clear. There were things Gregor could do in the office, taking some of the burden off him. But schooling required an expenditure of money. Still, it might be an investment that would pay off eventually. After all, the boy was entirely dependent on him, and if Vladimir was shrewd, he could keep it that way.

Ali Jabbar sensed what the old man was thinking, so, every time the opportunity arose, he dropped hints about the English missionary school that had recently been established in Baku.

Vladimir made his decision the day the important letter arrived from the British oil company. He could read only a few words of English, not enough to understand the full implications of the letter. He did not want to take it to an outsider to have it translated; he did not like outsiders knowing his business. He called Gregor to his office.

"Do you read English?" he asked.

"No, sir," Gregor replied, somewhat puzzled. "Only Persian, Russian, Torki, and a little Farsi."

"Then we shall have to remedy that," Vladimir announced. "I propose that we should send you to school. Oh, not full time, of course, just a couple of hours in the afternoon. This will cost me money, so I hope you appreciate that and work twice as hard to get all your chores done."

"Yes sir," Gregor replied, trying to keep from appearing elated by the news. "Thank you, sir."

For the first time since he had been told of his mother's fate, Gregor experienced a sense of hope. Gregor had always liked school; learning things outside his small world was what had given him ambition, opening up vistas of limitless possiblilities for the future.

This was something that Vladimir Mehdovi was not aware of, and would not have expected, for he knew very little about the human heart and soul.

* * * * *

With the passage of time, Tatiana ceased to feel like an adopted member of the Boustani family. She loved them as deeply as she had loved her own parents and brother, and they grew to love her as their own, for indeed that was what she had become. Eventually, Tatiana stopped having the nightmares that had been so frightening to her, and the memories of her true family faded, becoming like events that had happened to some other child.

Philip Boustani was a highly successful merchant, also having income from rice farms in the country. He spared no expense when it came to his family's happiness. Nadia and Tatiana were given the best of everything that was available in Rasht, and whenever Philip traveled, he invariably brought them things that could not be obtained at home.

There was one important thing lacking in Rasht, and that was a school.

While it was generally considered unimportant for daughters in Persia to be educated—indeed it was a luxury even for sons—Philip wanted Nadia and Tatiana to have the advantages that young ladies of good European families had, so he hired a governess for them. Because Nadia had shown a great talent for painting, Philip sought out a teacher with a background in art.

Madame Veronique was from Paris, an older woman who was widowed. She adored Nadia and Tatiana, and she fit very well into the Boustani household, but she quickly grew homesick. Rasht was not Paris, and she longed for the comforts and conveniences she was accustomed to. For that reason, Madame Veronique remained with them for only a little over a year, but both of her charges learned much from her in that time.

They were taught French and Russian. In both of these, they were introduced to European literature. Though neither of them showed talent for music, it was a part of their program, and naturally Philip bought them a piano. It was painting, however, that was Madame Veronique's great love, and under her tutelage, Nadia's talent grew considerably. Tatiana took instruction in art as well, but she knew very well that she was talentless.

Tatiana's interest lay in another field, and it was not one that Madame Veronique was prepared to teach, for science was not considered appropriate for women to study, even in Europe. She did share the little she knew of botany, zoology, and mathematics, and Tatiana was grateful.

The whole family knew of Nadia's dream—to be an artist. She talked about it openly, though her parents assumed she would give up the idea after she was older and became interested in marriage. Tatiana confided her ambitions only to Nadia, for they were highly impractical, if not outright impossible. Her greatest dream was to be a doctor, but she readily admitted that she would settle for being a nurse.

She shared this impractical dream with Nadia, as Nadia shared hers. That was the relationship of the two sisters and had been from the very beginning. They shared everything, withholding nothing from each other. In adolescence, the pretending that had begun with their dolls became fantasies of a time when Nadia would be a successful painter living in Paris, while Tatiana would work in a hospital, saving lives.

And gradually into their fantasies came great romances—incredibly handsome and impossibly rich men who would fall madly in love with them. When they imagined these things in the privacy of their rooms, they invariably broke into giggles.

When Madame Veronique left them, they were saddened. For a while it dampened their dreams, because the education they would need to accomplish their desires now seemed out of reach. Even if their father hired another tutor for them, they knew this would not be enough. The only way they could achieve what they wanted would be to go away to a European university, and that would mean Paris, London, Berlin, or Moscow, all of which were very far from Rasht.

Several times, Nadia suggested to Tatiana, "I'm sure Papa would allow us to go away to a university, if we asked him."

"Oh, but we mustn't ask," Tatiana protested. "At least, not for me. He has done so much for me already. Why don't you simply ask him to send you?"

"I couldn't go without you," Nadia told her.

So their lives continued—pleasantly but uneventfully—with aspirations remaining little more than dreams. Tatiana reached her fourteenth birthday and Nadia her twelfth; for each the future seemed to grow more unreachable.

Then, in the summer of 1905, an epidemic of cholera swept through Rasht, reaching rich and poor alike. The hospital and the infirmary were filled with the suffering and dying. There were not enough doctors, nurses, or medicines in the town to take care of the crisis. Philip and Judith Boustani were greatly concerned; they were among the wealthiest of the citizens of Rasht, and they believed that the blessings of their prosperity gave them a responsibility to those less fortunate.

Philip responded to the crisis by ordering shipments of medical supplies, which he donated to the hospital. Judith responded by organizing a group of women to help nurse the suffering.

As soon as she learned of this, Tatiana offered eagerly, "Of course, Nadia and I will help you."

"Oh, no, dear," Judith protested. "It's very good of you to offer, but you are both too young. "I'm afraid it would be too much for you. You have no idea of the suffering . . . "

"But I have seen suffering before," Tatiana said.

"And I'm sure I can bear up to it well," Nadia chimed in, for Tatiana's sake. "Please, Mama, we want to help."

"Well . . .," Judith hesitated. "Perhaps we can find something for the two of you to do. But we can't let you actually tend to the sick."

As the epidemic grew, Judith and her volunteers were sent out by the doctors increasingly into the homes of the suffering for whom there was no room at the hospital. Most of these were among the poor of the city, who in truly wretched conditions. In each household, Judith found there was far more to be done than one person could accomplish. The cholera was only a small part of the misery of the poor.

Because of that, she decided to allow Tatiana and Nadia to accompany her on her rounds. While Judith tended the cholera victims, the two girls looked after the other needs of the household, seeing that children were bathed and fed and trying to instill habits of cleanliness.

By the end of each day, all were exhausted, but Tatiana thrived on the work, feeling a great sense of accomplishment from even the smallest of her efforts. The suffering they witnessed affected both of the young women, each in a different way. Because she had seen it before, it was no shock to Tatiana. For Nadia, it was a profound emotional experience. Brought up in affluence, she had never realized such misery existed. Even though Tatiana had told her about her own experiences, Nadia did not understand what it was really like until she witnessed it for herself. Nadia found an outlet for her shock by spending a few hours each evening sketching the suffering faces she had seen. She kept these drawings separate from her other work, the pretty landscapes, still lifes, and portraits, showing them to no one but Tatiana.

It was Judith Boustani, however, who ultimately suffered most from these long, arduous days. At first, it was merely fatigue; then she began to lose weight and grow pale, developing a faint cough. The epidemic was at its peak when she came down with the cholera herself, and it was a severe case.

Of course the doctor came. He could do no less after all she had done to help. But there was little he could do, with so many others to look after. After leaving Judith's bedside, he stopped in the front hall to speak to Philip Boustani and his two daughters. "I will do what I can," the doctor said. "I cannot say what her chances of survival are. She needs constant attention."

"I understand," Philip told him, but Tatiana could see that he was frightened, perhaps even bewildered. He was a good and gentle man; he would not let himself use his wealth and position to demand more from the doctor than he would give to other patients.

It was then that Tatiana stepped forward and said strongly, "Doctor, If you will tell me what to do, I will look after her."

The doctor smiled benignly. "But you're just a child," he said.

"Some children my age are married with children of their own," she said. "And my goal in life is to become a nurse. I might as well begin to learn now."

Philip looked startled, but something in the doctor's eyes told Tatiana that be believed her. "All right, young lady," he said. "I will tell you what you must do, and you must listen very carefully."

Tatiana committed every instruction to memory. If she did not understand something, she asked questions of the doctor. She knew that she was taking on a grave responsibility, and she had to be prepared to handle it.

She made a small bed for herself in Judith Boustani's room, and she stayed there, by her mother's side, day and night. When she slept, it was only lightly, keeping her ears alert for any emergency. Occasionally, Nadia or Neriani would take her place at Judith's bedside, but both accepted instructions from Tatiana.

Judith's fever grew increasingly worse. She became delirious, and Tatiana began to be frightened for her. She never stopped applying the cold compresses to her mother's forehead, however, and when the basin of water grew warm, she called for Nadia or Neriani to replace it.

With her eyes closed tightly, she muttered over and over the Hebrew prayers she had learned as part of her adopted religion. One night, weary after a long day with little rest, she tried to recall a Christian prayer from her childhood, and she muttered through it as best she could. If one God was not enough, she thought, perhaps two would help.

When she opened her eyes, Tatiana saw that Judith's eyes were open and looking at her. "My child," Judith whispered weakly, "you must get some rest, or you will become ill yourself. I fear it is too late for me. I am going to die."

"No," Tatiana said firmly. "I will not let you die. I have lost one mother already; I cannot lose you as well."

Judith smiled, and her eyes closed. Tatiana returned to her Hebrew prayers.

Two days later, the fever finally broke, and Judith slowly began to grow stronger. Once she knew that her mother would live, Tatiana allowed Neriani to take over for a night so that she could go to her own bed for a full rest. But she did not sleep until after she had said two silent prayers of thanks—one to the Hebrew God and one to the Christian God, just in case.

The first evening the entire Boustani family was able to gather downstairs for dinner together was a festive occasion. Neriani prepared special dishes, and Philip brought out a rare wine he had been saving. Everyone dressed for celebration. The joy of this happy family seemed even more blessed, after the fearful threat it had survived.

It was after dinner when Nadia brought up the subject she had been planning to discuss all day. She did not tell Tatiana her intentions. She no longer felt that she was bound by her promise not to speak of Tatiana's dream, for Tatiana had now mentioned it herself.

When a pause in the conversation occurred, Nadia said decisively, "Papa, there is a favor I want to ask of you—a very special favor."

Philip smiled, and his eyes twinkled with mischief. "This sounds ominous," he said. "It must be something very costly for you to save for a moment when I am so satisfied with good food and wine that I cannot say no."

Nadia blushed. "It is very costly," she said, "and it is very special. I want to ask you to allow Tatiana and me to go to Paris to study. You know that I want to be an artist and that Tatiana wants to be a nurse. There is no way either of us can do that here in Rasht."

Philip grew serious. He studied Nadia's face pensively, and then looked at Tatiana, who was staring accusingly at her sister. Philip smiled apologetically at Nadia and said, "I wish I could grant your request, but I don't see how I could send the two of you off to Paris unchaperoned."

"I've thought of that," Nadia said. "We could stay with Madame Veronique. She is so much like one of the family, I'm sure you could trust us to her safekeeping."

"But she has another position now," Philip said, "a very good one. I don't think we could ask her to give it up."

"Please, Papa," Nadia pursued. "It's very important. To both of us."

"I know it is, "Philip said. "I think you could become a very fine painter, and I believe Tatiana could do very well at nursing. But . . . " He glanced down at the table in embarrassment. "What about marriage? Don't you think that will one day be more important to you?"

"I don't know," Nadia said. "But I don't think so."

There was a painful silence at the table. Finally, Philip said, "I can't send you to Paris. But I'll see if I can think of something I can do." He gave each of his daughters a loving look. "I want you to understand, it's not the money. It's your safety and your welfare I'm concerned about. Neither of you has ever been to a big city. You don't know what they're like."

Chapter 9

Gregor enjoyed school, and he wished that he could attend more than just a few hours each day. However, he also found that he did not dislike the work he did in Uncle Vladimir's office, for in that he was also gaining an education. It was not as much as he might have learned if he had been working for a less secretive and less distrustful man than his uncle, but it was a good introduction to business practices.

About some things he learned more than Vladimir would have liked him to know. One of Gregor's tasks was to keep the old man's files and records in order. This was no small job, for his uncle was as disorderly about his papers and documents as he was meticulous about money. This meant that Gregor often had to read a document before putting it away in its proper place.

It was in doing this that Gregor learned his uncle had lied to his father about the disposal of the family land. It had not been sold, as Alexei had been told by Vladimir, but merely leased to the oil companies. What was most startling to Gregor, however, was to learn that his father had been entitled to a one-third share in the land. On all of the oil leases signed before his father's death, the name Alexei Mehdovi appeared with Vladimir Mehdovi as lessor, and his signature was an "X." Gregor knew very well that his father could read and write and sign his name.

The fact that his family had been entitled to large sums of money did not make Gregor angry at his uncle. He already despised the old man. What upset him was the tangible proof that Vladimir was a liar. If he had lied so blatantly to his father, Gregor reasoned that he could as easily have lied to him about his mother and sister.

He was angry at himself for accepting his uncle's word so readily. In the beginning, he considered confronting Vladimir with the lies, but he decided that would be a mistake. He was totally within his uncle's power; he had no proof against the lies, and no guarantee that a confrontation would prompt Vladimir to admit the truth.

Gregor would have to deal with his problems himself.

He knew that the displaced children's center was not far from his school, so he decided to go there himself to ask about Tatiana. This was not an easy thing to do, because of his schedule of work and school. Vladimir barely gave Gregor time for school, expecting him back promptly after his classes were over.

He decided he had no alternative but to miss his classes for one day and hope Vladimir would not find out.

It was a bright, sunny day in autumn when he finally mustered his courage to walk through the front gates and enter the office building of the children's center. A group of little girls was playing in the yard at the time, and Gregor stared at them, searching to see if one looked like Tatiana. But then he realized that these girls were all too young; his sister would now be much older, just as he was older.

Inside the office building, Gregor found a matronly woman at the desk. He approached her, informing her he would like to see the director. She smiled at him sweetly, wrote down his name, and went into an office. Within a matter of moments, he was invited into the office and introduced to Haydar Gogoli.

To Gregor's relief, the director appeared to be a kind and gentle man, with sympathetic eyes. "What can I do for you?" Gogoli asked, as Gregor approached his desk.

"I'm tring to locate my sister," Gregor explained. "I believe she was brought here some years ago, during the time of the riots in Sabunchi."

"Oh yes," Gogoli nodded. "Those were terrible times, the worst I've ever known for displaced children. I would like to help you, but we have very strict rules about giving out information. You would have to have some proof of your identity, and your sister's."

Gregor had anticipated something of this sort, so he had brought with him the documents he had taken from his mother's Bible. They were carefully folded inside his schoolbook. He took them out and handed them to Gogoli.

The director was clearly surprised. He studied them carefully, then looked up at Gregor thoughtfully. "Tatiana Mehdovi," he mused. "I have heard that name somewhere, but I can't place it. I dont recall a child by that name. I mean, I can't put a face to it."

"Do you keep records?" Paul asked hopefully. "She may have used the name Tatiana Baranov."

"Of course we do," Gogoli replied, somewaht offended. "Excellent records—on every child who comes in here and goes out."

"Perhaps you might check them," Gregor suggested.

"All right," the director said, defensively, "but I have a very good memory for children." He got up from his desk and walked to a large filing cabinet against the wall, opening the top drawer and rifling through the folders inside. In very short order, he slammed the drawer shut and turned back to Paul, shaking his head. "No," he said. "We've had no Baronov child at all. And no Mehdovi." Then his eyes brightened. "Of course, that's where I recall the name."

"Where?" Gregor asked, his excitement rising.

"Vladimir Mehdovi," Gogoli said. "That old skinflint came here asking about her, a long time ago."

Gregor's hopes were dashed. His uncle had not lied about the inquiries.

"I had to tell him the same thing," Gogoli said with a satisfied smile. "We have no record of a child by either of those names."

"Perhaps her records were lost." Gregor suggested.

Gogoli shook his head. "Not likely. We're quite efficient. "He smiled sympathetically. "I wish I could help you."

"Is there someone else here who might remember her?" Gregor asked.

"Well, there is Nurse Afsar," Gogoli said pensively.

"Could I speak to her?" Gregor asked.

"I'm sorry," Gogoli replied. "She is making her rounds in the infirmary. We couldn't call her away from the sick children. And I assure you, her memory is no better than mine."

Gregor was determined not to give up hope until he had spoken to this nurse. After leaving Gogoli's office, he loitered outside the displacement center, watching the children playing on the other side of the fence. He searched for a woman who might be a nurse, but there was no one who seemed likely. He had almost given up hope when one of the children fell and scraped her knee. Another child quickly ran off to a building on the far side of the yard, returning within moments, accompanied by a woman Gregor was certain was the nurse.

Swiftly he entered the front gate and made his way onto the children's playground. He reached the scene of the accident only a moment before the woman had finished her ministrations to the small cut.

As she stood up, Gregor said firmly, "Nurse Afsar, may I speak to you?"

The small elderly woman looked at him with a mixture of curiosity and suspicion. "I must be getting back to the infirmary," she said guardedly.

"What do you want?"

Gregor identified himself and told her why he was there.

"I'm sorry," she said, moving away. "That sort of information can only be given out by Mr. Gogoli."

"Please," Gregor begged. "I've been to see him, and he has no record of my sister. I thought perhaps you might remember her."

She smiled. "I don't recall a girl named Tatiana. And our records are quite good." Again, she started to go.

But Gregor followed. "Let me describe her to you," he said.

The nurse stopped and studied Gregor curiously, looking him up and down and then gazing inquiringly into his eyes. "You love your sister very much, don't you?" she asked finally.

"Yes," Gregor said. "And I must do anything I can to find her—if she is still alive."

"All right," Nurse Afsar said. "Describe the child for me, and I will see if I can recall. But I assure you, our records are much better than my memory. After awhile, many children look alike."

"Tatiana was very fair," Gregor said. "She had blond hair, and Mama usually braided it and pinned the braids on top of her head. She had blue eyes and pale skin."

Suddenly recognition flashed in the woman's eyes, and she gasped, "Sarah."

"What was that?" Gregor asked.

Afsar hesitated, then she asked cautiously, "Was your sister a mute? Could she speak?"

"Of course she could," Gregor replied. "She could even read and write a little. We both attended the Christian church school, when we were small."

"Then you are Christians?" she asked, looking worried.

"We attended church with our mother long ago," Gregor said. "But we were of mixed parentage. Our father was Persian and our mother was Russian."

Asfar turned and started walking slowly toward the infirmary. Gregor followed. "This is a matter for Mr. Gogoli," she said.

"You know something," Gregor said urgently. "I can see that you do. Please, you must tell me. You remember my sister, don't you?"

"I recall a child very like the one you described," she said. "And we did not know her name because she did not speak. We called her Sarah. If she is your sister, we made an unfortunate mistake, and I do not think I should tell you about it. That decision should be made by Mr. Gogoli."

"No," Gregor begged. "Please, I must not take a chance that he would refuse. You must tell me. Is my sister alive?"

Afsar stopped and smiled at Gregor sympathetically. "She is alive," she said. "Or she was when she left here. But she was placed for adoption by a Jewish family. That is the mistake we made."

"I don't care about that," Gregor said excitedly. "I only want to find her to make sure she is all right."

The nurse sighed. "I should not do this," she said. "If anything should happen, I will deny that I ever told you. She was taken to Persia by a Jewish merchant, who used to help Mr. Gogoli find homes for children of Jewish birth. But he has not been here for several years."

"What was the merchant's name?" Gregor asked. "And where in Persia was she taken?"

"I don't know," Afsar said. "You would have to ask Mr. Gogoli, and to do that now you might get me into trouble." She shook her head wearily. "I know I should have said nothing."

"I won't go to Mr. Gogoli," Gregor promised. "But you must try to remember more."

Asfar thought long and hard. "I just don't remember," she said finally. "He was a very wealthy and influential man. I think perhaps he was from Tehran. But his name escapes me."

"All right," Gregor said. "I'm grateful you have remembered this much. Thank you."

There was no doubt in his mind that he would be going to Tehran to look for Tatiana. He had no idea how he would do this, but he had to manage somehow. Tehran was very far away, and it would cost a great deal of money to travel there. For all his work at Vladimir's he earned nothing beyond room and board, and he realized there was little use in asking his uncle to pay him his value.

After talking to Ali Jabbar, Gregor devised a plan. His absence from school was not reported to his uncle, and he found it easy to catch up on the lessons he had missed. He realized it was possible for him to miss classes and still keep up with the other students. He would continue to cut school one or two days a week. On those days, he would go to the docks and hire out his services as a porter to passengers boarding the boats. Whatever he earned, he could put away, saving his money until he had enough to leave Baku.

The only problem would be if his absences were reported to his uncle. But there was a way of dealing with this concern. Most things passed through

Ali Jabbar's hands before they reached Vladimir. Ali would endeavor to keep any reports from the old man.

Gregor's plan worked well. He kept up his lessons and remained at the top of his class. He continued to perform his duties in Vladimir's office, and did his household chores, though he often worked late at night to finish them. On some days, he stole time from these chores so that he could stay longer at the docks.

He was one of a number of young boys who hired themselves out to travelers, offering to carry baggage, run errands, or perform any services that might be needed. He had one special talent, however, that none of the other boys had: because he spoke several languages, he could translate for foreigners. For that reason, during the few hours he had each week, he invariably earned money.

By the spring of 1906, he had turned thirteen and had managed to put away quite a bit of money in his secret hiding place—a book that was one of the few possessions he had managed to acquire. He kept a careful count of that money, knowing always precisely how much he had, and how much more he would need before he could make his move.

One afternoon he rushed home excitedly and happily calculated that he would need only one more good day at the docks before he had enough money. Before settling down to the chores, he ran to his room to put his latest installment away. He opened the book, which always fell open to the page containing the money.

It was gone. Panic gripped him as he rifled through the pages. Someone had taken his money. There were only two people who could have come into his room, and Gregor knew that Ali Jabbar would not steal from him.

The only person who could have taken his money was Uncle Vladimir.

Gregor did not pause to question the rationality of this assumption. He knew it was true. Angrily, he ran down the stairs and burst into his uncle's office. "You have been into my room and have taken something that belongs to me," he charged. "I want it back!"

Vladimir looked at him coolly, unperturbed by Gregor's rage. "That is not quite true," he said. "It belonged to you, yes; but now it belongs to me."

"I earned that money," Gregor challenged. "It is rightfully mine!"

"Again not true," Vladimir cut back icily. "You earned it on my time. When you were supposed to be attending classes, which I had to pay for. Therefore this money is owed to me." Vladimir smiled malevolently. "You thought I didn't know what was going on. One afternoon I had to be at the Baku port on a matter of business. I admit I was surprised to see you there. It was very stupid of me not to realize sooner that I hadn't received a report from your school for some time. Your attendance record has been very poor."

"Yes," Gregor said defiantly. "But I have kept up my lessons. Didn't they tell you that as well?"

"Yes," Vladimir replied. "But that's not the point. You have been cheating me."

"No more than you cheated my father," Gregor accused, his voice trembling. "Did you think I was too stupid to figure that out, working here in your office?"

"No," his uncle said smugly. "I wanted you to know. I wanted you to realize what a stupid man your father was. He was ruled by his heart, not by his head. He deserved to be cheated."

Gregor was astonished by what he was hearing. He had expected his uncle to deny the charges, to try to excuse his actions, but he was admitting them blatantly. The astonishment, however, did nothing to calm Gregor's sense of outrage. "I see," he said hotly. "Like father, like son. In your eyes, I deserve to be cheated as well."

Vladimir shugged indifferently. "A man deserves whatever he gets."

Gregor had never felt such anger in his life. It was blinding him, and he feared if he remained in the room with his uncle much longer, he might strangle the old man. He had to have an opportunity to think calmly and rationally.

Without another word, he turned and stormed out of the office, rushed through the front hall, and literally ran out the front door. As he did so, he brushed forcefully against a man on the front steps, who was about to knock on the door. Gregor glanced back to make sure that he had not knocked the man down, and then hurried on. At the moment he did not wish to speak to anyone.

Gregor walked aimlessly, wrapped entirely in his thoughts. He had many things to think about. He had assumed that Vladimir was simply a miser, that he was like anybody else, except that he cared more for money than for people. Gregor now realized that this was not quite true—his uncle was not like anybody else at all.

Vladimir Mehdovi had more money than any man could possibly want or need. Yet he was also the cheapest, most miserly man Gregor had ever known. The only vaguely human emotion Gregor had ever seen in his uncle had been today—a pride and satisfaction in cheating or besting someone else.

Gradually Gregor began to realize that Vladimir lived for the joy of competition, of playing his financial games. The only other people he cared about were those who could beat him at his own rather shady rules. On reflection, Gregor began to recall transactions where his uncle had come out the loser. The Nobel brothers had bested the old man in some oil negotiations, and Vladimir had spoken admiringly of them afterward. The same had been true of the Russian cartel he had been negotiating with on a caviar sale.

But this sort of thing was not in Gregor's nature. He was a sensitive young man. He cared deeply about others. Yet he could see that these were the very things that others—like his Uncle Vladimir—could use to deny him whatever he sought in life.

As he walked, his feet eventually led him to the little house in Black Town where he had spent his happy childhood with his family. It was now terribly run down, and the children who played in the yard were thin and gaunt from malnutrition. They stared at him with blank, hopeless eyes.

Money. Suddenly, in a flash of insight, Gregor saw that it was the cause of most of the suffering he had seen in the world. Some had too much of it; others too little; but all were struggling to have as much as they could. Gregor had never valued money as highly as love and family happiness, but he could not have what he valued without having first what others valued more.

He knew now what he had to do. He must play his uncle's game by his uncle's rules. His objective was to go to Tehran to find Tatiana. To do that, he had to earn whatever money he could as quickly as he could. He could not even consider being fair to Vladimir. If his uncle threw him out of his house, he would still survive. Gregor knew he was capable of earning far more than his room and board.

He set out to the docks in search of opportunity. He now had no time schedule in mind; he would simply work as many hours a day as he could, and make his departure as soon as he had enough to get him to Teheran.

The other young men who worked the docks were surprised to see Gregor return for a second time in the same day, and they teased him good-naturedly, but Gregor did not stand about and talk to them. He set to work with determination, approaching one traveler after another. "May I carry our bags?" he would ask one. "Do you need an interpreter?" he approached another. "May I find you a carriage, sir?" If someone told him no, he moved on to another. If someone said yes, he performed his work swiftly, collected his money, and moved on.

"Here boy," a voice called out in heavily accented Russian, but Gregor did not pay attention to it. He was not used to the travelers approaching him. "You," the voice said, coming nearer through the crowd. "Boy," it persisted, now clumsily trying to speak Persian.

Gregor turned as the man came up to him. "Take care of your baggage for you, sir?" Gregor asked, first in Russian. Then, noting the man's fair hair, blue eyes, and heavy tweed suit, he asked again in English.

"You speak English?" the man asked, amazed.

"Yes," Gregor replied. "Do you need a translator?"

"As a matter of fact," the man replied, "I could use one. And I do need someone to take care of my baggage. However, I approached you for another reason. You're the young man who almost knocked me down in front of Vladimir Mehdovi's house, aren't you?"

Gregor looked at him suspiciously. He had been so blinded with rage at the time, he had not noticed what the man on the doorstep had looked like. "Why do you ask?"

"My name is Sidney Fleming," the man said. "I'm with the British TransPersian Oil Company. I came here to Baku especially to see Mehdovi, and I'm having a bit of a problem with him."

Gregor grinned. "That's not unusual," he said. "Most people have problems with my uncle."

"Oh?" Fleming's brows raised in surprise. "You are his nephew?"

"Yes," Gregor said. "But I don't have time to stand here talking. I have to work. Do you want to hire me or not?"

Fleming was slightly flustered by Gregor's bluntness. "Of course, I'll pay you for your time," he said. "I can use your services to get my baggage on board the boat, but what I would like even more is some information. It would be quite valuable to me."

"What kind of information?" Gregor asked cautiously.

Fleming looked around uncomfortably. "Perhaps we could find a place to sit down and have some tea while we talk," he said.

"This will take some explanation."

Gregor guided the Englishman to a small, outdoor teahouse only a short distance from the docks. Once they had been settled at a table and were served, Fleming laid out his problem to Gregor.

"Our company has been trying to obtain some information from Vladimir Mehdovi," he said. "We are quite willing to pay for the information, but so far Mr. Mehdovi has refused every offer we've made."

Suddenly Gregor remembered letters he had translated for his uncle, letters from the British TransPersian Oil Company's headquarters in

London. "Oh, yes," he said in recognition. "The surveys of the Batoum fields."

Fleming was so startled by Gregor's response he almost choked on a sip he had just taken of his tea. "You know about this?" he asked incredulously.

"I do some work in my uncle's office," Gregor explained. "He knows very little English."

"Could you speak to your uncle for me?" Fleming asked. "Unfortunately, he refuses to see me. You could explain to him that we are willing to pay whatever price he would ask. Within reason, of course. It would be very costly—both in time and money—if we had to do our own survey. I don't have a lot of time to spend here in Baku. I'm on my way to Teheran, and my boat sails for Enzeli first thing in the morning."

Gregor felt his heart pounding excitedly. His mind raced with ideas he would never have considered before. Sitting across the table from him he recognized opportunity, and it astonished him. If such opportunity had come to him only a few hours earlier, he would have dismissed it. He would not have considered what he was about to suggest.

"I might be able to do even better than that," he said guardedly to the Englishman. "How much would this information be worth to you?"

"As I said," Fleming replied. "Mr. Mehdovi can set his price, and we'll try to meet it."

"I'm not talking about my uncle," Gregor replied. "Would you be willing to pay me for the information? For example, would you be willing to take me to Tehran with you, in return for this information?"

The Englishman was clearly shocked by the question. "Do you mean you would steal the information?"

"It wouldn't exactly be stealing," Gregor said. "In a way, you could say that it belongs as much to me as it does to my uncle."

"I don't know," Fleming said hesitantly. "I don't think the main office would approve. And I don't think I could take on the responsibility of looking after a young boy in Tehran. Why would you want to go there anyway?"

"I can take care of myself," Gregor said. "And I have my reasons for wanting to go. That's why I've been working at the docks, to earn my fare. Now, do you accept my proposal or not?"

The Englishman was still reluctant to agree, but Gregor continued to press, arguing coolly and calmly against each of the moral qualms Fleming had. Finally, the man gave in and agreed to take care of all Gregor's expenses as far as Tehran, but he insisted the information had to be fully documented, and there must be no way Vladimir could seek legal action against his company.

Gregor assured Sidney Fleming there would be no problem. No original documents would leave his uncle's office, but Fleming would have a copy of everything he needed. Gregor would sit up all night if necessary, copying the information himself.

Chapter 10

Gregor could hardly believe that he might finally leave Baku. It had all happened so quickly, there had been little time to think about what he was doing. There was much to be done, and he had to move swiftly and carefully. To accomplish his objective, he would have to work through the night, after Uncle Vladimir had gone upstairs to his room to sleep.

Gregor did not have a lot of possessions to pack; he could tie everything he owned into a small bundle. What would take time and care would be copying all of the documents that Sidney Fleming needed. He would have to do this without being discovered by either his uncle or Ali Jabbar. Though the servant would not object to what he was doing, Gregor decided it would be best for Ali to have no knowledge of the theft of the information, just in case Vladimir should ask questions.

The strain of the copying was intense. Gregor was accustomed to sleeping nights, and for the copying work, he had to remain alert so as not to make mistakes. It also had to be done with a very dim lamp, so that the light would not attract attention to his presence in the office.

His ears were always alert to sounds in the house. Each time the floors or walls would creak, as they had a way of doing in old houses, his heart would pound fearfully, and he would strain to listen for footsteps or sounds of movement. Even the sounds from the street outside unnerved him, though usually it was only the nocturnal prowling of a cat or a dog.

It was very early in the morning when the sounds seemed to Gregor to be distinctly those of someone moving about in the house. But he had been startled so many times only to realize it was merely the wind or the house settling, and he was now weary with the fatigue of the strenuous and precise work. He was also very near the end; he needed just a few minutes more. So he did not get up to look out into the hallway.

He was sitting at Vladimir's desk, beneath the dim lamp, desperately copying the last page, when he was startled by the creaking sound of the office door opening.

In terror, he looked up at the figure in the doorway, disguised by shadows. He was sure that it was his uncle, and that all was now lost.

"Gregor," Ali Jabbar's voice whispered. "What are you doing in here?"

Gregor was so relieved he sat there speechless for a moment. "Ali," he said softly. "Go back downstairs, please. I will be down in a moment and explain everything."

Gregor dreaded saying farewell to Ali Jabbar. The servant had grown to be almost as dear to him as his true family had been, and he feared that Ali might try to persuade him not to leave.

He need not have worried. When Gregor told him his plans, Ali understood and accepted. "I knew that you would have to leave sometime," he said quietly, standing at the kitchen fire, preparing the morning's tea. "I pray that Allah will be with you and give you success in your search. What you are doing is right."

But when the moment came for parting, Ali embraced Gregor and wept openly. "I hope that I will see you again," he said.

Gregor turned in the doorway to reply, "We shall. I'm sure of it." But as he turned again and walked out the basement door into the still dark street, he was not so sure.

*　*　*　*　*

The sun was rising in a soft pink sky, as the steamer began to pull away from the Baku docks. Gregor stood at the railing alongside Sidney Fleming, looking back at the awakening city with no sorrow at leaving it. He was sailing toward a land that was unknown to him except in stories and his own imagination. As yet unsoiled by the everyday frustrations and conflicts of experience, it represented hope to Gregor. What lay behind was merely memory, most of which was unhappy.

Gregor did not know quite what to expect from Sidney Fleming. He had not given thought to the fact that the two of them would be traveling together. Gregor did not look upon the Englishman as someone to like or to dislike. He was merely an Englishman, a foreigner, a stranger with whom he had made a business deal, someone who would be used for a time and then forgotten.

Gregor had been taught to distrust foreigners, especially those connected with the oil business, but he had accepted the man's offer as a means to an end.

He certainly did not expect to like or respect the man, nor to develop a friendship with him, however casual it might be. But now, as they stood together on the deck of the steamer, leaving Baku together, the business arrangement that had brought them together had been completed. Gregor had turned over to Fleming all the information the oil company needed on the Batoum fields, and the Englishman had given Gregor the payment he had requested. There was really no reason for the two of them to remain in each other's company.

As the city of Baku faded into the distance, Gregor turned away from the railing to find Fleming staring at him curiously. "You're a very puzzling young man," he said to Gregor. "I have been trying to understand why someone like you should want so badly to go to a place like Tehran. You certainly don't have to tell me, but I would very much like to know."

Gregor looked at the man for a moment, silently deliberating about confiding in him. Finally, he decided it could do no harm. "It's nothing mysterious," he said. "Several years ago, I was separated from my sister. I would like to find her. I've been told that she was adopted by a family in Tehran."

"Why were you separated?" Fleming asked.

Again Gregor hesitated. This was a question he wasn't sure he should answer, for it involved politics, and he did not know how far this foreigner could be trusted. After a moment, he realized his thoughts were visible on his face, for Fleming looked flustered and said, "I'm sorry. I don't mean to pry into personal matters."

Gregor decided to trust the man. As they walked about the deck of the steamer, he told him the full story. In the telling, he sensed that he was gaining a friend and ally. The morning in Baku had been slightly overcast; by midday they were in fog. As the day passed and they drew nearer to Enzeli, that fog turned to rain, forcing the passengers indoors.

By the time the boat finally reached Enzeli, they were in the midst of a heavy downpour, with blustery winds.

Gregor had intended to take his leave of the Englishman at the port city. Fleming intended to stay there overnight, then go on to Rasht, which was only a short distance inland, to spend a few days to take care of some business. Gregor wanted to catch the first available coach overland to Tehran.

"I say," Fleming told him, as they sought shelter on the Enzeli docks, "you can't possibly go off in weather like this. You had better stay on with me until this clears."

Gregor did not know what a room at an inn would cost, but he was sure it would be more than he could afford. Feeling the money in his pocket, he replied, "No, thank you. I think I should go on. I'll be all right."

"If you're worried about the expense," Fleming pressed. "I'll take care of it. I got off very cheaply in our little business deal."

"It was fair," Gregor said.

"It's only a matter of a few days," Fleming argued, "and you could be very useful to me on the way, especially since you know the languages. You work for me, and I'll pay you fairly."

Gregor really didn't look forward to traveling in this weather, and Fleming's company did give him a sense of comfort and security in this unfamiliar country. He thought about the offer.

"In fact," Fleming pressed, "you could be very useful to me in my work. How would you like a permanent job? Or at least permanent for a few months."

Gregor forced himself to look into the man's eyes, trying to read his intentions. "What sort of work would this job involve?" he asked cautiously.

Fleming smiled. "Just about anything you could handle," he said. "You would travel with me, serve as my interpreter when necessary, run errands, perhaps take care of some of my correspondence."

"Thank you," Gregor said, "but no. I wouldn't be able to travel. I want to stay in Tehran for a while. You understand."

"How about working for me until we get to Tehran," the Englishman suggested. "I'll pay you well, and that will give you something to start out with there."

Gregor hesitated for a moment. "I suppose I can do that," he said. "When shall I start?"

"First thing in the morning," Fleming said with a satisfied smile. "We will work on my correspondence, and plan our schedule for Rasht."

*   *   *   *   *

The short journey from Enzeli to Rasht was pleasant. The rains had abated, and the early summer sun warmed the travelers. They crossed a green plain, with the Elburz Mountains in the distance to their right and sand dunes to their left leading to the sea. They passed fields where rice was growing, and groves rich with lemons and oranges.

Sidney Fleming had set aside only two days to conduct his business in Rasht. From Gregor's assessment, the Englishman should have planned for a week there. Gregor's concern that he was being hired out of kindness or charity was quickly dispelled. Fleming kept him busy with work. Gregor hardly had time to savor the realization that he was finally in Persia.

The weather remained unpredictable throughout their stay in Rasht. Thunderstorms caused numerous delays in the business Fleming had to conduct, causing people to miss appointments. As the second day began to draw to a close, it became clear that everything could not be accomplished. Yet they could not postpone their departure, for Fleming had to be in Tehran for a very important meeting with government officials and a representative of Russian oil interests.

One important matter that had to be taken care of before they left was the delivery of some signed contracts and leases. "I don't have to see the man personally," Fleming told Gregor. "Do you think you could deliver them to his home for me?"

"Of course," Gregor assured him confidently. "Just give me the directions."

"I'm not able to," Fleming told him. "I have the address, but it's a part of town I know nothing about. You'll have to ask someone on the street for directions."

Gregor had learned his way around the central section of Rasht, including the bazaar and the business section, but he had not ventured into the residential areas. Finding his way at night would present some difficulties, but Gregor felt he could make the delivery.

When he set out with the important envelope, the sky gave the impression that the rains had ended. The address for his delivery was in the wealthiest section of Rasht, an area that resembled White Town in Baku. The only important difference was that the streets were not laid out in a grid pattern. Some streets cut at odd angles, and others turned and meandered erratically.

Gregor asked directions and managed to find the address without much difficulty. However, before he had managed to find the house, it began to drizzle. The heavy rain began on the way back. It blew in suddenly with a strong wind from the sea, and it was so heavy that Gregor could not see more than a few feet in front of himself. Within a matter of moments, he was soaked, and he realized he had become lost.

It was pointless to try to go further until the rain subsided. He had to seek shelter.

His first opportunity was a large, elegant mansion that had a portico at the front door and small sheltered porches running off on either side.

With a guilty sense that he was trespassing, Gregor ran up to the portico and hid himself in the shadows, hoping he would be able to leave before anyone sought to enter or leave the house.

The wind against his wet clothes made Gregor shiver with chill. He huddled behind a marble column for protection. On the side porches, light from the windows flooded out into the night, warmly inviting. Gregor wished he could knock on the door and ask to be sheltered from the wind and rain, but he knew he could not.

He was shivering uncontrollably when he noticed a closed carriage draw up in front of the house. Its door opened cautiously; someone was preparing to get out, clearly intending to approach the front door where Gregor was huddled.

Frightened, he acted swiftly, darting from the portico onto one of the porches, squeezing himself into the shadow of one of the pillars that bordered the windows. It was only then that he realized the window next to him was open a few inches.

Gregor's heart beat fearfully as a tall, well-dressed man dashed up the front steps to the portico and swiftly let himself into the house with a key. The carriage moved off down the street, and Gregor breathed a sigh of relief. He had not been discovered.

Suddenly, from inside the house, he heard the man's voice call out excitedly, "Nadia! Tatiana! I have some good news for you!"

Gregor was astonished; the man had spoken his sister's name!

Could it be his sister? The name could not be that common in this part of the world. Gregor was sure that it must be only coincidence, but his curiosity was piqued. Cautiously, he repositioned himself to peer in the window.

He could see that there were two people in the room, but he could not see them clearly, because the sheer curtains, which were blowing slightly in the wind, were in the way. In the middle of the window they were parted. Gregor moved still further into the light so he could see clearly.

"Tatiana!" he heard the man call again. "Nadia!"

"In here, Papa," a young woman's voice called back. "In the parlor!"

Gregor could see clearly as the man entered the room, now divested of his wet hat and cloak. Two women stood to greet him. One was older, clearly the man's wife. The other was about Tatiana's age, but she could not possibly be Gregor's sister. She had dark hair and smooth skin, which was almost olive in complexion. Tatiana would be fair, with blond hair and blue eyes.

Gregor stood transfixed, torn with conflicting emotions. He was disappointed that the girl was not his sister, but he was also drawn to stare at her beauty, as if mesmerized. Because the man had moved into the room and was standing a short distance from the window, with his back to Gregor, the girl was now facing him, allowing Gregor to gaze at her warm, dark eyes.

Suddenly, a gust of wind blew the curtains apart, and Gregor found himself completely exposed in front of the lighted window.

The girl's eyes were looking straight into his.

She screamed in terror, and her hand flung out to point at Gregor.

The man whirled around, but Gregor did not wait for his reaction. He turned, rushed to the porch balustrade, and leaped over it onto the sidewalk, rushing desperately out into the driving rain. He had no idea where he was going; he knew only that he must get away before he was caught. He must not get into trouble with the law after he had managed to get this close to his goal.

Behind him, Gregor could hear the man's voice calling out, "Wait! Boy, come back!"

For a time, there seemed to be running footsteps following him, but Gregor quickly left them behind.

Just as quickly, he found that he was completely lost in unfamiliar streets of a strange city.

*   *   *   *   *

Tatiana came downstairs to find the Boustani household in confusion. She had been dressing for dinner when she heard Philip calling her excitedly from the front hall, and had hurriedly finished to find out what he wanted. Now, as she descended the stairs, she noticed the front door wide open, with the chill, damp wind blowing in from outside.

Philip came in the door, hatless and coatless and soaked from the rain, a perturbed look on his face.

"What is it, Papa?" Tatiana asked. "Is something wrong?"

"We had an intruder," Philip said. "There was a boy looking through the window. It frightened Nadia, and he ran away. I tried to catch him, but he ran too fast."

Nadia came out from the parlor, somewhat embarrassed. "I'm sorry I screamed, Papa. I was just startled to see him there. It was almost as if he were in the room with us."

Philip smiled. "That's perfectly understandable," he said. "He may only have been trying to find shelter from the rain."

"He was staring right at me with such a strange look," Nadia said. Then she turned to whisper to Tatiana with a soft giggle, "He was very good-looking, even if he did rather resemble a wet puppy dog."

"Let's all forget about this boy now," Philip suggested, "and go back into the parlor where it's warm and dry. I do have something to tell you."

As the girls followed their father, Nadia whispered to Tatiana excitedly, "Wouldn't it be wonderful if this boy is a secret admirer? Perhaps he's been watching me for days. I think I could like him very easily. He had fair skin like yours, but his hair was a little darker."

Tatiana giggled, "How can you even think such a thing?" she asked. "It would make me awfully uncomfortable to have someone watching me without my knowing it."

"I hope he comes back," Nadia said. "I would like to meet him."

"Be quiet, girls," Judith Boustani admonished. "Your father has an announcement to make, and I think it's something that will please you both very much."

Their curiosity aroused, Nadia and Tatiana sat down on the red plush sofa obediently, waiting to hear what Philip Boustani had to say.

Philip cleared his throat self-consciously, aware that he must look somewhat in disarray after his run in the rain. He combed his hand through his black wavy hair, then wiped moisture from his lush handlebar mustache, endeavoring to regain his dignity. "I received a letter this afternoon from a friend of mine in Moscow. You may have heard me speak of him— Gromyko Kominek. He and his wife Tanya are very dear people. They are almost like family, even though we have not seen each other in some years."

He paused to glance at Nadia and Tatiana, to see if either suspected the surprise he was leading up to. Both looked at him with blank expressions, and this gave him satisfaction. It would be a complete surprise. "We have been corresponding quite a bit these past few months, trying to make the arrangements."

"What arrangements?" Nadia asked impatiently. "What are you trying to tell us, Papa?"

Philip grinned with pleasure. "I am trying to tell you that you and Tatiana are to go to Moscow—perhaps to study at the university."

With a squeal of delight, Nadia leaped from the sofa and rushed to embrace her father. Happily but quietly, Tatiana followed to thank him as well. Then the two sisters hugged each other excitedly. "This is so wonderful!" Nadia exclaimed. "I don't believe it's actually happening!"

"You will be staying with the Komineks," Philip told them. "They will look after you as if you were their own daughters."

"Do they have children of their own?" Tatiana asked.

"They have one son," Philip said soberly, "named Vanitoff, a rather unfortunate boy who was born with a deformity of some sort. They rarely mention him in their letters."

This information did nothing to lessen the excitement of the sisters. They were too elated by the prospects of being able to fulfill the dreams they had possessed for so long: dreams they had, until now, believed were impossible. They immediately began to make plans for what clothes they would have to take, asking Philip questions about the weather in Moscow, how they would travel, how long they would be there before they could come home to visit, what sort of preparation they would need to pass the university's entrance examinations, and when classes would start.

The strange boy at the window was quickly forgotten.

Chapter 11

Gregor wandered through the rain-soaked streets of Enzeli for over an hour before he was finally able to get his bearings and return to the inn where Sidney Fleming was waiting for him. By that time, he had caught a chill and fever. He hurried to his bed, fervently hoping he would be better in the morning, since they had to make their departure for Tehran.

When Fleming awakened him at daybreak, Gregor felt even worse. His fever was extremely high, and he was dizzy when he tried to stand up.

"This is terrible," Fleming said. "I should not have sent you out last night. You can't possibly travel in this condition."

"I'll be all right," Gregor assured him. "We must leave today, and we will."

"I wish you could stay behind until you're better."

"I wouldn't, even if I could," Gregor said firmly. "It's just a cold. I'll get over it."

Under the best of circumstances, overland travel in Persia was difficult. The coach—which was hardly more than a large sheltered wagon—had none of the comforts of the boat they had taken from Baku to Enzeli, and the road it followed was merely a rough, rutted path. The passengers felt every bump through the hard seats. In the hilly and mountainous regions, just after leaving Rasht, it was cold. Gregor tried to look at the scenery, at the tea plantations and the great forests, which people here called jungles, but he felt miserable. On the almost desertlike plains, after leaving Kazvin, it was hot. Sweat made their bodies clammy, and the ever-present dust from the road clung to them in heavy layers. And getting fleas was inevitable. The scenery there, too, was interesting, with mile after mile of grape vineyards, but Gregor still did not feel well enough to enjoy it.

At night, the coach stopped at small hotels along the way, first at Roudbar, then at Kazvin, but even these were uncomfortable. The beds were lumpy and foul-smelling. Water was scarce, so baths were impossible. The best the travelers could hope for was to quench their thirst and to wash their faces and hands. At least the food served at the teahouses nearby was adequate, but because of his illness, Gregor had little appetite.

His cold and fever did not improve; if anything, they seemed to grow worse. Each day of travel seemed to be a test of his endurance and determination.

When they finally arrived in Tehran, entering by the Kazvin Gate, in the southwest part of the city, all Gregor felt was relief at reaching their destination; he was in no condition for joy or elation. Even if he had been in the best of health, the city would have seemed strange to him. Through his fevered eyes, it was bizarre and frightening. He had expected Tehran to be like Baku, only larger, but there was little resemblance between the two places. There was virtually no European influence at all in Tehran, except in the hotels. The huge crowds on the streets were mostly Moslem, wearing the traditional robes. A few men were dressed in western suits, but they invariably wore the traditional woolen hats as well. Occasionally, Gregor saw uniformed Russian officers or soldiers among the crowds.

When they arrived at the Grand Hotel, where the Englishmanh had reserved a room, Sidney Fleming insisted that Gregor go directly to bed. Gregor did not have the strength to argue; he was grateful for the clean room and the comfortable bed and the chance to sleep without interruption. The next morning, Fleming told him there was a bathroom down the hall, and instructed him to take a long, hot bath. This lifted Gregor's spirits, even if it did nothing to improve his health.

After the bath, Fleming sternly told Gregor to rest, while he went to his series of meetings with the Persian government officials. The Englishman said firmly, "You must not think of getting out of bed until you are completely well. I will be in Tehran a full week before going south to Khorramshahr and Abadan. That should be plenty of time for you to regain your strength."

"But I can't take your charity," Gregor argued. "If I am to be dependent upon you, I must do my work."

"I can manage without you," Fleming told him, then smiled. "It's not that I don't need you. You are a very big help to me. But you're of no use when you're sick. You must promise me that you will rest and get well. Then we'll talk about your work."

"You've done enough for me already," Gregor said. "I'm grateful, but I must take care of myself now."

Fleming did not have time to argue. "We'll talk about it this evening," he said. "I don't know how late I'll be, but I want you to be here when I return."

Gregor said nothing in reply. He had no intention of depending upon his friend any longer. After Fleming had left, Gregor wrote him a lengthy note, thanking him for all his help and telling him he hoped one day they would meet again. Then he gathered his few possessions together and set out on the streets of Tehran on the mission that had been delayed far too long.

He was feeling somewhat better, so he was now able to appreciate some of the wonders of the city. It truly was beautiful, lush with trees and gardens. Gregor recognized poplars and pines and plane trees, though many of the flowers were totally foreign to him. In the distance, rising above the city, he could see snow-topped mountains.

It was midday before Gregor succeeded in locating the bazaar. He had wandered the teeming, crowded Tehran streets for hours, getting lost several times and having to ask for directions from people who were more suspicious than friendly. The crowds, the noise, and the unfamiliarity of the surroundings combined with his fever and weakness to confuse him. Self-consciously, he was certain everyone recognized him as a foreigner because of his European-style clothes and his accent.

The bazaar seemed an astonishing place to Gregor. It was unlike the market where he had worked in Sabunchi, and it did not resemble the one in Baku. Sheltered by an arched brick roof with openings spaced at regular intervals to let in air and light, it was a city unto itself—a vast enclosed city containing a maze of narrow streets and countless shops that were tended by countless merchants.

Gregor was dismayed; he had not expected such numbers. It might take weeks—even months—to find the one specific Jewish merchant who had adopted a daughter named Tatiana, especially if he had to go from one shop to another, talking to one merchant at a time.

For a moment, he considered returning to the hotel and taking Sidney Fleming's advice. But he considered that only for a moment. He told himself that he could not turn back now. He had made his decision, and he had to go on, no matter how difficult it might be.

Wandering aimlessly through the bazaar, he thought about his prospects. The best course, he decided, would be to find work in the bazaar, preferably work for a merchant who was Jewish. Even if he did not find the right merchant immediately, he reasoned that one Jewish merchant might lead him to another, and eventually he would find the one he was looking for.

After wandering through the bazaar for a while, Gregor discovered that there was a certain order and organization to the place. One street contained the shops of the rug merchants; another brass and silverware; still another carried fabric and clothing. Because Gregor had worked for a food merchant as a boy in Sabunchi, he chose to look for a similar job here. But the food markets were themselves specialized according to the type of merchandise, with sections for meats, fish, grains, fruits, and dried vegetables.

Gregor was confused and weary by the time he mustered the courage to begin inquiring for work. The first few shopkeepers he approached refused him curtly, giving him no reason or explanation, but eyeing him with suspicion and distrust. After a while, his courage began to flag, but he persisted.

It was an elderly merchant who specialized in dried fruit who finally took the time to speak to him and offer advice. There was no activity in his shop at the time, and the old man was casually stacking small sacks of dates. "I'm sorry," he said in reply to Gregor's inquiry, "but I don't need any help." However, as Gregor started to walk away in dismay, the man stopped him. "You're a stranger here, aren't you?" he asked.

"Yes, sir," Gregor nodded.

"It's hard for a stranger to get work in the bazaar," the merchant told him. "Most people hire only family or friends. They don't trust strangers, especially foreigners."

"I'm honest," Gregor said hopefully. "And I'm willing to work hard."

The old man eyed him appraisingly and nodded. "I do know of someone who's looking for some help," he said. "His name is Rajik Sarkissian. He's a grain merchant, and he doesn't have any sons of his own. He might take a chance on you."

"Thank you, sir," Gregor said gratefully.

"But don't tell him I sent you to him," the old man added, as Gregor was walking away. "If you don't turn out to be as honest as you say, I don't want him to blame me."

Gregor located Sarkissian's shop in the street of the grain merchants, but when he entered, setting a bell to ringing on the door, he found the shop unattended.

"Hello," he called out, looking around. "Is anyone here?" Noticing a back door propped open, Gregor gravitated toward the rear of the large room. As he approached the door, he almost collided with a short, plump, black-bearded man, carrying a heavy sack of rice. Gregor took it as a good sign that the man was wearing a western suit.

"I'll be with you in a moment," the man grunted. "As soon as I put this bag down."

Gregor followed quickly. "Let me help you with it," he offered.

"Thank you," the man said, "but I've got it." He thrust the large sack of grain onto a stack against one wall of the shop, then heaved a sigh of relief, wiping sweat from his brow, and turned to face Gregor. "What can I do for you, young man?"

"I'm looking for Mr. Rajik Sarkissian," Gregor said.

The man smiled. He was middle-aged, but there was something boyish and trusting about his smile. "You've found him," Rajik Sarkissian said.

"I've heard you might have some work available," Gregor ventured. "I'm looking for a job."

"Well, you've certainly come to the right place," the merchant told him. "Do you think you can lift fifty-pound sacks of rice? I've got a whole lorry-ful in the back alley." Sarkissian looked Gregor up and down, but not disapprovingly. "The last helper I had disappeared two days ago, along with the money in the till. I hope he's not the one who sent you to me."

"No, sir," Gregor said earnestly, then added. "It was just a man in the bazaar."

"Well, it doesn't matter," Sarkissian said. "I need help, and you're here. You can start to work right now if you're willing."

"Yes, sir," Gregor said happily. "Just tell me what to do."

Gregor's strength had been depleted by his illness. Normally he could have unloaded all of Sarkissian's grain with no problem at all. However, as weak as he was, every sack seemed a struggle. At first, the merchant did not notice; he was occupied with matters in the shop, with doing his paperwork and with waiting on customers. But, as the afternoon wore on, his small dark eyes would gaze at Gregor, drawn there by a cough or by a moan as Gregor heaved a heavy sack into place.

Finally, Sarkissian approached Gregor, saying, "You aren't well, are you, boy?"

"I'm all right, sir," Gregor replied, attempting to give a good appearance. "I've just got a little cold." But he could not control the shivering from his fever.

"You should go home to bed," the merchant said, with a sympathetic smile. "You could start to work tomorrow or the next day. Whenever you're feeling better."

"I appreciate your kindness, sir," Gregor said. "But I would prefer to finish the work I've started. Truly I'm all right, just a little weak."

Sarkissian did not press the matter, and Gregor went back to unloading the lorry. He had almost finished the task when suddenly, as he was about to thrust a sack of rice from his shoulder to the stack in the shop, his knees gave way and he collapsed on the floor in a faint

When he opened his eyes again, he wasn't quite sure where he was or whose round, bearded, kindly face it was hovering over him. Then he realized what had happened, and he was gripped with anxiety that the job he had tried so hard to obtain and that he needed so desperately might be taken from him.

"You are a very sick young man," Rajik Sarkissian said. "You have a fever. I am going to take you home and put you to bed. Where do you live?"

"Please, sir," Gregor said, trying to get to his feet. "I'm all right."

"You're not all right," Sarkissian insisted firmly, forcing him to lie back. "Now, where do you live?"

"I don't have a place," Gregor confessed reluctantly. "I've just arrived in Tehran, and I was hoping you might permit me to sleep in the shop."

Sarkissian appeared shocked. Then he shook his head in wry consternation. "You certainly are a strange one," he said. "Why is it that every lunatic, thief, or runaway boy in Tehran seems to come to me seeking work?"

Tears of indignation welled up in Gregor's eyes. "I don't mean to cause you trouble, sir," he protested. "I am honest and trustworthy. I just have a little cold."

"Sure you do," Sarkissian said skeptically. "And you flew in here on a magic carpet." He shook his head woefully. "I suppose there's nothing to be done but to take you home with me. I don't know what my wife will think when I come home with a strange sick boy, but I'm sure she'll be willing to give you some soup and find a bed for you."

Until he actually met Jeanous Sarkissian, Gregor did not realize that Rajik was being facetious about not knowing how his wife would react. If there was anyone who was more kind and trusting than Rajik Sarkissian, it was his wife. Like her husband, Jeanous was short and plump. She had the manner of a mother hen anxiously looking for baby chicks to take care of. She had only to hear that Gregor was homeless and sick, and she took charge of him totally. She would accept no protests.

She fed Gregor with ash, a thick soup, and freshly baked bread. Then she put him to bed, covering him with layers of warm, downy quilts, instructing him firmly not to get up again until she gave him permission.

The fever continued for three more days, gradually increasing. At times, Gregor was delirious, and in such a state, it was impossible for him to recognize the people around him. One was clearly a doctor. Another was a woman, who would come periodically to spoon-feed him hot broth and mop his brow with a cold wet cloth. In his fevered mind, there were moments when he thought it was his mother, and he cried out to her, asking her how she had found him, wanting to know where she had been, and begging her not to leave him again.

On the third day, the fever broke, and Gregor awakened with a clear mind, but he had only vague memories of how he had gotten to this strange room in an unfamiliar house. He tried to rise, but found his legs were too weak for him to stand. So he lay back down, to try to recall what had happened to him. He had a feeling of contentment and happiness. He sensed that he had seen his mother, that she had come to him at last, but that was not rationally possible. His mother, he knew, was in Siberia, and he was in Persia.

However, there had been a kindly woman looking after him.

It was only a few moments before Jeanous Sarkissian came into the room.

Gregor looked into her plump, pretty face inquiringly. "Who are you?" he asked. "I'm sure I should know your name, but I can't remember."

She smiled. "You must be feeling better," she said. "My name is Jeanous Sarkissian. For a time you thought I was your mother. You kept calling me 'Mama.' "

"I'm sorry," Gregor said, embarrassed.

"You needn't be," Jeanous told him sincerely. "I didn't mind. I've always longed for a child to call me mother, but I've never been fortunate enough to have one."

* * * * *

Gregor was grateful to the Sarkissians, and he wanted to be able to repay their kindness. He worked very hard at Rajik's shop, and tried to help Jeanous at home as much as he could. That is, as much as she would permit him to do. However, he felt that everything he did was inadequate. Nothing seemed to make them happier than doing things for him.

They could not have treated him with greater kindness and love if they had been his own parents. For that reason, he felt a continuing sense of guilt that he was deceiving them. It may have been a mistake, but he had chosen not to tell them the truth about himself. He had admitted that he had come to Tehran from Baku. That had been necessary to explain his accent and his manner of dress. He had told them, however, that his parents were both dead and that he had no other family, choosing to keep his mission in Tehran a secret.

Perhaps if he had realized how deeply they longed to have a child to shower their love upon, he would have known the truth was less cruel than the lie.

After Gregor had recovered from his illness, Rajik and Jeanous refused to allow him to move out of their house into a rented room. They insisted that he dine with them as a member of the family, accepting no payment or reduction in his wages for his room and board. They gave him gifts of clothing and books. And they inquired frequently about his health and his happiness.

Gregor remained single-minded in his purpose. Trying not to appear too curious, he would ask Rajik and Jeanous about the other merchants at the bazaar, particularly about those who were Jewish. He was disappointed that they were not themselves Jewish, but were Armenian Christians, for that meant that their circle of close friends did not include many Jews.

In order to meet Jews, Gregor had to stop and speak to them himself. "How are you today?" he would ask, trying to appear casual. After they replied, he would pursue, "And how is your family?"

As Gregor came to be known and accepted in the community, these solicitations usually prompted detailed accountings of the health of each family member.

He learned that a great many of the merchants had daughters; some were around Tatiana's age, but none fit her description.

Weeks passed, and Gregor began to fear that the information given him by Nurse Afsar was false. After all, she had been reluctant to divulge the information. Would she have deceived him purposefully? Gregor didn't think so, or rather he didn't want to think so. The woman had seemed so kind and caring. But, as time passed, there remained very few Jewish merchants in Tehran that he had not met. And even those he had heard about and knew that they had not adopted his sister.

Perhaps Afsar had not known the truth. She had first told him that the girl had been taken to Persia. She had told him Tehran only after he had pressed her the name of a city. Persia was a very large place. He wished now that he had not been so hasty; he regretted that he had not gone to the head of the ophanage, the man named Haydar Gogoli, to ask for details. But now it was too late. There was no way he could return to Baku.

Gregor did not realize that Rajik and Jeanous were aware of his growing despondency, until Rajik approached him one day in the shop. Gregor was helping to take inventory; it was an afternoon with very little activity. Gregor had counted the sacks of rice three times and come up with three different numbers.

"What's wrong?" Rajik asked him. "I can see that something has been troubling you."

"It's nothing important," Gregor replied with a shrug.

"You know, don't you, that you can talk to me about anything that's on your mind?" Rajik pressed. "Jeanous and I want you to be happy here."

Gregor was embarrassed. "Yes," he said. "I know." And he went back to count the sacks of rice for a fourth time.

But Rajik interrupted him. "Gregor," he said, almost shyly. "There's something I've been wanting to talk to you about."

Gregor stopped what he was doing and looked at the merchant curiously. He knew from Rajik's manner that this was something important.

"Jeanous and I have grown to be very fond of you," Rajik proceeded to explain. "And we hope that you feel a fondness for us as well . . . "

"Of course," Gregor interjected. "I'm very grateful for . . . "

"We aren't looking for gratitude," Rajik cut in. "It's something more than that. Jeanous and I have discussed the matter at length, and we both feel the same. We have come to think of you as if you were our own son." He took a deep breath, sighed, and looked down at the floor. "We would like to propose adopting you legally."

He looked up into Gregor's eyes inquiringly.

Gregor was stunned. He realized suddenly that he should have anticipated this, but the thought had never really occurred to him, so intent had he been on his own concerns. "I don't know what to say," he stammered. "I'm deeply honored, but . . . "

"You don't have to give us an answer immediately," Rajik pursued. "You can think about it. There are many advantages to such an arrangement— for you as well as for us. Although I am not an extremely wealthy man, I am not poor by any estimation. I have no heir. Naturally, if you were my son, I would want you to have every possible advantage. I would want you to finish your schooling, and . . . "

"Rajik, please," Gregor interrupted gently, embarrassed. "I know your generosity. If I were to make such a decision, it would not be for material reasons. There are other things I must consider."

"I understand," Rajik replied, but a question remained in his eyes.

It was a decision Gregor did not want to make, but it was one he could not avoid. He had to give the Sarkissians some sort of answer. He could not choose to ignore their offer, for that—in itself—would be a decision, perhaps the worst decision of all because it would hurt them.

For so many years his life had been devoted to one purpose. All his efforts in achieving that purpose had failed, and it seemed now that he might never be able to accomplish it. Should he give up in trying to locate Tatiana? Was it really as important as he had believed it to be? He sensed that a door was closing in his life and another was opening. Should he go forward through that new door? Or should he turn around and retrace his steps before the first door was closed?

To do that, he knew he would have to turn his back on the Sarkissians forever. Refusing their offer would be cruel, so it would be necessary to leave them. In fact, it would be advisable for him to leave Tehran, to try to return to Baku. But how was that possible?

It amazed him that strangers had been so kind to him. The Sarkissians had not been the first; there had also been the Englishman, Sidney Fleming. He, too, had made Gregor an offer, but Gregor had turned him down. If he had accepted, he would have had a job that would have allowed him to travel all over Persia. He would have been able to look for Tatiana in places other than Tehran. But it was too late for that now.

Or was it? Gregor knew Fleming's travel schedule. He would be coming back to Tehran soon from Khorramshahr. Gregor wasn't sure how the Englishman would feel about him, after the way he had left, but he thought he would at least talk to him. He decided to go to the British Embassy and leave a note. If Fleming still felt kindly toward him, he would come to the bazaar to see him. A talk with him would at least help Gregor to put his new situation into perspective.

Two days after Gregor left the note at the embassy, Sidney Fleming appeared at the Sarkissian shop, asking for him. Gregor was in the back alley checking a shipment of goods at the time. When Rajik came out to tell him there was an Englishman asking to see him, there was a curious look on his face, but he did not ask questions.

Gregor hurried into the shop to greet Fleming, who smiled warmly as he approached. "I didn't think I would ever see you again after the way you left," Fleming told him genially. "You know, that wasn't exactly cricket of you."

Gregor blushed self-consciously. He was aware that Rajik was listening intently, even though he was trying to appear unconcerned. "At the time, it seemed to be the right thing to do," Gregor said. "Come out back with me where I'm working, and we can talk."

As they retreated through the back door of the shop, Gregor could feel Rajik's eyes boring into the back of his head, and he knew that his employer was as hurt as he was puzzled. But there was no way Gregor could explain the matter to him. At least, not yet.

Gregor told Fleming all that had happened in the past weeks—of his illness, of the Sarkissians' kindness, of his fruitless search for Tatiana, and finally of the offer that had been made to him. "I just don't know what to do," he said. "I feel I should continue to look for my sister. She is the only family I have. At the same time, I feel a responsibility toward the Sarkissians; they've been like a family to me."

Sidney Fleming listened sympathetically throughout Gregor's explanation. When he had finished, the Englishman said, "If you found your sister and she was happy in her life, would you want to change things?"

Gregor hesitated. "No, but . . . "

"If you found your sister, and she was not happy," Fleming broke in, "would you be able to do anything to help her, without money or a position of your own?"

"I could try," Gregor said, though there was doubt in his voice. "Especially if I had the job you offered me before."

Fleming smiled in sympathy. "That job would not last forever," he said. "In a couple of months, I have to go back to England."

Gregor's face fell. "I see," he said.

"You've made every possible effort to locate your sister," Fleming told him. "No one could have done more; you have to start thinking of yourself. Think of your future, so that—if you ever do find her—you'll be in a position to help her, if she needs help. You might never find another opportunity like this one. Certainly not one in Baku."

"But I can't continue to lie to the Sarkissians about my family," Gregor said. "It wouldn't be fair."

"No," Fleming agreed. "It wouldn't. Tell them the truth. If they care about you, as you say, they'll understand."

"But it will hurt them that I've lied to them," he protested.

"Not as deeply as it would for you to refuse their offer," Fleming said firmly. Then he smiled. "I'm very pleased for you, Gregor. A family is what you need."

"They might change their minds," Gregor suggested.

"They might," Fleming agreed. "But I don't think they will."

"If they do," Gregor asked, "is that job offer still open—for as long as it might last?"

"Of course," Fleming said.

That evening at dinner, Gregor gave his decision to Rajik and Jeanous. "There is something I have to confess to you first," he said. "I have lied to you. It is true that my father is dead, but my mother is alive, imprisoned in Siberia. At least, as far as I know, she is still living."

"I'm sorry," Rajik said sympathetically. "But there was no reason to keep that from us. We have no interest in Russian politics."

"That's not all," Gregor continued. "I have a sister alive somewhere. It's why I came to Tehran, to look for her. I had been told she was adopted by a Jewish merchant here."

Jeanous gasped. "Now I understand why . . . "

"You asked all those questions all the time," Rajik completed the statement.

"It's clear to me now that she isn't here," Gregor said, his voice trembling with emotion. "I don't think I'll ever be able to find her. I must give up my search."

Rajik Sarkissian gazed at Gregor sadly. "Why didn't you tell us this?" he asked. "We would have helped you."

"I don't know," Gregor said. "It just seemed easier not to talk about it." He paused, then said almost tearfully, "I'm sorry to have lied to you."

"That doesn't matter," Rajik soothed. "All we want is your happiness. If you don't want adoption, we understand. It would hardly be fair to your mother—or your sister. We'll do what we can to help you."

Gregor blushed. "That's not necessary," he said. "If you still want to adopt me as your son, after all I've told you, I'm willing to accept the offer."

There was a moment of incredulous silence at the table; then Jeanous and Rajik both leaped from their chairs simultaneously to rush to him, to embrace him, tears of joy welling into their eyes.

Chapter 12

The change from Gregor Baranov to Gregor Sarkissian involved much more than the legal transfer of a name. In one way at least, it was somewhat like turning time back ten years and starting over as a child. When he had promised Rajik and Jeanous that he would go back to school to improve his education, Gregor did not fully realize what that would involve.

Gregor's accumulation of knowledge had been irregular. In some subjects he was advanced; in others he had little background at all. He had learned quite a bit of mathematics, which he had used in his Uncle Vladimir's business, along with some engineering, though in both cases he had only a weak basic framework for the bits and pieces of practical information he had gathered. His teachers were amazed at his facility for foreign languages, but his background in history and in reading literature was almost nonexistant.

The Sarkissians enrolled Gregor at the Christian school in Tehran, and it was organized strictly according to educational level. Although all the students of one level were not precisely the same age, most were within a few years of each other. There were a few students in the school who were as old as Gregor, who was now fourteen, but he looked considerably older than his years. He had grown very tall, and his broad shoulders had filled out from the manual labor he had performed. His voice had changed to a deep baritone, and he already had a small mustache. He felt very much out of place.

At first the teachers and administrator were perplexed about what to do with him. Since the Sarkissians were important in the church and had made large donations to the school, even before they had adopted Gregor, it was decided that an exception would be made for the young man. He would take his various classes at different levels. In some cases, he would be with students who were his own age; in others, he would be studying with nine- or ten-year-olds.

That was embarrassing for Gregor. He was shamed by the whispers and muffled laughter from the children and those of his peers who secretly—and some not so secretly—made fun of him.

Mercifully, Gregor progressed very rapidly, and he was soon mostly in classes with the older children, but there was so much to be assimilated in the history and literature courses that he remained with eleven- and twelve-year-olds in those classes. His teachers treated him well. They were impressed by his eagerness to learn, by his seriousness.

However, only Gregor knew how difficult it was to maintain a calm appearance. Many times he wanted to say nasty things to those who taunted him, but he restrained himself. He wanted to do nothing that would reflect badly on his new parents.

There were adjustments to be made at home, as well as out in the world; learning to be a son after so many years of independence and self-reliance was not easy.

His restraint became more difficult though when the taunting passed from the children to a group of street toughs Gregor passed every afternoon on his way home from school. He understood these indolent types very well. There had been a time in Baku when he had known such groups, and some of the boys who worked the docks were part of one. Although he knew there was little real malice behind their words, which were spoken partly out of boredom and partly out of a need to feel superior to someone, their words cut through him nevertheless and touched his own thoughts and feelings about his situation. The words hurt because he felt there might be some truth in them.

There was one heavy-set boy about his own age who seemed to be the ringleader. He always started the catcalls as soon as he saw Gregor, shouting, "Hey, here comes the big baby!" Then the others joined in with calls of "Sissy," and "Maybe he's really a girl," and "Better hurry home to mommy."

In the group, there were never fewer than four and never more than six. Gregor was aware that if he ever responded to their taunts and there were a fight, he would be heavily outnumbered. If only he could get the ringleader alone sometime, he felt he could end the problem.

Gregor was also aware there was a degree of racial hatred in their taunts. The street toughs were clearly Moslems, and they assumed that he was Christian, because virtualy all of the students at the school were. Those who were not Christian were Jews, whom the Moslems hated even more. Although Gregor had long been aware of the animosity among the religions and races, he had always felt above it because he was not really a member of any particular religious group. Now that he was a Sarkissian, he was automatically a Christian, and therefore the enemy of Moslems and Jews.

It was not a good feeling. It made him angry to have to hate and be hated for such a foolish reason.

The taunts changed their nature one afternoon during the spring term, making them impossible to ignore. He didn't have any idea which one threw the first stone, but it was most likely the ringleader, whose name he new was Ahmed. The small rock struck Gregor on the leg, and almost immediately afterward another hit his arm.

Reflexively he began to run, attempting to dodge the barrage of pebbles hurtled at him. And almost immediately he was ashamed of himself for doing so. He was not a coward; he really should have faced them, he felt. But how could he explain to Rajik and Jeanous, if he got into a fight?

The laughter and jeering of the boys smarted in his ears as he ran down the street, slowing to a walk again, once he was out of sight of the street gang.

For the sake of his pride and dignity, Gregor would not permit himself to turn around to make sure he was, indeed, safe from his tormentors. Instead he straightened himself, kept his eyes ahead, and pretended his bruises did not hurt at all.

Suddenly, he felt a sharp pain as a rock hit the back of his head, causing him to lose his balance and fall to the ground. When he looked up, he saw that the ringleader, Ahmed, had followed him, separating himself from the group, which still hovered near the streetcorner. Ahmed was only a few yards away, and was bending to pick up another stone from the street.

Gregor's rage blinded him. He did not pause this time to reason with himself. Instead, he leaped to his feet and rushed headlong toward the boy, who was so startled he did not move. Gregor lunged at Ahmed, knocking him down and falling on top of him, pummeling the tormentor with his fists.

Taken by surprise, Ahmed could do little but attempt to defend himself. Immediately his friends rushed to his rescue, attacking Gregor, who was now outnumbered.

With effort, Gregor was able to extricate himself from the situation to run away, aware that people had stopped in the street to watch the altercation. The group of boys pursued him for several blocks before giving up the chase.

Once he was safe, Gregor stopped to catch his breath and to survey the damage. He had several minor cuts and bruises, and his clothes were torn and soiled. Now the only thing he could think of was how to explain this to Rajik and Jeanous. He was sure it would hurt them to tell them the truth.

Rajik, he knew, would still be at his shop, and Jeanous would be home with the servants, preparing for the evening meal. Gregor would have to try to slip into the house without her seeing him, so that he could wash and change his clothes. Then he could easily excuse the bruises and cuts as some simple accident at school.

He entered the house through the front door, hoping Jeanous would be back in the kitchen, as she was. However, as he was about to climb the stairs, the housekeeper—an elderly woman who had been with the family for years—was passing through the hall from the parlor. She looked at him with a shocked expression, and started to exclaim something, but he put a finger to his lips and whispered, "Please don't say anything to Mama about this."

She hesitated a moment, then said, "All right, Master Gregor," and went about her business.

With that concern resolved, Gregor began to consider what he could do to avoid another altercation with the group of street toughs, for he was sure they would be waiting for him the next day, and the next. He knew he could not avoid facing them again, for they could wait as long as they had to in order to get their revenge for the indignity Ahmed had suffered. Gregor could not even consider staying away from school.

The most reasonable solution would be to approach the group directly and challenge Ahmed to a one-on-one fight, though he wasn't sure the other boys would see this as particularly fair. However, Gregor could see no other solution.

The next day, at school, Gregor was unable to concentrate as well as he usually did on his studies; his mind was on the anticipated confrontation he would have when he started home. He was not afraid of the group of street toughs, but he dreaded the fight.

To his surprise, Ahmed and his friends were not waiting for him on their usual street corner. In fact, they were nowhere to be seen. Gregor felt a strange combination of relief and disappointment. He would not have to face a confrontation today, but he was sure it would occur sooner or later; in a way, it would have been better to get it over with.

He proceeded on his way toward home, occupied with his thoughts, wondering why the boys were not waiting for him on this of all days. If he had been in their place, his pride would have demanded another fight today.

Gregor had gone little more than a block when it happened. With his guard down, he was taken totally by surprise.

They rushed out at him from an alleyway suddenly, all six of them together. Before he could even make an attempt to defend himself, he was on the ground, and they were on top of him, pummeling him with their fists. He tried to fight back, but his efforts were futile, overpowered as he was.

He had no idea when or how the other boy came to his aid. He realized only that, at one point, he seemed suddenly to have a fighting chance, that he was no longer completely pinned down and his blows were finding a mark.

Then he heard someone shouting, "Get up, boy! Get up and run!"

Somehow Gregor managed to get to his feet and begin to run down the street. He heard the sound of running footsteps behind him, but he did not turn back to look. His heart was beating fiercely, and his muscles ached from the blows they had sustained. His one hope was that his attackers would eventully stop their pursuit as they had the day before.

But this time the footsteps continued behind him, growing ever nearer. His breathing became increasingly painful and forced, and he wasn't sure how much further he could run before collapsing.

Then, through the roar of his heartbeat in his ears, he heard the voice behind him calling, "Wait, boy! Wait!" It was the same voice that had urged him to run.

Unable to go further, Gregor stopped, falling against the wall of a house for support. A boy about his own age, perhaps slightly older, one he had never seen before, collapsed against the wall next to him, gasping for breath as painfully as Gregor was. It was only then that he fully realized that someone had come to his aid. But Gregor was puzzled; why would this young man help him? He was obviously a Moslem; that was clear from his manner of dress. If he were to have chosen sides, he should have been with the other boys.

"Are you all right?" the young man asked, between gasps for breath.

Gregor nodded. "Yes. Thanks for your help." He studied the dark intelligent eyes for an explanation. "But why did you do it? Help me, I mean?"

The young man grinned and shrugged. "I hate to see an unfair fight," he said. "You were outnumbered." He looked away for a moment, and then added. "Anyway, I've seen them teasing you before, and I admire you for trying to ignore them. You're getting yourself an education—a real western education—and that's something I wish I could do."

"Why can't you?" Gregor asked, then realized it was a rather personal question to ask of a stranger.

The young man looked embarrassed. "My religion permits one kind of education," he said. "I can study only the Koran, and I've had that schooling."

Gregor understood. He should have known without even asking the question. "Thank you for helping me," he said. "Whatever your reasons."

Again the young man grinned. "I enjoyed it," he said. "How about having a cup of tea with me? There's a teahouse I go to near here, and we can talk . . . That is, if you have time, and . . . "

Again, Gregor understood. By race and religion, they should not really be friends. "I'd like that," he said impulsively, "and I think I can manage the time. But, after that fight, I must look pretty bad."

"No worse than I do," the young man said. "This teahouse isn't very fancy; we'll be all right there."

"Well, I guess I should introduce myself," Gregor said. "My name is Gregor Sarkissian." He extended his hand.

"Kouroush Jalali," the young man responded, hesitating only a moment before accepting the handshake. Then he looked at Gregor curiously. "Sarkissian? Isn't that an Armenian name? You don't look Armenian."

It was Gregor's turn to be embarrassed. "I'm adopted," he said. "It's a long story."

Kouroush smiled. "Then you can tell it to me over tea."

*   *   *   *   *

The teahouse was a very small, ill-kept cubicle in a storefront near the outdoor market. As Kouroush had told him, it was not fancy, but as all of its customers were Moslem, Gregor felt somewhat out of place.

It was behind an outdoor shop in a rather poor neighborhood, set up on the street under a crude awning where the owner sold tea and coffee and spices. They entered through the large open door and found themselves a space on one of the large, carpet-covered platforms in the rear. Kouroush sat down comfortably on the platform, slipping easily into a cross-legged position. Gregor was unaccustomed to such a place, so he sat uneasily on the edge, allowing his feet to rest on the floor, about a foot below the platform.

Almost immediately, a young boy about their own age came by with a tray containing glasses of tea in saucers to serve them. Gregor asked for his tea sweetened, but Kouroush ordered his lumps of sugar on the side, choosing to suck on the lumps and wash the sweetness down with strong hot tea.

On a platform in a corner, near the bar, a couple of old men sat smoking a water pipe and talking. Behind the bar was a row of about half a dozen water pipes ready for customers, and on the bar, the pots of tea and hot water were steaming, ready to serve.

"I come here because it's cheap," Kouroush said. "Until I finish my schooling, I'm dependent on my father for support, and I hate asking him for money."

Gregor thought he understood, but he was wrong, for after only a moment's hesitation, Kouroush explained, "It's not that he can't afford to give me everything I need; he's got plenty of money. The reason I don't like asking is that he uses money as a way to try to control me. He's in the military—the Persian Cossack Brigade—and he wants me to be just like him."

"You mean, he wants you to go into the military?" Gregor asked.

Kouroush nodded, "Into the cossacks. But I hate the Russians; I would like nothing better than to have them driven out of Persia. I certainly wouldn't want to serve them and their puppet army."

"What would you like to do?" Gregor asked.

Kouroush shrugged. "I don't know," he said. "Almost anything but the military. What really interests me is politics and government, but I wouldn't want to have anything to do with this pro-Russian government we've got now."

Gregor found that he liked Kouroush Jalali, and within only a few short minutes began to look upon him as a friend, the first real friend near his own age he had acquired since arriving in Tehran. Kouroush exuded an energy and vitality that was infectious; he was as excitable and as talkative as Gregor was subdued and quiet. Only two years older than Gregor, he was as dark as Gregor was fair, with a mass of thick black curls and lively dark brown eyes. On his upper lip were traces of the beginning of a mustache. He had a strong, determined chin and a very pleasant smile.

But as different as they were in looks and personality, they were very similar in their ideas and opinions, especially when it came to politics.

Gregor was surprised to learn that Kouroush's father was Pasha Jalali. His name was well known in Tehran, for he had risen about as high in the Persian Cossack Brigade as it was possible for a Persian to do. He was one of only a handful of Persians to reach the rank of sergeant. Gregor also found that the two of them had something in common; Kouroush had been about ten years old when he had lost his mother, who had died in childbirth.

But Kouroush was really impressed when he learned that Gregor's real father had been a socialist leader in the refinery and oil field strikes in Baku, and that he had been killed in the riots. "A Persian can truly be proud of a father like that," he told Gregor passionately. "A true patriot."

Kouroush told Gregor about a holy man who was attempting to rally Persians toward independence. "You must come with me to hear him speak," Kouroush said. "His name is Mirza Kuchik, and I think he is our real hope for the future."

But Gregor declined. "I don't want to get involved in politics," he said. "It would be very difficult for me after what happened to my father. And I don't want to do anything that will reflect badly on my new family."

"I'm not asking you to *do* anything," Kouroush said. "Just come and hear him speak."

Gregor shook his head. "I'd rather not." By the tone of his voice, it was clear to Kouroush that he meant it. Kouroush did not press the matter.

When they parted company, they agreed to meet again the following day, outside the school. With Kouroush at his side, Gregor should have no trouble with the street toughs again.

*   *   *   *   *

Until he left Kouroush, Gregor did not realize how much time he had spent with his new friend. He would be very late getting home. In fact, it was almost time for Rajik to be arriving from his shop. Gregor hoped he had not been missed.

He looked even more of a mess than he had the day before, and he would again have to attempt to slip into the house unseen.

As he entered the front hall, there seemed to be no one around. He closed the door silently behind him and moved toward the stairs, trying to keep from making a sound. But the parlor door was open, and as he passed it, Rajik's voice called out, "Gregor, would you come in please. I would like to talk to you."

Gregor turned and saw that Rajik was standing in the open doorway, looking at him, an expression of concern on his face. Gregor's mind began to race, searching for an innocent, harmless explanation for his condition. He walked slowly into the parlor, with an increasing fear that he could think of nothing that would not upset his parents.

"I guess I don't have to ask if it's true," Rajik said simply. "It appears that you've been in a fight today, so reports of your appearance yesterday must also be accurate."

Suddenly he smiled. "Are you all right? Have you been hurt?"

"It looks worse than it was," Gregor said. "It's my clothes that are ruined."

"Clothes can be replaced," Rajik said. Then he gestured toward the sofa. "Come sit down and tell me about it."

"It's nothing really," Gregor began to protest. "I can handle it without it concerning you and Mama." But he sat down as Rajik had asked him to do, though he could not allow his eyes to meet those of his adopted father.

"I know what it is to be a young man," Rajik said gently. "And I did grow up here in Tehran. I am capable of understanding."

Gregor looked up into Rajik's eyes, and in them he saw not only concern, but the love of a father. Tears began to well inside and threatened to roll forth from his eyes; he struggled to hold them back.

There was nothing he could do but tell Papa all about what had happened. Papa. Yes, for the first time, he really accepted that Rajik was now his papa, and he must share such things with him.

PART II

EMBERS—1907 to 1913

Chapter 13

As the weeks before Tatiana and Nadia were to depart for Moscow dwindled into days, there was increasing excitement in the Boustani household. Philip Boustani had recommended that the girls wait until they reached their destination to purchase new clothes, but they could not keep themselves from going on shopping sprees in Rasht, adding to the number of trunks that had to be packed. They read everything they could about the city of Moscow, and they practiced speaking Russian for hours each day. For Tatiana, recalling the language was easy, and she coached Nadia, helping to refresh her memory on what Madame Veronique had taught them.

It would be over six months before they would have to face their entrance examinations for the university, and the reason they were going to Moscow early was so that the Komineks could see that they were tutored in the subjects they would need before being admitted, but they were already concerned about their lack of adequate education.

The trip from Rasht to Moscow would be a long one, taking many days. There were two ways of traveling the great distance. They could take a Russian boat most of the way from Enzeli, sailing across the Caspian and up the Volga River as far as Novgorod, then going overland from there to Moscow. Or they could take the boat to Baku, and go by train from there, traveling the greater distance by land.

After lengthy consideration and much discussion with his daughters, Philip decided on the latter route. He would have to accompany them on the trip, and there would be some difficulties in taking so much time away from business. However, to compensate for the loss, he set up a few appointments with Russian merchants in Moscow in hopes of arranging a few import contracts that might be lucrative.

The day of departure arrived, with much activity and confusion. The trunks had been delivered to the Enzeli docks the day before, but there was still last-minute packing to be done for the hand luggage, which was supposed to consist only of the items they would need during the trip, but which was rapidly being filled with things that one or the other of the girls remembered they had forgotten to put into the trunks. Everyone was running up and down the stairs, calling to each other from room to room and driving the servants frantic.

They changed clothes several times, trying to decide what would be best to wear for the boat trip, finally deciding on their identical white organdy dresses and hats, with their lightweight, gray ankle-length coats.

Philip was the only one who kept calm throughout it all. At one point, he told Nadia, "You aren't leaving forever, you know. You can't take the entire household with you."

"Oh, Papa," Nadia said, throwing her arms around him, "I didn't think it would be so difficult to leave. I'm going to miss everyone so much."

"I understand," Philip replied, comforting her. "But it's a bit late to change your mind now. You aren't thinking of that, are you?"

"No," she said.

"Then we must go," he told her. "The longer we delay our departure the more difficult it will be for you and Tatiana to say goodbye."

As it was, the parting was extremely difficult. The two girls first said farewell to the two elderly servants, Serash and Neriani, who had looked after them since they were small children. Then, when they embraced Judith Boustani, they broke into tears. Philip had wisely suggested that his wife not accompany them to Enzeli to see them off at the docks, for he knew that she was the one who was suffering most greatly, although she was trying in vain to restrain her emotions. Judith could not help but weep, for much of her life during the past few years had been centered around her daughters.

By the time they reached the Enzeli, Nadia and Tatiana had managed to calm themselves. The trip by carriage to the seaside town was an adventure in itself for two sheltered girls who were accustomed to their own town and neighborhood. They alternated between gazing at the mountains on their left and trying to glimpse the sea in the distance on their right, beyond the sand dunes.

At the docks, they were caught up in the bustle and excitement of the crowd. There were people of all races and nations, wearing all manner of dress, milling about. There were wagons and carts filled with trunks and luggage. And there were vendors selling food and trinkets to the people boarding the ship. The sense of adventure quickly banished all sadness or sorrow that Nadia and Tatiana felt.

Philip took time to exchange some toumans for the Russian currency, so that he could give the girls manat and rubles for pocket money on the trip.

There was even more noise and excitement as the Russian steamer cast off from the dock late in the evening. Nadia and Tatiana stood at the railing with Philip, watching the crowds of people waving goodbye to each other. For Nadia, the boat trip was a new experience, and she was fascinated by every detail—the people, the steamer, the sea-birds, the water, and the routine on board the ship.

For Tatiana, however, the trip northward brought back memories. They had a berth so they could sleep through the night, but she merely dozed off and on. As they drew nearer to Baku early in the morning, a feeling of melancholy grew. Thoughts of how different she was from the small, frightened child who had traveled this route in the other direction so many years before filled her mind. She had not thought of her real mother in a long time, and she strained to recall Maria's face.

But all she could remember was a comforting physical presence, and a soft gentle, caring voice. And that made her sad, as if she had somehow betrayed her heritage.

After they got up and dressed that morning before dawn, Nadia saw what was happening to her sister, and she tried to cheer her up. With Philip's permission, they took a walk on the deck together. They played games, trying to guess where passengers had come from and what their professions might be. When they saw young men of their own age, they talked about what they liked and disliked about them.

It was on the walk that they noticed a tall man in a European suit, with reddish blond hair and mustache, who seemed to be staring at them. Heeding their parents' warnings to beware of strangers, they did their best to avoid him, but he seemed to turn up almost everywhere they went. And he continued to watch them. They decided to tell Philip about the man, and he advised them not to walk on deck again except when he accompanied them.

When the steamer whistle finally announced the approach to Baku, Nadia, Tatiana, and Philip joined most of the other passengers at the railing to watch the city gradually grow nearer. Tatiana was amazed at how dark and dingy Baku looked, with its heavy cloud of smoke hanging overhead. As a child, she had not realized how ugly the place was.

As she stood at the rail looking toward land, she sensed someone staring at her. She turned to see the tall European man who had followed her and Nadia on their strolls. He smiled and nodded to her, then looked away.

She returned her gaze to the city, her heart pounding with fear. Should she tell Philip? Yes, she decided, she should.

As the steamer was pulling into it berth at the Baku dock, Philip went over to speak to the man. Tatiana could not hear the words they spoke, but she noticed that the man glanced at her and Nadia from time to time, nodding.

The conversation was halted abruptly as people began to move away from the railing, preparing to disembark. The stranger disappeared into the crowd.

When Philip returned, he had a puzzled frown on his face. "Who was he?" Tatiana asked. "And why was he staring at us?"

"He's an Englishman by the name of Fleming," Philip said. "He's with one of the oil companies. For some reason, he wanted to know if you were really sisters, if you were both my daughters. He asked all sorts of questions about Tatiana's fair complexion."

"Oh," Tatiana said, understanding. She was familiar with people who wondered how she and Nadia could really be sisters and so different in appearance. "What did you tell him?"

Philip smiled. "I told him you were, of course," he said. "Sometimes Europeans are much too curious. Why should he need to know something as personal as that?"

* * * * *

The customs inspection on the Baku docks took hours. With every passenger, the inspectors felt compelled to investigate each item in each trunk or piece of hand luggage. Nadia and Tatiana were offended at this, but Philip told them to be patient and endure it.

But it was the vaccinations that upset the girls the most. Tatiana was especially offended by the unsterile conditions utilized by the gruff, unkempt doctor. They noticed the Englishman protesting the procedure, and the doctor merely laughed at him and stuck his instrument quickly through a flame.

They stayed overnight at a small inn in Baku and boarded the train the following morning. Philip had reserved a compartment with sleeping accommodations so that they would be able to travel in relative comfort and privacy. Tatiana had ridden on a train once, when she was very young, but it had been only the short distance between Baku and Sabunchi, and she could barely remember it. Certainly that train had had none of the luxuries of this one; this seemed like a hotel on wheels. It even had a special car just for dining. There were carpets on the floor, and it had highly polished brass light fixtures.

It was an exciting and thrilling experience for both girls. When the train jolted to life and began to ease along the rails, Nadia and Tatiana opened the window of their compartment to look out at the crowds on the platform, waving goodbyes to passengers. The locomotive engine spewed out great clouds of steam; its bell clanged loudly; and its whistle shrieked. Then abruptly there was a second jolt, and a noisy shudder wracked the cars. There was a pause, another jolt and shudder, and they began to move slowly out of the station.

Gradually the train moved faster and faster until the platform and the crowds were left behind. Philip made Nadia and Tatiana put their heads back inside the compartment and close the window, but the girls continued to look out at the passing landscape, with their noses pressed to the glass like children at a candy store window. They gazed out at the rugged beauty and awesome enormity of the Caucasus Mountains. Passing a village, they could see farmers herding their sheep near mud-covered cottages, with friendly wisps of smoke coming from chimneys, indicating that the women were busily cooking. Nadia pointed out to Tatiana a flock of geese flying in perfect formation across the sun-scorched sky.

In cities and large villages, the train would stop, and the passengers permitted to get off to walk around. At every station, crowds would surround the train. Vendors would sell bread, soup, tea, and souvenirs. Ragged children would approach them, begging for money, or offering to carry luggage or packages.

The first day passed with surprising swiftness. Between looking out the window and going back to the dining car for meals, the evening came sooner than they wished. The porter came to their compartment to prepare their beds, and the girls changed into their nightgowns reluctantly.

After Papa had turned out the lights, Tatiana lay in her bed, fully awake for some time before the gentle rocking of the railway car lulled her to sleep. Her mind drifted back to the past, to memories of childhood, for this was her native land. By birth, she was Russian, though it now seemed a foreign place. She remembered the train her mother had been put upon, a rude open boxcar. That train had been going north, too, perhaps even on these very rails.

How her life had changed; she marvelled at that. And what lay ahead promised even greater changes. Hopes and dreams and aspirations were far more than fantasies. They could be realized. In the future, anything was possible. The future was magical; the past hardly real at all.

* * * * *

The arrival in Moscow was an incredible experience for Nadia and Tatiana. So much of what they had seen on the long train ride seemed marvelous to them. By the time they stepped off the train onto the Moscow platform, they felt as if they were in a dream world. They had never realized that a city could be so vast or so incredibly beautiful.

The train station itself was astonishing to them: a vast structure that resembled a palace more than a public building. The girls had never even envisioned a building so large that locomotives could pull inside to unload passengers who were protected from the elements. It was built of steel and glass and stone. The steel girders reaching far overhead created a vaulting to support the glass roof, making it seem as if they were in some sort of a cathedral.

And the puffs of steam that were wafting across the platforms from the rows of locomotives added to the impression they were stepping into some fantasy world.

They were met on the platform by Gromyko Kominek, Philip's friend and former business associate. Kominek was a short, plump, scholarly-looking man with a gray beard and uncontrollable gray hair. He wore thick, rimless glasses and had a habit of peering over them to look at people when he talked to them.

Kominek had a servant with him who took care of the Boustanis' baggage, getting it to the carriage, which was waiting on the street outside the train station. Nadia and Tatiana tried to be proper and well-behaved young ladies on the ride to the Kominek home, but it was impossible to hide their excitement and wonder at the sights of Moscow. The buildings, the parks, the shops were unlike anything they had ever seen.

Though it was not directly on their route from the Kazan Railway Station, Gromyko took them by the Kremlin on their way to his home. The churches and palaces beyond the stark red brick walls were more fantastic than anything either of the girls could have envisioned in their wildest imagination—brilliantly colored, onion-domed towers on churches, vast colonnades of Ionic columns on palaces and public buildings. The early spring weather gave the impression of a city just coming to life, as if everything had been born at the moment of their arrival.

The people riding in the carriages they passed were elegantly and impeccably dressed. The women were especially beautiful, wearing incredibly colored fabrics, and hats with feathers and silk flowers. It was cooler here than it had been in the south, and some people still wore fur hats and fur-trimmed coats. Nadia and Tatiana realized now why Philip had wanted them to do their shopping after getting to Moscow. Their new finery was ordinary by comparison.

The Kominek home was in the eastern section of the city, facing on one of the small parks along the Neglinnaya River and built of limestone, brick, and marble. It was a spacious mansion, and its furnishings were of the finest quality, though somewhat understated in style. The only sign of excessive wealth or ostentation was the collection of paintings by the European masters of art during the last century. This was especially fascinating to Nadia, and she was surprised to learn that it was Tanya Kominek, Gromyko's wife, who had put together the entire collection.

She had works by Vermeer, Monet, Matisse, Bonheur, Manet, Van Gogh, Utrillo, Kandinsky, and numberous others, artists known to Nadia only through books.

Both girls were enchanted by Tanya Kominek. She was a small, almost frail-looking woman with thick black hair and black eyes that sparkled with life and vigor. The boundless energy she exuded was a strong contrast to her rather delicate appearance. In welcoming Nadia and Tatiana, she exclaimed delightedly: "At last I have the daughters I've always wanted."

They felt at home instantly. Each girl was given her own room, which they suspected had been redecorated especially for them. Tatiana's was decorated in gray and blue, and Nadia's was in green and beige. The rooms were adjoining, and they would share a maid, a young girl name Catherine, who had a round face and pale gray eyes.

They did not meet the son, Vanitof, upon their arrival. When Tatiana asked about him, she was told he would be down for dinner. Nor did they see anything more of Gromyko for the rest of the afternoon. He retired to his study to work. The girls understood that this work was of a scholarly nature rather than business. Philip had explained to them that Gromyko was "retired," that he had spent fifteen years working extremely hard at business, acquiring a vast fortune so that he could cease work at an early age to pursue his real interest—reading and study. He still had to do a small amount of work, managing his fortune so that it would continue to produce money for him, but he spent only a few hours a week at this. Though they did not see it on the first day, the girls were told that Gromyko had a huge library of rare books adjoining the room that was his study.

The Kominek family dined formally in the evenings, so the girls had to change every night for dinner. As they seated themselves at the beautifully appointed table, the Komineks seemed unusually restrained. There was a wariness or apprehension, a formality the couple had not expressed earlier. In honor of their guests, Tanya Kominek had planned a special meal, served on fragile gilt-edge china, with gold tableware, and finely cut crystal. The table was lit with candles in a gold candelabra, and there were beautiful red roses in a vase in the center.

Then they realized there were only five people at dinner, and there were to have been six. Vanitof was not present. There had been no evidence of him since their arrival. Tatiana wondered where he mignt be, but she had already asked for him earlier and did not think it would be polite to ask again.

Nadia, however, was not shy. They had been seated at the table only a few moments before she asked, "But where is your son? Won't he be dining with us?"

The Komineks glanced uncomfortably at each other, and a sadness clouded their eyes. After a momentary silence, Tanya replied, staring at the centerpiece, avoiding their eyes, "He's not feeling well. He's having dinner upstairs in his room."

"I'm sorry to hear that," Nadia said. "I hope it's nothing serious."

Tanya Kominek smiled warmly. "I'm sure he'll be feeling better by tomorrow."

Immediately, Tatiana understood. Philip had told them that he was deformed in some way. Vanitof would surely be shy and insecure about his appearance. It was clearly a matter of embarrassment and concern for his parents as well. She felt a great warmth for them. "Papa has told us about him," she said, endeavoring to keep pity from showing in her voice. "We have been looking forward to meeting him."

"Yes," Nadia broke in brightly, as if reading her sister's mind. "We've brought him a gift. Perhaps we can send it up to him after dinner."

Tanya Kominek's eyes brightened. "Oh, no," she said. "You must give it to him yourself. If not tonight, then tomorow."

"We hope it's something he'll like," Tatiana said. "It's a book of Persian legends and stories that Mama illustrated and translated into Russian."

"I'm sure he'll love it," Gromyko Kominek said kindly. "All Vanitof does is read. As much as I like books and enjoy reading myself, I think the boy goes too far. He hardly ever leaves the house, and sometimes he stays in his room for days without leaving."

Tanya gave her husband a disapproving glance, then smiled at the girls. "I'm sure having you here is going to do him a lot of good. It will be like having sisters."

After dinner, their host escorted them into an elegant parlor containing a beautiful grand piano. Gromyko Kominek persuaded his wife to play for their guests, then excused himself, explaining that he would be back directly. Tanya's playing was so enjoyable that they hardly noticed their host was gone over an hour before returning. When he did enter the parlor, he was followed hesitantly by a dark-haired young man who kept his face averted from the guests, as if studying a painting on the wall to his right.

Tatiana's first impression was that this was a very handsome young man, and she wondered who he might be. After what she had heard about the Komineks' son, it did not occur to her that this might be Vanitof. Then abruptly, Tanya stopped playing and rose from the piano, going to the boy and pulling him into the light, forcing him to look at the guests as he was introduced.

Perhaps it would not have been such a shock if Tatiana had seen the ugly side of Vanitof first, but the sudden change from beauty to distortion was too startling for her to avoid showing some sign of recognition. It was as if Vanitof Kominek were two totally separate young men—the left side gentle and attractive, the right side fearful and misshapen. It was not just his face, which had an overly large cranium and narrow jaw on the right side, but his right shoulder was narrow and his right leg ended in a clubfoot. Vanitof did his best to hide it by walking slowly.

Tatiana recovered her composure quickly by focusing on Vanitof's warm brown eyes. The beauty of his spirit shone deeply from within them as he gazed at her, seemingly knowing everything she was feeling. She realized immediately that he averted his ugly side not from vanity but out of a desire to spare others the unpleasantness that he lived with always.

Tatiana smiled warmly at him and held his gaze, saying, "It's very good to meet you, Vanitof. I hope we shall be best of friends."

"I know we shall be friends," Nadia echoed, as she took Vanitof's hand. "I'm glad you're feeling better. We've looked forward to meeting you very much."

Nadia presented him with their gift. It was wrapped neatly in plain paper, but Vanitof caressed it lovingly, as if it were the most beautiful present he had ever received. "What is it?" he asked softly.

"Open it and see," Nadia replied. "Half the fun of presents is being surprised."

Vanitof removed the paper carefully, without tearing it. When his eyes saw the book, they widened in delight. "It's beautiful," he exclaimed, running his hand over the tooled leather cover, then opening the book to look at the brightly colored illustrations.

"Mama did the illustrations," Nadia explained. "I think it's some of her best work. Of course she works in the Persian style, which may seem old-fashioned to Russians."

"I think they're lovely," Vanitof said, his eyes entranced by an illustration of Scheherazade that Tatiana had posed for. "I can't wait to read it."

Vanitof looked at his father questioningly.

"All right," Gromyko smiled sympathetically. "You may go back to your room now."

Vanitof clutched the book to his chest and turned to the two girls, saying, "Thank you, Nadia. And Tatiana."

As he left the room, Tatiana saw that there were happy tears welling in his eyes. From that moment the restraint that had earlier been evident in the Komineks' manner disappeared. Nadia and Tatiana were treated not as strangers in the household, but as members of the family.

Chapter 14

It was possible to travel for miles through Moscow without leaving the stone-paved streets and rows of limestone or red brick houses and public buildings. Everywere there were things to delight the senses. There were churches that resembled mosques, but were brightly painted with contrasting colors, and with gilded domes. There were palaces built in the European style that seemed to stretch for acres behind strong walls and ornate iron gates. In the public squares and parks were statues so finely crafted that the horses and riders seemed merely still for a moment.

Through the middle of it all ran two rivers that intersected—the Moskva and the Neglinnaya—with elegant stone bridges connecting the various parts of the city. In traveling all the way across Moscow in a straight line, Nadia and Tatiana were surprised that they could cross the Moskva River three times, because of the way it wound around.

At the very center of the city, its heart, was the Kremlin, built as a fortress against Tatar invaders. As Moscow had grown over the centuries, the city had been built gradually out from the Kremlin with other walls, always retaining the circular pattern.

But more exciting than the structures and physical appearance of the city was the life of Moscow. Neither of the girls had ever experienced a place that seemed to be a living thing, pulsing with movement, ever changing, breathing with expectancy for the next eventful moment. This sensation—Papa explained to them—was one that all the great cities of the world shared, though the character of each was quite different.

Philip Boustani remained with his daughters in Moscow for a few days before setting off on his return trip to Rasht, just long enough to see that Tatiana and Nadia were settled in comfortably with the Kominek family, and to be sure they had everything they needed. He arranged finances with Gromyko so that they would have a regular allowance to cover their expenses.

He took care of his business appointments and came out of them with profitable trade agreements. Before he left, the Komineks took them all on a river outing, to have a picnic in the country. They boarded a river boat at Serebryanny bor, taking it past one of the most breathtaking views in Moscow—the Church of the Holy Trinity at Lykovo, situated on a bluff overlooking the river. The gleaming white church, with its elaborate ornamentation resembling a wedding cake, was reflected perfectly in the water.

The picnic was a peaceful and pleasurable way to spend their last afternoon with Philip before his departure. It was made melancholy for Nadia and Tatiana only by the realization that it would be the last chance they would have to spend time with their father for many months or even years.

With all they had purchased before leaving Persia, the two girls truly needed very little. However, Tanya Kominek—as soon as Philip had left—insisted on taking Nadia and Tatiana on numerous shopping trips, advising them on the latest fashions in Moscow. On several occasions, when the girls decided against some piece of apparel as too expensive, Tanya would purchase it as a gift. If Nadia or Tatiana protested, Tanya would invariably say, "Let me do this for you. I've never had a daughter of my own to spoil."

The Komineks did everything they could to help prepare Nadia and Tatiana for the day when they would be signing up for their classes, Nadia at the Art Institute and Tatiana at the Institute of Science. Their acceptance by the university was a conditional one, dependent entirely upon a period of tutoring that would bring their educations up to the level of Russian students.

Gromyko's greater concern was for Tatiana, who had more obstacles to overcome. Not only was her preparation less than the standard for entry into a Russian university, but she was a woman seeking to study what was considered entirely the domain of men. While women were not prohibited from studying for medical careers, their lives were made difficult, not only by the professors but by the other students as well.

Tatiana spent many mornings and afternoons with Gromyko in his library, reviewing chemistry, biology, anatomy, and math. When they had exhausted his books and his knowledge, he called in a friend of his who was a professor at the Institute. Professor Turchaninov was reluctant about tutoring Tatiana, and frankly skeptical about her chances at the Institute, but as a favor to his friend Gromyko he accepted the task.

It was necessary for both Nadia and Tatiana to pass examinations before being accepted as students at their respective schools. Tatiana would be required to pass a written test and an interview; Nadia was required to show her work to a jury of art professors and to answer questions about it. However, both had the same concern—that their respective committees would be prejudiced against them because they were women.

The two girls discussed this matter openly with the Komineks, including Vanitof, and they found that the young boy was especially sympathetic to their problem. He understood far better than most people what it was to face prejudice, and that understanding drew him out of his reclusivenesss to talk to them. He had always been a recipient of sympathy; it was a new experience to offer it to others.

Tatiana quickly came to realize that Vanitoff had a brilliant mind as well as a sensitive soul. In the summer, while the weather was warm, they frequently sat outside in the garden—just the three young people—in the evenings, talking. For someone who was supposed to be shy and a recluse, Vanitof became very vocal when he was alone with the young women.

On the evening before Nadia was to face the jury at the Art Institute to show her work—and two days before Tatiana's exam—the three of them sat together watching the sun set in a haze of violet clouds, surrounded by the sweet scent of late summer roses. On this evening. Tatiana was as anxious for Nadia as she was for herself, and she tried to say things that would help calm her sister, but everything seemed to make Nadia's anxiety worse.

"Oh, I wish I hadn't come to Moscow," Nadia said despairingly after a time. "If I had stayed in Persia, I could have gone on painting to my heart's delight, without ever having to be judged."

"You mustn't say that," Vanitof protested. "You must think of being judged as a wonderful opportunity, not something frightening."

Nadia tried to smile. "Perhaps if I borrowed a suit of your clothes, Vanitof," she said, "I could make them think I was a man, and they would at least take me seriously."

"I'm afraid my suits wouldn't fit you," Vanitof replied, with a trace of embarrassment. "The hump on my coats is on the back, not the front." Suddenly, realizing what he had said, he blushed.

Nadia and Tatiana broke into giggles, and soon Vanitof began to laugh with them. The tension of the momentous day that was to follow quickly faded with the laughter.

"Perhaps you could wear my coat backward," Vanitof suggested, prompting more giggles.

Until this moment, Vanitof's physical deformity had not been mentioned. Now, because of the laughter, it was as if a barrier had been broken between him and the girls. When the laughter finally subsided, Vanitof spoke seriously. "It is not good to try to pretend you are something you are not. You are what you are, and you can't deny it. I know that only too well. If you show them you are afraid, you help them to defeat you."

"It is very difficult not to be afraid," Nadia said, "knowing what will be in their minds."

"But that is what should make it easier," Vanitof said. "Not knowing is worse. It took me many years to realize how most people react to me. It's still not easy to meet strangers, but it's not possible."

The sunlight had almost entirely left the garden now. Vanitof's face was hidden in shadow, but Tatiana could see it in her mind. Silence followed his words and Tatiana knew Nadia was thinking the same thing she was— that the prejudice they faced as women was slight compared to what Vanitof faced, and they were foolish to complain.

No more was said that evening about Nadia's appearance before the jury. The next morning, Nadia was calm as she left for the Art Institute, carrying her portfolio of drawings and paintings, and wearing her simplest, most understated gray wool suit, with her hair pulled up and tied in a plain bun on top of her head. "You will do well," Tatiana told her sister, embracing her warmly. "I know you will."

A few hours later, however, Nadia returned, and Tatiana knew from the expression on her face that it had not gone well at all. "I wasn't accepted," Nadia announced, trying to hold back tears. "It was horrible. I think they had decided to reject me even before I walked into the room. They hardly even looked at my work."

Nadia was devastated. Tatiana tried to tell her not to be defeated, explaining that there were plenty of other places in Moscow to study art, but that did not help. The professors at the Art Institute were the very best in Moscow. But what hurt the most was that they had not judged her art at all; the judgment had been based entirely upon the fact that she was a woman and a foreigner.

There was nothing that could be said to cheer Nadia. An atmosphere of gloom descended over the household that evening and the following day. Tatiana realized that this was not auspicious for her own chances before the committee of the Institute of Science. If anything, the artists were known to be far more liberal than the scientists in accepting students. Even if Tatiana was accepted, she wasn't sure that she should go through with her studies.

If Nadia should return home to Rasht—and there was no point in her staying if she was not studying—Tatiana would have to accompany her.

Tatiana attended her committee hearing with an attitude that approached indifference. Indeed, if it had not been for the trace of anger that stirred within her, she would not have bothered to attend at all. The anger she felt was not for herself, but for Nadia; it was a sense of outrage that her talented sister should be dismissed so easily, especially after the long and expensive trip. That alone should have conveyed to the committee that Nadia was serious about her studies.

Tatiana transferred these feeling to her own committee, assuming they were cut of the same cloth as the artists. She was neither fearful nor shy when she stood before the group of six scientists and doctors. In defiance, she had chosen not to dress conservatively as Nadia had done. She wore her green plaid wool suit with a white silk blouse, tied at the collar with a large jabot. It would be impossible not to notice that she was a woman. Indeed, she was an attractive young woman, now a mature seventeen years old, soon to turn eighteen.

The chairman was Dr. Anatoly Strelenski, a thin wizened old man with gnarled hands and an unkempt shock of white hair and unruly white mustache. He peered at her over bifocals without a trace of sympathy, and she returned his gaze in kind. He introduced each of the members of the committee to her—Professor Sarkov, a rotund man, who did not look at her; Dr. Petrovich, also large and heavy, who looked at her with one eyebrow raised quizzically; Dr. Alexandrovich, a small man who seemed more interested in folding and unfolding a piece of paper than in acknowledging her presence; and Professor Abramovitz, whose dark eyes gazed at her with more than curiosity. The last member of the committe was the youngest and was someone she knew; it was Professor Turchaninov, whom Gromyko Kominek had called on to tutor her.

The room was filled with mysteries she longed to understand. In one corner was a full skeleton on a stand; on shelves were glass jars containing organs preserved in liquid; on the walls were charts diagramming the working of the heart, the circulatory system, and organs which she could not identify.

The professors fired questions at her in voices that were harsh and unfeeling, and she snapped back her answers just as coldly.

"Why do you want to study medicine?" Dr. Strelenski asked in opening the session.

"Because I want to help overcome human suffering," Tatiana replied without hesitating.

"Have you ever witnessed human suffering at close hand?" Dr. Petrovich asked, his eyebrow still raised.

"Yes," Tatiana leveled her gaze at him. "As a child, I was orphaned by the riots in Baku. At the displacement center, I assisted the nurse in her rounds; and when I was older I assisted my adopted mother in treating the victims of a cholera epidemic."

"Then you have wanted to study nursing for some time?" Professor Sarkov asked.

"Yes," Tatiana replied. "I would like to be either a nurse or a doctor, whatever my talents and my sex will permit."

"You do not have the sort of extensive formal education we normally require," Professor Abramowitz commented. "You realize that is a considerable handicap, don't you?"

"I do," Tatiana said simply. "However, I am intelligent and studious. And I can be tutored."

They proceeded to ask her questions covering her knowledge of science, medicine, and math. Some of them Tatiana could answer, some she could not. If she did not know an answer, she told them so; she made no attempt to guess or to cover up her lack of knowledge, feeling that she could retain her dignity through bluntness and honesty.

For almost an hour she stood on her feet, facing the group of men seated behind the long table. Finally Dr. Strelenski rose shakily to his feet to signal that the interview was over, saying, "If you will wait outside, we will discuss your case and give you our decision."

The wait in the small anteroom was worse for Tatiana than the hearing had been. The room was completely barren except for two uncomfortable straight-backed chairs and a narrow bench, and the walls were painted an ugly institutional green. The smells from the laboratory rooms down the hall wafted by her enticingly, smells that—to someone else—might seem noxious, but to her meant excitement. There was the vague odor of antiseptic, the pungent whiff of formaldehyde, the sharpness of iodine, and others that had no association for Tatiana.

There was one narrow window overlooking the grounds and buildings of the Institute. Tatiana knew that she would be rejected by the committee, and she wanted desperately to leave so that she would not have to face that rejection.

But she sensed that doing so would be a far greater humiliation than confronting them again. If nothing else, she would show these men that she had courage. So she waited, gazing out the narrow window at the lead-gray sky and listening to the sounds of the first autumn wind beating at the glass windowpanes.

It was almost another full hour before the door of the committee room opened. Professor Turchaninov smiled at her and asked, "Miss Boustani, would you come in, please?" He held the door open for her.

For the first time since the hearing had begun, Tatiana felt the fear grip her. Her heart was pounding in her breast, and her knees felt weak as she stood up to walk back through the door. The only thing she could think of was, "What should I do and say when they tell me I am rejected?"

So intent was her mind on this that she hardly understood when Dr. Strelenski announced. "Despite strong reservations by some members of our committee, we have decided to admit you as a student at the Institute."

For several moments, Tatiana stared at him, stunned and unable to reply. Finally, she found her voice and said simply, "Thank you, sir."

There was almost a sparkle of mirth in the old man's eyes and something approaching a smile on his thin lips as he told her. "If you will report to the main office next Friday, you will be given a schedule of your classes."

Under other circumstances, Tatiana would have been overjoyed, but now she could think only of Nadia. How could she possibly stay in Moscow to study if Nadia had to return to Rasht. On the other hand, how could she possibly tell Nadia that she had been accepted but would turn it down for her sake? It was a terrible dilemma.

By the time she arrived at the Komineks' house, she had decided what she must do. She had no choice but to tell everyone that she had been rejected by the committee. It would be difficult, even painful, but it would have to be done.

They were all waiting for her in the music room—Nadia and Vanitof and Mr. and Mrs. Kominek. Nadia leaped to her feet and rushed to Tatiana as soon as she entered. Tanya Kominek, seated at the piano, stopped playing and turned to her expectantly.

Tears welled up in Tatiana's eyes as she hesitantly, "I didn't make it. We can both go home to Rasht."

"Oh, my dear...," Tanya exclaimed. "I'm sorry."

"Those old men at the Institute must be very stupid," Vanitof said.

Gromyko simply stared at Tatiana with a puzzled expression.

Nadia embraced her. "We shall write to Papa tomorrow. Perhaps he will have something to suggest. Perhaps we can go to St. Petersburg or to Berlin."

"No," Tatiana replied. "I think we should go home. I couldn't go through this again."

They dined in silence that evening; even Tanya and Gromyko felt saddened by the defeat of the girls' dreams. The excellent food seemed tasteless; each ring of silver against china seemed the tolling of a sorrowful bell. After dinner, they retired to the music room, but Tanya, for the first time, did not feel like playing the piano to entertain them.

Vanitof excused himself and went to his room to read. Tatiana and Nadia were about to retire early themselves when there was a knock on the door, and the Komineks' manservant, Viktor, entered.

"There is a Professor Nichola to see Miss Boustani," he announced.

Immediately, Tatiana feared it might be someone from the Institute, and she did not want her lie to be uncovered. "Which Miss Boustani?" she asked.

"Miss Nadia Boustani," Viktor replied.

"Show him in, please," Tanya Kominek said eagerly. Then she turned to Nadia, "Could this be *the* Professor Nichola? He is the most highly regarded portrait painter in Russia. He's a favorite of the Czar."

"I believe there was a Professor Nichola on the committee," Nadia said, bewildered.

The professor was well into his sixties, but there was something of a childlike innocence in his face, almost a shyness. He seemed rather embarrassed to find the room filled with people, and he endured the necessary introductions with a trace of nervousness and discomfort.

Once the formalities were out of the way and he was seated in a brocade-covered Louis Quinze armchair, he turned to Nadia and said, "I have been very disturbed about the committee's decision concerning you. I feel we were entirely unfair."

"Does that mean the committee will reconsider her application?" Tanya Kominek asked hopefully.

"No," Professor Nichola replied. "Actually I feel it would be a mistake for the young lady to study at the Institute. I feel it might destroy her talent." He turned to Nadia. "You see, the art world is in the midst of changes— great changes. Much of it is occurring in France,but some are taking place here in Russia. I admit that I do not understand all these changes; after all, I am an old man and set in my ways. But I do recognize that it is taking place, unlike most of my associates in the Institute. I'm afraid what we do there is to take very talented young people and train them to turn out work that all looks alike. That would be a terrible mistake for you, my dear, for your work has originality. It is unlike any that I have ever seen." He paused, then asked gently, "Do you understand what I'm saying?"

"I think I do," Nadia replied hesitantly.

"What I have come here to suggest," the old man continued, "is that you study with me, personally. I do take on a student occasionally outside the Institute—in my own studio. That way you could learn technique from me, without losing your own special spark of originality. Would you be interested in doing that?"

Briefly there was a look of excitement on Nadia's face, then she glanced at Tatiana, and her face fell. "No," she replied. "I'm afraid I can't accept. My sister and I have to return to Persia."

"No, we don't," Tatiana broke in. "You mustn't turn down this opportunity."

"But what about you?" Nadia asked. "What will you do?"

Tatiana's eyes fell to her lap; she knew she was blushing. "I have a confession to make," she said. "I lied to you. I was not turned down by the committee today. I was accepted."

She lifted her gaze to meet Nadia's, and she recognized that her sister understood the reasons for the lie.

With a happy smile, Nadia turned to Professor Nichola. "I'll accept your offer," she told him. "I would be very honored to study with you."

Chapter 15

Winter in Russia quickly followed fall, and it bore no resemblance to the cold season in Rasht. Nadia and Tatiana were not accustomed to heavy snow in the city; that was something that occurred only in the mountains, and did not last long. But from the first snowfall, Moscow was covered with a powdery blanket that was deep and did not go away. If anything, it grew deeper and deeper as the season lingered. And winter did linger, for months.

Yet the people of Moscow did not look upon the freezing weather as adversity. It was simply a fact of life, and they went about their business as usual, merely dressing a bit warmer, in thick coats and furs.

Nadia began her study under the guidance of Professor Nichola easily and enthusiastically. She had no difficulties at all. Tatiana, however, was faced with problems from her first day. She was the only female in her classes, and for that reason, she was shunned by the other students and singled out by the professors as a curiosity. Usually this was only an embarrassment for her; occasionally, it was something that outraged her.

To her surprise, the older professors treated her well, while the younger professors resented her presence. It was her anatomy teacher, Professor Pavlovich, a young man in his early thirties, who made her life most difficult. When it was necessary to make some reference to one of the more private parts of the male or female body, he invariably prefaced his comments by saying, "With apologies to Miss Boustani." Or "I hope the lady present will forgive me . . . "

These comments caused her to seethe with unexpressed anger, and she grew to dread his lectures. His behavior reached its most outrageous one afternoon when he was reviewing the lessons of the first few weeks by questioning the students on what they had learned, calling each before the class to point out on charts the structure of some part of the anatomy. When

Tatiana's turn came, she made the long trek down the steep steps of the lecture hall, apprehension rising within her and growing to fear. The smug smile on the professor's face told her that he intended some special way of embarrassing her.

After she reached the front of the lecture hall and turned to face the other students, standing alongside the two charts of the male and female figures, Professor Pavlovich narrowed his cold blue eyes, smiled, and said, "Miss Boustani, will you describe the various parts of the male and female genitalia, pointing them out for us?"

Tatiana refused to allow this to embarrass her. No matter how childishly he behaved, she was determined not to descend to his level. Calmly, she detailed each anatomical part of the female genitalia, then proceeded to do the same with the male genitalia.

When she had finished, Professor Pavlovich said mockingly, "You surprise me, Miss Boustani. I would not have expected a lady to be so familiar with the male anatomy."

At this, Tatiana could no longer control her anger. "Professor Pavlovich," she said angrily, "I cannot help but be aware that my sex is different from yours. I am a student here at the Institute, and it is my duty to learn everything the other students learn. What I know about the male and female genitalia I have learned in this class. Outside this class, I have learned that there are common euphemisms for both. I will endeavor not to behave like the female euphemism if you will stop behaving like the male euphemism."

Laughter broke out in the lecture hall, and the professor flushed a crimson red, first with anger, then with embarrassment. He stammered, struggling to find something to reply. Finally, realizing that there was nothing he could do to save face, he said merely, "You may sit down, Miss Bonstani."

Tatiana realized that she had made an enemy of the professor, but she hoped she had put an end to his snide comments. Her action did have its beneficial results. For the first time since her classes had begun, some of her fellow students spoke to her, coming over to her after the class was over, with comments such as, "Well done, Miss Boustani," and "He deserved everything you gave him."

One student lingered after the others had moved on. "That was wonderful the way you handled the professor," he said. "I'm very much in favor of equality for women."

"I don't know much about politics," Tatiana replied. "I just want to study and learn."

"May I walk with you to your next lecture?" the boy asked. "I'm in the same class."

"If you like," Tatiana said, really looking at him for the first time. He was about her own age and attractive in an unkempt boyish way. He was tall and slender, and he slumped his shoulders the way young men do when they suddenly grow several inches in a short time. He was attempting to produce a beard and mustache, but clearly had a few more years to go before he would be able to succeed.

"My name is Fyodor," he said. "Fyodor Vachtangov. I've been wanting to speak to you since the first day of classes."

"Why didn't you?" Tatiana asked.

Fyodor blushed and shrugged. "I don't know," he said. "You just seemed unapproachable. I mean, being the only female in the class. I thought you might suspect my motives."

Tatiana smiled. "Should I suspect your motives?"

Fyodor grinned. "Probably," he said, then blushed.

Tatiana laughed. "At least you're honest enough to warn me."

Fyodor ducked his head shyly. "That isn't exactly what I meant. I was thinking of asking you to attend a political meeting with me."

"What kind of political meeting?" Tatiana asked guardedly.

'Socialist," Fyodor replied. "We're very much interested in women's rights. A lot of women are involved."

Tatiana felt a sudden chill run through her. Memories she had long kept submerged tried to rise up within her, and she had to fight to keep them back. "I don't think so," she said faintly, aware of a slight trembling in her voice. "I really don't want to get involved in politics."

"Have you ever been to a political meeting?" the young man pursued. "I think everyone should get involved. Revolution is the wave of the future."

"Please," Tatiana said stiffly, "I don't want to hear anything about either revolution or politics."

Fyodor studied her with a puzzled expression. "I'm sorry," he said. "I didn't want to offend you."

His boyish manner made Tatiana regret her harsh tone. "You're forgiven," she said with a smile. "Why don't you tell me where you came from or how you grew up or why you decided to study medicine? That would be much more interesting to me than talking socialism."

By the time the two of them reached Pavlov Hall for their next lecture, Tatiana had learned that Fyodor had lived all his life in Moscow, that his father owned an apothecary shop in a middle-class section of the city, and that he had three sisters and one brother, all younger than he. As for his studying medicine, that was what his parents had wanted for him. He would not have chosen it for himself; he was much more interested in politics.

Tatiana decided she liked the young man despite his political interest. He was attractive, with dark wavy hair, intense brown eyes, and a sensual mouth and chin. Also, he was someone she could go home to tell Nadia about. The two of them had long speculated about the possibility of finding romance in Moscow, wondering if handsome young men might come along to sweep them off their feet. So far, this was the closest either of them had come to romance. Fyodor was no prince charming, but he was attractive, pleasant, and clearly interested in her.

That evening, Nadia was delighted by Tatiana's report. "At least," she said, "you are surrounded by young men all day. Except when we have a model coming in to pose, I'm alone with Professor Nichola. I'll probably never have a romance."

"If it's any comfort," Tatiana said, "I doubt if anything will come of this. Fyodor is much more passionate about politics than he is about girls. And he's certainly not the sort of young man I would want for a husband."

Notwithstanding these first impressions, the friendship between Tatiana and Fyodor grew, and it increasingly began to resemble a romance. At first, Fyodor called on her only to walk her to class or to escort her to the library, where they would study together. One day, on their way home from the library, he suggested they stop for tea at a small cafe, along the way. From that day forward, it became a favorite spot to visit after study hours.

But Fyodor did not invite her out to the kinds of places and events she dreamed of attending with a young man—to the theater, concerts, or the opera. He claimed that he was opposed to these as bourgeois entertainments, but Tatiana suspected he might have been more favorably inclined toward them if he could afford the seats. She enjoyed this "bourgeois" entertainment, and she could afford it. So, she and Nadia attended together, just as she frequently went to art exhibitions with her sister.

One evening the two of them had tickets to the opera to hear *Boris Gudunov*, which Tatiana had especially been looking forward to. However, that morning, Nadia woke up with a cold and fever, and Tanya Kominek advised her to stay in bed for a few days. Tatiana was prepared to stay home that evening as well, but then a thought occurred to her—why not ask Vanitof to escort her?

They were sitting together in the parlor, just the two of them, keeping warm in front of the fireplace, when Tatiana brought up the matter.

"Oh, no, I couldn't possibly do that," Vanitof protested. "You understand, don't you?"

"I know why you wouldn't want to go," Tatiana said. "But I don't think it's a good reason for not going. Don't you think you would enjoy the opera?"

"I would probably like it very much," he replied. "But I don't think I would like having so many people staring at me."

Tatiana smiled and said teasingly, "Everybody stares at everybody else at the opera. It's something to do during the boring parts, and you're supposed to take it as a compliment that they want to know who you are."

Vanitof blushed, trying to smile. "I don't think they would be payiing me a compliment."

"You know, you really should take your own advice," Tatiana chided. "You gave Nadia and me the courage to face our problems when we were trying to enter the university. It shouldn't take any more courage for you to go out into the world and meet people." She smiled. "And besides, if you don't take me, I won't be able to go."

Vanitof looked hesitant. "You really want it that much? It's really important to you?"

Tatiana nodded.

"All right," he said with a sigh. "I'll go with you."

Tanya and Gromyko Kominek were astonished and delighted at the news. All their efforts to draw their son out into society had failed. They now did all they could to encourage him to enjoy the evening. Vanitof already had the necessary white tie and tails, which he wore to dinner at home. But he did not have a top hat, opera cloak, or cane, so his parents promptly went out that afternoon and bought them for him.

That evening, Vanitof was very nervous and worried. For a while, Tatiana thought he might change his mind and not go, but once he was fully dressed, it seemed clear he was going to go through with the evening, no matter how much pain he might have to endure. When he came downstairs, wearing everything but the top hat, which he carried, he was more attractive than any of them had ever seen him. The opera cloak hid much of the deformity of his body; and—when he put on his top hat—it did the same for his face and head. The entire family, including Tatiana and Nadia, praised his appearance, and that seemed to give him confidence.

Tatiana's new evening dress also drew praise, and, indeed, she felt she would be as elegantly attired as anyone at the opera that night. It was a dark blue velvet with black and gold trim and a high waist. Tanya Kominek offered her ermine coat to wear over it, with the matching ermine hat.

As Tatiana and Vanitof descended the front steps to the carriage, breathing in the brisk, cold winter air, Tanya and Gromyko stood in the doorway to watch proudly, tears welling in their eyes. As they rode through the dark, snow-filled Moscow streeets in the enclosed carriage, Tatiana sensed that Vanitof was both excited and apprehensive. He seemed as delighted by the view outside the window as she had been on her first night outing in the city. The almost full moon cast a blue shadow on the snow, and the soft lights from streetlamps and the windows of houses seemed mistily warm.

When they stepped out of the carriage at the theater, Vanitof was trying hard to give the impression he was not afraid, but Tatiana knew that he was terrified. She took his arm and felt it trembling slightly. His face was pale, and his jaw was set with determination. She took Vanitof's disfigured side to shield him as much as she could.

Some people stared at them as they climbed the grand staircase to the box seats, but Vanitof had been prepared for this, and he kept his eyes proudly on Tatiana. She looked at him and smiled fondly, giving sustenance to his courage. He smiled back at her in understanding.

The stares were most obvious as they sat in the box, waiting for the opera to begin. However, Tatiana sought to distract Vanitof by chattering constantly about Chaliapin, who would be singing the title role, about Mussorgsky's music, and about the original play by Pushkin. She was surprised that Vanitof knew the play very well, having read it several times. He confessed to her that he liked reading the dramatic form because it was so succinct, and then added—with some embarrassment—that he had even tried his hand at writing a few plays himself.

Once the opera began, Vanitof lost himself completely in the drama and the spectacle, forgetting entirely that there were other people present in the dark theater. By the time the evening was over, his fears had disappeared, and he was eager to go out again. The next time, he told Tatiana, he wanted to attend the theater, if possible to see a Chekov play. He loved reading Chekov's work.

After that evening, they went out together regularly, sometimes just the two of them, sometimes with Nadia. Gradually a transformation was taking place in Vanitof. He began to behave like a normal young man, no longer quite so self-conscious about his disfigurement. Though Tatiana looked upon their relationship as one of brother and sister, the romance of attending the opera, theater, and symphony on the arm of a young man made up somewhat for the lack of romance in her relationship with Fyodor.

Tatiana was grateful for Fyodor's friendship, if only because it kept her from being so totally isolated from the other students. She liked him well enough, and he was physically attractive, but he was not the sort of man she could fall in love with, because he had no sense of romance.

She knew she was sexually attractive to him, but to him sex was purely a biological urge that had to be satisfied, as cold and dispassionate a view as was his political view. For her, romance was far more important than any biological need. She chose to ignore his overtures, behaving as if she hadn't understood what he was saying.

One evening, however, he refused to be ignored. As he was walking her home from the cafe, along a quiet darkened street, their feet making crunching sounds in the tightly packed snow, their breath making visible clouds of steam, he announced unashamedly, "Tatiana, I want to have sex with you."

For a moment, Tatiana was too stunned to reply. Then she said hotly, "Fyodor, that is not something a woman wants to hear."

"Why not?" Fyodor asked, genuinely puzzled. "I'm sure a woman's needs are as great as a man's."

"Perhaps," Tatiana replied. "But saying it that way is very unappealing. A woman needs a gentle caress, a touch on the hands, a kiss. A woman needs to hear how much you love her."

"Love!" Fyodor exclaimed with distaste. "That's pure sentimental, bourgeois nonsense!"

"It may be to you," Tatiana said coldly. "But it is not to a woman. Without love, human beings would be like dogs on a street corner."

Fyodor shrugged. "I don't see that we're any different."

"If that's your attitude," Tatiana told him, "I don't think we can possibly be friends."

After that, they walked in silence for a few blocks. Clearly Fyodor was thinking about what she had said. At the corner before the Komineks' house, they had to wait to allow a carriage to pass. Suddenly, Fyodor grabbed Tatiana by the shoulders, turned her to him, and kissed her harshly on the mouth. To Tatiana, there was nothing pleasurable about the kiss; it was a shock, an assault, nothing like love at all!

She pulled away angrily, and slapped Fyodor's face. Almost immediately, she regretted her reaction, for she knew he meant no harm.

"I'm sorry," she said. "But that is not the way to kiss a lady."

Fyodor rubbed his cheek, casting his eyes down to the ground in embarrassment. "I guess I need someone to show me how," he said

"Well," Tatiana smiled. "I'm certainly not going to do it here on a street corner."

They crossed the street and walked on to the Kominek house in silence.

At the top of the steps, Tatiana turned to her friend and said softly, "Here, I'll show you." She reached up and took his face gently into her hands, pulled him down to kiss him softly, on the lips. At first, his mouth was still tightly clenched, but gradually it softened to meet her gesture.

When their lips parted, Fyodor said breathlessly, "You must have a lot of experience with men."

"No," Tatiana said with a smile. "That was my first kiss. But I know by instinct how it should be."

Fyodor bent to kiss her again, but Tatiana pulled away gently, shaking her head. "No," she said. "I think we should say good night."

Chapter 16

As they had always done, Tatiana and Nadia talked to each other about all of the important things that happened in their lives. Tatiana described in detail Fyodor's clumsy advances, and they laughed together about it. Then Tatiana said seriously, "Of course, he is rather nice, despite everything. He just needs to grow up a bit."

"What will you do if he wants to do more than kiss you?" Nadia asked.

"I don't know," Tatiana replied. "I don't think I should encourage him to go any further. He's certainly not the sort of man I would want to marry."

"But it's some sort of excitement in your life," Nadia said wistfully. "At least you aren't spending your days with a seventy-year-old man."

"Don't you like Professor Nichola?" Tatiana asked.

"Of course I do." Nadia said. "Hes a wonderful teacher, and I adore him like a grandfather. But he's certainly not my romantic ideal."

Tatiana did have a problem keeping Fyodor at his distance after that first kiss. "Please, Fyodor," she said repeatedly, "let's just be friends. We both have careers to think about."

He accepted her rejection, but it was clear that he was not happy about it. He was more persistent about getting her to join him in his political activities. After turning him down numerous times, she finally agreed to attend a Friday evening meeting in which a doctor was to talk on the subject of the "The People's Right to Medical Care." The subject was at least of some interest to her. She hoped they would stay off the subject of revolution.

The meeting was held at a basement cafe in a rather seedy area of Moscow. The place was dark, dirty, and filled with smoke. The people who were gathered there were a strange assortment. Tatiana felt very much out of place. Though she had dressed in her simplest street clothes, a gray wool walking suit with no ornamentation, she was by far the best-dressed person there, and she was one of only six women in the group of over thirty men.

They were predominantly workers, peasants, and members of the intelligentsia. Tatiana felt ashamed of herself for looking on them with a degree of disdain. After all, she tried to remind herself, she had been born into a working-class family and had come to privilege only by accident.

Most of the people were known to Fyodor, and he fit in with them perfectly. They wore the same ill-fitting uncoordinated clothes, almost threadbare in appearance.

After being introduced to several of them, Tatiana no longer felt as guilty about the disdain she felt, because she recognized a similar attitude directed toward her. Though Fyodor invariably told them she was a fellow student at the Institute of Science and Medicine, they clearly looked upon her as a rich, spoiled dilletante.

She was grateful when the speakers stepped up onto the small stage and the audience began to take their seats at the cafe tables. While waiting for the proceedings to begin, Tatiana's eyes were attracted to an imposing-looking man in his early to middle thirties, who had thick dark hair, a mustache, and heavy black brows. There was something about his dark intense eyes that was familiar to her. Turning to Fyodor, she asked, "Who is that man? I think I've seen him before."

Fyodors eyes followed her gesture. "Oh, I doubt if you would know him," he said. "He's one of our most important leaders. His name is Stalin."

"I'm almost sure I've met him," she said, puzzled. Something about the man made her think of her childhood. But then, the entire atmosphere of this meeting brought back flashes of memories of her father and mother, of attending the rally in the square at Baku, when the violence broke out, of meetings in their living room, her father talking in conspiratorial tones with men such as these.

Tatiana found the lecture, given by a doctor named Vishinsky, very interesting. She had great sympathy for the plight of the poor and workers as he presented it, citing examples of people who had died because they could not pay for medical care and others who had become invalids or cripples. She believed everyone should be entitled to medical care, but she was reluctant to accept a political solution.

She was aware that she blamed socialist politics for the tragedy of her childhood, while also realizing that her attitude was unreasonable. There was nothing specific to warrant her view.

As she listened to Dr. Vishinsky, her eyes kept wandering to the man named Stalin, sitting with two other men on the stage behind the speaker.

Tatiana was certain that she had a memory of this man, and it had something to do with her father. Suddenly, a name came to her—Koba, Josef Koba. And she was able to recall a scene that had taken place in their living room at Baku, before her father had made the speech in the public square—before her father had even gotten involved in the political demonstrations.

Tatiana was sitting on the floor in the corner, playing with her brother Gregor. The man Koba came to their house with another man to try to persuade Papa to join them, to take an active part in the socialist movement. Papa had been reluctant at first, but the man Koba had been persistent. He made promises. Yes, that's what she remembered.

Now there was another memory—a recollection of Papa, after the trouble had begun, after he had lost his job and they had to move. He had talked about the man Koba being responsible for their move, and for their new name. She recalled her father cursing Koba for deserting them, for disappearing just when they needed him to fulfill his promises of assistance. He had gone from Azerbaijan without a trace. When asked about him, the party leadership had no record of a man named Koba. Papa had talked to Mama, saying he suspected Koba was not his true name.

Anger began to build inside Tatiana. She turned to Fyodor and whispered into his ear, "When this is over, I would like to be introduced to this man Stalin."

Fyodor seemed puzzled by her request, but Tatiana refused to explain. Coming to this meeting had opened up memories that had long been hidden, and she had mixed feelings about that. They were painful memories, and better left forgotten, yet recalling them helped her to understand herself. She could not talk of them to Fyodor, yet she felt compelled to say something to this man Stalin—Koba.

When, after the speech was over, Fyodor introduced them, Tatiana was trembling with controlled rage. "Mr. Stalin and I have met," she said coolly. "Though his name then was Josef Koba and mine was Tatiana Baranov."

"Oh?" Stalin met her eyes with a stare as cold as her own. "I don't think so."

"It was in Baku," Tatiana prompted his memory. "Just before the riots. You came to my parents' home. My father you should remember. Alexei Baranov?"

Stalin's heavy brows furrowed. Then there was clearly recognition in his eyes. "Oh yes," he said cautiously. "And how is your family?"

"Of course you wouldn't know, would you?" Tatiana said. "You didn't stay in Baku long enough to see the results of your work. My father was killed in the rioting, and my mother was taken to Siberia. I don't know what has happened to my brother."

"But you seem to have survived very well," Stalin said, eyeing her expensive clothes.

"I have been fortunate to have the love of my adopted family," she said. "But that hardly makes up for the loss of my real one, however humble it was." She hesitated a moment, took a deep breath, then added. "You may think I was too young to realize what you did to my father, but I remember your betrayal. And I won't forget it. Ever."

Again, Stalin's brows furrowed. "I'm sorry," he said. "But I don't understand what you're talking about."

"I think you do," she said, then turned and walked away, followed by a mystified Fyodor, trying vainly to get her to explain.

"I want to go home," she told him simply. "And I never want to come to one of these meetings again. If you persist in inviting me, we will have to stop seeing each other."

"All right," he said. "I won't press you to come with me to the meetings. But I'm your friend. Why have you never told me about your family? I might be able to help. I have contacts in high places. I might be able to locate your mother for you."

"What good would that do?" Tatiana asked. "You could not have her set free. And besides, by now no one will know what happened to her."

For a time, neither of them mentioned her true family again.

* * * * *

In Moscow, the two girls were growing quickly into mature young women. Much of what they experienced was normal for Russian girls of their age, but some was not, for their studies were extraordinary by any standards. However, all of it would have been shocking to their friends back home in Persia. While Tatiana was learning in technical terms about the biological functioning of the human body—male and female—Nadia was studying anatomy from the aesthetic point of view.

Professor Nichola was most noted for his works utilizing the human figure—for his portraits and for his paintings of nudes. He was steeped in the classical tradition, so precise in his perspective and his use of light and shadow that the figures on his canvasses seemed almost to breathe with life.

The young artists who studied with him, either at the Institute or privately, were required to learn the fine subtleties of the male and female form, beginning from the human skeleton, applying the musculature, and then appreciating the finer points of skin coloration. In the early stages, some of this was gained from books and charts, but eventually all students had to draw and paint from live models.

Nadia could be no exception, despite her sheltered upbringing.

Her first nude model was a woman—a plump, middle-aged lady with straw-colored hair. Her name was Sophia, and she had been modeling for art classes so long that she thought nothing of sitting for hours being scrutinized. In the beginning, Nadia had some difficulty overcoming her embarrassment, but she discovered that the more intensely she concentrated on her technique the less aware she was that what she was drawing or painting was a naked woman. Yet it did seem strange that she was covered from head to foot in a formless gray smock, gazing constantly at someone whose body had no covering at all. Indeed, at times, the model would suffer from goosebumps because of the chill seeping in from the snow-covered windows.

Nadia worked from several female models before Professor Nichola brought in the first male one. Nadia realized that this was deliberate on her teacher's part, intended to lessen her discomfort. Nevertheless, it was something of a shock when Boris removed his robe on the modeling stand, preparing to pose.

Boris was only a few years older than Nadia, and he was very attractive. He was an engineering student, and he helped earn his tuition by modeling for the art classes. His musculature was well-defined, and his classically sculpted face was truly beautiful and accentuated by curly black hair and gray eyes. But the thing that shocked Nadia was that his genital area was not as small nor unnoticeable as that of most of the nude statues she had seen.

Her first drawing of Boris was terrible, for she could not relax and concentrate properly. Her teacher and model both seemed to be aware of the problem, but Nichola did not know quite how to deal with the situation. All of his criticism simply seemed to make both of them more uncomfortable.

Then Boris climbed down from the modeling platform. "Let me see what you've done," he said in a jocular manner. "I'm not much of a critic, but I know what I like."

Nadia flushed hotly, aware of the beautiful naked man standing at her side, wishing she could turn and run away, but knowing that she could not.

"Well," Boris said pensively, "it doesn't look much like me. Except maybe for one part, and that seems overly large."

"But it is overly large," Nadia said defensively, before she realized what she was saying. Then she hid her hands in her face to hide the crimson blush she felt rising.

Boris laughed. "I guess it is at that," he said.

Then Nadia laughed, Professor Nichola chuckled softly. And that ended everybody's discomfort. After that, Nadia could look at the nude man with more clinical eyes. Her next drawing was excellent, and the painting she did of Boris was one of her best figures so far.

After some time of drawing and painting a number of models, Nadia talked to Tatiana about the cold, dispassionate view that was developing within her. "I look at a nude man now," she said, "and I don't feel anything sexual at all. My eye is analyzing, looking for patterns of color, measuring light and shadow. I'm beginning to wonder if it will affect my ability to love. If my prince charming should come along right now, I wonder if I will be so busy analyzing that I won't even recognize him."

Tatiana laughed. "I don't think that will happen. I'm not sure love is totally dependent upon physical attraction anyway. It's something that comes more from the heart than from the eye. If it weren't so, then all of the ugly people in the world would never know love at all. I think the heart can see beauty where the eye cannot."

Still Nadia longed for the experience of love and romance. At least, she reasoned, Tatiana had Fyodor, though she admitted he wasn't much of a prince charming. She was now seventeen years old, and many of her friends back home were already married.

She was progressing rapidly in her studies, and Professor Nichola praised her daily. She could see the progress herself, and she was invariably amazed when she made some new insight, discovered some new technique. The more she learned, the greater was her realization that she had known very little about art when she had appeared before the committee at the Institute. Her colors were no longer the pure bright pigments of Persia; her figures were no longer stiff and crude, but seemed to be living, breathing persons.

With her best work, it was almost impossible for a stranger to distinguish whether it had been done by her or Nichola.

Nadia was not really aware of this until it was called to her attention by the owner of a Paris art gallery, who was a close friend of her teacher.

Roscow Molinar was in Moscow on one of his regular buying trips, collecting new works of art for his gallery. As always, he called on his good friend, Nichola, who always guided him toward the promising new artists on the Moscow art scene. Though Nichola's style was conservative and traditional, he appreciated the new experimental artists who were opposed to his style. The Molinar Gallery in Paris was one of the most successful outlets for these young artists.

"I want you to meet Molinar," Nichola told Nadia. "I want him to see your work, but I don't want to be present when he comes. I want you to meet him entirely on your own."

"But why?" Nadia asked.

"I don't want to prejudice him for or against your work," Nichola explained. "I want it to speak for itself. Do you understand?"

"I think so," Nadia said uncertainly.

She was apprehensive about meeting such an important figure in the art world, and she would have felt much more comfortable showing him her work if Nichola were there to give her moral support. In her mind, Nadia envisioned Molinar as a very intimidating man. After all, he was one of the most important gallery owners in Paris, the very center of the art world. His eye, she knew, would be able to pick out her every weakness and failing.

To study with Nichola, Nadia had rented the studio adjacent to his, a studio with connecting doors, but entirely her own. All of her works were there, as well as all of her painting supplies and equipment. On the appointed day, she set out all of her best works for viewing; she put all of her early works, those done before her study with Nichola, into the shelves and racks where they would not be noticed. She prepared tea in the samovar to try to make his visit as pleasant as possible.

The man who arrived at her door was nothing like the Molinar she had expected. Since he was an old friend of her teacher's, Nadia thought he would be around the same age as Nichola. But to her surprise he was only in his early thirties. There was nothing harsh or severe in his appearance at all. Though there was definite strength and assurance in his manner, he seemed a warm and genial man.

Molinar was tall and quite handsome, with straight black hair graying at the temples. He had a strong chin, a rather long straight nose, sympathetic dark eyes, and a mouth that seemed always on the brink of smiling with secret mirth.

Nadia's heart, beating anxiously as she opened the door, changed its rhythms, taking on the churning rush of excitement. For the man who stood before her seemed to be everything she had ever dreamed of in a Prince

Charming.

Nadia was hardly aware of the pleasantries they exchanged, she was trying so hard to control her emotions. She served tea, and he sipped it silently as he wandered about her studio gazing at her paintings without expression.

She took this to mean that he did not like her work, that he was trying to find ways to tell her so without offending her. Perhaps they were too amateurish; she had learned much from Nichola, but she was sure there was still so much she had to learn. Her teacher should have waited another year or two before allowing her work to be seen.

After Molinar had looked at all of the paintings hanging or propped against the walls, going back to study a few of the smaller ones a second time, he said finally, "They are all very nice, but not quite what I'm looking for."

Nadia's heart sank, but she mustered courage to put the best face on. "Could you offer criticism?" she asked. "I would like to learn."

"There is nothing to criticize," Molinar said kindly. "Without a doubt, you have talent, and your technique is beyond criticism." He hesitated. "But I could not sell your work. It is too obvious that you are a student of Professor Nichola's. If I did not know these were yours, I would swear he had done them himself. I already sell Nichola originals; I could not take on Nichola imitations."

"I see," Nadia said, though she did not truly understand as yet. "Thank you for your time and your comments." She set down her cup with finality, preparing to see her guest to the door.

"Please don't be offended," Molinar said gently. "This is frequently a problem for art students. With time, you may find your own distinctive style. You are unquestionably one of the best students I've ever seen. No one has ever mastered Nichola's style as you have. I would like to see your work again after you have stopped studying with him and have been on your own a few years."

"Of course," Nadia said, again trying to dismiss him so that she could be alone. She could sense pity in Molinar's face, and she did not want that, for it might bring tears to her eyes. She felt a complete failure. "I'll see you to the door."

Reluctantly, Molinar picked up his hat and coat, which he had draped over the racks of Nadia's early canvasses. As she helped him into his coat, his eye was drawn to a large canvas that was partially visible. "Whats this?" he asked, sliding it out of the rack. "Are these more of your works?"

Nadia was embarrassed. "I'm sure those won't interest you," she said. "Please don't waste more of your time."

"I'm not wasting my time," he said, pulling another painting out. There was a strange excitement in his voice. "Whose paintings are these?"

"Those are some that I did before I came to study with Professor Nichola," Nadia said, trying to hold back tears of shame. "They are very crude and amateurish."

"But they're not," Molinar said. "They are magnificent. They have everything your other works lack—originality, excitement, color, attitude. I want these. I want them very much."

"I'm sorry," Nadia said. "But I couldn't possibly sell those." She was sure that he was acting out of pity, and her pride could not bear it.

Molinar turned to look down at Nadia. "You don't understand, do you?" he said, and there was warmth and kindness in his dark eyes. "With these paintings, I could make you a very successful artist."

"I don't think so," Nadia said. "I don't think I'm ready for my work to be seen by the public."

"Please," Molinar pressed, "let's discuss it further. Have dinner with me this evening, and give me the chance to persuade you."

Nadia hesitated. A romantic dinner was enticing; it was the first chance she had to be taken out by a handsome man. But she could not let him take these crude paintings to Paris, for she now knew how truly bad they were. "All right," she said finally, "I'll have dinner with you. But I'm not going to change my mind about selling these paintings."

Chapter 17

That evening Nadia dined with Roscow Molinar in his suite at the Metropole Hotel. She was, of course, somewhat concerned about being alone with him, and she knew that the Komineks would object if they knew. However, she felt that she was mature enough to take care of herself, so she lied to Gromyko and Tanya, telling them it would be a dinner party and that Professor Nichola would be there.

Truly, Nadia felt safe in Molinar's suite, for throughout dinner there was always at least one servant present, sometimes as many as three attending them. And Molinar was, after all, a gentleman.

The evening was as romantic as Nadia had dreamed it would be. He called for her in his carriage, bringing her flowers—a beautiful spray of violets—which he pinned in her hair. They matched the color of her dress so perfectly, it was almost as if he had known instinctively what she would choose to wear, a violet satin and chiffon creation she had bought in Moscow, but which had come from Paris and was the very latest style.

He was extremely solicitous toward her, offering his arm as they walked down the front steps, and assisting her into the carriage. It was dusk as the carriage took them through the streets of Moscow to the hotel; as they rode along, Roscow pointed out interesting architectural sites and talked knowledgeably about the history of Russia and its ancient architecture.

"To me," Nadia commented,"Moscow seems the most beautiful city in the world." She blushed."But, of course, I haven't seen many cities."

Roscow smiled."It is beautiful," he said."But of course I'm partial to Paris." He paused for a moment, then added,"Since so much of Moscow was burned in 1812, many of the buildings you see now, especially those with classical facades, are new or reconstructed, using styles borrowed from other European cities. From an aesthetic point of view, I prefer the native Moscow style, though you don't see much of it anymore."

"I have no way of comparing," Nadia said."All I know is that the buildings of Moscow are the most magnificent I've ever seen."

They fell silent, gazing out the carriage windows at the peaceful evening scenes. There was a hint of spring in the air. The snow was beginning to melt, and the city was at its quietest period of winter sleep, just before awakening."Many of the buildings, churches, and residences, and some of the commercial buildings, are actually log structures," Roscow continued."Though you wouldn't know it from the magnificent facades. Wood is one of the natural resources Russia has in great abundance."

It was the first time Nadia had ever been inside a truly fine hotel, and she found the glamor and elegance of the Metropole exciting.

The people in the lobby, as they passed through, were all beautifully dressed—men in tuxedos and uniforms, and women in elegant dresses and costly jewels. Nadia and Roscow rode up to the top floor of the hotel in an elevator—a cage of brass and glass that lifted them soundlessly and smoothly in a matter of minutes.

An impeccably appointed table had been set up in the sitting room of Roscow's suite, glittering with a silver candelabrum and gleaming china and crystal. There were red roses that scented the air, and a violinist played. The waiters served from a polished brass cart, perfectly anticipating their every need, whether it was wine or the necessity to remove or place another course.

The food was French, not Russian, and Nadia loved it. She had never tasted flavors such as these, whether it was the fish in aspic or the beef bourgignon, or the dessert, which was chocolate mousse.

Molinar talked of developments in the world of art, concentrating on Paris."Of course," he said rather apologetically,"there are fine painters in other parts of the world. But in Paris, young painters are able to keep up with the trends, with what other important young painters are doing, so there is considerably more opportunity."

"I understand," Nadia told him."I always wanted to go to Paris to study, but Moscow was the best my father could manage. Actually I'm grateful to be studying with Professor Nichola."

Roscow nodded and smiled."He is one of the best teachers in all of Europe," he said."At least, for the old-fashioned style of painting."

There was a brief moment of silence. Roscow's eyes gazed into hers, knowing that she was aware of what he wanted to say. When he finally spoke, his words were soft and gently pleading."You know, Professor Nichola is not the right teacher for you," he said."Your natural primitive style is far more exciting. You should be developing that, rather than learning to copy and imitate."

"You shouldn't speak of Profesor Nichola that way," Nadia said."He's supposed to be your friend."

"He is my friend," Roscow said, reaching across the table to take Nadia's hand in his."If he thought about it, he would agree with me. He knows the art world is changing, and hes behind the times."

"I am very grateful for all he has taught me," Nadia told him staunchly."And I know he has much more that I have to learn."

"I wish you could come to Paris," Roscow said wistfully."Then you would see what I mean. You truly might have a future in art."

"I think I might as easily have a future here in Moscow or at home in Persia," Nadia said haughtily.

"Ah," Roscow sighed."But it would not be quite the same." He hesitated, glancing down at his wine glass, then lifting his eyes to speak."Besides, I have other reasons for wanting you to come to Paris. You are not only a talented painter, but you are also a fascinating woman. I would like to see more of you."

Nadia felt herself blushing. He had taken her completely by surprise."I'm flattered," she said, looking down at the table."But that's hardly a reason for me to come to Paris."

"I don't know why not," Roscow said with a shrug."I certainly look upon it as a reason to come back to Moscow. Much sooner than I had originally planned."

After the dinner was cleared, the waiters left, but Nadia and Roscow were still not alone, for the violinist remained, playing for them. However, Roscow escorted her out onto the hotel balcony to look at the view of the city. Although they could still hear the music, they were out of the musician's sight. The panorama of Moscow was breathtaking in the moonlight. In the distance, they could see the Kremlin, the fortress palace of the czar, and St. Basil's, with its gilded and brightly colored domes. In fact, the view was filled with spires and domes as far as the eye could see.

Nadia felt very happy. She was experiencing a blissful sense of contentment, mixed with an excitement she had never known before. There was something wonderfully romantic about being alone with Roscow Molinar, gazing at the beautiful vista and listening to the soft lilting music from inside. It felt right, being with him. It was a feeling that she did not want to end.

Now there was a longing within her breast to have him touch her, to be even closer than they were.

Almost as if he read her thoughts, Roscow suddenly reached out and put his arm around her waist, pulling her to him so that her head cradled on his shoulder.

"I think I will stay in Moscow a bit longer than I had planned," he said softly."I really don't want to leave."

Nadia felt her heart beating faster."When are you supposed to return to Paris?" she asked, her voice breaking slightly.

"In three days," he replied."But I think I shall delay my return."

"I'm not sure that's wise," Nadia said in little more than a whisper. And she tried, rather feebly, to pull away from him."I don't think we should see each other again."

"Why not?" Roscow asked."Don't you like me?"

"Of course I like you." Nadia replied, somewhat embarrassed."But we are from two completely different worlds. We can be friends, but nothing more."

"Your objection is that I am French?" he asked, puzzled.

"No," Nadia said, shaking her head."You don't understand. You see, I'm Jewish."

Roscow laughed. "I knew that," he said. "Professor Nichola told me. I'm also Jewish." He looked at her quizzically, saw that she was confused. "It's the name, isn't it? I changed it for business reasons."

Nadia was taken aback by this revelation, but she quickly recovered, standing firm in her purpose."Still," she said,"there are other differences. You are considerably older than I am, and you do live in Paris. When my schooling is completed, I shall be returning to Persia."

"But I would like to change that," Roscow said.

"No," Nadia told him firmly."I could never leave my family." This time, she managed to pull away from him and walk to the balcony railing.

Roscow followed, but kept a respectful distance."I realize we hardly know each other," he said."But the moment I saw you, I sensed that you were a very special woman. I felt something inside. It may be too soon to say this, but I think it's love. I must see you again so that I can find out. Again and again and again."

Nadia gave him a skeptical look."At your age," she said,"I would think you would have some experience with love, and should be able to recognize it."

Clearly her comment had startled Molinar, for a look of pain crossed his face momentarily."I have known a great many women, yes," he said, with some embarrassment."And on several occasions I have thought I was in love. But invariably it proved to be merely passionate infatuation. Truly, I have never experienced what I am feeling for you." Again he reached out to touch Nadia, to pull her to him.

But she pulled away. "I admit that I am rather innocent, Mr. Molinar," she said. "But I am not naive. I have heard about Frenchmen."

She turned to smile at him coyly, and was surprised by his swift movement, grasping her by the waist and pulling her to him, kissing her passionately on the mouth.

Nadia struggled to break away, but he was too strong and persistent for her efforts to be successful. Then the sensation of his lips on hers began to fill her with warmth, and she ceased to struggle, overwhelmed by what she was feeling. Wasn't this what she had dreamed of for so long? Hadn't she wanted this from Roscow Molinar? Wouldn't she have been disappointed if he had taken her home without at least making the attempt to kiss her?

She found herself not wanting the kiss to end, yet she knew it must.

With effort, she managed to break away, saying hoarsely,"I think I should go home now. Will you please take me?"

"If you wish," Roscow said softly."But I insist upon seeing you again."

*   *   *   *   *

Tatiana was already in bed that night, but she was not yet asleep when Nadia came in to tell her about her evening with Roscow Molinar. In fact, Tatiana had been trying not to fall asleep, so that she could hear about her sister's romantic dinner.

With Nadia perched on the foot of her bed, Tatiana listened to every detail, asking questions when her sister was not specific enough to suit her curiosity.

When she had finished, Tatiana asked,"Will you see him again?"

Nadia shrugged and smiled."I suppose so," she said."I know I shouldn't encourage him, but it is the only romance I've had in Moscow. And he will be returning to Paris soon. After that, I'll probably never see him again."

Nadia did see Roscow almost every evening for the next week, going out with him to the opera, the theater, and to dinner. On Saturday and Sunday, there were walks in the park and a picnic in the country.

As she got to know Roscow Molinar, Nadia's feelings for him grew. Was she in love? She didn't really know. She knew only that she enjoyed being with him, and that she wanted to be with him even when they were apart. She would miss him when he returned to Paris, but not so much that she would want to give up the rest of her life in order to follow him.

It was this awareness that enabled her to maintain a distance between them. Several times, she permitted Roscow to kiss her, but she would allow him to go no further, no matter how much her body ached for more.

Now it was Tatiana's turn to be jealous of her sister. Nadia's romance was far more exciting than her own friendship with Fyodor. Of course, she was pleased for Nadia, and she enjoyed the romance vicariously, but she was also eager to have the experience for herself. It was perhaps this eagerness that prompted her to soften somewhat toward Fyodor.

Late one afternoon, after an examination at the Institute, she accepted Fyodor's invitation for a walk in the park by the river. When he took her hand and held it as they strolled along, she did not object; and when they stopped to look down at the river and he put his arm about her waist, she accepted that as well. And finally, when he made the attempt to kiss her—less clumsily than his earlier efforts—she allowed his lips to press themselves upon hers, welcoming their warmth.

The sensation this time was pleasureable. Tatiana closed her eyes and imagined that Fyodor was the man of her dreams, her romantic ideal. It was only for a moment that she indulged in her fantasy, but she enjoyed it, responding to Fyodor's kiss with feelings that matched his.

When their lips parted, Fyodor whispered,"Oh, Tatiana, I do love you so much. I want you to be mine."

Only then did Tatiana realize her mistake. She pulled away abruptly."You mustn't say that," she told him curtly."We're just good friends, nothing more."

"That was not the kiss of a good friend," he said."I could tell that you feel something for me."

"It was a mistake," she said, shaking her head vigorously."It should not have happened."

"If it's marriage you're concened about," Fyodor said impulsively."I'll marry you."

Oh, no," she said."I couldn't possibly marry you. You're too much like my father." Then, realizing how that sounded, she blushed."I mean . . .," she stammered."I'm sorry, I cant explain . . . " She paused, then said almost angrily, "Besides that's hardly the way to propose marriage."

Fyodor gave her an embarrassed, frustrated look."I know I never say things the right way," he told her."They just don't seem to come out the way I intend. But I mean well. It might help me to understand how you feel if you would only talk about your parents. If you would tell me about your father. I mean, about your feelings toward him . . . and your mother."

Fyodor's discomfort and his apparently genuine concern, made Tatiana feel guilty."I'm sorry, Fyodor," she said sincerely."But I'm not sure I even understand my feelings about my parents, myself."

Perhaps it might do you good to talk about them," he suggested.

"I can't," she said honestly."I just can't."

Fyodor nodded in understanding."If you ever can," he said,"I'd like to listen."

*   *   *   *   *

As the day neared for Roscow's departure, Nadia began to realize how greatly she would miss him. In a very short time, he had become an important part of her life. Although she knew that there was no way they could share their lives, she did not want their time together to come to an end.

For Roscow's last evening in Moscow, Professor Nichola gave a formal dinner party at his home, and Roscow insisted that Nadia be invited as his dinner partner. Nadia's teacher was well aware that she was seeing the Paris art dealer. Though he had said nothing to her about it, she sensed that he disapproved in some way.

When she arrived at Nichola's home, escorted by Molinar, the professor was gracious and charming. There were twenty guests, all of the most important figures of the Moscow art world, painters, teachers, gallery owners, and museum directors. Nadia had, of course, heard of all of them, though she had met only a few.

It was a wonderful evening. Somewhat in awe of the other guests, Nadia found them fascinating. She was conscious, throughout the evening, of her youth and inexperience; she felt she did not truly belong among these people. By their standards, she was a mere child, and she knew it. It made her even more aware that her relationship with Roscow was far from ideal.

After the party was over, as Roscow helped Nadia into his carriage, he told her, "We must talk. Will you come back to my hotel with me?"

"It is rather late," Nadia replied. "Couldn't we just talk in the carriage?"

Roscow gave her a pleading look. "I would rather it be in more comfortable surroundings," he said.

"All right," Nadia relented. "But I mustn't stay long."

Once they had arrived in his hotel suite, Nadia realized this had been planned all evening. He had a bottle of champagne iced down and waiting for them, clearly set up on the serving cart no more than half an hour before their arrival. With a trace of fear, Nadia wondered about his intentions. For protection, she chose to seat herself in an armchair rather than take a loveseat or sofa.

If this disturbed Roscow, he did not show it. With the calm and graciousness of the perfect gentleman he was, he opened the champagne bottle, poured two glasses, and handed one to Nadia. Then he seated himself on the loveseat opposite her. He took a sip of champagne and said, "It is difficult for me to leave you. If there was any way I could, I would stay longer. But, since I must return for business, I plan to come back as soon as I am able—I hope within two months."

Realizing his intentions, Nadia felt a sinking sensation within her breast. But she hesitated only a moment, took a deep breath, and spoke with determination. "Please don't return on my account," she said. "I think it is best that we do not see each other again."

"I can't accept that," Roscow said firmly. "I won't. Because I know now that what I feel for you is love. True love. It is the first time in my life I have experienced it, and I will not give it up. I will persist until you admit that you feel love for me and you agree to marry me."

Nadia's heart leaped. Roscow was proposing marriage, and something within her wanted to say yes, but she maintained her control. "You know that cannot be possible," she said, her voice trembling slightly. "And you know the reasons. That is why we should not see each other again."

"I know there are obstacles," Roscow persisted. "But love can find a way to surmount them."

Nadia shook her head vigorously. "There are just too many obstacles," she said. "Not the least of them is that I am not ready for marriage."

"I can wait," Roscow said, "as long as you agree to see me again."

Nadia began to falter in her resolve. She felt a great compassion for this man, deep within her. His behavior toward her had been impeccable. He had done nothing to hurt her or to harm her in any way. And she did feel something for him; she did not know if it was love or not, for she did not really know what love was. Was it possible that what she feared was her own feelings for him? Perhaps. She did have a longing at that moment to have Roscow hold her in his arms, to kiss her, possibly even to make love to her.

"All right," she said. "I will see you again. But I cannot guarantee that I will ever love you or that marriage will ever be possible."

"That is fair," he said with a smile, rising from the loveseat. He walked across the room to her and took the champagne glass from her hand. "Now,

I should take you home. It is getting late."

Nadia felt a strange disappointment. She had expected him to attempt to make love to her, and it was disconcerting to her that he had not. Was he not even going to kiss her?

She rose shakily to her feet, embarrassed by her thoughts. As she did so, he bent down and kissed her on the cheek.

"I have been waiting for you all my life," he whispered. "If necessary, I will wait for the rest of it, for you are truly worth waiting for."

Suddenly, impulsively, Nadia threw her arms around him, hugging him tightly. He responded by giving her a kiss on the lips, filled with passion, but far too short to satisfy Nadia's longing for him.

Chapter 18

On his weekends and holidays from school, Gregor continued to help Rajik in the shop. He enjoyed these days, because he again felt like a responsible adult instead of a young schoolboy. Indeed, as the spring of 1907 approached, his schooling was almost complete. He would soon be sixteen, of an age when young men entered the world of adults or—in some cases, in other parts of the world—went on to college or university. He now wore the full suit of a man, with the long coat, vest, and tie that was typical of the Armenian shopkeepers.

He performed the shop work with confidence and assurance, keeping a record of the stock, making sure the wares were displayed attractively, assisting customers, and occasionally allowing them to bargain for the price.

Gregor enjoyed meeting people, and he usually tried to greet them cheerfully. For the most part, they responded in kind, confirming his belief in the inherent goodness of people, whatever their backgrounds or traditions. Only occasionally was he disappointed.

Almost always, those who failed to confirm his faith in human nature were Russians, those foreigners living in Tehran in order to maintain power over the natives. Gregor did not like to think that he was developing a prejudice, but he was definitely beginning to be wary of anyone who appeared to be Russian.

Gregor was somewhat ashamed of this feeling, and he tried not to let it show when he waited on customers who were Russian. Late one Saturday in February, however, he found it extremely difficult to keep his view silent. He was alone in the shop, because Rajik had gone to transact business with an importer.

It was almost closing time, and Gregor was waiting for Kouroush to come to meet him. By this time, they had been friends for several weeks, and it had become their habit to see each other at least once a day, usually only to go to the little teahouse for tea and conversion.

He was torn with conflicting feelings from the moment the young woman walked into the shop. She was approximately his own age, and she was—without a doubt—the most beautiful young woman Gregor had ever seen. Her hair was golden and was wrapped about her head in an intricate network of braids. Her eyes were a deep sea green, and filled with mystery. Her lips were full and firm and sensuous, as were her breasts. She wore a hat with feathers and a veil, and her stylish blue and white dress was loosely covered by a fur coat, even though spring was in the air.

Her manner was representative of everything he considered bad about the Russian intruders. He could tell she was Russian from the way she dressed and the way she carried herself. She was accompanied by an elderly Moslem woman who was obviously a servant, and whom she treated as if she were a beast of burden, without feelings or soul. The frail old woman was laden with packages and bags when they came in the door, and it was clear the young woman intended to make her carry more, although she herself was burdened only with a small purse.

The young woman led the older one through the shop, surveying and examining the grains in their bins and the dried fruits neatly laid out in the stalls. She had not looked at Gregor since entering the shop, nor did she look at her servant, maintaining the attitude that native Persians would offend her eyesight. However, she spoke loudly to make sure that he could hear her every word.

"Look at these dates," she said disdainfully. "They must have been here at least a year! They're as hard as rocks! It would break a tooth to bite into one!"

Gregor felt his temper rising. He knew there was nothing wrong with the dates. She was preparing her case for talking him down in price, even before she knew the price he would ask.

She moved on toward the rice bins. Pausing, she picked up the wooden dipper and scooped up a small amount, letting it fall slowly back into the bin. Dropping the scoop, she gave a disparaging glance heavenward. "I don't see how a merchant can stay in business with such poor quality merchandise," she said. "There doesn't seem to be anything here we can use; we might as well go." The young woman started slowly toward the door, followed by her servant.

Gregor knew she wanted him to go to her obsequiously, to try to sell the wares at bargain prices, but he remained behind his counter, even though there was no one else in the shop. His anger was increasing with every minute that passed. He wished that she would reach the door and leave before he said something unwise.

Realizing that Gregor was not going to respond as she wanted, the arrogant young woman paused to survey the bin of dried beans. She reached out a gloved hand and ran her fingers through them. "Well, I suppose these aren't really too bad," she said. "Though they seem a bit small."

Gregor knew that the beans were as good as any availabe in any of the shops in the bazaar. They had arrived only the day before. She began to scoop beans into bags, filling three, then adding them to the burden already borne by the servant, doing it so carelessly that the old woman had difficulty in balancing everything. Why doesn't she look at what she is doing, Gregor wondered.

The young woman hesitated a moment, then walked back reluctantly to the dates. She paused indecisively before turning to Gregor and asking imperiously, "Young man, how much are your dates?"

Impulsively, Gregor replied, "Ten toman a tcharak."

"Ten toman?" the young woman exclaimed in astonishment. "Don't you mean ten shahis?"

"I meant what I said," Gregor responded gruffly.

"That's outrageous," she said shrilly. "You can't expect people to pay that kind of price for these."

"I don't," Gregor replied. "For most people, they're only ten shahis. For foolish young women who don't know how to treat their servants, they're ten toman."

It took a moment for his meaning to register with the Russian woman. When she finally understood, she looked at the old servant for the first time and realized what she had done. Her face turned crimson; then she reached out and removed the bags of dried beans from her arms, tossing them into the bin of dates. "You obviously don't wish to do business with me," she said angrily.

As she was doing this, Kouroush entered the shop, surveying the scene silently. He could see that his friend and the young woman were in the midst of a dispute.

The young woman stalked up to the counter where Gregor stood and confronted him. "If you knew who you were talking to," she said furiously, "I don't think you would be quite so fresh."

"I don't care who you are," Gregor replied calmly, feeling somehow that he had won. "If you can't be considerate of others, I don't wish to sell you anything."

The young woman stormed out of the shop, followed by her servant.

As soon as they were gone, Kouroush studied Gregor curiously. "You really don't know who she is?" he asked.

"No," Gregor replied. "Why should I?"

"I thought everybody in Tehran knew about Sylvia Zinoviev," Kouroush told him. "She's the daughter of Major Zinoviev, the Russian military attache, who is probably more powerful in this city than Muhammed Ali Shah himself. Everybody says he rules Persia, and his daughter rules him."

Gregor shrugged. "That explains her arrogance," he said calmly. "But it doesn't excuse it."

Kouroush grinned. "You sound like Mirza."

"I'm not a revolutionary," Gregor protested. "I just don't see that the Russians have the right to look down upon Persians. They aren't our rulers; they're here only by treaty."

"That's exactly what Mirza says," Kouroush pressed. "And he doesn't want to be a revolutionist either. He believes that force should be used only when all other alternatives fail." Kouroush smiled. "You really should come with me to hear him speak sometime."

Gregor could not help but smile at his friend's persuasive manner. "I suppose it wouldn't do any harm to listen to a speech," he said. "Especially if it only confirms what I already think."

Kouroush slapped his friend on the back affectionately. "At last you've come around," he said happily. "I was sure you would, sooner or later."

Gregor grinned sheepishly. "You just happened to catch me at the right time," he said. "You have Sylvia Zinoviev to thank for it."

* * * * *

On the evening he was to accompany Kouroush to hear Mirza, Gregor did not tell Rajik and Jeanous where he was going. He said simply, "I'm going out with Kouroush for a while." So his parents did not ask for an explanation, for which he was quite grateful; he did not want to lie to them as he had before.

Mirza did his speaking at one of the mosques in Tehran, the Masjed Shah, near the bazaar, in the southern part of the city. He gathered his listeners in the courtyard outside the meeting rooms where the mullahs spoke, for his talks were not sanctioned by the religious leaders. In his youth, he had been in training to be a mullah, and though many considered him to be one, he had angered too many by his calls for revolution and so had not been elected to the rank of holy man.

He had only recently returned to Tehran after a period of exile, and there were indications his presence would not be tolerated for long, before he was again expelled from the country.

Gregor feared that he would be out of place at the mosque, among a predominantly Moslem group. However, no one seemed to object to his presence. There were a few others in the group of about thirty who were clearly not of the Moslem faith.

Mirza Kuchik was still a young man, though he was some years older than Gregor and Kouroush. Gregor could see instantly that there was something charismatic about the man; he was a born leader. Mirza dressed in the robes of a mullah, and wore the full beard, so it was natural for people to think of him as one. When he spoke, his voice was powerful and his words eloquent. There was a blaze in his eyes that could draw people to him like moths to a flame.

He spoke of Persia's glorious past, calling it the fountain of civilization, a fountain that had been shut off by foreigners. He accused his fellow Persians of weakness for permitting the intruders to control them. He was particularly vigorous in his attacks on the weakling Muhammed Ali Shah for allowing himself to become a puppet of the Russians, and for permitting the British to come into the country in the south.

Throughout, his speech was punctuated by the cry, over and over, of "Persia for the Persians!"

With all of the other listeners, Gregor found himself swept along by the words, in full agreement with all that Mirza said, feeling the passion and the urgency of the cause he espoused. At the same time though, he could not dispel the memories of his childhood, the awareness of where such passion could lead—the violence, the death, the sorrow. In his heart was a conflict he could not resolve.

Gregor had expected only to hear Mirza speak and then leave, but Kouroush had other plans. As the crowd began to disperse, and a few people were going up to speak to Mirza, Kouroush took his friend's arm and said, "Wait with me. Mirza wants to meet you."

"Why should he want to do that?" Gregor asked. "What have you said to him?"

"Don't be angry," Kouroush said pleadingly. "I know you will like Mirza as much as I do."

"It's not a question of liking him," Gregor tried to explain. "It's simply that I can't get involved, and you know that."

After a few minutes, Mirza separated himself from his group of admirers, and walked over to greet Kouroush, then turned an appraising eye on Gregor. "So this is your friend," he said. "The son of Alexei Baranov."

Gregor looked accusingly at Kouroush. "You told him about my father?"

Mirza smiled. "Don't be upset with him," he said kindly. "Your father was someone you should be proud of. His name is legend among the Persian people."

Gregor was skeptical. "How can you know about my father?" he asked. "He lived in Baku, not in Persia."

"By rights, Baku should belong to Persia," Mirza said. "Come, let us go for tea, and we will talk. It may surprise you how much I do know about your father and your mother.

Indeed, Gregor was astonished at Mirza's knowledge; he had not simply been flattering him by talking of his father. The teahouse they went to near the bazaar was larger than the one Kouroush frequented, and it was more crowded and much busier. There were several young men in Moslem robes moving through the customers, who were seated on there platforms, serving tea and sugar.

And there were a great many of the customers smoking water pipes, some of them clearly using opium rather than tobacco. A few of the customers were eating dizi, a goulash made of meat, garbanzo beans, and lentils, with saffron rice.

There were attractive, colorful Persian rugs on the walls, along with pictures of Mohammed, his son Ali, several contemporary mullahs, and even one of Mirza.

As they sat drinking their tea, Mirza revealed things about Gregor's father that even Gregor did not know.

"Your father was one of the great martyrs to the Persian cause," he told him. "Why do you think the Russians have kept your mother imprisoned in Siberia all these years? She was guilty of nothing more than being the wife of Alexei Baranov."

"I don't really remember very much about what happened," Gregor admitted. "I know only that my father spoke in favor of the strike, and that he was killed trying to stop the rioting in the oil fields."

Mirza nodded. "If he had not been killed in the tunnel, he would have been killed by the cossacks," he explained. "The Russians did not want him alive, for what he was advocating was dangerous to them. He sought to unite people in opposition to their rule; he wanted people to forget ancient racial and religious hatreds for their common good. And that was the most powerful thing the Russians have to maintain their control over us. As long as they keep us divided, we are weaker than they are."

Mirza's words recalled a memory to Gregor—a memory of the visit to the Zoroastrian shrine, and of the words spoken by his father and the old priest. He knew that what Mirza said was true.

He could also sense what Mirza was leading up to, and that increased his sense of frustration. He liked Mirza, as much as Kouroush had promised he would. Under other circumstances, he knew that they could be good friends. Under these circumstances, Gregor would have to refuse.

It was late before Mirza came to the point. The mixture of scents in the teahouse—the spices, teas, coffee, tobacco smoke—that had seemed so pleasant before now seemed cloying. Gregor was struck by a sense of claustrophobia. He wanted to leave, but he could not be rude.

Finally, Mirza said, "Do you know how much it would aid our cause to have the son of Alexei Baranov among us?"

"I understand," Gregor replied. "But I am now Gregor Sarkissian, the son of Rajik Sarkissian, a merchant who cannot afford to have a son who is a revolutionary."

Mirza nodded. "The day may come," he said, "when Gregor Baranov and Gregor Sarkissian are one and the same, for the evil that we fight will ultimately affect both."

*   *   *   *   *

Gregor walked home alone that evening, deep in thought. The things Mirza had said had affected him far more than he had wanted to admit. When he had agreed to the Sarkissians' adoption, he had attempted to put the past behind him, to bury Gregor Baranov forever. But the past would not stay buried.

He was sure he had done the right thing. He had set himself upon a new course, and he must follow it to its end. He could not go back, no matter what old feelings and loyalties had been brought back to the surface.

He owed so much to Rajik and Jeanous—not just for what they had done for him, but for their deep loving and caring as well. He had almost completed his schooling now, and they had been extremely pleased to learn that he had shown a distinct talent for writing. They had encouraged him to pursue a career as a journalist, despite the fact that Rajik had looked forward to having him take over the shop when he grew too old to continue himself. Rajik's generosity and concern for his adopted son's happiness had been very touching to Gregor.

Still, he hated the Russians, and there was nothing that could change that.

* * * * *

Mirza's prediction came true, even more quickly than he had expected. The course that Gregor Sarkissian had set himself upon was altered irrevocably by events beyond his control, events brought about by the courses of others who were completely unknown to him. In August, only a few months after Gregor's meeting with Mirza, the Shah's handpicked prime minister, the hated Atabak-i-Azam, was assassinated, increasing the hostility between the Shah and the parliamentary body, the Majlis. Within a matter of days, word reached the Persian people of a secret agreement between Russia and England, concluded in St. Petersburg, partitioning Persia into two spheres of influence, the Russians to have the north and the British the south.

Although the signed document professed to guarantee the "independence" of Persia, its very existence was a mockery of this idea. It had been concluded without the consent of the Majlis, and was well known that Muhammed Ali Shah accepted anything the Russians demanded.

The people of Tehran were outraged. The Majlis protested the action, and the newspapers denounced the agreement and the Shah for accepting it.

The Shah mobilized the Cossack Brigade and threatened to disband the Majlis.

The increased visibility of the cossacks on the streets and in the shops of the city aggravated the dissatisfaction of the populace. An outbreak of violence seemed inevitable.

In December and January, when there were already shortages, the cossacks seemed determined to buy up all the supplies of food in Tehran, refusing to pay the merchants fair prices. They were accustomed to paying wholesale prices, but now they were cutting even that in half.

Merchants began to dread the sight of cossacks moving through the bazaar.

One Saturday in January 1908, when Rajik and Gregor were both in the shop, and they were busy with customers, they noticed a group of cossacks entering the shop across from them. Merchants and customers all sensed trouble, and they left their transactions to go to the door to see what would happen. The shop the cossacks had chosen was tended by an elderly man, who could not put up much resistance if force became necessary.

The shouting began almost immediately. "No!" the old man yelled. "You cannot take the rice! It has been sold!"

"Then what is it doing here in the shop?" a cossack sergeant demanded. "If it is here, it is for sale, and we're taking it!"

"You can't," the merchant cried. "They're coming this afternoon to pick it up! They've paid for it already!"

"You can give them their money back," the sergeant said adamantly.

Gregor was outraged by the officer's manner. He was obviously not a Russian but a Persian. His olive skin, dark eyes, and well-groomed handlebar mustache betrayed his heritage. He should have had sympathy for his countryman.

"They've paid me full value," the merchant protested. "You won't even pay me half!"

The sergeant laughed. "You can afford it! You could afford it even if we paid you nothing!" He turned to his men. "Take the rice and start loading it into the wagon."

"You'll have to kill me first!" the old man yelled, running to try to prevent the soldiers from taking the grain.

One of the cossacks struck the merchant, knocking him down.

Before Gregor fully realized it, Rajik had rushed from his own shop to help his fellow merchant. Then Gregor followed; by the time he arrived, the old man was on his feet again and struggling with the soldiers. Together, the three men fought the six cossacks, but they were greatly overpowered. Even when two other men came to their aid, they were no match for the trained soldiers.

Gregor suffered blow after blow, not fully aware of what was happening to the others, conscious only that their struggle was violent, with bins of rice and flour and dried fruits being overturned, and that there were shouts of encouragement from the crowd that had gathered, as well as jeers at the cossacks.

The last thing he remembered was being hurled against a bin and landing with a blow that took the breath out of him and caused sharp pain in his head.

Gregor regained consciousness slowly, vaguely aware of a beautiful face hovering over him, a woman's face, the face of an angel. There was something familiar about it, but he couldn't place it. As recognition came to him, he wondered if he really was conscious at all, for it was not a face that he associated with kindness or gentleness, certainly not that of an angel. It was the face of Sylvia Zinoviev.

Gregor tried to get up.

"Lie still," Sylvia said. "Your head is still bleeding."

Only then was he aware that she was in the process of bandaging his head. "My father . . . ," he said, lying back down.

"He's all right," she replied. "You were both luckier than the old man."

What do you mean?" Gregor asked.

"I'm afraid he's dead," Sylvia said gently.

"The cossacks . . . ?"

"Yes," she replied sadly. "I witnessed everything. They behaved outrageously. I intend to report Sergeant Jalali to my father."

"Sergeant Jalali?" Only then did Gregor realize that the officer was Kouroush's father. He had been the one to strike the blow that had knocked Gregor unconscious.

"He exceeded his authority," Sylvia said, almost angrily. "There is sure to be trouble as a result of this. It was a foolish, senseless act."

By this time, the young woman had finished her bandaging, and he was able to sit up. "I don't understand," he said. "Why are you . . . ?" Then he stopped, realizing his question would be impertinent.

She smiled. "Why am I helping you?" She finished the question for him. "Because I owe you an apology. After thinking it over, I realized you were right that day in your shop. I have not been very considerate of the feelings of others. I am trying to change." She hesitated, obviously embarrassed. "Do you think you can forgive me?"

Now it was Gregor's turn to be embarrassed. "I hardly think it's necessary now," he said. "Instead, I owe you my gratitude for looking after my wounds."

"That's the least I could do," she said sincerely. "You see, I haven't gotten to know any Persians, even though I've been here for several years. I mean, I haven't gotten to know them as people. I would like to correct that." She hesitated. "I hope perhaps you will help me."

Gregor didn't know quite how to respond. "That's easier said than done," he said cautiously.

She smiled. "Perhaps you could start by letting me get to know you," she said.

Sylvia's bluntness disturbed Gregor. He felt defensive. He wanted to tell her that he could not be a friend to a Russian, but he knew that would be as rude and as unfeeling as she had been the first time he saw her. At the same time, he found her fascinating, and that frightened him.

Confused, he said finally, "There's not much to know."

"Let me be the judge of that," she said confidently. "If you have no objection, I'll visit you in your shop."

"Why should I object?" Gregor responded evasively.

* * * * *

The death of the old shopkeeper incensed all the merchants of the bazaar. Men who were normally calm and conservative were now threatening violence, demanding the abdication of the Shah and the expulsion of the Russians and British. Gregor was shocked at how forcefully the gentle and mild-mannered Rajik condemned the actions of the Shah's regime.

On the day of the old shopkeeper's funeral, the merchants closed the bazaar and marched in the funeral procession to symbolize their unity.

Obviously, the government had expected some sort of reaction, as the funeral route was lined with armed cossacks on horseback. It was also apparent that they were surprised at the number of people who turned out, because they made no move to disperse the thousands of ordinary citizens, as small demonstrations in the past had been handled. On this occasion, the cossacks were greatly outnumbered. It was an impressive show of unity against Muhammed Ali Shah and his Russian advisors and for the Majlis and the constitution. The demonstrators were pleased with themselves, dangerously euphoric with power.

After the funeral, Rajik invited a group of the leading merchants to his house to discuss an idea that had occurred to him. Gregor sat with the group and listened. Rajik's idea was that closing the bazaar for the day had been an inconvenience, nothing more. But if they continued to keep it closed, it would be a hardship for many people. If they kept it closed for several days, the economy of the city would come to a standstill. The entire populace would be crying out for the Shah to abdicate.

At first, several of the group wee skeptical about the idea; there could be too many problems. Not only would they be hurting themselves financially, but the people's anger might be turned on them. Somehow it would have to be made clear that they were demonstrating against the Russian influence over their ruler.

In response to this, one of the merchants suggested that they not only close the bazaar, but march as a group on the Russian embassy, which was at the northern limits of Tehran, adjacent to the British embassy, both of which were set in the midst of gardens, surrounded by high walls for protection.

Listening to the lengthy discussion, Gregor felt he had been taken back to his childhood. It was all very much like the meeting that had taken place in his parents' house in Baku before the refinery strike. And it frightened him. He could not bear to have the same thing happen to Rajik that had happened to his real father.

At the same time, he knew their plan was right; he believed in their goals. Their objectives were the same as those of Kouroush and Mirza, and their actions would free him to join in the efforts of his friends.

After the meeting was over, Gregor went to the teahouse, where Kouroush and Mirza were waiting for a report on the results. They were sitting at their usual place, on the broad bench against the far wall. They looked up at him expectantly as he approached.

"Well?" Kouroush spoke. "Tell us quickly; what happened?"

Gregor smiled. "They've agreed to close the bazaar tomorrow," he said as he sat down. "And possibly the next day as well."

"That's wonderful!" Kouroush said. Mirza simply smiled.

"That's not all, though," Gregor continued. "The merchants all plan to march on the Russian legation to demonstrate in protest against the partition pact."

"Even better," Kouroush exclaimed.

Mirza looked pensive. Kouroush glanced at him and asked. "Aren't you excited? This is just what we've been hoping for."

Mirza said solemnly, "I didn't expect it so soon. I'm not sure we're ready for it. There is certain to be bloodshed, and it will be innocent people who will be hurt. We don't yet have a militia to meet to Shah's forces."

"We can raise one," Kouroush suggested encouragingly.

"There isn't much time," Mirza said. "And it must be trained. The cossacks will have to move against the people, not against a revolutionary force. There is no way we can divert their attention in the next few days."

"Should we try to stop the demonstration?" Gregor asked.

"No," Mirza said. "What must be must be. If there are to be martyrs, it is Allah's will."

"We could join one of the other *anjumans* that already exists," Kouroush suggested. "They have had time to organize their opposition."

"No," Mirza said decisively. "They are too weak and too radical. The people will not follow them. Look at how badly they managed the assassination of Atabak. No, we must begin a new force, one that can gain the people's sympathy."

That evening in the teahouse, the three of them began to plan a truly organized resistance movement, establishing the beginnings of the Committee for Islamic Union. Mirza would be in command of all aspects of the revolutionary force, with others taking on specific responsibilities. Kouroush would handle military recruitment, aided by Gregor, who would be responsible for propaganda leaflets and a revolutionary newspaper, using the name "Baranov."

Eventually, when the time came, they would move north to the province of Gilan, where Mirza already had a lot of followers and influential friends who would join them.

Gregor was caught up in the excitement of the cause, but he was also frightened of the step he was taking. Even though he would be operating under a pseudonym, and he would not be engaged in the actual fighting, he was taking a definite stand, just as his father had done. Now, he could still hear his mother's urgent warning to stay out of such matters, predicting that any kind of involvement could only lead to sorrow.

* * * * *

As Mirza had predicted, the demonstration of the merchants provoked violence.

The day began peacefully and according to plan. All of the merchants had been notified by the leaders, and without exception had agreed to closing. Almost all of them, along with families and many friends, agreed to join in the march. Early in the morning, at the time the bazaar normally would have opened, the throng gathered outside the bazaar.

Gregor and Kouroush were there to participate, though Mirza thought it would be better for them not to be involved.

There was some confusion as early-morning customers arrived to do their shopping, unaware that the bazaar would be closed. Many of the shoppers, mostly men but also some women, decided to actually join the group as it set out for the Russian embassy. It took over an hour for the organizers to set up cadres and explain the plan and the manner in which they were to behave. Everyone understood that it was to be a peaceful demonstration and they were all to attempt to avoid any dispute with the military, if—or when—they arrived.

The cossacks arrived even sooner than they had expected, before the group had begun its march,. A small troop, led by Sergeant Reza Khan, rode into the crowd peacefully, and the commander asked to speak to the leadership. Rajik and two of the others were located to meet with him.

Though the crowd was quiet while this was taking place, Gregor heard very little of the conversation. He did hear Reza Khan demand strongly but respectfully that the merchants cancel their march and open the bazaar. Gregor did not hear the response, but he knew the leaders were refusing, just as firmly and respectfully.

Reza Khan's strong voice resounded clearly, "You understand, we must preserve the peace. There must be no violence, for your sake as well as ours."

Gregor was sure he heard one of the leaders say, "There will be no violence, so long as your men are not violent."

After that, the sergeant spoke softly to Rajik for a few moments and then led his troops away.

Shortly after that, the march began, moving slowly up the street to the north, toward the Russian embassy.

It was a thrilling experience for Gregor. He had never imagined what it could be like being a part of a massive movement of people, one of hundreds, perhaps thousands, joined in a common goal. The silence and the solemnity of purpose produced a sense of exhaltation unlike anything he had known before. After much thought—and there was time to think as they walked—he realized it was a sense of being a part of history in the making. For he had no doubt that this expression of the people was the beginning of something much larger.

It took almost two hours for the massive group to arrive at its destination. Gregor and Kouroush were not in the front ranks and could not clearly see what was ahead, though they could see the legation building and the tops of the walls around it. On the walls were cossacks, with rifles aimed at the crowd, and the word quickly spread through the ranks that the entire Persian Cossack Brigade was mounted in front of the legation, facing the demonstrators. In command was the Russian Colonel Liakhoff, a fact which could only anger the crowd further.

For a long time, nothing happened. The demonstrators merely stood in place, showing their force and their unity. Word came back that the leaders were talking to Liakhoff, and he was demanding that they leave and disperse. The talk continued for an hour before the cossacks made their move.

Gregor saw the soldiers on the walls aim their rifles above the heads of the demonstrators, and then he heard the firing. It seemed only moments before the crowd began to surge back toward him. Like everone else in the tightly packed group, he had no choice but to turn and push back in the direction from which they had come. No one had to tell him what had happened. The mounted cossacks were moving on the crowd, forcing them by their sheer numbers to retreat or be trampled by the horses.

But quick retreat was impossible. People in such numbers could not move faster than horses could attempt to move them. Panic resulted. There were screams behind Gregor and Kouroush, screams of anger and of pain. He knew that people were being trampled.

After that, there was chaos. People pushed and shoved, knocking each other down, trying to run. It was not that they were cowards; under the circumstances they had no other choice, for they were being pushed and shoved as well.

Few people got away without some minor scrapes and bruises; several dozen were injured severely enough to require medical treatment, among them Rajik. Three people were killed, trampled by the horses or by other people.

The next day, the bazaar opened. Rajik was able to go to his shop, though he wore bandages on his head and one arm was in a sling. The merchants felt that their effort had been a failure, but it had achieved something. The Russians had become aware of how much opposition there was among the Persian people. And the response of the cossacks served only to reinforce the determination of the people to continue their opposition.

Shortly before noon on the morning of the bazaar's reopening, the cossacks moved through the streets, stopping at certain shops to arrest leaders of the demonstration.

Among those arrested was Rajik Sarkissian.

Chapter 19

Rajik and the other leaders were kept in prison only a few days before being released. This was surprising to everyone, and taken as a sign of appeasement on the part of the authorities in hope of forestalling further protests. As Gregor later learned, this was not the ultimate reason, but it may have played some part in the decision.

The merchants had not been treated as badly as they expected, though they were greatly in need of rest, food, and washing. Rajik did not return to work immediately, needing a few days to rest and recover from his wounds, leaving Gregor alone to look after the shop. After getting a good night's sleep, he called Gregor in to his bedroom to talk to him.

He was still lying in bed, looking pale and weak. "I will try to come back to work as soon as I can," he told Gregor. "I'm sure you can take care of everything necessary until I do. I have notations in the account book for deliveries that are expected this week; just check them and note them in inventory."

"Don't worry about a thing," Gregor said cheerfully. "Just rest and get better."

"There's only one thing I'm worried about," Rajik said with a smile. "I know you can handle the shop without a problem. But I'm sure the Shah's men will be watching my place as well as those of the other leaders. You must be very careful of what you do or say for a while, especially if there are strangers about."

"I understand," Gregor said.

"It will be impossible for me to be active politically after this," Rajik said sadly. "They will be watching me for any sign of activity. But that mustn't stop your involvement in the cause."

"But . . .," Gregor started to protest.

"I insist," Rajik said. "Just be careful. What you and your friends are doing is important." He smiled. "And I'm pleased you will be able to use your writing talents."

Gregor was deeply touched by his adopted father's kindness and generosity, as well as his wisdom and understanding. He vowed to himself that he would do all he could to protect Rajik and to make him proud of him. He would be very careful about anything he did or said in the shop, and he would be cautious in his dealings with printers and paper suppliers while setting up the new newspaper, making sure everyone he talked to would be trustworthy.

Everyone in the bazaar was being guarded in speech and activity. Though customers came and went as usual, there was an unnatural quietness throughout all of the markets. Disputes and loud bargaining were noticeable by their absence. Customers and merchants determined that it was not worth the few shahis to call attention to themselves.

For Gregor, the days that followed were almost boring. That is, until the third day after the demonstration.

That morning, Gregor was occupied with a rather large transaction, and he was only vaguely aware of a young woman who had stepped up into line behind his customer. Only after he had finished his sale did he look at her and realize it was Sylvia Zinoviev.

"Hello," she said, smiling. "How is your father?"

On his guard, Gregor replied. "He's fine; why do you ask?"

"Are his wounds healing satisfactorily?" she asked sympathetically.

Gregor was suspicious. How did she know about his father's wounds? Had she been sent here by her father to spy? "What do you mean?" he asked. "What wounds?"

Again she smiled. "It's natural that you should distrust me," she said. "I know you think I am your enemy, but I'm not really. I am trying to understand you and your people. That's why I spoke to my father and to Colonel Liakhoff to ask them to release your father and the others."

Gregor was astonished. "How could you . . . ?" he began, but could not complete his question.

"I work in their offices," she explained. "Doing clerical work, handling filing and correspondence. I know everything that goes on."

At this, Gregor became even more cautious. Kouroush had not told him this fact, only that Sylvia was very influential with her father.

Obviously his reaction showed on his face, for Sylvia laughed. "Don't worry," she said. "I'm not here to spy on you. I don't think I would report you, even if I learned you were planning to bomb the cossack headquarters."

She looked at him coyly. "You know, I can get myself into a lot of trouble if my father knew I was talking to you like this. He would be very unhappy to learn I've been trying to make friends with an attractive young Persian. That sort of thing isn't done among my people."

Gregor could not help smiling. He blushed at her direct compliment. She was admitting that she was attracted to him, just as he was attracted to her. He was sure she could not be suggesting that they could be friends that way. That was unthinkable, for him as well as her. Then he began to grow angry; she was always saying things that left him speechless, then leaving a silence as if expecting a response.

Foolishly, he said, "Did you come to do some shopping? We have some fine dried figs today, a new shipment from the south."

"No," she said bluntly. "I came to see you." She paused, a look of sadness or disappointment crossing her face. "What can I do to convince you I want to be your friend?"

Gregor heaved a sigh of exasperation. "How can we be friends?" he asked. "You are Russian and I am Persian. We are of different worlds."

"No," Sylvia replied. "It is the same world. We may be different peoples, but isn't there a chance all people are really the same?"

These were words Gregor might easily have uttered, for they expressed what he believed—with one exception. He would have added, in his thoughts, "All people except Russians." But confronted by Sylvia Zinoviev, he could not utter them, for he was ashamed to acknowledge his prejudice.

Gregor shrugged. "People may all be the same," he said. "But they are also different, and these differences may not be easy to overcome."

Sylvia smiled. "Let's try," she said. "Spend your midday break with me. I have a picnic basket in my automobile outside. Come share it with me, and let's get to know each other a little."

Gregor hesitated. He felt a surge of desire within his breast; he was strongly attracted to this young woman. She was beautiful and charming and intriguing. But she was also dangerous. Could he take the risk?

"Please," she smiled sweetly. "Say you will." She reached out and touched his hand softly.

"All right," Gregor replied, and he felt a strange electricity run through him at the touch.

*　*　*　*　*

Gregor was still innocent when it came to women. He felt attractions and urges like other boys of his age, and he did know what men and women did together, but he assumed that would all be far in the future, after he was married—after a marriage that would be arranged for him.

The possibility that something might happen sooner was both thrilling and frightening.

Gregor had no idea where Sylvia intended to take him, for he could think of no place in Tehran where they could eat together without calling attention to themselves. For a Persian man to be alone with a Russian woman was unthinkable, especially for them to be sharing a meal.

However, Sylvia had thought it all out. As they climbed into her automobile, which was waiting outside the bazaar, she instructed the driver, "Take us to the Shah's Gardens and stop on the street, but not near an entrance. A nice shaded area will do." The back seat of the auto was completely closed off by curtains.

"We aren't going to eat in the gardens, are we?" Gregor asked cautiously.

"No," Sylvia replied, "We'll eat in the automobile, where we can be entirely private—just the two of us."

"What about the driver?" Gregor asked.

Sylvia smiled, "He's paid not to see or hear anything."

As the automobile began to move through streets to the west of the bazaar, Sylvia said, "Now, I want to hear all about you, where were you born, how you grew up, what your interests are—everything."

Gregor was beginning to get used to Sylvia's bluntness, but still it was difficult to respond. He started slowly, telling her about his childhood in Baku, but he carefully avoided revealing his parents' names, and he said only that his father had been killed in the oil field riots; he did not tell her that he had been a leader of the socialist movement, nor did he mention his mother's arrest. He felt that these things would be too revealing, and he still did not entirely trust her.

By the time they had reached the Shah's Gardens, he had told her most of what he felt he could safely reveal. The driver stopped the auto at a pleasant shaded area, where there were not too many passersby, and Sylvia took her picnic basket and began to prepare a plate of food for each of them, neatly placing a white linen napkin on his lap and then one on her own. She poured two crystal glasses full of white wine.

Gregor was not accustomed to wine, but he could not refuse, and found the taste was pleasant. The meal consisted of fruit, cheese, and bread, all quite good.

As they began to eat, Gregor said, "Now it's your turn. You must tell me about yourself."

"I'm afraid there's not much to tell," she said. "My life has not been as exciting as yours. I was born in St. Petersburg; I have two younger sisters. My father wanted a boy, but my mother didn't give him any sons, so I've been the son in the family, being closer to my father than to anyone else. My mother is a typical Russian matron of good family; she does nothing but sit at home and entertain friends, with servants to do everything for her. Since I was six years old, we've moved with my father's assignments—first to the Ukraine, then to Afghanistan, and finally here. I have few friends, and I work in my father's office to keep from being totally bored. I help my mother by supervising the household staff. There's really nothing more of interest I do."

"But the traveling must be enjoyable," Gregor said. "Getting to see different places."

"I haven't gotten to see that much," she explained. "As a woman, I've been protected and sheltered, watched constantly by my parents or by servants."

"I see," Gregor said. They fell into an uncomfortable silence, eating their food and pulling back the curtains of the automobile window to gaze out at the happy people enjoying the public gardens.

After a long time, Sylvia said, "Do you know what the worst thing is about being Russian?"

Gregor, chewing a piece of bread, shook his head.

"Not having something to believe in, the way you Persians do," she said. "Wanting something so much you would be willing to die for it. I have everything I want; and if I don't have it, I can get it."

"That's not being Russian," Gregor said. "That's being rich. I'm sure there are Russians who don't have everything they want."

"I suppose so," Sylvia said. Then she smiled at him very sweetly. "And lately, there is one thing I've found that I want and I'm not sure I'll get."

"What is that?" Gregor asked.

To his surprise, she blushed. "I'll tell you that when we know each other better," she said.

When they finished eating, she had the driver take them back to the bazaar and let Gregor out so he could reopen the shop. Just before the automobile stopped near the entrance to the bazaar, Sylvia suddenly reached over and took Gregor's hand.

"Do you believe now that I want to be your friend?" she asked.

"I guess so," Gregor replied in embarrassment.

Then she leaned over and kissed him briefly on the lips. "Then will we do this again," she whispered. "Very soon."

"Thank you for the meal," Gregor said politely, "and the automobile ride." Then, his heart pounding, afraid she might again try to kiss him, he got out. "I mustn't be late."

"Of course not," Sylvia said with a smile.

Gregor turned and hurried into the bazaar, his head spinning with confused thoughts. How could he possibly be doing this? Feeling what he was feeling? He must be insane to become involved with a Russian, the daughter of a Russian officer.

*　*　*　*　*

There was not a repeat of the midday outing in the days that followed. Events again took control of people's lives, and there could be little thought of such things as romance or love, though the brief experience with Sylvia was never completely out of Gregor's mind. Once Rajik was able to return to the shop, much of Gregor's time was occupied elsewhere, with making arrangements for the revolutionary newspaper, which had now acquired a name—*Voice of Freedom*. If Sylvia had come to the bazaar looking for him, she would not have been likely to find him.

Gregor's first task was to obtain funding. He was able to get some contributions from sympathetic merchants, including Rajik. Once they had sufficient money to begin, Gregor's next task was to find a printer willing to turn out their first few issues. This was a delicate matter, for not only did the printer have to be sympathetic to their cause, but his employees had to be trustworthy, or the printing had to be done when the shop was supposed to be closed. After talking to several possible printers, Gregor decided on one who chose the latter course.

And finally, he located a source for paper that could not be traced. It was extremely difficult, but he found an importer who acquired supplies from Turkey that he brought overland and not always subject to customs.

They were ready to begin, as soon as he had written the necessary articles.

He would have plenty to write about. He was just beginning his work when there was an assassination attemp on the Shah.

*　*　*　*　*

The hated despot would have been killed if he had been riding in his offical car rather than in the one behind it. Instead, he was only slightly injured by the bomb that was thrown from the crowd on the street. All efforts to determine the identity of the would-be assassin failed.

In retaliation, Muhammed Ali Shah set his personal ruffians, known as the *lutis*, loose on the city, allowing them to attack and loot at will. Their random acts of violence were particularly fearful for the populace, for it was impossible to know when or where they would strike.

Accompanied by Kouroush, Gregor went to the Baharistan, the house of deputies, to cover the confrontation that developed after the *lutis* had rioted in Gun Square. The *lutis* had not managed to close off the entrances of the Baharistan before hundreds of enraged citizens came to the aid of their elected representatives, guarding the doors and the deputies. There were several minor skirmishes, but the Majlis was able to meet and conduct business.

The Shah used these skirmishes as an excuse to send out the Cossack Brigade. However, once he had arrived on the scene and saw precisely what was taking place, even Colonel Liakhoff hesitated to attack the constitutional parliament and the citizens who were protecting it.

The confrontation was a standoff, with no significant violence—until a large black automobile with curtained windows attempted to make its way through a nearby street. There were cries from the crowd of, "The Shah! Muhammed Ali!"

Immediately a group of citizens attacked the auto, attempting to overturn it, rocking it back and forth violently and clambering on top of it.

Gregor sensed that he recognized that automobile, and he found himself fearing for the person inside. He prayed it wasn't who he thought it was.

He rushed toward the scene, pushing his way through the crowd. He was aware that the cossacks were going to the rescue as well, but he was nearer and his reaction was automatic. "Stop it!" he shouted at the men who were attacking the auto. "It's not the Shah!"

He struggled with a man who was attempting to break a back window. "Don't be a fool!" he yelled. "You don't want to hurt a defenseless woman, do you?"

Startled to be facing one of their own, an ordinary citizen, the men began to cease their violent attacks.

"This isn't the Shah's car," Gregor continued to say loudly. "It isn't anybody important."

"How do you know?" a man called back. "Prove it! Get them to open the door!"

Once the car had ceased its violent rocking and had settled back down onto its four tires, the curtain on the rear window was pulled back slightly. Then, when Sylvia Zinoviev recognized Gregor, she opened the door and got out shakily.

Attempting to smile, Sylvia said to Gregor, "Thank you for coming to my rescue."

"Are you all right?" Gregor asked.

"Yes," she replied. "Just a little frightened."

Gregor turned to the troublemakers. "Do you see now?" he asked, frowning. "It would have been a big mistake! I don't think any of you would have wanted to hurt a defenseless woman, would you.

In embarrassment, the group began to move off, a few of them calling out apologies to Sylvia before doing so. The altercation was over before Colonel Liakhoff had made his way across the square with his men.

This was the first time Gregor had ever seen the head of the Persian Cossack Brigade at close quarters. Vladimir Liakhoff was a very impressive-looking man, tall and with a bullet-shaped head. With his blond mustache and his elegant, heavily decorated black Cossack uniform, he seemed the epitome of the grandeur and power of Russia.

As Liakhoff got down from his horse and approached, he said sternly, "Sylvia, I warned you not to drive through this area today!"

"I know," Sylvia said, embarrassed. "But I didn't think there would be any harm."

"I hope next time you listen," Liakhoff said. Then he turned and looked at Gregor. "Who is this? Do you know him?"

"Yes," Sylvia replied. "He's a friend."

*   *   *   *   *

Gregor and Sylvia did become friends. The act of rescuing her from the angry mob did far more to break Gregor's resolve to stay away from her than all the favors or entreaties she might direct his way. Paradoxically, her indebtedness to him gave him more reason to trust her than his indebtedness to her. However, although he now trusted her, he did not let down his guard entirely. He remained aware of who she was and what her connections were to those in authority, so he kept secret his work with the revolutionary newspaper. Gregor felt he was leading a double life. Not only must he keep his revolutionary associations secret from Sylvia, he sensed also that it would be unwise to tell Kouroush and Mirza about his friendship with Sylvia.

They met in the shadows, and what they had together was entirely between the two of them, and, of course, the chauffeur who was paid to hear and see nothing, for almost always, the only place they could be sure to be together without being seen was in the automobile. Occasionally, as the weather grew warmer, they would have the driver take them outside the city so they could eat their picnic in the light under trees, as ordinary lovers do, and take walks in the open fields.

They did not see each other as often as they would have liked, for they could meet only in stolen moments, when they would not be missed by family or friends. Gregor was entranced by the beautiful Russian girl; he thought he might even be in love with her. However, the knowledge that a life together would be impossible remained a barrier between them.

On a beautiful sunny day in late summer, they took their picnic outing to a lush wooded area in the mountains outside the city. The chauffeur remained with the car a good distance away, allowing them complete privacy. After they had finished eating their meal, Gregor and Sylvia lay down on the carpet they had set out for the food, and gazed placidly at the tree limbs intertwining above them.

Sylvia rested her head on Gregor's shoulder. Her nearness, her warmth, and her softness were intoxicating to him. He could not resist turning his head and kissing her on the ear. Almost immediately, she turned to him, offering her lips, which he took eagerly.

Within moments, their hands were caressing each other, exploring their bodies, touching with excitement the most private of places.

Gregor began to undo the back of Sylvia's dress, but then hesitated, not sure he should go further.

"Yes," Sylvia whispered breathlessly. "I want you. Don't stop."

Gregor proceeded, eagerly seeking to touch her nakedness, eager to expose his own. They made love with complete abandon, joining their bodies in sublime union, blissfully happy together. And after they had finished, they lay for a long time in each other's arms, unwilling to accept the fact that the sun was retreating far into the western sky.

It was stolen happiness, they both knew. It was something that must one day end. However, Gregor did not realize the depth of Sylvia's love for him—even after she attempted to tell him.

On another afternoon, a few weeks later, they were lying in each other's arms under a tree after making love, aware that they must soon be walking back to the automobile to return to the city. Sylvia looked up at him lovingly and asked, "Do you remember I once said there was one thing I wanted that I couldn't have?"

Gregor nodded. "Yes."

"This is what it was," she said, in barely more than a whisper. "But I want it forever. Do you think that's possible?"

"I don't know," Gregor said, though he firmly believed it could never be. "I don't know if anything can be forever." He was not being cruel or unfeeling in what he said; he merely assumed that she saw the difficulty of their situation the way he did.

Gregor was not unappreciative of Sylvia. He realized that she had the right to demand much more of him than she did. He was especially grateful that she did not ask him questions about his activities; she did not seem to want to know what he did on those days when he disappeared for hours with Kouroush and Mirza. It was as if she knew he was involved in political activities and deliberately avoided the subject in order to prove to him that she was not a spy for her father or Colonel Liakhoff.

With the passage of time, those absences grew more frequent, for the deadline was growing near for the appearance of the first issues of the *Voice of Freedom*. Gregor worked very closely with Mirza in producing the final copy, which had to be carefully hand-scribed on the printing plates. While Gregor would be using the name Baranov for his investigative articles on the Russian influence over the Shah, the real call for revolution would appear under Mirza's name.

Because of the Shah's continued suppression of the regular newspapers, they felt sure the *Voice of Freedom* would receive a wide readership, not just in Tehran, but in Gilan in the north and Tabriz in the south, where Mirza had numerous contacts. It would be circulated free, delivered to the various regions and neighborhoods at night by some of Mirza's loyal followers.

The first issue came off the press and was delivered in April, with an even greater response than they had hoped for. People all over Tehran were talking about the news and articles it contained. It seemed to revive the energy and dedication of the constitutional supporters, increasing the talk of driving both the Russians and British out of Persia.

By the time the second issue reached the streets two weeks later, the Russian authorities and the Shah's enforcers were already attempting to determine where the paper was being printed so they could put a stop to it. They were also trying to locate Mirza and "Baranov." As a result, Mirza had to stop speaking at the mosque and limited his movements in the city.

On one of their outings after that, Sylvia said to Gregor, "My father and Colonel Liakhoff are looking very hard for this 'Baranov' who's publishing the *Voice of Freedom*. If any of your people know him, they should warn him to be careful."

Gregor wondered if she knew more than she was saying—or if perhaps she suspected the truth.

By the time the third issue was out, relations between the Shah and the Majlis had become increasingly strained. The Shah blamed the Majlis for fomenting unrest among the people, and the Majlis demanded the ouster of several of the Shah's more ruthless and corrupt ministers.

Frustrated at his inability to silence either the Majlis or the *Voice of Freedom*, the Shah set the *lutis* on the populace again, causing even more unrest and resentment.

But the Russians and the British were also frustrated by what was happening. In June, they decided to take matters into their own hands. The Russian Minister de Hartwig, accompanied by British Charge d'Affaires Marling, called the Persian Minister of Foreign Affairs and threatened to take matters into their own hands if the Majlis did not stop their opposition to the Shah.

The next day, the ultimatum was passed along to the Majlis, which capitulated, fearing the prospects of a Russian invasion.

Gregor and Kouroush learned of what had happened only a short while after the session of the Majlis was over. They kept in close touch with several of the members, and one of them reported to Gregor immediately upon leaving. He, in turn, notified Mirza, and it was decided that an extra edition of the *Voice of Freedom* must be published to inform the people.

This was a blatant breach of Persian sovereignty, an acknowledgement by Russia and England that the guarantees of Persian freedom specified in their agreement meant nothing to them. Their partition of Persia was for more than "spheres of influence."

In writing this issue, Gregor held back nothing. He attacked the Russians as treacherous, and accused the British of cowardice and duplicity. He called on the Majlis to display courage, demanding that they stand up to the foreigners and guarantee Persia for the Persians. And finally he called for the abdication of the Shah. He worked all night so that the issue would be on the streets of Tehran the following day and reach the far regions of the country before the week was over.

The people were incensed by the news; by midday a large crowd had gathered outside the Shah's palace, shouting for him to abdicate. Fearing for his life, Muhammed Ali fled the city, seeking refuge in the Bagh-i-Shah outside the walls, making his departure under protection of the cossacks.

Leaving Colonel Liakhoff in charge of Tehran, he began to make preparations for war against his subjects, collecting arms and closing down the telegraph office in hopes of keeping news from reaching the provinces. This move was too late, for copies of the *Voice of Freedom* had already taken the news north and south.

Once he felt securely ensconced in the Bagh-i-Shah, however, Muhammed Ali acted even more foolishly. Calling leaders of the Majlis to a conciliatory meeting in his garden palace outside the city walls, he had them arrested and imprisoned, thereby angering the populace even further.

Gregor and his friends were busy day and night producing issue after issue of the newspaper, spreading word of every treacherous action of the Shah and of Colonel Liakhoff, who had proclaimed martial law in the city. The paper and word of mouth had become the only means of keeping people in the provinces abreast of the daily events that were threatening their constitutional rights. Gregor, Kouroush, and Mirza felt the weight of this responsibility, and they knew that they were placing their lives at great risk.

Gregor saw very little of Sylvia, and when they were together, he was preoccupied. Whether she understood or not he had no idea, but she accepted and did not question his silences.

The people throughout Persia began to arm themselves in opposition to the Shah and his foreign "advisors," though they were not yet ready to offer armed resistance. For the moment, they merely continued to gather in public squares to express their views vocally. Reasonably, the people wanted to exhaust all other alternatives before resorting to violence.

Typically, it was the Russians who began the violence.

The demonstrations outside the Baharistan had gone on for little more than two weeks before Colonel Liakhoff could stand the tension no longer. It was like a test of who could stare longer without blinking first. He issued an ultimatum to the Majlis; they must order the people to cease their demonstrations, or the cossacks would use force to disperse them. This force might include the use of cannon against the crowds in the square and against those at the Masjed Shah mosque, where the mullahs spoke out against the Shah and the Russians.

As always the elected representatives sought a compromise to avoid a direct confrontation, but Colonel Liakhoff was impatient. On the morning of June 23, 1908, before sunrise, he moved over one thousand cossack troops with six cannon into the square outside the parliament buildings, getting them into place before either the demonstrators or the representatives could arrive. The Majlis members were allowed to enter their building, but no one was permitted to leave.

Just over an hour later, when the demonstrators began to arrive, the bombardement of the parliamentary building began. Gregor was at the small basement room they used for the newspaper office when he heard what was happening, having been awake all night preparing the next issue of the *Voice of Freedom*. Kouroush and Mirza arrived together to tell him, and to discuss what they should do.

Kourosh, the man of action, had no doubts about their course; they must all take arms and join the forces fighting the cossacks. Gregor agreed with him. But Mirza was more cautious. "The work Gregor is doing here is more important," he said to Kouroush. "You and I will take arms, but he must stay here. We do not know how long the battle will last. He must keep the people in the provinces informed"

Gregor realized the truth of what Mirza advised, but he felt that his contribution was somehow lesser. While his friends were risking their lives in battle, he would be hiding in a cellar preparing plates for printing. He wished he could turn his task over to someone else so he could join his friends. But that, he knew, was not possible. Reluctantly he allowed Kouroush and Mirza to leave without him.

To his regret, his knowledge of the events of that day had to come to him secondhand, from Kouroush and others.

A force of little more than one hundred poorly armed citizens attempted to defend their elected government against over a thousand cossacks with six cannon. Yet the battle lasted for eight hours, as the Baharistan was barraged by one heavy shell after another. From his cellar office, Gregor was able to hear the roar of the explosions, as cannon shells found their marks, and the anxiety made it difficult to continue concentrating on his solitary work.

When the sound of shelling stopped, the terrible silence was even worse for Gregor. It was late in the afternoon, and he knew that it meant the battle was over. He was afraid of what that might mean for his friends and his country.

Gregor had heard only silence for over an hour when Kouroush suddenly burst into the room. His friend was badly injured from a saber wound in his side. He was bleeding severely, and he was so weak he could barely speak as he attempted to tell Gregor what had taken place.

Collapsing on the floor and leaning against the cellar wall, Kouroush told him, "The cossacks have won. The Baharistan is completly destroyed."

"The Majlis?" Gregor asked anxiously.

Kouroush shook his head sadly. "Almost all killed," he said. "A few have managed to escape. The others have been arrested."

"Mirza?" Gregor questioned. "What about Mirza?"

"I don't know," Kouroush replied. "The last I saw him he was still fighting valiantly in a small group in Sarcheshmeh Square."

"We must get you to a doctor," Gregor said. "Your bleeding must be stopped."

"Not now," Kouroush said. "It's not safe to be on the streets. The cossacks and the *lutis* are everywhere, arresting people and pillaging. Just see if you can stop the bleeding for me."

Gregor did the best he could, ripping off a piece of Kouroush's robe to stuff in the wound, then binding it by tearing off another piece to wrap around his waist as a bandage. This did stop the bleeding, but Gragor was aware that it was not a very sanitary bandage. He was also aware that his friend was in great pain. Finally, he decided he must risk leaving him in the newspaper office to go for help.

The only person he could think of to go to for help was Rajik, though he knew he should not risk getting his father involved. Gregor was sure that the bazaar would be closed and that Rajik would be home with Jeanous. Kouroush was right about the dangers of being out on the street; the city was in chaos. Gregor attempted to make his way through alleyways and back streets, but he could hear the sounds of fighting and pillaging, and the smell of smoke told him fires had been set.

He reached his home without incident, but what faced him there was entirely unexpected.

Breathless from running the last few blocks, Gregor burst into the parlor, expecting to see only Rajik and Jeanous. But there was a guest, sitting on the sofa facing them. It was Sylvia Zinoviev.

As soon as she saw Gregor, she rose to her feet and exclaimed, "Oh, thank God! You're all right!"

Immediately Gregor was on his guard. "Of course I'm all right," he said. "Why shouldn't I be?"

"Oh, Gregor," she said anxiously. "I know about your newspaper, and about your friends. I've known from the beginning. The only reason you haven't been arrested before this is because I've kept the information from my father and Colonel Liakhoff."

"But how . . . ?" Gregor looked at his parents in embarrassment, then at Sylvia.

"Never mind how," she said impatiently. "The reason I've come look-ing for you is because your friend Mirza Kuchik has been arrested, and he's scheduled for execution."

Gregor looked at Rajik questioningly. "It's true," his father said solemnly. "People all over the city have been arrested, whether they had anything to do with the fight today or not. They are to be excuted without trial."

Suddenly Gregor felt very weak. He sat down on a chair and massaged his forehead with his hand. "How could it come to this?" he asked of no one in particular. "Mirza under arrest, and Kouroush badly wounded." He looked up at his father. "That's why I came home, to get your help, because Kouroush needs medical attention."

Until that moment, Jeanous had remained silent and still. Now she rose to her feet and announced simply, "I will get my medical bag, and you will take me to him."

"No, my dear," Rajik said. "You mustn't go out. I will go."

"No," Jeanous said firmly. "You must not take the chance. They will be less likely to bother two women." She turned to Sylvia. "You will go with me, won't you?"

"Of course," Sylvia said. "It is the only way. I must have time to talk to Gregor; we must decide what we will do to save his friend Mirza."

What was happening seemed unreal to Gregor. Not only was his mother risking her life to help his friend, but he was taking the daughter of a cossack officer to his secret office, where he prepared the revolutionary newspaper. And she was talking of helping him.

With the lives of both of his friends at stake, he could not protest, even when Sylvia insisted they have her chauffeur drive them in her automobile.

To Gregor's amazement, Sylvia had already formulated a plan, but it would require that he work feverishly throughout the night. She would atempt to persuade her father and Colonel Liakhoff that the Mirza Kuchik was not the same one who wrote articles in the *Voice of Freedom*. To sup-port her argument, Gregor must get an issue of the newspaper on the streets the following day with an article about the attack on the Majlis, written by "Mirza Kuchik."

If she could not convince them that Mirza could not be in two places at one time, she might be able at least to create sufficient doubt to keep him from being executed.

As soon as Jeanous had finished cleaning and dressing Kouroush's wound, she and Sylvia left the newspaper office so that Gregor could set to work. Sylvia wanted to stay and help him, but she realized it would be better not to arouse her father's suspicions by being out without explanation on this of all nights.

Gregor was tired from a night and day of ceaseless work, and he was feeling the strain of the day, but he forced himself to stay awake and to continue working. Though Kouroush was in no condition to do much to help, he contributed by talking and keeping his friend company. To Gregor's chagrin, Kouroush teased him unmercifully about his secret love affair with the young Russian woman.

* * * * *

The ruse worked, not sufficiently for Mirza to be set free, but well enough for his life to be spared. He was to be exiled from Persia. When Sylvia reported to Gregor what had happened, she was apologetic. "I'm afraid I could not do more without arousing their suspicions," she told him. "As it was, they wondered why I was taking an interest in this particular prisoner. I had to tell them I had met him in the bazaar and that he had been very kind to me."

"It's a miracle that you have managed to do this much," Gregor said. "I want you to know that I'm very grateful." He smiled. "Actually, I'm amazed that you would even think of doing such a thing."

Sylvia smiled and blushed. "I'm somewhat amazed myself," she said. "I suppose, in a way, I might be considered a traitor to my country."

"Why did you do it then?" Gregor asked.

Sylvia bit her lip and looked away. She shrugged. "I suppose love can make someone do strange things," she said.

Chapter 20

Without Mirza, Gregor and Kouroush lost much of their impetus for the revolutionary cause. Of course their feelings about the Russians and their puppet Shah did not change; if anything, the outrage of the destruction of the Majlis intensified their feelings. However, they were leaderless, without direction, much the way all of the people of Tehran were, for the fight in the Baharistan Square had resulted in the death, imprisonment, or exile of practically all the constitutionalist leaders.

Colonel Liakhoff had become the virtual dictator of Tehran. To reinforce his victory over the Persian people, he destroyed all the records of the Majlis, along with the buildings and the representatives themselves. If the people wanted to return to a constitutional government, they would have to begin all over again.

Gregor did not cease publication of the *Voice of Freedom*. He remained committed to issuing an edition at least every two weeks, not only to maintain the impression that Mirza Kuchik was still active in Tehran, but also to aid the efforts of the revolutionaries in the provinces. The defeat in Tehran had been total, but the constitutionalists in Tabriz and in Rasht were still effectively holding off the Shah's forces, and they were still fighting valiantly in Kirman and Isfahan.

Life became very difficult for all citizens of Tehran, and especially for those who were known to be opposed to the Shah and the Russians. Although Rajik had not been politically active since the closing of the bazaar and the march on the Russian legation, the cossacks would not leave him in peace. They came often to his shop, appropriating whatever grain or rice or dried fruits they might require, telling him to send a bill. None of the bills were ever paid, and as time passed, what had once been a profitable business began to show losses of such magnitude he was not sure how long he could continue.

At supper in the evenings, Rajik began to talk to Jeanous and Gregor about the possibility of moving from Tehran to one of the cities in the provinces.

But there were signs of imminent change everywhere. One that was more upsetting to Gregor even than the prospect of moving from Tehran involved Kouroush. It had been impossible to keep Kouroush's revolutionary activities secret from his father, especially after his injury.

Pasha Jalali was enraged, considering his son a traitor, and threatened to disown him. Kouroush and Pasha argued and fought continually. Pasha demanded that his son give up all opposition to the Shah and Russian rule; when Kouroush refused, his father cut off all financial aid and attempted to lock Kouroush in his room to prevent him from going out. When Kouroush managed to escape, supporting himself by getting a job in the bazaar, Pasha found him and tried to persuade him to return home.

After several months of father and son not seeing or speaking to each other, Pasha persuaded a favorite family servant to go to Kouroush to convey a threat. If Kouroush persisted in his rebellion, Pasha would have him arrested and imprisoned for treason. If Kouroush would return home and join the Persian Cossack Brigade as a dutiful son, Pasha would restore all financial aid.

At first, Kouroush wanted to refuse the ultimatum. But then he asked for time to consider the matter. He talked to Gregor about an idea that had occurred to him.

Sitting at the teahouse one evening, he said, "Joining the cossacks might not be such a bad idea after all. I wouldn't have to stay in the regiment forever, and the training might ultimately be helpful to us when Mirza returns."

"I don't know," Gregor said. "By that time, you might find you like the Brigade."

Kouroush was offended. "I could not be a traitor," he said. "I would never turn against the constitutional cause for the sake of my own comfort. It's just that I think we might be able to use the enemy; the more we know about the Russian ways the more likely we will be to defeat them eventually."

"Perhaps," Gregor said. "If you think it's a good idea, do it."

So Kouroush bowed to his father's wishes. Gregor continued to see his friend, but less frequently than before. However, they were of an age where five years seemed a long time, and Gregor believed this was the beginning ot the end of the friendship he had known with both Kouroush and Mirza.

By dividing them, the enemy had defeated them.

Then came the big chance in Gregor's life, making the division seem even greater.

The winter of 1908 was a difficult one for Rajik and some of the other merchants. The battles in the provinces, particularly at Tabriz and Rasht, were raging. Many of the cossack troops from Tehran were dispatched to try to quell the determined revolutionaries, and they required increased food supplies, particularly for those troops at Tabriz, where there was famine.

Their demands and their lack of payment had driven Rajik Sarkissian to the brink of bankruptcy. He could no longer afford to keep his shop in Tehran. A move was necessary before he lost everything he owned and could no longer afford to set up another business. By the spring, it was merely a question of where he and Jeanous would relocate.

There was also the question of whether Gregor would go with them or not.

One evening in March, the family gathered in the parlor after supper to discuss their alternatives. Rajik had potential buyers for the shop and the house. He favored moving to Rasht, but he did not want to make the decision without consulting his wife and son.

"There are both good and bad points about Rasht," Rajik explained. "Ephraim Khan and the Sipahadar-i-Azam have been very effective in holding off the cossacks there. And there is still a free flow of goods in and out of the city, unlike Tabriz, where the cossacks have cut off all roads. But there is one drawback—if the Russians should try to invade, they would be sure to move on Rasht first."

"If the Russians should invade," Gregor said, "I doubt if there will be a safe place in all of Persia."

"That may be true," Rajik acknowledged. "I am inclined to take a chance. There is a shop available in the bazaar at Rasht at a reasonable price. But . . . " He looked at Jeanous.

She smiled. "Where you go I go," she said. "I will trust your instincts."

Rajik smiled; this was as it had always been with his wife. He looked at Gregor and hesitated. As he spoke, he looked down at his hands almost shyly. "Of course, you will not have to come with us, Gregor," he said. "You are now of age and must make your own decisions. Your work with the newspaper is important."

"The newspaper could be moved," he said. "In fact, I think it would be advisable to move its location soon, if only to another place in the city." He fell silent; Rajik and Jeanous waited expectantly. Gregor was aware that his parents wanted him to go with them, and he felt he should. There was little to keep him in Tehran now that Mirza was in exile in Azerbaijan and Kouroush was with the Cossacks besieging Tabriz. There was, in fact, only one reason to stay—Sylvia.

Looking at that relationship realistically, he knew that it could not last forever. Certainly marriage between them was impossible. Perhaps it would be wise to end it now, while there was still time for both of them.

He looked at Rajik and smiled. "I will go," he said. "But I will need a few weeks to make arrangements to move the newspaper."

"We can go ahead," Rajik said happily. "And you can follow when you are ready. I think I can afford the second lorry to take your newspaper equipment. If not, there will be no difficulty getting the financing. There are many wealthy men who value it as the only voice for freedom we have."

* * * * *

It was going to be difficult to tell Sylvia. Gregor dreaded facing her, but he felt it had to be. Since the day she had assisted Jeanous in treating Kouroush's wounds, the Sarkissians had been aware of the friendship between Gregor and Sylvia, and she had been welcome in their home, though Gregor could tell that they had reservations about his connection with a Russian. Only occasionally would Sylvia visit Gregor at the newspaper headquarters, and then she would be extremely careful not to be seen entering or leaving. She would have her automobile wait at least a block away.

However, Gregor chose to give her the news on one of the occasions when they took the auto outside the gates of the city to be alone with nature.

They were sitting beneath their favorite tree, sharing cheese and wine, when he told her. "I hope you understand," he said. "I feel I must go with them." He paused uncomfortably. "I will come back from time to time to visit."

He could see the disappointment in Sylvia's eyes, and it may have been much more than disappointment. "I will miss you," she said softly, sadly.

"And I will miss you" he responded, leaning over to kiss her on the cheek. "But I will be back. I promise."

It was then that tears began to show in her eyes. But Sylvia would not allow herself to cry; she was too strong for that, too much in control. She knew as well as he did that promises of visits would not be fulfilled; the distance between Rasht and Tehran was too great. She know that this was goodbye, though she was willing to go along with Gregor's pretense.

"Let's go for a walk," she said, getting to her feet.

Gregor followed, uncomfortably.

"I wish I had known about your father's problems," Sylvia said. "You should have told me. Perhaps I could have done something about getting the bills paid."

"You've done too much already," Gregor said. "You must be careful not to arouse Colonel Liakhoff's suspicions."

A silence fell between them. The warm sun of the March afternoon beat down on them comfortingly. A gentle breeze ruffled their hair. It was such a beautiful day, a day for lovers, they ought to be happy. But the prospect of parting was too great a sadness.

When Sylvia spoke again, she was in complete control. "You are right, of course," she said. "Eventually my father would find out about us. But I'm not really sure I would care. I love you so much, I'm willing to risk his disapproval."

"I think his reaction might go beyond disapproval," Gregor said. "He would certainly never permit you to marry a Persian."

It was the first time the subject of marriage had been mentioned between them. Sylvia stopped walking and stared at Gregor questioningly, almost expectantly. "There are ways of marrying without permission."

"There are," he admitted. "But they can create more problems than they solve." He hesitated. "There is something I haven't told you. My parents were of different backgrounds; they married without family approval. I don't think it hurt my father too much, but whenever my parents would argue, my mother would always bring up the break that had taken place with her family by marrying him."

"But weren't your parents happy together?" Sylvia asked.

"I don't know," Gregor replied. "I don't think their happiness made up for the pain of being isolated from their families and from friends and neighbors."

"I think I would be willing to risk that," Sylvia said. "I love you so much, I would risk anything."

"I know," Gregor said gently, pulling her into an embrace. "But I love you too much to want you to risk it. I want you to be happy; I don't want to cause you pain."

They stood, holding each other tightly in an embrace, on a hilltop overlooking Tehran, nestled by the sun and breezes of spring. Around them birds sang. Sylvia looked up into Gregor's eyes; she could no longer hold back the tears. "When you're in love," she said, "There is no way of avoiding pain."

*   *   *   *   *

The move to Rasht was accomplished, but with difficulty.

In April, as the lorries filled with the Sarkissians' furniture and possessions moved north from Tehran, the citizens' army of Ephraim Khan and the Sapahadar-i-Azam moved south from Rasht to face the government forces, their objective being the holy city of Qum. The Sarkissians were stopped numerous times by cossack troops, and several times were forced to unload their lorries for inspection, to make sure they were not transporting supplies to the revolutionaries.

It had proved fortuitous that Gregor had not accompanied them, for the equipment and supplies of the *Voice of Freedom* would surely have been discovered.

As they approached Rasht, they began to hear the sounds of battle. Sometimes the sounds were so close they feared the next turn in the road might bring them directly into the fighting itself. However, only once did they come so close that they chose to stop and wait until the battle was over before proceeding.

When it was time for Gregor to follow them, Rajik wrote to him to advise him to ship his supplies by a circuitous route to avoid discovery. Even so, Gregor almost did not make it to his new home. Surprisingly, it was not the cossacks who stopped him, but the revolutionaries.

It required two wagons to carry all the printing equipment, the presses, the platemakers, the type, the paper, and supplies, to Rasht. Gregor was able to hire two wagons, with men to drive them, through an old and trusted friend of Mirza's, one who believed in the cause. They knew what they were carrying, and they knew to beware of trouble.

To avoid the government forces, they took a mountain road, little more than a goat path.

They were just about to leave a mountain pass and return to the vast plain below, when suddenly the wagons were surrounded by men on horseback. There was no mistaking these men for cossacks; for they wore robes and rode up on them wildly. At first, Gregor thought they were bandits.

But no, they were revolutionaries, and their leader was Ephraim Khan. Gregor breathed a sigh of relief when he recognized him from pictures he had seen.

"Who are you and where are you traveling?" Ephraim Khan demanded.

"My name is Gregor Sarkissian, and we are on our way to Rasht," Gregor said. "We are friends."

"Let me be the judge of that," the leader said gruffly. He studied Gregor for a moment. "You don't look like an Armenian."

Gregor tried to smile, but he suddenly realized he might have difficulty. "I am Armenian by adoption," he explained. "I was born . . . "

"What is in the wagons?" Ephraim Khan demanded. "Munitions?"

"Machinery," Gregor said. "For my business."

The leader turned to his men and snapped an order. "Uncover the wagons! Let's see what's in them!"

The men did as they were told, rudely ripping off the canvas covers, exposing the press and the plate-makers.

Ephraim Khan scowled. "What kind of machinery is this?" he demanded of Gregor.

"It's a printing press," Gregor said. "I publish a newspaper."

"You work for the Shah?" The revolutionary scowled at Gregor angrily.

For a moment, Gregor thought he might leap at him from his horse and cut his throat, the man looked so fierce.

"No," Gregor said shakily. "I publish something called the *Voice of Freedom*." He hesitated. "I am known by the name Baranov."

Ephraim Khan still scowled at him skeptically. "Can you prove it?"

Gregor was grateful that he had not destroyed the plates of the last issue he had printed. "Yes," he said, getting down from the wagon. "If you will permit me to take something out of the wagon."

"All right," the leader said gruffly. "But if you make a wrong move, you will be shot on the spot."

Gregor climbed into the back of the wagon and found the heavy lead plate and pulled it out. He lifted it up for the leader to see.

"That doesn't look like any language I've ever seen," Ephraim Khan said.

For a moment, Gregor was puzzled. "It's backward," he said. "So that it can print on the paper. You have to imagine it like in a mirror. Read it this way." His finger pointed out the reverse order.

"Oh, I see," Ephraim Khan said with interest. "Yes . . .," he smiled. "It says 'Voice of Freedom.' "

Suddenly, his face lit up. "And you are Baranov?" he asked. "The friend of Mirza Kuchik?"

"Yes," Gregor replied.

"Why are you taking this to Rasht?" the leader asked.

"Because it seems safer there than in Tehran," Gregor said. "Especially with you here, keeping the cossacks occupied."

Ephraim Khan smiled proudly. "That is a good reason," he said. "You may go on your way. But be careful near Menjil. There may still be cossacks there."

They went on their way, with no further incidents.

After Gregor was established at Rasht, once more producing his newspaper on a regular schedule, he realized the full power of the provincial revolutionary army. The reports that had earlier reached Tehran had given no indication. The cossacks and the Shah's militia were no match for them.

As summer approached, the provincial forces from the north, the west, and the south gradually moved closer and closer to Tehran, giving the Shah's army one defeat after another. The situation appeared so desperate for the puppet regime that on July 8, Russia took extreme measures, dispatching an invasion force of 2,000 troops from Baku. However, even that did not prevent the people's victory.

On July 13, the revolutionary army entered Tehran, forcing the Shah to take refuge in the Russian legation. On July 16, 1909, his abdication was announced. His twelve-year-old son, Sultan Ahmad Mirza, ascended the throne, with the head of the " ajar family, Azudu'l-Mulk, serving as regent until he was of age. The constitutional goverment was restored, with a new Majlis.

Muhammed Ali Shah lived out his exile in Russia. The Persian Cossack Brigade swore allegiance to the new ruler.

The transition of power took months, with lengthy, involved negotiations, during which time the country sank into increasing disorder and financial chaos. The greatest delay was caused by the Russian demands that the new Shah assume the heavy indebtedness incurred by the old Shah, most of which was for his personal use and which he was determined to take with him into exile.

While this matter was being resolved, the Russian army remained on Persian soil, waiting like vultures at Tabriz, Kasvin, and Rasht. And, as long as they were there, Gregor was determined to continue publishing the *Voice of Freedom*, unwilling to give up until he was sure the promise of hope was true.

* * * * *

The news of the troubles in their homeland reached Nadia and Tatiana in Moscow by various routes, and there were conflicting versions of what was happening. According to the Russian newspapers, the chaos and disruption were caused by a small band of criminals and anarchists, and the Russian troops had come to the aid of the people to restore order. According to the letters they received form Philip Boustani, the Russians were largely to blame for the difficulties.

Though Philip sympathized with the revolutionaries, he did not become involved in their activities. As a Jew, he had enough difficulties in the community without taking sides in this dispute.

The disparity in the stories merely added to the homesickness the two girls felt after having been away from home for two years. They both loved Moscow, enjoyed their studies, and adored the Komineks, but they missed their parents and their old familiar surroundings. In their letters, Philip and Judith Boustani acknowledged that they missed their daughters as well.

It was not possible for Nadia and Tatiana to take a lengthy leave from their studies to return home for a visit, but in the summer of 1910, the situation in Persia had calmed sufficiently for Philip and Judith to make a trip to Moscow. They had a wonderful visit together for a full week before the parents had to return home.

Nadia and Tatiana were both progressing well, though the medical courses were getting increasingly difficult for Tatiana, now that she had moved form the earlier preparatory classes into those directly involved with medical practice. Nadia was experiencing exactly the opposite—her studies with Professor Nichola had reached the point where each new revelation seemed to come easier to her.

However, there was one thing that disturbed Nadia. For some time, her teacher had seemed in poor health. Throughout the winter of 1910, he lost weight, and his complexion acquired a pallor that seemed almost gray in color. He had reached the age when most men would have wanted to stop working, or at least to slow down, but Nichola was determined to keep to his busy schedule, teaching and accepting commissions for portraits.

In the summer of 1911, he was given a commission by Czar Nicholas to do a combined portrait of his four daughters—Olga, Tatiana, Maria, and Anastasia—to be hung in the Winter Palace. This was to be life-sized and would be a major work, requiring numerous trips to St. Petersburg for sittings with the young girls. Nichola did not look upon this as a hardship, but an exciting challenge.

It had to be completed by Christmas as a special gift for the Czarina.

On his trips to St. Petersburg, Nichola did numerous sketches, both in pencil and in oil, so that he could do the work on the enormous six-foot by eight-foot canvas in his studio in Moscow. To Nadia, each time he returned from Moscow, he seemed more weakened and frail. In September, he even acquired a trembling in his hands that slowed his work considerably, but he kept going, working on the painting obsessively.

Normally, he would permit his students to watch him work. With this painting, however, he permitted only Nadia in the studio, keeping it covered when the others were around. Nadia was more than a student now; she was a friend and fellow artist, having commissions of her own. While Nichola worked on the four czaretzas, Nadia was completing a portrait of the wife of a wealthy merchant.

She tried to work side by side with him as much as possible, for she was extremely worried about his health. There had been several occasions when he had been forced to sit down to recover from a sudden faintness or dizziness. He ignored her suggestions that he see a doctor.

One evening they were working late, long after the natural light was gone, and they were entirely dependent upon lamplight. Nadia knew that anything she did might have to be changed the next day, for hues and shadings altered with the quality of the light.

She set down her brush and cloth and walked over to where Nichola worked feverishly, attempting to adjust a delicate shadow on the face of the Grand Duchess Olga.

"Don't you think we should stop for the night," she suggested. "It's really very late."

"You go ahead, my dear," he said, not even looking away from the canvas. "I have to work a little while longer. I want to get this shadow right."

"Do I have to remind you of your own teaching?" Nadia asked cajolingly. "You've always told me never to attempt anything subtle by artificial light. 'Anything you do at night will have to be undone in the morning.'"

"I know, my dear, I know," he said, still not looking away from his work. "But there is so little time, and this is such an important commission."

She did not press the matter, but went back to her own portrait, studying it to see if there was some unimportant area she could work on just to occupy the time. There really wasn't that much she could do, but she pretended to work, while keeping an eye on her teacher.

Nichola muttered to himself as he tried time and again to work the same patch of canvas, each time rubbing it out with his cloth and starting over, his palsied hand growing more and more uncontrollable, and his frustration and agitation increasing with it.

Nadia was looking at her painting when it happened. There was a sudden sharp cry from Nichola, followed instantly by a series of thuds and crashes as he fell against the painting, knocking it and the easel to the floor and falling on top of them.

Nadia let out an involuntary scream and rushed to Nichola. The teacher was alive, but clearly in terrible pain, for he was clutching his chest and there was an expression of agony on his face.

Nadia recognized instantly that there was nothing she could do to relieve the pain, and she certainly could not take him to a doctor; the only thing was to go for one and pray that Nichola would be all right while she was gone.

Locating a doctor at this time of night seemed to take an eternity, but in fact she was gone from the studio hardly more than half an hour.

The professor had suffered a heart seizure, a very serious one. The doctor insisted he be taken to a hospital for observation and close care. Nadia simply nodded her understanding, and the doctor made all arrangements.

Nichola's painting was ruined. However, when Nadia visited her teacher in the hospital during the next few days, she did not tell him this fact. She knew it would upset him, and he did not need to be upset in his condition. To her surprise, he did not ask about the work. It was almost a week later, after he had been removed to his home but still confined to bed, that he brought up the subject.

Nadia was sitting at his bedside on one of her daily visits, when Nichola said suddenly, "You must finish the painting of the Czaretzas for me."

Nadia's immediate reaction was that Nicholas mind had been affected by the seizure. "You mustn't worry about the painting right now," she said. "You will be recovered in time to...to finish it."

"No," he said. "It isn't possible to recover from old age. Even if I do get over this, I've had to recognize that I wouldn't be able to do the work justice. You must complete it for me. It's the only way of avoiding a terrible embarrassment. There isn't really a lot left to do. And you know my style perfectly."

Nadia couldn't find the words to tell him, so she did not try. "I will do my best," she said, having no intention of touching the work, which she knew was beyond salvaging, for there were two actual rips in the canvas. Somehow, she believed, the Czar must be informed of what had happened, and the part of the commission already advanced must be returned. There seemed to be no other solution.

"Bless you, my dear," Nichola said, reaching out to grasp her hand tightly. "You don't know how important this painting is to me."

"But you have done other works, great works, for the royal family," Nadia, argued. "For two generations."

"Yes," Nichola said solemnly. "And this was to have been the third generation. Do you know, there has never been a painter to remain in favor that long? I was to be the first, and I wanted this painting to be as fine a work as those done at my prime. But perhaps it was just an old man's pride."

Nadia felt tears welling in her eyes. Finally she understood the intensity with which he had worked on this painting. She wished desperately that she could do as he wished. If only the canvas had not been ruined . . .

It was these thoughts that prompted Nadia to make the attempt.

She began just to see if she could recreate the composition on a new canvas, not really believing she could duplicate his style sufficiently for people to believe it was his work. However, the more she worked, the easier it became. She could recall precisely how he mixed each shade of his colors; she could feel in her hand the way he made each stroke of his brush. Nichola's composition had truly been inspired. In the grouping of the four girls, he had achieved a relationship of four distinct personalities, from Olga's imperiousness to Anastasia's shyness.

She worked on the painting every day, postponing commissions of her own in order to make this attempt for her beloved teacher. And, on her visits to Nichola's, she could truly answer, "It's going well," when he asked about it. Indeed, it was going well, far better than she ever could have imagined. It might just work after all.

The test would be Nichola himself. If he disapproved, it would be shown to no one else. Only one other person even knew what she was doing, and Tatiana would never reveal her secret.

Nadia worked on the painting with even greater care than she did her own, for she was putting into it all the love and admiration she had for the man who had taught her everything, hoping she could repay even the smallest amount of what she felt she owed him.

Nevertheless, when it came time to show him the completed work (she had even duplicated his signature), she was terrified. Placed in its frame, it was extremely heavy, and had to be transported by wagon to Nichola's home. It was then carried up to Nichola's bedroom by the two lorrymen, who held it while Nadia nervously removed the protective drape.

Nichola stared at the painting in silence for a long time. "It is perfect," he said finally. "I knew you could do it." Then he grinned at her like a mischievous boy. "I might even go so far as to say it's my finest work." He reached out and took Nadia's hand, squeezing it tightly. "Thank you, my dear, for assuaging an old man's vanity."

As far as Nadia could see, he believed this was the canvas he had begun.

The painting was packed and shipped to the Czar well before Christmas, and not long afterward, a letter came from the Czar to Nichola. It praised the work as Nichola's finest masterpiece, and it thanked him for his many years of service to the royal family, expressing the hope that there might be many more years of such service.

Nichola kept the letter by his bedside and read it every day, until it became well worn. It was the old man's most treasured possession.

*   *   *   *   *

Christmas in Moscow was a magical time. Even Jewish families like the Komineks were caught up in the spirit of the season. Of course, they would not go so far as to decorate a Christmas tree or to sing carols, but they did adopt the practice of giving presents, using their holiday of Chanukah as an excuse. It was the joy of giving that the Komineks loved, a joy quickly picked up by Nadia and Tatiana.

Sometimes Tatiana thought she could recall Christmas as a small child in Baku with her real parents, but the memories were slight and uncertain, little more than smells and vaguely familiar sounds. Because of those memories, she had longed to go to a Christmas party, but had always turned down invitations, feeling somehow that to go and celebrate a Christian holiday would be a betrayal of her adopted parents and her acquired religion.

During that winter of 1911, the desire to experience Christmas became acute. As part of her medical studies, she had begun intern work that fall at a Christian hospital, run by nuns. As the Christmas season began, the workers had decorated a tree for the patients, and they had planned a special party for the patients and staff on the Saturday before Christmas, with presents and singing. That party would be followed by the traditional students' party at the university.

Each year before, Tatiana had managed to avoid the student party, making one excuse or another, though she was sure everyone knew the real reason was that she was Jewish.

But this year was different.

Tatiana admired the nursing nuns very much. Until she had met them and worked with them, she had assumed nuns were women who had retreated from reality into a private spiritual world. These women were not like that at all; they were closer to reality than women who married and had children. They looked forward to the Christmas party with such enthusiasm, Tatiana wanted to be a part of it.

It was, after all, she rationalized, a part of her work at the hospital, caring for the patients.

When she tried to talk to Fyodor about her dilemma, he laughed. "Religious differences are such nonsense!" he said disparagingly. "To me, a party is a party, and should have nothing to do with religion. I certainly intend to go, and I hope you'll go with me."

"But the exchanging of gifts . . . ," Tatiana protested. "The singing of carols. They have religious significance."

Fyodor shrugged. "They're nothing but gifts and songs. Do you think they make a difference to a God, if there is one."

In the end, Tatiana decided to attend both parties, but she remained self-conscious about it. And she felt she had to tell the Komineks and Nadia that she was going. They voiced no objection, and Nadia even joined in her shopping trip, having fun helping to select the presents for special patients and hospital staff.

Tatiana did not like the cold of winter, but she loved the snow. Moscow was beautiful covered in a blanket of white, at least at Christmas time. Within a month or two, the white blanket would be gray and slushy and miserable to walk through. But while it was still fresh, there was joy in it, as there was joy in trudging through it to buy presents for people she cared about.

When it came to wrapping the presents, Tatiana and Nadia were like little girls again, having great fun with the bright colored paper and ribbons. Vanitof helped, and he clowned with the ribbons, putting on a little show with a bow he made, using it alternately as a hair ribbon, a mustache, and a bow tie to create three different characters.

On the evening of the party, Gromyko arranged for her and her armful of gifts to be delivered in the sleigh, which was complete with festive bells on the horse's harness. Tatiana felt like Saint Nicholas.

She gave out most of her presents at the hospital party, saving Fyodor's and a few others for the student party later. She had a delightful time, and was surprised to receive several gifts herself. One that particularly delighted her was from one of the patients; it was a fountain pen on a little chain that she could wear around her neck. Its special significance was that she was almost always without a pen when she had to make notes at the bedside. It had become a joke among some of the patients and staff, and everybody laughed when she opened the present.

She even enjoyed the carol singing, even though she stumbled over the unfamiliar words, while everybody else seemed to know them. However, one or two of the songs were almost familiar to her, as if she recalled them from her childhood, associating them with the fresh smell of the fir tree that had been set up in the middle of the room and decorated colorfully.

The second party was quite different from the first. It centered more around the punchbowl—containing a spicy vodka concoction—than around the Christmas tree, though there was one, and the group did sing a few Christmas carols, before they switched to drinking songs.

All of the guests here were young and boisterous. After a few drinks of the spicy vodka punch, there was dancing, which was accompanied by loud shouts and laughter. Few of the students had brought gifts, for most lived on such small budgets that the expenditure for Christmas was beyond their means, and Tatiana felt almost embarrassed about giving out those she had brought. However, no one was embarrassed to accept them, except perhaps Fyodor.

Tatiana had bought him a long woolen scarf in bright revolutionary red. She was aware that his winter clothes had become a bit threadbare, and the scarf he wore had numerous holes and ravels.

They were standing in a corner of the crowded room, near the punchbowl, when she gave it to him. The sounds of the party were so loud they could barely hear each other talking.

Fyodor was pleased with the gift. "It's beautiful," he shouted to her. With some embarrassment, he added, "I didn't buy anything for you, I'm afraid. But I do have a sort of present for you."

Tatiana gave him a puzzled look. "What do you mean by a sort of present?" she asked, straining her voice to be heard above the din.

"I have something to tell you!" he shouted back.

"About what?" she asked.

"About your mother," Fyodor said. "I've learned where she is! You'll be happy to know she's alive and well."

Tatiana suddenly felt faint. Everything around her seemed unreal— the people, the noise, the Christmas joy. She was not even aware that she asked, "Where is she?"

"Still in Siberia!" Fyodor replied loudly. "She's working as a cleaning woman in a hospital!"

The image of the scrubwoman at her own hospital came to her mind, a poor, pitiful woman with a bedraggled appearance. Tatiana felt a sense of anguish overcoming her. She felt she wanted to scream. If she did not get out of this room, with all of the loud dancing and laughter, she would faint, she would break into tears. "Why did you do this to me?" she screamed at Fyodor. "Why did you have to tell me here, now?"

Then she turned and rushed from the room as hysterical tears began to break. She ran out into the wintry night, the heavy snowflakes stinging her tear-streaked face. She did not know where she was running, only that she could not stop, even though for some time she could hear Fyodor running after her, calling her name and begging her to wait.

She kept running long after he had given up following her. And when she finally did pause to think, she was by the river, the great icy Moskva, bleak and ugly and threatening in the wintry night.

She sat down on a bench on the walkway overlooking the river, ignoring the fact that she was sitting on ice and snow. Somehow she had to understand the feelings that were cutting deeply at her heart. She realized that Fyodor had meant no harm, but she really had not wanted to hear the news he had given her so proudly. She did not really know why, except that the truth about her mother made her feel guilty at being free, ungrateful for all the luxuries she had been given.

If only there was something she could do for her mother. If only she could trade places. But no, she would not really want to do that; she could not bear to be scrubbing floors at a hospital in Siberia. She could not bear to give up all the happiness that had been given to her; she could not give up her dreams of being a doctor.

That was the problem; she was a selfish, ungrateful child. She had not even bothered to find out about her mother for herself. It had taken Fyodor to do that. If he could find out so easily, she could have done so.

That was what made her feel so guilty, what made her so angry at Fyodor.

Tatiana was still sitting on the bench by the river, thinking, when Fyodor and Nadia finally found her. Fyodor had gone for Nadia's help when Tatiana had managed to escape from him, and they had been searching the city in the sleigh ever since.

They took Tatiana home and put her to bed, assuring her that everything would be better after a good night's sleep.

Chapter 21

But everything was not all right in the morning. It was not all right for a very long time. Tatiana continued to be upset about the revelation, not so much what she had learned about her mother as what she had discovered about herself. There was a marked change in her personality, and it affected everything she did. There was less laughter, less joy, less enthusiasm for life. The change even affected her studies; she seemed to have difficulty concentrating.

As she approached her last year of medical studies, she was in danger of failing.

Nadia and Vanitof tried to talk her out of her depression, but it did not seem to help. Fyodor tried as well, but she no longer even wanted to see him; she did everything possible to avoid him when he approached her at the university or at the hospital.

Finally, one evening in early spring, Gromyko Kominek called her into his study to talk to her. "My dear," he told her solemnly, "there are a great many people who are concerned about you."

"I know," Tatiana told him. "And I'm very sorry if I'm causing any unhappiness, but I don't know what to do. I feel I don't deserve the good fortune I've had; I feel there should be something I can do for my mother, but I don't know what. Why should she be kept a prisoner? What could she have done to deserve such punishment? If only I could see her and talk to her."

Gromyko nodded in understanding. "You know, I do have a few connections in the government," he said. "Would you like me to see what I could do? I don't guarantee I would have her set free, but I could try."

Tatiana's face brightened. "Oh, would you?" she asked. "I would be so grateful. Even if you could find some way for me to see her, it would mean so much."

For the next few weeks there was an improvement in Tatiana's manner and attitude; she was not the joyful Tatiana of old, but she was pleasant and more attentive at her studies. She even spoke to Fyodor, though she still would not go out with him.

It was almost the end of the spring session at the university when Gromyko again called Tatiana into his study.

"I received a response from the authorities," he told Tatiana. "And I'm afraid the news is not good. I have hesitated to share it with you, but I don't feel it is fair to withhold the truth. You must simply try to be brave, my dear, and accept what is."

"I understand," Tatiana said faintly. She could not imagine what Gromyko Kominek was preparing her for. Had her mother died? "I want to know whatever you can tell me."

"There is no way the government can be persuaded to release your mother," he said with a sigh. "Though they admit that she is not dangerous herself."

"Then why won't they release her?" Tatiana asked.

Gromyko hesitated. "Because of your father," he said. "There are rumors—merely rumors, mind you—that he is still alive and leading revolutionary activities in Persia."

Tatiana felt faint. "But that's impossible!" she said. "Why should they think he is alive?"

"There is someone who calls himself Baranov, who publishes a newspaper called the *Voice of Freedom*," Gromyko explained. "No one knows who he is, but the revolutionaries themselves believe he is Alexei Baranov, whom they consider a great hero of Persian nationalism."

"It can't be my father," Tatiana declared flatly. "He is dead. I know he is dead. He must be. Otherwise . . . " Tears began to fill her eyes. She could not bear to think her father would have abandoned her and her mother and brother.

Gromyko rose from his desk, walked around to Tatiana's side, and placed a comforting hand on her shoulder. She rested her head against him and wept uncontrollably.

As she began to regain her composure, Gromyko told her softly, "Permission has been granted for you to see your mother, if you wish. Of course, you would have to travel to Siberia, which is a great distance and would take a long time to get there. But I know it is very important to you."

Tatiana looked up at him, her weeping over. "But how could I posssibly go?" she asked. "My studies . . . ?

Gromyko smiled. "I'm sure arrangements could be made for you to take a leave during the summer months," he said. "But only if you do well in the spring examinations."

"Do you really think it would be possible for me to go?" she asked, a brightness returning to her.

"Of course you couldn't go alone," Gromyko told her with a smile. "Someone would have to go with you. I might enjoy a trip myself, and Nadia, and perhaps Vanitof would like an outing. He's never traveled at all."

* * * * *

That spring of 1912 was a difficult one for Nadia as well as for Tatiana. Professor Nichola's health did not improve, and he suffered a series of small seizures, growing more frail with each one. When the final payment on the commision for the portrait of the Czaretzas arrived, Nichola insisted that Nadia accept it. She tried to refuse, but Nichola told her that she would offend him greatly if she did not take it.

It was far more than she had ever received for a work herself.

"You earned it," the elderly teacher said. "You may think I don't know how much work you put into the painting, but I do."

"Oh, but I didn't do enough to earn this," Nadia protested.

Nichola smiled. "Do you think an arist cannot recognize his own work?" he asked. "Especially an artist of my years?" He was silent a moment, then said. "My canvas was damaged, wasn't it? That's why you had to start over?"

Nadia started to lie, but knew it would do no good. "Yes," she admitted. "There were two very bad rips. I just didn't feel I could tell you."

Nichola sighed wearily. "You know, my dear," he said sadly, "time is a very cruel thing. It is so deceptive. When you are young, it seems you have all the time you need to do everything you want. But it passes so swiftly, before you even realize it, you have very little time left, and you feel you have done nothing at all that you truly wanted to do."

"How can you feel like that?" Nadia chided him affectionately. "After all you have achieved in your life?"

"Achievements are not everything," the old man said. "Looking back, I think love and companionship would have been far more important. But I was always too busy for that." He paused pensively, then said, "No, that isn't quite right. I never met anyone I cared more for than I cared for my work. Not until it was too late."

Nadia smiled, not fully understanding what he was trying to say. "But it's never too late for love."

Nichola returned her smile sadly. "Yes it is. When the man is old enough to be the woman's grandfather. When the man has a few weeks or months left to live, and the woman has years."

Finally Nadia understood what he was saying, and she did not know how to respond. "Perhaps time is unjust in that way," she said hesitantly. "But time has also been very good by allowing me to know you and to have your friendship for the few years we've had. It is something I will treasure always."

"Bless you, my dear," Nichola said, reaching out and taking her hand in his.

In April, Nichola died. The artistic community of Moscow and St. Petersburg and even Paris mourned his passing. Despite the fact that he was of the old school, the young artists who were now taking the world by storm expressed respect and admiration for his skill, as well as affection for the man. The Czar proclaimed the day of his funeral as a day of mourning for the entire nation.

But no one was more heartbroken than Nadia. She felt completely lost without him. She truly had loved him, as one loves a kindly grandfather. For days she was unable even to stand at her easel to attempt to paint, because she had worked so closely with him and she missed his presence.

She had begun to look for another studio when she was notified that Professor Nichola had willed a very large part of his estate to her—his studio, a large amount of money, and all of his unsold paintings. Only then did she truly realize how deeply he had loved her, and how painful it must have been for him to maintain his silence.

Roscow Molinar was not able to arrive in Moscow in time for Nichola's funeral, but he did come to pay his respects a few weeks later. He had also come to attempt to purchase as many of Nichola's paintings as were available. He was surprised to learn that he would be negotiating with Nadia to obtain them.

"I don't know if I want to sell them," Nadia told Roscow honestly, "at least right now. I've been considering an exhibition of his work somewhere. I would like to honor him in some way."

"That's an excellent idea," Molinar said. "Perhaps I might be able to help you. A Nichola retrospective. I'm sure I could persuade some of the collectors who've bought his works to loan them for such an exhibition."

With Roscow's help, the plans developed swiftly. The Moscow Art Institute agreed to house it; collectors came forward to offer loans of works in their possession; and the Czar heartily approved, agreeing to show all of the many paintings done for the royal family.

It was scheduled for the spring of 1913, and during the months of preparation, Molinar made many trips to Moscow to work with Nadia. Naturally, they saw much of each other, and he continued to profess his love for her, pressing her to marry him and come to Paris.

Nadia refused to consider marriage. To try to keep from offending him, she began to joke with him affectionately. "You aren't looking for a wife," she would say. "You're just trying to get all of Nichola's unsold works for free."

And he would always answer seriously, "I would pay double the value for those paintings if I could get you for a wife."

The state of being loved and admired was something Nadia had difficulty adjusting to. It was true that she cared for Roscow, and she had loved Professor Nichola in a way, but she was still not sure of what her feelings truly represented. Were they signs of the kind of love that could be shared a lifetime? Certainly this was not the way she had thought love would be. She had expected an instant recognition, an electriciy to sweep through her the moment she saw her one true love.

She had expected to make the choice of whom she would love, not to have the choice made for her.

Professor Nichola had spoken to her of time. She still had time to make her choices.

* * * * *

That summer, Tatiana managed to acquire the time to make the trip to Siberia. She did extremely well on her spring examinations, and the university granted her a month's leave from her studies.

To her disappointment, Nadia would not be able to accompany her on the trip. Because of the short period of pleasant weather in Siberia, they could travel there only in the summer, and during that time Nadia and Roscow Molinar were very occupied with the plans for the Nichola retrospective, arranging with collectors all over Europe for the loan of paintings.

However, both Gromyko and Vanitof would go, though Tanya would remain in Moscow with Nadia. Surprisingly, Vanitof looked forward eagerly to the long train excursion. He had gradually grown out of his shyness and self-consciousness about his appearance, and now wanted to see and learn about the world first hand.

Tatiana had never really conceived of the vastness of Russia until that trip. The distance from Moscow to Yakutsk was more than twice that from Rasht to Moscow. After the excitement of the first few hundred miles, the days of riding on the train seemed to stretch out endlessly. Of course, they were not uncomfortable, for Gromyko had obtained a compartment for the three of them, and there was a lavatory, though an actual bath was impossible and washing hands and faces was all any of them could manage. Also, the food sold on the train was not as good as what they were accustomed to at home. However, at some of the stops, they were able to get off and purchase fresh fruits and cheeses from vendors at the stations.

Vanitof and Tatiana had grown as close as a brother and sister; with this trip, that closeness increased. They delighted in each other's company, sitting by the window of their compartment watching the passing land- scape and talking about the people, towns, and farming communities they saw, for the people of Russia were as varied as the landscape.

As the day drew near for their arrival in Yakutsk, Tatiana began to be apprehensive. For years, she had longed to see her mother again, but now that the dream was becoming a reality, she was afraid. What would she say to her mother, and how would her mother react to her? Since her mother could not be set free, would this meeting not actually be cruel and painful? How could Tatiana possibly leave her there and return to her life of privilege and luxury?

It had been eight years. Tatiana knew that she had changed greatly in that time. She had become a woman, of an age when other young women would already have families of their own. She had been educated, and she had acquired ambitions.

Would her mother approve of what she had become? That was the ques- tion that plagued her the most.

The last few nights on the train, Tatiana did not sleep well. The old nightmares, which she had not had in years, came back. Though their sleep- ing berths were hidden by curtains, she and Gromyko and Vanitof slept in the same compartment in the train. The last night, she awakened in tears, after the nightmare, in which her mother was wrenched from her.

Embarrassed, she listened to determine if her violent dream had awakened anyone else. There were no sounds except those of the train, gently rock- ing on the rails, moving ahead through darkened countryside at a steady pace.

She relaxed and dried her eyes. At least no one had been aware of her nightmare.

Then suddenly, Vanitof's voice came to her softly out of the darkness. "Tatiana, are you all right?" he asked.

"Yes," she whispered back. "I was just having a bad dream."

"Would you like to talk about it?" he asked.

"I don't know if it would do any good," she replied.

There was a moment of silence, then Vanitof asked, "Are you worried about seeing your mother again?"

"Yes," she admitted. "I'm frightened." She hesitated before admitting, "I'm afraid she won't like me. Who I am. What I've become. I don't know how to say what it is I feel. Even though I know it's impossible, I would like to go back to being her little girl again, to have her guide me into being the woman she wanted me to be."

"I understand," Vanitof said soothing. "At least I think I do. But your mother can't help but love you, just the way you are."

"I hope so," Tatiana said. "I truly hope so."

Tatiana had imagined the meeting in many different ways, but none of them were like what actually took place in the grim uncomfortable waiting room of the prison hospital.

It was a bleak, oppressive place, surrounded by gray stone walls, patrolled by guards, and even in summer it was cold inside the ugly, sordid buildings.

The travelers had spent the night before in their lodgings, so they could be washed and rested. However, Tatiana had slept little because of the anticipation. She chose to wear her simplest dress, a gray shirtwaist, because she did not want to show off her good fortune in the face of her mother's misfortune.

They spoke to the doctor who was in charge of the hospital briefly before they were permitted to see Maria Baranov. He was kind to Tatiana, but guarded. "I want you to know that your mother is content here," he told her. "I hope that you will try not to upset her."

"I don't want to do that," Tatiana told him. "I would like to do what I can to see that she is happy." She hesitated a moment. "I have brought her a basket of fruit and cheese. May I give it to her?"

"Of course," the doctor smiled.

Tatiana did not at first recognize the woman who was brought into the room. She bore no resemblance to the mother Tatiana remembered, the strong and beautiful woman who had sheltered and protected her as a child. The Maria Baranov she faced looked far older than her years; her thin body was bent with toil, bending over day after day, year after year, scrubbing floors, her face gaunt and wrinkled, and her hair was almost completely white.

There was a wariness in her eyes as she confronted the three strangers. She curtsied obsequiously, saying, "Good day, sirs, mistress. What can I do for you?"

Tatiana moved across the room, her objective to embrace her mother, but the old woman cringed and backed away. It was then that Tatiana was able to bring back her mother's face as it once had been. The lovely blue eyes had not changed. The expression about the mouth was again familiar. Her heart pounding painfully and tears beginning to form in her eyes, Tatiana asked, "Mother, don't you recognize me?"

Maria studied her warily. "Do I know you?"

"It's your daughter," she replied, trying to hold back the tears. "Tatiana."

Maria became even more guarded. "Yes, I have a daughter named Tatiana," she said. "How do you know about her?"

"Mama," Tatiana said gently. "I am Tatiana, grown up now."

The old woman would not understand. "I pray for my little Tatiana every day," she said. "They took her from me. I don't know where she was taken, where she is. Have you seen her? Is she all right?" Maria Baranov was growing agitated. "Is she happy? She isn't dead, is she?"

The tears began to flow down Tatiana's cheeks. Gromyko stepped forward and put a comforting hand on her shoulder. Then he addressed Maria. "No, she's not dead," he said. "She is very well and happy. She was adopted by a fine family who loves her very much."

"Thank God for that," the old woman said tearfully. "It is what I have prayed for. If you see her, will you tell her I love her and think of her every day?"

"Of course," Gromyko said

"And my son?" Maria asked. "Is my Gregor well?

Gromyko hesitated. "Yes," he replied, knowing it was what the woman wanted to hear. "You have no need to worry about either of your children."

"Thank you, sir," Maria said, going to him and kissing his hand. "Bless you." Then she rose and began to back away toward the door. "Now, if you will excuse me. I have much work to do. The hospital needs me, and I am so grateful to be of use. God has been good to me."

Tatiana could not bear to let her go like this. Controlling her tears, she went to her mother with the basket of fruit and cheese. "This is for you," she said, "from your daughter."

Maria Baranov looked at the basket incredulously. "All this for me?"

she asked, her eyes glistening with happiness. "From my Tatiana?"

"Yes," Tatiana nodded. "She loves you dearly."

"Bless you, mistress," her mother said. "You are a kind lady. I hope when my Tatiana grows up, she will be as fine."

"I am sure she will," Tatiana said, and impulsively reached out and embraced her mother, giving her a kiss on the cheek.

Tatiana nodded, and her mother left the room.

It was not easy for Tatiana to accept this unsatisfactory reunion with her mother. Gromyko tried to tell her that it was best for Maria Baranov to remain in the small contented world she had found for herself, but Tatiana could not accept that. Somehow, she felt she had to get through to her mother, to have her recognize her, to express the deep love she felt.

"I have to see her again," Tatiana said desperately. "I have to be alone with her, just the two of us. I can't leave her this way."

"I understand," Gromyko said kindly. "I'll talk to Mr. Shumiatsky again and see if it can be arranged." He took Tatiana's hand gently. "But if you can't make her understand, don't press it too hard. You don't want to hurt her any more than she's already been hurt."

The permission was granted, but with reluctance. It was against the prison rules for prisoners to be alone with guests without supervision, but Shumiatsky realized that Maria Baranov was harmless. And the prison medical director assured him there could be no serious risk to Maria, even if she became upset.

This time, Tatiana chose to wear a pretty summer dress, a white organdy that made her appear young and feminine. She was allowed to use Shumiatsky's office, where she and her mother could sit comfortably and talk.

This time, Maria's face broke into a warm smile when she saw Tatiana. For a moment, it seemed she recognized her daughter, but she said, "Oh, it's the lady who brought me the fruit. How nice of you to visit me again. Where are the others?"

Tatiana moved to her mother gently. "They didn't come with me," she said. "I wanted to spend some time with you alone." She paused, then added, "I would like to talk to you."

"Oh?" Maria asked. "What do you want to talk about?"

"About your daughter, Tatiana," she replied.

They sat down in two straight-backed chairs near the window of the office, where the sunlight could warm them. Tatiana began as softly and gently as she could. "Do you remember the doll you made for your daughter?"

she asked. "You used two blue buttons for the eyes and some yellow wool for the hair."

"Yes," Maria smiled. "And I made it a pretty dress, blue and white. As nice as a real dress. I used to be a very good seamstress; I liked to sew." A wistful look came over her face. "Tatiana loved that doll. She was so proud of it."

"She used to sit on the hearth and play with it for hours, didn't she?" she asked cautiously.

Maria nodded. "She pretended she was the mother, Maria, and the doll was the child, Tatiana. I used to laugh sometimes, because she would reprimand the doll with the same words I would speak to her."

Tatiana had forgotten that. She had to strain to hold back tears. "She was a naughty child sometimes, wasn't she?"

Suddenly Maria stiffened. "Oh, no," she said. "Not Tatiana. She never meant to be naughty; she always tried so hard to please. Gregor was the naughty one, but boys are always that way, aren't they?"

"Do you remember the flowers you and Tatiana planted in the back yard one spring?" Tatiana asked. "By the cook-house?"

Maria thought for a moment, her brow furrowed. Then, suddenly, as she recalled, she smiled. "Oh, I had forgotten," she said. "Tatiana thought she was planting daisies, but what came up were poppies. "Then she stared at Tatiana, puzzled. "But how did you know that?"

Tatiana felt herself beginning to tremble. She took a deep breath to calm herself, then reached over and took her mother's hand in hers. "Look into my eyes," she said softly. "Just my eyes, nothing more, and think about your Tatiana. Remember how long you have been here, eight years. Remember how old your Tatiana was when you last saw her."

Maria looked puzzled by what she was saying, but she did as she was told. She gazed into Tatiana's eyes.

"Try to recall where you've seen my eyes before," Tatiana said in little more than a whisper.

Maria stared. Her brow was furrowed, as she strained to recall.

Tatiana braced herself with a deep breath, knelt down on the floor before her mother's chair, then said in the most childlike voice she could manage, "Mama, can we have sweetcakes for dinner tonight?"

Suddenly, Maria's face turned pale, her mouth dropped open, her eyes widened and became misty. "Tatiana!" she said. "My little Tatiana!" Abruptly she broke into sobs. "You are my Tatiana!"

She reached down and grasped her daughter by the shoulders, pulling her up into an embrace, holding her tightly, as each broke into sobs.

When their happy tears were spent, they talked as mother and daughter. Tatiana told her all that had happened to her in the years, explaining about the Boustanis, and about how she had come to be in Russia. She could see that Maria was truly happy about her good fortune, and she was proud of all that her daughter had accomplished, though she did not understand how a young woman should want to become a doctor.

When they parted, Maria was content, and so was Tatiana.

Returning to the university that fall, for her last year of study, she was determined to work even harder to achieve her degree.

* * * * *

The collection of Nichola's paintings acquired by Nadia and Roscow for the exhibition at the Moscow Art Institute was a truly impressive one. Having known her professor's works only in his later years, Nadia had not realized the scope of his long career.

Once the exhibition opened, in the early spring of 1913, it was a similar realization for most of the artistic community of Moscow. Seen fragmented, one piece at a time, Nichola's talent was impressive; seen collected under one roof, it was overwhelming.

A center of much attention at the show was Nichola's last work—the "Portrait of the Czaretzas," considered by many to be his finest masterpiece.

After the weeks of the exhibition were over, and as they were preparing to dismantle it and return the paintings to their owners, Nadia and Roscow stood in front of the "Portrait of the Czaretzas" for a final look. Suddenly Roscow startled Nadia by saying, "What you have done is truly amazing."

"What do you mean?" Nadia asked. "If you're talking about the exhibition, we've done that together."

"I'm not talking about the exhibition," Roscow replied with a smile. "I'm talking about this painting. If the public only knew that Nichola did not paint it."

"You aren't making sense," she said harshly. "Of course he painted it."

Roscow shook his head sagely. "I know his work, and I know yours," he said. "Perhaps better than anyone else alive. And this is your work, from start to finish."

Nadia blushed. "Please," she said, "never say anything about this to anyone."

"I won't," he assured her. "Because I hope eventually you will return to your native style and far surpass anything of this sort."

"I don't think I could ever be better than Nichola," Nadia said.

"But you already are," Roscow told her.

Before Molinar returned to Paris, he and Nadia came to an agreement for the sale of Nichola's unsold works, with Nadia keeping only one painting—a portrait he had done of her, which she would treasure always. She did not feel that she could keep more. Not only were they too numerous for her to take back to Persia with her, but she felt it would be unfair to deprive the art world of them.

Again Roscow told her, "I would be much happier if I were taking you back to Paris with me than I am taking these paintings."

"I'm afraid you must be satisfied with the paintings," Nadia replied.

* * * * *

At the end of that spring of 1913, Tatiana received her medical degree, a major achievement for a woman, and especially for a Persian woman. She did not go on to the apprenticeship in medicine, which was the usual course in Russia, for she did not intend to practice there, but in her own country. She had come to Moscow only for the study, and with the completion of their education, it was finally time for her and Nadia to return home to Rasht. They had grown to love Moscow and the friends they had acquired there over the years, so it was with a mixture of sadness and happiness that they made the plans to leave.

They were mature young women now, so it was decided they would be able to travel alone, as long as they had the security of their own train compartment. Philip Boustani would not have to come to Moscow to accompany them.

The Komineks took the two girls to the train station to see them off. It was a tearful farewell, for they did not know if they would see each other again. It was most difficult for Vanitof; Nadia and Tatiana had been not only his sisters for the past few years, but his best friends as well.

The train station was crowded, bustling with activity, for it was now summer, the time when many Russians traveled. Vanitof and his parents helped them settle into their private compartment, giving them a basket of food to enjoy during their first few days of the journey. Vanitof had a parting gift for each of them. He had handwritten and handbound two books of stories, each quite different. The stories were his own, written secretly in his room.

Nadia and Tatiana had given him his gifts before leaving the Kominek house. Nadia's was a painting she had done of sunflowers, one he had particularly admired, and Tatiana's was a pair of opera glasses.

When the train conductor came through to advise guests that they were about to make their departure, Vanitof did not want to leave. Only when the steam began to billow outside the windows did he finally embrace each of his dear friends, with tears streaming down his cheeks, then scurry to get off.

Almost immediately, his face appeared at the window of their compartment, still weeping uncontrollably. Tatiana opened the window, and both girls stuck their heads out, each taking one of Vanitof's hands and squeezing it tightly.

"We will see each other again," Tatiana told him. "I know we will."

"I hope that's a promise," Vanitof said, straining to be heard over the sound of the train, which was now beginning to jolt into movement.

"It is," Nadia said. "We love you."

Vanitof did not let go of their hands, but as the train began to move slowly, steadily out of the station, he ran along the platform. He shouted, "And I love you! I love you both!"

Finally, the train was moving too fast and he had to let go, but he continued to stand on the platform, looking toward them until he was finally lost from sight.

Nadia and Tatiana settled into their compartment, saying little to each other, both absorbed in their thoughts of the sad parting. Eventually they picked up the books that Vanitof had made for them and read some of the stories, which they found revealed a fine talent.

Nadia and Tatiana recognized themselves as characters in many of the stories.

It was while they were traveling on the train, bound toward home, that Tatiana read one of the stories about a deformed boy who falls in love with a beautiful young medical student. Only then did she realize how deeply Vanitof had cared for her.

Chapter 22

For almost two years after Ahmad Mirza Shah ascended the throne, there was relative peace in Persia—though, truthfully, the only kind of peace that was possible was relative peace, so long as Russia and England remained determined to control the country.

Although Russian troops remained in Tabriz, they made no overt moves to control the new Shah and his regents. However, Russia and England continued to attempt to exert economic pressures to keep their spheres of influence, particularly related to the new oil business. In 1911, in an attempt to gain economic stability, the Shah and his representative government brought in an American financial advisor, a man named Morgan Shuster.

It remained a struggle for the fledgling government to survive against the two powers, but with Shuster's help it did gain strength.

With an elected parliament and a free press, there was no need for Gregor to continue publishing the *Voice of Freedom*. Mirza had been the impetus for his creating the newspaper, and it had not been intended as a commercial venture but as a temporary voice for change in the country. Now that its ends seemed to have been achieved, Gregor felt he had to look to more practical matters. He was now a man, and he must assume responsibilities.

He deemed it unwise to use his journalistic experience to seek a job on a newspaper, though that was what he really wanted to do. It might still be too risky to reveal the identity of "Baranov," so he went back to work for Rajik, tending the shop and keeping the financial accounts.

It was a time in Gregor's life that was uneventful and routine.

But by June of that year, Morgan Shuster's financial program for Persia began to show signs of overcoming the Russian and British efforts to bring the young Shah to his knees. Rumors spread that the two powers wanted to depose Ahmad Mirza and return Muhammed Ali to the throne, so that they could again have full control of the country.

This was confirmed in July, when the deposed Shah and the troops he had mustered in Russia landed at Astrabad to attempt to overthrow his son's regime. Divisions of Persian Cossacks were sent to meet them, and other divisions were mobilized in other parts of the country, preparing for extensive fighting.

One good thing came of this. Gregor was reunited with his old friend Kouroush, whose division was sent to protect Rasht.

Though they had rarely seen each other rarely in the last two years, Gregor and Kouroush had kept in contact. Kouroush did not let Gregor know that he would be in Rasht, but Gregor recognized the division that arrived there and was expecting his friend when he came to the shop.

Kouroush looked very impressive in his cossack uniform, very dashing and handsome, with his neatly trimmed mustache and strong jaw.

Their friendship was renewed, but on a different basis. The were no longer young boys; their youthful idealism had been tempered by pragmatism, and their lives had taken different courses. Yet they shared a common bond in these exciting days in Teheran.

It was not a particularly busy day in the shop, so Rajik insisted Gregor take time off to go to a teahouse with his friend. They had much to talk about and news to share about mutual friends and acquaintances.

In reviewing these friends, eventually Kouroush said guardedly, "You know, I have seen Sylvia Zinoviev on several occasions."

Gregor felt his heart leap at the mention of her name. The old feelings for her were still there. "How is she?" he asked.

Kouroush smiled. "As beautiful as ever," he said. "And she always asks about you." There was a long silence, then he offered, "As far as I know, there has been no one else since you left."

Gregor chose to change the subject. "Has there been any word of Mirza?" he asked. "Do you have any idea where he is?"

"There have been no reports of him in many months," Kouroush replied, "but he is still supposed to be in Baku."

Gregor offered, "I wrote to him several weeks ago to ask him to visit the Zoroastrian shrine to see if it is still tended, but I've had no reply from him."

"That's the shrine you visited as a child?" Kouroush asked. "The one you told me about, with the eternal flame?"

Gregor nodded. "It made a great impression on me. I've longed to go back, but of course there is no way I can now."

Eventually their talk turned to politics and the current situation. Kouroush was as filled with fire as he had been in his youth, though he now served the government rather than opposing it. "Morgan Shuster is doing great things," he told Gregor. "But the Russians and the British are very unhappy. This move by Muhammed Ali is certainly backed by the Russian government. If he doesn't succeed at retaking the government, there is every indication that the Russians will invade to overthrow Ahmad Mirza. Either way, there are difficult times ahead. All of our work may prove to be for nothing."

"That sounds very pessimistic," Gregor said.

"It's merely facing the truth," Kouroush told him sadly. "I wish we had Mirza here. There really ought to be something that could be done."

Kouroush shook his head. "The government is nothing without the people standing behind it. That's been evidenced in the past."

His words proved to be true. In September of 1911, Muhammed Ali was defeated and driven back by the Persian troops, and in December, Russia made its move, sending an invasion force to Persia. Within weeks, they had again forced the Majlis to be dissolved, to be replaced by a directorate of influential politicians who would do their bidding. Morgan Shuster was expelled, and the young Ahmad Mirza Shah unwillingly became a puppet of the Russians, just as his father had been.

The Persian Cossack Brigade was again under the indirect command of Russia, a fact that Kouroush was very unhappy about. His division remained stationed at Rasht, however, and he continued to see much of Gregor, with whom he confided his feelings. "There doesn't seem to be anything I can do about the situation," he told his friend. "It would be pointless to resign. As long as we are not used against the Persian people, I have no problem. But I could not kill a Persian to defend the Russian interests. Perhaps the time will come when the tide will again turn in our favor."

Yet, as always under the Russian domination, the Persian people suffered, taxed unmercifully to repay the debt that Russia claimed from the reign of Muhammed Ali Shah. For over a year, the people endured without complaint.

* * * * *

In the summer of 1913, something happened, however, that would change the lives of Gregor and Kouroush irrevocably.

When the invitation came, Gregor did not really want to attend the party.

It was being given by a business acquaintance of Rajik's, a wealthy Jewish merchant who was involved in the import and export of goods. Gregor had promised to go with Kouroush to Enzeli that evening, and he knew if he canceled, Kouroush, who had gotten leave from his division for the trip, would be faced with nothing to do.

"You know I wouldn't insist if it weren't important," Rajik told him. "But Philip Boustani is the most important importer of goods in Rasht. He also owns a great many rice farms. If there is any way you and Kouroush could postpone your plans, I would appreciate your accompanying us."

There was no way Gregor could refuse. "Of course I'll go," he said. "I just wish there were some way to avoid disappointing Kouroush." He was silent, pensive, for a few minutes. "Papa, is there some way Kouroush might be allowed to go with us?" he asked. "Would it be a terrible imposition?"

Rajik smiled. "I think it could probably be arranged," he said. "A young cossack officer is certainly acceptable in society, and the party is in honor of Boustani's daughters, who are returning from their schooling in Moscow. I understand they are just about the same ages as you and Kouroush."

When Gregor told Kouroush that he would have to cancel the plans for the trip, Kouroush was disappointed.

"But you're invited to the party, too," he said, trying to cheer up his friend. "It should be just as enjoyable as an evening in Enzeli."

"But I couldn't possibly go to the party," Kouroush protested. "I know of the Boustanis. They are Jewish. As a Moslem, I could not even enter their house."

Gregor frowned, surprised at Kouroush's reaction. "I don't think it will make a difference to the Boustanis," he said. "After all, they did invite you when Papa spoke to them. They were aware of who you are."

Kouroush looked annoyed. "It's not their religion that prevents it," he explained patiently. "It's mine. A Moslem is defiled by dining with a Jew. Even entering the home of a Jew is prohibited."

Gregor was astonished. "But I thought you were much more broad-minded than that," he protested. "I thought you believed as I do that all people are basically the same."

"I do," he said, "up to a point. I am still a Moslem, though. To my people, Jews are unclean."

"I can't believe you're saying what you're saying," Gregor told him, almost angrily. "You, of all people, my best friend, believing that superstitious nonsense."

"It's not nonsense!" Kouroush replied hotly. "I don't ridicule your religious beliefs!"

"I don't see why not," Gregor retorted, just as hotly. "Some of them are just as ridiculous as yours!"

"So you think I'm ridiculous!" Kouroush exploded.

"Right now you're being very ridiculous!" Gregor cut back just as angrily.

Kouroush stormed away without another word, leaving Gregor feeling not only angry but bewildered. This was the first serious fight he and his friend had ever had, and he did not feel he had been in the wrong. This was just a side of Kouroush he had never seen before. Or was it that his friend had changed in the last few years since he had been in the military?

About an hour later, Kouroush returned, looking rather embarrassed. "I must apologize to you," he told Gregor. "You are right; I am being ridiculous. We both believe in a new enlightened Persia, in which all Persians will be equal, whether Moslem, Christian, or Jew. The Boustanis are Persians, not Jews. I must get rid of some of the old ideas of my people. I will go to the party." He hesitated. "That is, if you still want me to go with you."

Gregor smiled. "Of course I still want you to go. We'll have a good time. Perhaps Boustani's daughters will be beautiful, who knows?

* * * * *

On the evening of the party, the air was unusually clear for July. Normally, it would be humid and overcast, if not actually raining in Rasht. But it was mild and pleasant, perfect weather for a party.

As the Sarkissians and Kouroush arrived at the front of the Boustani home in their carriage, Gregor stared at the house. It looked strangely familiar, with its columned portico and veranda extending on either side. He felt he had seen it before. Suddenly he remembered—he *had* seen it before, on the rainy night when he had gotten lost in Rasht, delivering papers for the Englishman.

This was the house where he had sought refuge from the rain.

He felt a degree of embarrassment in entering this house, though he was quite aware that there was no way the owner could recognize the boy from so many years ago; he would probably not even recall the incident.

It was a magnificent home, even more luxuriously furnished than the Sarkissians' and done in the European style. The guests were admitted to the house by an elderly manservant, who escorted them to a large front parlor, where he announced them to the host and hostess, and to the two daughters, who stood in a formal receiving line, following the European custom.

As Gregor and Kouroush were introduced, Gregor stared at the dark-haired daughter, the one named Nadia, and she stared back at him curiously. It was the face Gregor had seen in the room that night, the face that had seemed so entrancing. He still found it beautiful, setting his heart to racing. But she was not the one named Tatiana, as he had thought that night. Tatiana was fair, like his own sister had been.

Nadia extended her hand to Gregor, and he took it. At the moment of contact, there was a spark of electricity, and they both withdrew their hands abruptly, startled. Then they laughed. "It's the wool carpeting," Nadia explained. "It always does that."

Other guests were arriving behind them, so they did not linger, but as they mingled in the parlor with acquaintances, Gregor's eyes were drawn back to Nadia. Once or twice, he saw her glancing at him. But the other daughter, Tatiana, looked at him even more often.

There was something strangely familiar about her as well, but she had not been in the room that night.

A sense of unreality began to creep in and overtake him. Was it possible? Or was it merely that it was what had been in his mind that night? Surely this girl could not be his sister.

But she was just about the right age for Tatiana. And the hair, complexion, and eyes were similar to hers.

Still, he tried to tell himself, it was just his imagination playing tricks on him. He had given up looking for his sister years ago; he must not go back to that old obsession.

Kouroush noticed his glances toward the Boustanis and his distracted manner. "I agree," he said with a smile. "They certainly are beautiful."

"Yes," Gregor acknowledged. "They certainly are."

"The fair one seems especially nice," Kouroush pursued, but Gregor did not reply.

Gregor concentrated on mingling with the other guests, dismissing the disturbing idea that the girl might be his sister. Within a few minutes, all the guests had arrived, and the Boustanis and their daughters began to mingle as well. Nadia and Tatiana started across the room toward Gregor and Kouroush, pausing only momentarily to speak to one person or another.

Gregor, with Kouroush at his side, had just finished a brief conversation with a silk merchant whom he knew slightly, when he turned to find the two Boustani girls waiting to speak to him.

"You're the one named Gregor?" Nadia asked. "Gregor Sarkissian?"

"Yes," Gregor replied, somewhat puzzled. "And my friend's name is Kouroush. Kouroush Jalali."

"I know this may sound strange," Tatiana broke in, "but I have a brother named Gregor."

"Oh?" Gregor looked around. "Is he here? I thought your parents had only the two children. The two of you."

"They do," Nadia said quickly.

Tatiana blushed. "You see, I'm adopted," she explained. "What I mean is, I used to have a younger brother named Gregor . . . " She paused expectantly.

Gregor could hear his heart pounding in his ears. Again, the sense of unreality overcame him. Was he truly hearing this? Or was he hearing only what he wanted to hear?

"My real name," Tatiana continued, "my original name, was Tatiana Baranov or Mehdovi. I was born in Baku, and . . . "

"Tatiana!" Gregor heard himself exclaiming. "Is it you? Is it really you? My sister?"

"Yes," she said, breaking into a happy smile. "I kept looking at you, and you looked so much like my brother Gregor, and I kept asking myself if it was possible, and . . . " Tears began to roll down her cheeks. "You really are my Gregor, aren't you?"

Gregor did not answer the question. Instead, he threw his arms around his sister and hugged her to him tightly, as if to let her go would be to lose her again.

Kouroush stood staring at the two of them in astonishment.

Nadia rushed across the room excitedly to her parents, to tell them the incredible news.

The other guests fell silent, turning to look at Tatiana and Gregor, trying to understand what was happening.

They would break their embrace, then exclaim happily about their unbelievable joy at finding each other again, only to return to an embrace. The Boustanis and the Sarkissians gathered around them, delighted for their children. Philip and Rajik had known each other slightly through business for some years, but had never discussed their children.

"The most incredible thing," Gregor told them all, "is that I almost found Tatiana years ago—when I first came to Persia." He pointed to the front parlor window, open as it was on that night so long ago, and explained.

"I sought refuge from the rain, just outside that window one night, and I heard Tatiana's name called. I looked in and frightened Nadia, then ran away."

"That boy was you?" Philip asked. "The boy I ran after?"

Gregor laughed, then blushed. "Yes," he admitted. "I really meant no harm."

"If only you hadn't run away . . .," Philip mused.

"Yes," Tatiana broke in. "All our lives might have been so different."

Rajik Sarkissian nodded. "For one thing, Jeanous and I would not have had a son," he said. "In one way, I'm glad you didn't catch Gregor that night," he told Philip. "But I know that is rather selfish of me."

Gregor embraced his adopted father. "I understand," he said. "It has all come out for the best. You have a son; I have a father; and I have a sister again."

"Two sisters," Nadia broke in impulsively. "And I have a brother."

It was a joyful evening. Seating arrangements for dinner were changed so Tatiana and Gregor could sit next to each other and talk, and their conversation lasted long after dinner was over. They had so much to tell each other, so many years of being apart to share. After dinner, Nadia and Kouroush sat with them in a corner of the parlor, keeping them company and chatting idly, but mostly listening to the brother and sister getting reacquainted.

Both Gregor and Kouroush were fascinated by the Boustani home. Because of Philip's travels, the house was filled with items from other countries. They especially liked the western invention, the phonograph. Kouroush and Nadia played one phonograph record after another.

Gregor was pleased that Tatiana had seen their mother, but saddened to hear of Maria Baranov's condition. When Tatiana mentioned the suspicion that their father might be alive, Gregor assured her it was not true. However, he did not tell her the true identity of the "Baranov" who published the *Voice of Freedom*; he did not tell her of any of his revolutionary activities. He was troubled though to hear that this was used as a reason to keep their mother imprisoned.

He was astonished to learn about her education in Moscow. He would never have expected his shy big sister would have an interest in medicine.

Each was delighted that the other had found a new family. Their reunion as adults would not alter the new lives they had found for themselves, but would help to reinforce them.

PART III

SPARKS—1913 to 1916

Chapter 23

Gregor and Tatiana saw much of each other in the months that followed. In fact, the four of them—Nadia, Kouroush, Tatiana, and Gregor—spent almost all their free time together. Most often, the evenings would be spent at the Boustani home, listening to records on the phonograph, with the girls trying to teach the boys to dance the way people did in Moscow.

In the beginning, Kouroush was reluctant to learn. Dancing in public with a woman was entirely new to him, but after chiding from Gregor and cajoling from Nadia and Tatiana, he gave in.

When they paired off for these dance lessons, it would usually be Kouroush with Tatiana and Gregor with Nadia.

Occasionally, Nadia and Tatiana would come to the Sarkissian home for an evening, and Kouroush would inevitably join them, if he could be freed from his regiment.

These evenings were happy times; they gave meaning to the days of work; they helped Gregor and Kouroush forget the problems of their world, problems that were growing more severe, as the Russian abuses increased.

When their days were free, they would go for rides in the country or take picnic baskets to the beach, when it was warm enough taking a swim in the Caspian's water.

Their times together were relatively uneventful, filled with the quiet happenings and gentle discoveries of getting to know each other—and of falling in love.

Kouroush was the first to recognize what was happening, though he and Tatiana had exchanged no words of love and he had made no physical overtures of his affection. There would be none of that, he knew; it would create too many problems. Marriage between a Moslem boy and a Jewish girl would never be possible. This happiness had to end before it went too far.

One evening early in September, Kouroush came very close to

overstepping the bounds he had set for himself. They had been listening to records and dancing in the Boustani parlor, and afterward he and Tatiana had gone for a walk in the garden. The balmy night air, the soft moonlight, and the fragance of roses had been too much for the two of them. For a few moments, Kouroush believed that this peace and tranquility was representative of reality and that love could conquer all opposition.

They sat down on the edge of the small fountain that fed a pool containing goldfish. Gazing down into the dark water and listening to the splash from the fountain, Kouroush was overcome by the joy of Tatiana's company. He reached out and took her hand and lifted it gently to his lips, kissing her fingertips softly; and then he said, "Do you know, these weeks with you habe been the happiest of my life?"

Tatiana smiled at him and replied, "They have been a very happy time for me as well."

At that moment, Kouroush wanted to sweep her into his arms, and it took all his effort to keep from doing so.

That night, while walking home with Gregor, he suddenly announced to his friend, "I must not go back to the Boustanis with you any more."

"Why?" Gregor asked. "Is something wrong?"

"Yes," Kouroush told him. "I have fallen in love with your sister."

"That's wonderful!" Gregor exclaimed. Then he looked puzzled. "But I would think that would make you want to go back even more often." He could not conceive of a better match for his sister than his best friend.

"It can't be," Kouroush said. "The difference in our religions is too great an obstacle."

"Is she in love with you?" Gregor asked.

"I don't know," his friend replied. "And it's better that I not know. If she does love me, it would make it even more painful than it is."

* * * * *

While Kouroush was telling Gregor about Tatiana, she was talking to Nadia about him, telling her about what had happened in the garden. They were sitting in their room upstairs, getting ready for bed and sharing the events of the day as was their custom.

"Are you in love with him?" Nadia asked excitedly.

"I don't know," Tatiana replied. "I think so. At least I've never felt this way about a man before."

"Well, tell me about it," Nadia said eagerly. "What do you feel?"

Tatiana was flustered. "It's a little scary," she said. "When he's around, I feel all warm inside. I want to be near him; I want him to touch me. When he's not around, I can't wait until I see him again."

Nadia grinned. "You're in love," she said flatly. "You've got all of the signs."

"But I mustn't be in love," Tatiana said, sitting down on the bed wearily. "I don't want to be in love. I have so much I have to do. Falling in love wasn't in my plans for a long time."

Nadia shrugged. "That's not the sort of thing you can plan for."

"What can I do?" Tatiana asked pleadingly.

"Well," Nadia replied, "you certainly can't think of marrying him. After all, he's a Moslem."

Tatiana looked at her sister strangely. "I hadn't thought of that."

"I have," Nadia said with a sigh. "Because, you see, I think I'm falling in love, too."

"You are?" Tatiana asked brightly. "With whom?"

Nadia laughed. "You must be in love not to have seen it," she said. "With your brother, of course."

"That's wonderful!" Tatiana exclaimed.

Nadia smiled sadly. "No, it's not," she said. "It's just as impossible for me to think of marrying Gregor as it is for you to think of marrying Kouroush. We are of different race and religion."

Tatiana looked confused. "But he's my brother."

Nadia laughed again. "If we look at it that way," she said, "he would have to be my brother too, and I still couldnt think of marrying him. In fact, that would be even worse."

"Then, what can we do?" Tatiana asked. Her expression suddenly became downcast. "Do you think we should stop seeing them?"

"We probably should," Nadia admitted. "But I don't really want to."

Tatiana grinned. "Neither do I."

* * * * *

The next time Gregor went to visit Nadia and Tatiana, Kouroush did not go with him. Nor did he go the time after that. Gregor made excuses for him, telling the sisters that his friend could not get away from his barracks. He sensed that Tatiana did not believe him, and he could see that she was disappointed.

The evenings were not as enjoyable without Kouroush. They played records on the phonograph, but they did not dance. They talked, but it was not Gregor talking to Nadia, but to Tatiana and Nadia. He was restrained, and so were they. A spark was missing. As a result, Gregor went home early.

The following week, he managed to persuade Kouroush to accompany him again, and the laughter and joy returned. Kouroush spent most of his time with Tatiana, as before, and Gregor talked to Nadia and danced with her. That was much more satisfying to him.

Was it possible that he was falling in love with her? He tried to convince himself that he was not; he merely enjoyed her company, like a brother and sister. But when he held her in his arms to dance, he felt something special, something that was not what a brother feels for a sister.

If it was not precisely the same, it was at least very similar to what he had felt for Sylvia Zinoviev.

That evening, it was very late when Gregor and Kouroush left the Boustani home for the walk across town. It was a dark moonless night, and it was foggy. The city was quiet, and there were few people on the streets. The autumn air was chilly.

They always took the same route home, before they came to the parting of the ways, Gregor to the Sarkissian home and Kouroush to his barracks, a short-cut through a rather poor neighborhood with warehouses and livestock storage areas, which generally saved them a good ten minutes. This night they did not talk much, but walked quickly, wrapped in their own individual thoughts,.

They were passing through the poor neighborhood, on a particularly deserted block, between two warehouses, when suddenly a man stepped out of an alleyway and confronted them. He stood facing them, his hands on his hips, about four yards away, waiting for them to approach. They could not see his face, but his manner and dress did not resemble anyone they knew. He seemed to be a few years older than they, and considerably larger and more muscular. He wore a long dark coat over trousers, and he wore a large woolen cap. They could see enough of his face to tell that he was clean shaven except for a mustache.

Reflexively, Gregor and Kouroush stopped for a moment, then moved out into the street as if to pass the stranger with plenty of room.

"Wait," the man called out to them in a loud whisper. "There's no reason to fear me."

The two young men hesitated, glanced at each other cautiously, then waited for the stranger to approach them.

"You don't recognize me," the man said smiling. "I thought if anyone would know me, you two would."

There was something familiar about the man's voice, but Gregor could not recognize the appearance. His instincts told him the voice did not belong to this man but to someone he should recognize.

The man laughed. "If I can fool you, I suppose I shouldn't worry about the authorities recognizing me."

Gregor recognized that laugh. "Mirza?" he asked. "Is it you?"

"It can't be!" Kouroush exclaimed. "You're supposed to be in Baku!"

"That's where I'm supposed to be," Mirza told them. "And that's why I've had to change my appearance."

Gregor and Kouroush happily embraced their old friend.

"How did you happen to be here at this time of night?" Kouroush asked.

"I was waiting for you," Mirza explained. "I've been wanting to see you two for several weeks, but I'm also trying to keep my presence here a secret. When I learned about your visits to the young ladies, this seemed the best way." He began to guide his friends down the street. "But we mustn't stand here talking," he said. "Let's go where we won't be seen or overheard."

Mirza took them to the place he was staying, an unused warehouse in which a corner had been sectioned off to make a fairly comfortable living area with a bed, a desk, a kerosene lamp, and a few chairs. There were two men waiting for them there, new friends of Mirza's. One was a doctor named Heshmat, and the other a revolutionary whom Gregor and Kouroush had heard of, but never met, named Ahmed Kasmayi.

To their surprise, there was also a beautiful young woman as well. Mirza introduced her to them as Zahra. The most amazing thing about her was that she did not wear the traditional robes and chador, though she was clearly a Moslem. Instead she wore western dress and was obviously well educated for a Persian woman.

As the three old friends talked, Zahra served tea, which she had made on a small burner. Heshmat and Kasmayi did little but listen.

Mirza explained that he had returned in order to begin to plan the revolution to push the Russians out of Persia, once and for all. He had removed the beard and the robes of the mullah in the hope that the authorities would not recognize him by appearance, though he fully intended to continue using his own name. After telling them this, he grinned at Kouroush and said, "I trust that you will not betray me to your superiors now that you are a cossack."

Kouroush was embarrassed. "Of course I would not betray you," he said.

"You are my friend. This uniform is merely a temporary compromise."

Mirza studied him, "Then, when the time comes," he said, "you will have no objection to removing the uniform and joining forces with me again?"

Kouroush smiled. "I am willing to remove it now," he said.

"Keep wearing it a little longer," Mirza said, then turned to Gregor. "And you? Are your journalistic ambitions gone completely?"

"No," Gregor replied seriously. "I have all the equipment stored away. It wouldn't take long to put the *Voice of Freedom* into print again."

Mirza shook his head. "Not the *Voice of Freedom*," he said. "We will want a different name. This time we will call it *Jangal*."

Gregor gave him a puzzled look. "That's a strange name," he said. "What does freedom have to do with a 'jungle'?"

Mirza smiled. "You will soon find out," he said. "I have already begun to organize forces with an encampment in the Elburz mountains. We can hide in the forests there forever if necessary. And we are calling ourselves *jangali*."

Kouroush frowned. "You are already training forces?"

Mirza did not realize how deeply Kouroush had been hurt by this, but Gregor understood. Mirza had made other friends during the past five years. Two of them were sitting silently in this room, listening to all they were saying. After the closeness they had enjoyed before, Kouroush was jealous of his position in Mirza's revolution. He wanted everything to be as it was before.

Mirza explained that he had made connections among Russian socialists who were planning a revolution in their own country. He had also contacted several leaders in the German government who were interested in helping rid Persia of Russian influence. They were willing to send military advisors to help train the rebel troops.

There was also much talk of a war in Europe, a war that Russia could not help but become involved in. If it should occur, the Persian people could take advantage of the situation to make a strike for freedom.

Gregor, in his excitement, was ready to take on his responsibilities immediately. However, he knew that Kouroush was reluctant. Mirza had not yet told him what his place in the new organization would be. He was growing more and more agitated as the evening progressed, for it had become clear that Kasmayi had taken the place he wanted as the close military aide to Mirza. Finally, he could stand it no longer.

He asked Mirza anxiously, "And what am I do do in the movement?

What responsibility do I have?"

Mirza finally caught the resentment in his old friend's voice. He studied Kouroush a moment. "I'm sorry I did not tell you," he said. "I was just too overcome by the joy of seeing you again. You have a very special place. You are the only one who can keep us informed of what is happening in the government and the military. We need you to keep watch and guard us from discovery until we are ready. Then you can take off your uniform and take command of one of our divisions."

"You want me to be a spy, then?" Kouroush said hotly.

Mirza realized he had offended his friend even further, but he tried to assuage the hurt. "There is no dishonor in what I ask," he said. "It is extremely important to us. It is for the ultimate good of our country and our people."

"I don't think I can do it," Kouroush told him angrily. "I want to fight for Persia; I do not want to lie and cheat and steal."

"It is not yet time to fight," Mirza said pleadingly.

"Then I am not yet ready to join you," Kouroush replied.

Mirza was disappointed. "I trust you will not betray us," he said.

"Of course I won't," Kouroush assured him.

*   *   *   *   *

Gregor arranged to meet with Mirza often in the weeks that followed, both at the warehouse and at his encampment in the Elburz mountains. At this point, relatively few volunteers had moved to the location, which was known as the Valley of the Trees, but those who had were considered among the core group of leaders. They were preparing a settlement for large numbers. Doctor Heshmat had begun to set up a medical cinic to take care of the volunteers and their families, and there were already numerous tents and small structures erected to house the people.

Gregor would have the newspaper printed in the city, but they had plans for eventually doing everything at the encampment.

As far as Mirza knew, the authorities were not aware of his return, nor of the *jangali* encampment, but he was sure it was only a matter of time before they learned of what was happening. However, he hoped they would never be able to find the exact location.

Things moved slowly but deliberately, with each person following his assigned tasks, maintaining secrecy so that—when the time came—the *jangali* could spring forth fully formed as a powerful movement.

Gregor's involvement with Mirza's plans did not cause an outright rift between him and Kouroush, but it did create a degree of strain. Koruoush refused to talk to him about his activities and about Mirza, and that lack of openness made them less close than they had been.

They continued to vist Nadia and Tatiana, but they did not always go together. Sometimes Kouroush would visit them alone, while Gregor was with Mirza; and at other times Gregor would go when Kouroush was unable to leave his barracks.

*   *   *   *   *

Nadia and Tatiana were aware that something had changed with Gregor and Kouroush, but they were not sure what it was. They assumed the difference in manner was in some way connected with them. The most logical explanation for their new reserve was that the two young men were concerned about the religious differences, as aware of the difficulties they faced as they were. Yet they had never dared bring up the subject, for fear it would put an end to their enjoyable times together.

They each had their own concerns during this time. To pursue her painting, Nadia had to have a studio to work in, and the ideal place was an unused part of the carriage house behind the Boustani home. However, it needed considerable renovation to open up the space and to create a skylight on the north side. It took the workmen several months to do all the work to her satisfaction.

It was also difficult to establish herself as a portrait artist in Rasht. Other than a few wealthy merchant friends of her father's, there were no people coming to her with commissions. Most of her time was spent in doing paintings for her own pleasure, a step down for her after the professional status she had enjoyed in Moscow.

Tatiana faced even greater problems. While the medical establishment in Moscow had looked on a woman doctor with skepticism, the hospital administrators in Rasht viewed her with outright prejudice and hostility. She had hoped her medical degree would automatically assure her a post on the hospital staff. Though they were greatly in need of doctors, the director of the hospital continually made excuses for not hiring her, the most serious one being the lack of sufficient budget. Yet, even when Tatiana offered her services without payment until funds were available, the doctor turned her down, finally admitting the truth. "I'm afraid none of our patients would want to be treated by a woman," he told her.

Despondently, Tatiana realized that the only way she would be able to practice medicine in Rasht would be to set up her own clinic. But that would be costly, if she did not have paying patients, and she feared that she would face the same prejudice from the people, no matter how poor they might be.

Finally, with Philip Boustani's help, she found employment as a nurse for the family doctor. It was not what she wanted, but at least she could use some of her training.

Chapter 24

In August of 1914, war broke out in Europe. The Russians and the British had to concentrate all their efforts in opposing Germany. They would, of course, have to maintain their power in Persia, for they were greatly dependent upon the oil supplies the country provided.

It was as Mirza had expected and hoped, but it had come too soon; he was not yet ready to make his move. However, it provided the impetus for him to press forward more quickly with his plans. And it also made it more urgent for his allies to offer him promised aid. Because of the war, he found natural allies in the Germans and the Turks, who were fighting the Russians and British. The military advisor from Germany, Colonel von Passchen, arrived that fall, along with Lieutenant Ernst Kaouk, from Austria, and Mirza began negotiating with Turkey for the purchase of arms, through their emmissary Effendi.

Gregor was ready to begin printing the newspaper, but Mirza held him back. He was not yet prepared to let the authorities know that he was in Persia.

However, with the increased activities, it was inevitable that they would earn of his presence and of his plans.

The first indication that the Cossacks knew anything came in February of 1915, when Pasha Jalali made a sudden visit to Rasht. Kouroush was sure that his father had not come just to visit with him; there was no affection between the two of them. When his father invited Kouroush to dinner, he was suspicious.

He did not, however, think it had anything to do with Mirza; he assumed rather that the incessant questions were connected to his interest in a Jewish girl.

Pasha began subtly, asking simply, "What have you been up to here in Rasht?"

Kouroush was guarded. "Not much," he replied. "There isn't as much to do in Rasht as there is in Tehran."

Pasha smiled, obviously trying to make himself seem friendly, but Kouroush recognized that there was nothing pleasant behind his effort. "I'm sure a young man like you can find plenty of trouble to get into," he said. "Even in a place like Rasht."

"What do you mean?" Kouroush asked, his temper beginning to rise.

The anger made his father uncomfortable. "Well," he hesitated, "how do you spend your evenings?"

"If you don't like the fact that I'm seeing a Jewish girl," Kouroush snapped suddenly, "why don't you just say so? Why do you have to go in circles around a subject?"

Pasha was startled. "You're seeing a Jewish girl?" he asked. "Do you mean you're serious about her?"

"Yes," he retorted hotly. "I'm in love with her!"

Pasha was still astonished, still assimilating the information. "Do you intend to marry her?" He was clearly shocked by the idea.

"That's my business!" Kouroush said furiously. "I'm a man now, an adult, and I'm capable of knowing the consequences of my actions!"

"I never said you weren't," Pasha stammered. "But a Jewish girl? I'm surprised you would even see one!"

Kouroush rose abruptly from the table. "I've eaten with her," he said curtly. "I've even kissed her. I suppose you think that makes me unclean! Perhaps you don't want to dine with me! Perhaps I should go!"

"Sit down, boy," Pasha said cajolingly. "This has just come as a shock to me. If you're an adult, sit down and talk like one. Finish eating your food."

"It's impossible to talk to you in an adult manner," Kouroush said. "With you, a conversation is an interrogation, nothing more than questions and answers."

"Have I asked any questions about this girl?" Pasha inquired.

Kouroush had to admit that he had not. In fact, he was surprised that his father was not more upset than he was. It was only then that he realized that Pasha had begun to question him for some other reason—and the only reason it could be was Mirza.

He sat back down and continued the meal, but he became even more guarded. He told his father about Tatiana, and he even confessed that he was in conflict about what he should do, admitting that he knew marriage was impossible, but that he could not deny his feelings.

To his surprise, his father was sympathetic, telling him, "It is a problem, and I don't know what advice to give you." The only criticism he offered was, "The mistake, of course, was in meeting her in the first place. You knew better than to have entered a Jewish home."

Pasha seemed impatient to change the subject, to ask about any other friends Kouroush might have seen. At that point, Kouroush became certain that he was trying to learn about Mirza.

The following morning, Kouroush was summoned before his commanding officer, Sergeant Reza Khan. When he entered the sergeant's office, he was not suprised to find his father there with Reza Khan. And he knew why he had been called.

His father was of the same rank as Reza Khan, but there was a considerable difference between the two men. Kouroush had a great deal of respect for his sergeant; Reza Khan was a fair man, an ethical man, unlike his father, who would do anything for his own security or advancement, and who did not really care what master he served.

Kouroush stood at attention and saluted. Reza Khan instructed him to stand at ease, then studied him a moment before beginning. "The government is interested in gaining information about a man name Mirza Kuchik," he began slowly. "According to Sergeant Jalili, you know this man. Is that true?"

"Yes sir," Kouroush replied. "I knew him over five years ago in Tehran."

"He was your friend," Reza Khan asked, "is that correct?"

"Yes sir," Kouroush replied.

"Have you seen him since that time?" the sergeant asked.

Kouroush did not hesitate. He did not want to betray the lie. "No sir," he said. "He has been in exile since that time. In Azerbaijan, to the best of my knowledge."

Reza Khan smiled. It was not an unfriendly smile. "He was in Azerbaijan until very recently," he said. "We have reason to believe he is now in Rasht. You have not seen him here or in the vicinty of Rasht?"

"No sir," Kouroush answered. "I was not aware that he was here." He hesitated. "Until you informed me."

Kouroush could see that his father was growing impatient with Reza Khan's gentle line of questioning. Now, Pasha Jalali broke in to ask a question. "Doesn't it seem strange that your good friend would be in the same city with you and not contact you?" he asked curtly.

"No sir," Kouroush answered, with a trace of anger in his voice. "Not under the circumstances. As a cossack, I am now his enemy."

"You admit then that he is a revolutionary?" Reza Khan asked.

"I admit that he is interested in restoring Persia to the Persians," Kouroush said stiffly. Then he added, "Or, at least he was when I knew him."

Reza Khan smiled. Something about the sergeant's manner made Kouroush think he knew the truth and that he did not entirely disapprove.

"He's the worst kind of revolutionary," Pasha Jalali interjected angrily. "He wants power for himself! Whether it's for the good of the country or not!"

Before Kouroush could reply to this, Reza Khan broke in calmly. "His politics are not at issue at the moment. We merely want to locate him for questioning. Obviously Private Jalali will not be able to help us."

"The boy knows where he is!" Pasha blustered irritably. "I would swear to it! I know my son, and I know when he's lying!"

"A cossack does not lie," Reza Khan said evenly. "And without proof, a cossack officer should not accuse a fellow cossack of lying."

Rebuffed, Pasha said nothing.

Reza Khan continued, turning back to Kouroush. "You have a friend named Gregor Sarkissian, who was also a friend to Mirza's?"

"Yes sir," Kouroush replied, growing tense. He hoped they would not bring Gregor in to interrogate him. "But I don't believe he has seen Mirza. He would have told me if he had."

"Can you be sure of that?" the sergeant asked.

"Yes sir," Kouroush answered. There was only a moment's hesitation, but a moment was long enough for Reza Khan to notice. "I am as sure of Gregor as I am of myself."

Reza Khan smiled. "That is as it should be between friends," he said. He paused pensively for a moment, then asked, "Do you know of anyone else in Rasht who might have seen Mirza?"

"No sir," Kouroush replied automatically. "We had no other mutual friends."

"Then I think that's all," Reza Khan said.

Pasha was outraged. "You're not going to let him get away with this, are you?" he demanded angrily. "He knows where the man is. Leave me alone with him for five minutes, and I'll get it out of him!"

Reza Khan remained calm. "I have asked the questions," he said, "and he has answered them. We can do no more."

"Well, I certainly could!" Pasha exploded. "Just turn him over to me!"

"I am his commanding officer," Reza Khan replied calmly. "And I am satisfied with his answers."

"I am his father, and I'm not satisfied!" Pasha shouted.

Reza Khan studied Pasha for a moment, then said, "Sergeant Jalali, would you leave the office for a moment. I would like to speak to Private Jalali alone."

Pasha started to protest, but realized it would do no good. He stormed out of the office.

Once he was gone, Reza Khan looked at Kouroush and smiled. "It is difficult being a father," he said kindly. "Sometimes as difficult as being a son."

Kouroush laughed, then caught himself. "Yes sir," he said, trying to maintain military dignity.

"I do not wish to suggest that you have not told the truth," Reza Khan said seriously. "There must be honor among cossacks as there must be among friends and among good Persians. Unfortunately, sometimes a man's loyalties may come into conflict, however, and he may be unsure where true honor lies. If that is the case with you, then you must decide for yourself. But you must realize that the Persian Cossack Brigade and the Persian government strive to serve the Persian people."

Kouroush hesitated, then asked, "May I speak freely, sir?"

"Yes, you may," Reza Khan replied.

"Sometimes," he said cautiously, "because of the intervention of imperialist powers, the Persian government has no choice but to act against its own people."

"I understand that," Reza Khan replied. "All good Persians want Persia to be free and independent of imperialist powers, but that is not practical at the moment. Under these circumstances, a good Persian has to search his own conscience and decide how best he can serve his people. Your friend Mirza may be serving in his own way, just as you and I and your father are serving in ours. Ultimately we all want the same thing."

"I understand, sir," Kouroush replied. He truly did understand, and he admired his commanding officer even more than he had before.

"If you have anything to tell me," Reza Khan added, "you may come to me at any time." Then he rose from his desk and said "You may go now."

* * * * *

Kouroush was sure that his sergeant had not intended him to interpret his words as he had, but they had made him recognize the course he must take. He saw truly, as he had not seen before, what he must do, no matter the consequences.

He returned to his barracks and packed his belongings, saying nothing to anyone. Then he went to the bazaar to find Gregor.

When Gregor learned what Kouroush intended, he was very worried. "Of course you know what will happen if you're caught," he said. "You'll be shot as a deserter, if not hanged as a traitor."

"I know what I'm doing," Kouroush, assured him. "I realize my life will be in danger even if I enter the city again. But it is what I must do. And, once it's done, even Mirza cannot stop me."

"Well," Gregor sighed, "if your mind is made up, I'll take you to him."

"First I want to remove my uniform," Kouroush said. "May I change clothes in the back room?"

Gregor nodded. "Go ahead," he said, "while I speak to Rajik about getting the rest of the day off."

They had to travel by horse to reach the Valley of the Trees, taking the road southeast from Rasht toward Tehran, but cutting off the road after a couple of hours to take a goat path up into the mountains. It was well past sundown when they arrived at Mirza's encampment.

Mirza was surprised to see Kouroush with Gregor. He wondered why Kouroush was not wearing his uniform, but assumed that he had removed it temporarily so as to avoid attracting attention coming into the mountain hideout.

There was a tension between Kouroush and Mirza, each expecting the other to say something. It was Kouroush who spoke first. "I have come to join you," he said, his voice trembling, "on whatever terms you wish. The only exception is that I cannot return to the cossacks or to Rasht, for I am now a deserter."

Mirza smiled warmly and moved to Kouroush to embrace him. "You are welcome," he said, "on whatever terms you wish to come."

After they broke from the embrace, Kouroush told him, "I have brought you the news you have been waiting for. They now know you are in Persia, somewhere in the vicinity of Rasht, and they suspect that Gregor and I have been in touch with you."

"I see," Mirza said pensively. "They have questioned you?"

Kouroush nodded. "My father was sent from Tehran," he said. "He and Reza Khan conducted the interrogation."

"And you told them nothing?" Mirza stated.

"I denied that I had seen you," he replied, "but they were sure I was lying." He paused, then added, "I felt the only thing I could do was to leave Rasht and join you. Otherwise I would be watched, and I would be useless to you as a spy."

Mirza nodded in understanding. "You did the right thing," he said. "But we must now all be guarded. Especially Gregor, for he may be followed, and he must remain in the city for a while."

Until this moment, Gregor had not even thought of the danger to himself as a result of Kouroush's decision. There might even be trouble for those close to him—for Rajik and Jeanous, and perhaps Tatiana and Nadia as well. At this point, it could not be helped.

Mirza invited Kouroush and Gregor into his tent, and they sat and discussed plans for their next moves. They talked far into the night.

"There is no point in postponing printing the newspaper now," Mirza told Gregor. "How quickly can you get the first issue out?"

"Whenever you want it," Gregor told him. "It's ready for the printer now. We can have it within a few days."

"Two weeks will be soon enough," Mirza said. "Or three."

"I will need help on distribution," Gregor said. "Some volunteers to take copies to the provinces."

Mirza nodded. "You'll have them." Then he turned to Kouroush. "Eventually you will be commanding a division of the militia," he said. "But at this point there aren't enough volunteers. Right now, I will want you on my personal staff to be in charge of tactics. You know better than anyone the way our opposition thinks. You will be invaluable in advising us how, when, and where they would be most likely to strike."

Kouroush smiled happily. "Whatever you wish," he said.

"Tomorrow I will introduce you to von Passchen," Mirza said cautiously. "He is the advisor from Germany, and I think you will like him and his associate, Liuetenant Kaouk." He paused. "It is important that you get along with them. The German aid is critical to our success."

"Don't worry," Kouroush assured him. "I am committed to the cause, not to my own ambition." He hesitated a moment, then said softly. "I am sorry I allowed my personal feelings to come between us. I was wrong."

Mirza smiled warmly. "We are all human," he said. "It is best to leave mistakes in the past."

*   *   *   *   *

The following morning, before Gregor left to return to Rasht, he and Kouroush took a walk in the forest. There was one matter that had been left unsettled, and Kouroush wanted to talk to Gregor about it.

"Under the circumstancs," he told Gregor, "it is best that I not see Tatiana again." He handed Gregor a letter in a sealed envelope. "I would appreciate it if you would take this to her. It is my farewell."

Gregor took the envelope and looked at it sadly. "I understand," he said. "Did you tell her the reason?"

"I did not tell her specifically what I'm doing," Kouroush said. "I said only that I was leaving to pursue a matter of conscience."

Gregor frowned in contemplation. "I'm sure she will want to know the specifics."

Kouroush nodded. "Tell her whatever you think is best," he said. "I don't want her to feel that it's her fault, but at the same time it is better that we end our friendship now. In the long run, it will be less painful for both of us."

*   *   *   *   *

Tatiana realized something had happened the moment she saw Gregor's face. He came into the Boustani parlor in his usual manner, with a smile of greeting; and it was no longer surprising that he came alone. But there was something in his eyes—a sadness, an apprehension, something different—that told Tatiana to expect upsetting news. Perhaps it was that he greeted her before he greeted Nadia, as had become his custom.

"Where is Kouroush?" she asked anxiously. "Something has happened to him, hasn't it?"

Gregor looked at his sister in astonishment. "He has made a decision," he acknowledged, "and has sent you a letter." He reached into his pocket and pulled out the envelope, then handed it to Tatiana somewhat reluctantly.

Her heart pounding, Tatiana ripped open the envelope and unfolded the single sheet of paper. "Dearest Tatiana," she read, "I am leaving the Cossack Brigade and leaving Rasht. I cannot give you the reason for my decision, but it has nothing to do with you. It is a matter of conscience. It will be impossible for me to return to Rasht, so I will not be able to see you again. I will miss you, as I know you will miss me. But parting now is for the best. I have grown to love you too much to want to cause you pain, and that would have been inevitable if I had continued to see you." It was signed simply "Kouroush."

Tatiana could not hold back tears. She turned to Gregor. "Why has he done this?" she demanded. "Where is he?"

He looked at her with a mixture of sadness and embarrassment. "It is better that you not know," he told her.

"Why?" she asked angrily. "Am I a child?"

"No," Gregor admitted. "It has nothing to do with . . ." He stammered in frustration. "It would be dangerous for you to know."

"That means it's political," she said. "It *is* political, isn't it? Just like our father?"

Gregor was astonished that she had guessed so accurately. He stared at her, not knowing how to respond, not wanting to lie to her but unable to tell her the truth.

"It is," she said. "I can see it in your eyes." Her heart tightened in anguish. She turned away to hide the pain she knew would show in her face. "Why is it that every man I care about must have a passion for politics? Is it some sort of curse I carry around with me?"

Nadia came to her to embrace her, to try to comfort her. "It has nothing to do with you," she said softly. "Gregor said it was his own decision."

Gregor moved toward them. "It is something that began long before he ever met you," he told Tatiana. "Years ago."

Tatiana turned on him accusingly. "You're involved in it too, aren't you?"

Gregor hesitated. Then he nodded. "Yes," he admitted, "but I must remain in Rasht, at least for a time." He looked at Nadia and saw a sudden flash of despair before she looked away from him.

Tatiana's anger returned. "Where is he?" she demanded. "I must go to see him."

"I can't tell you," Gregor said. "It's too far for you to travel."

"Don't be ridiculous," Tatiana told him cuttingly. "It can't be further than Siberia, and I've been there! How long would it take? Days? Weeks?"

"No," Gregor admitted. "Less than a day . . . Each way. But you would have to travel horseback."

"That doesn't matter to me," she said defiantly. "I ride very well."

Gregor heaved a sigh of exasperation. He looked at Nadia and then back to Tatiana, trying to decide how much to tell them. "You don't realize how dangerous this is," he said. "We are all sworn to absolute secrecy. It is far more serious than what our father was involved in."

Tatiana turned pale. She sat down suddenly on the sofa.

"Then it's revolution," she said softly.

Gregor sat down beside her. Nadia seated herself in a chair facing them, fear written in her face as well. "Yes," Gregor told her. "We will begin our moves in the next few months." Tatiana looked into his eyes accusingly. "The Baranov who published the newspaper?" she asked. "The one they thought was our father, that was you, wasn't it?"

Gregor sighed painfully. "Yes, it was. It still is. We will be printing again in a few weeks."

Tatiana rose to her feet, walked over to gaze out the window at the darkening street. "Life is too short to spend so much time in pain and suffering," she said. "I am in love with Kouroush. He is my happiness. I can know no other. I thought for a time I could be happy by helping people through medicine, but that, too, has been taken from me."

She turned decisively to face Gregor. "War and revolution have always been the business of men," she said strongly. "But times are changing. If you and Kouroush can dedicate yourselves to this, so can I. You are going to take me to him. I will not accept any arguments. I have made my decision, just as he has. The only way I can be persuaded not to join him is for him to tell me he does not want me at his side."

* * * * *

It was difficult persuading Philip Boustani to allow Tatiana and Nadia to leave the city with Gregor, especially since they would not tell him where they were going, except that it was to see Kouroush. It was Nadia's entreaties that finally convinced him it would be all right, for she assured their father that she would not allow anything to happen that could not take place in their own home.

The three of them left before dawn on horseback. It was a damp chilly spring morning, with the fog surrounding them like a shroud. They did not speak more than was absolutely necessary, all intent upon their own thoughts.

By midday they were traveling under sunny, blue skies, and they stopped beside a mountain stream to have their picnic. For a brief time, they felt like nothing more than three good friends on a holiday outing, laughing and joking, as if nothing serious could ever threaten them.

They arrived at the Valley of the Trees in the afternoon. When they passed the sentry on duty, the guard was skeptical of Tatiana and Nadia, even though Gregor gave the correct signal and password. As they entered the encampment, people stared curiously at the two beautiful well-dressed young women who obviously did not belong there.

Mirza and Kouroush both came to greet them, but Kouroush was clearly upset that Gregor had brought Tatiana to see him. Dr. Heshmat was also with them, and he seemed somewhat amused by the situation, though he was astonished when he learned that Tatiana was also a doctor.

Tatiana's heart melted the moment she saw Kouroush. She leaped down from her horse and rushed to him. But she did not embrace him; instead she stopped just before she reached him and said reproachfully, "You should have come to say goodbye. You should have told me."

Kouroush looked at Gregor, and there was anger in his eyes. "Why did you tell her?" he asked. "Why did you bring her here?"

Tatiana broke in before Gregor could attempt to explain. "Because I forced him to do what you should have done," she said.

"You don't belong here," Kouroush protested.

"I think that's for me to decide," Tatiana said. She looked around uncomfortably. "Could we go for a walk and talk, just the two of us?"

Their walk took them back and forth along the dusty streets of the encampment, for it was not advisable to wander in the forests or up the mountains that ringed the valley.

The people who lived and worked in the tents and huts along the streets stared at her curiously, but she was just as curious about them, for they were not what she expected.

This did not look like an army, but like a small rural town. There were more men here than women, but the surprise to her was that there were women at all—Moslem women in chadors—and that there were quite a few small children. Most of the children were dirty, but that was not unusual for children; what disturbed Tatiana was that quite a number showed signs of illness or sores that needed treating.

If she should come here to stay, this was something she could tend to.

However, she kept these thoughts to herself for the moment; now, there were things she and Kouroush had to work out between themselves. At first, they argued about Kouroush's departure and about Tatiana's following him there. Tatiana could see that these recriminations were getting nowhere, and her objective in coming had not been to fight.

Finally she told him flatly, "I will not let you walk out of my life this easily. The fact is I love you, and I know you love me. That is something that we have to face together, not apart."

These words forced Kouroush to stop and look at her honestly, letting down his defenses. She knew that it was the first time either of them had voiced their love so directly; that was why she had done it.

He sighed and shook his head wearily. "We cannot spend our lives together," he said. "You should know that as well as I do. There is no way a Moslem can marry a Jew."

"We can try to find a way," Tatiana said encouragingly. "We would be cowards not to make the effort."

"Would you really do that for me?" Kouroush asked tenderly. "Go against your family's wishes, against all of society?"

"Yes," Tatiana admitted. "But it would be as much for me as for you, for my happiness is a part of your happiness."

Kouroush pulled her to him and kissed her passionately, holding her in his arms, as if he could never let her go, oblivious to the curious eyes of the people on the street. There was both fear and excitement in their first kiss, for theirs was a forbidden love, yet one that must exist despite the consequences. Tatiana returned the kiss, welcoming his love, inviting it.

From that point on, they were of one mind, talking of practical matters, concerned about resolving the difficulties they would face together.

"We must give your parents every opportunity to approve of our marrying," Kouroush told her. "They are good people, and you owe them your respect. We must pray that their respect for you will help them to understand and to give their blessing."

"It will be difficult for them, I know," Tatiana told him. "It may be impossible."

"Of course you must return home and talk to them," Kouroush said. "It will take time, and—until I can find some way to see them to talk to them—it will be up to you to convince them."

Tatiana nodded in understanding. "And what about your parents?" she asked. "Would they ever approve of me?"

"I don't think, so," Kouroush said sadly. "But that doesn't matter. I am sure my father has already disowned me for what he will consider my traitorous actions."

"That saddens me," Tatiana told him. "To me, family is so important. You truly can't value parents until you lose them."

Kouroush shrugged uncomfortably and changed the subject. "What about your career?" he asked. "I know that practicing medicine is important to you."

Tatiana smiled sadly. "My prospects are not very good," she said. "As a woman, I might never be accepted doing anything more than nursing, or perhaps delivering babies." She shrugged. "But earning money in medicine isn't what's important to me; it's much more important to be of help to people, to relieve suffering. And I can do that here as well as in Rasht. As we've walked today, I've noticed children greatly in need of medical attention."

Suddenly Kouroush's manner brightened. "There is a clinic here," he said. "It's very crude, and greatly in need of supplies, but perhaps you might help with it. Dr. Heshmat is in charge of it. We must talk to him."

"Do you really think he would accept me?" Tatiana asked, trying not to hope too much for fear of being disappointed.

Kouroush grinned. "He needs help so badly, he'll have to accept you."

It was when they talked to Dr. Heshmat and Mirza that their plans for the future began to take shape. Tatiana found that she liked Dr. Heshmat very much, and she sensed that he liked her as well. He was a pleasant man, who always seemed to be on the verge of breaking into a mischievous smile. He was delighted at the prospect of having assistance in the clinic.

"As it is," he explained to her, "I have to divide my time between my practice in the city and the clinic here. It is all too much for one doctor." Suddenly his face lit up. "I have a wonderful idea. Perhaps you might be willing to assist with my practice in Rasht as well. It wouldn't pay much, but it would be far better than working as a nurse. You could be in the office there when I have to be here, and you could be here when I'm there."

"But wouldn't your patients object?" Tatiana asked. "I mean, to being treated by a woman."

Dr. Heshmat shrugged. "Some would, I suppose," he said. "Especially some of the men. But I would imagine many of the women would prefer a woman doctor. Moslem women have difficulty talking about certain things to a man, even a doctor."

"Wouldn't they object to my being a Jew?" she asked.

Dr. Heshmat's eyes twinkled. "When you become Mrs. Jalali, who is to know you are a Jew?"

Mirza approved of the idea. "Continue to live in the city as long as you can," he told Tatiana. "Until traveling back and forth becomes a threat to our security, we need people who have access to Rasht. We are still dependent upon the city for many of our supplies and information." He smiled. "And your being the daughter of one of Rasht's most important merchants will do us no harm. If he can be persuaded, we would like to do business with him."

It was decided that Tatiana should not return to the Valley of the Trees until she had obtained Philip Boustani's approval for her marriage and for her work in the clinic. However, she would begin working immediately in Dr. Heshmat's Rasht office. Much depended upon Philip's ability to accept and to understand his daughter's hopes and wishes. Tatiana knew he was a kind and generous man, but this might strain his generosity too greatly.

However, she would begin working immediately in Dr. Heshmat's Rasht office. Much depended upon Philip's ability to accept and to understand his daughter's hopes and wishes. Tatiana knew he was a kind and generous man, but this might strain his generosity too greatly.

However, she would have Nadia's help in approaching him, for Nadia approved of what was beginning to develop. While Tatiana had been with Kouroush, she and Gregor had spent time with Mirza. She very quickly grasped what he was attempting to achieve, and she approved of it wholeheartedly. While she loved the Russian people, she was aware that the Russian government was a tyrranical one, especially toward the people of nations under its sphere of influence.

Mirza permitted Nadia to take out her sketchbook and do some drawings of him to use in painting a portrait, though he advised her not to display it publicly. Nadia wished she could have also done sketches of the *jangali* encampment, but she did not even ask, aware that it would be too great a risk to their security if the sketches should fall into the wrong hands.

* * * * *

It would not be easy for Tatiana and Nadia to confront Philip Boustani with what had happened, though there were several factors in their favor. He was already aware that Tatiana and Kouroush were very close friends, and so far he had voiced no objections, even though he must have suspected that their feelings went beyond mere friendship.

There was also the fact that he had, throughout the girls' lives, displayed an amazing capacity for wisdom and understanding, always expressing concern for their wishes and well-being before his own. Neither Tatiana nor Nadia had ever been given reason to fear displays of rage or anger. They had always felt free to talk to him about anything that concerned them.

Of course, this was the most serious matter that either of them had ever had to confront him with.

Nervously, Tatiana sat in her father's study, presenting him with the entire story of what had happened, helped occasionally by Nadia. Philip Boustani listened to it all without comment, trying not to let the pain he was feeling show in his face. There was only a sadness in his eyes that told Tatiana how deeply this was hurting him.

After she had finished, he said calmly and slowly, "You know that I only want your happiness. That is what every father wants for his children. I am aware that it is impossible to live life without some degree of sorrow and tribulation, but a father hopes for more happiness than sorrow. I am afraid that what you want will give you greater troubles than joys in life, but to attempt to hold you back from it would be as bad if not worse."

He heaved a sigh and rose from his desk to walk around to Tatiana's side. "It is very difficult to decide what I should do; I do not want to do anything lightly or hastily. You can understand that, can't you?"

Tatiana nodded.

Philip continued. "A father always knows that one day he must give up his children, but he also hopes he can still hold onto some part of them. The custom of arranging marriages permits him to do this, by making sure a daughter's husband is of the same class, of equivalent wealth, of good family, and—yes—of the same religion."

He knelt down by Tatiana's chair and took her hand in his, looking into her eyes with affection. "Judith and I have been blessed to have you as a second daughter," he said, "and we don't want to do anything that would make us lose you."

He smiled at her. "Would you permit me to talk to Kouroush and to see this place where you will live," he asked, "before I decide whether to give my approval or not?"

"Yes," Tatiana said gratefully. "That is the least I can do."

She threw her arms around her father and embraced him tearfully. But they were tears of joy, because she knew that ultimately he would give his approval.

Chapter 25

As it transpired, Philip Boustani's approval was the least of the obstacles to marriage between Tatiana and Kouroush. After talking to the young man, Philip was satisfied that Kouroush loved Tatiana deeply and was as much concerned for her welfare as he was himself.

"Of course, you know it won't be easy," he told the two young people. "If you can find a way to be married under these circumstances, you have my blessing. It will be impossible for you to have either a Jewish or an Islamic wedding, and I don't see how the marriage can be recorded officially, so long as you, Kouroush, are a fugitive."

That was a problem neither Kouroush nor Tatiana had thought of.

"We may have to wait a while," Kouroush told Tatiana apologetically.

"I can wait," Tatiana said with a smile, taking her lover's hand and squeezing it encouragingly. "So long as I can still see you."

"I know you want to come to work in the clinic here," Philip told her. "And you may do it, but I don't want you traveling between here and Rasht without a chaperone. If Gregor cannot accompany you, then I must come, or perhaps your mother and sister."

Before Tatiana could protest, Kouroush said, "I agree. I would not want you to travel alone, even if we were married. The roads here are dangerous."

"That makes it very difficult," Tatiana said despondently. Then she brightened and added, "Perhaps I could simply move here."

Kouroush frowned. "Not until we are man and wife."

Philip Boustani smiled proudly. "He's right," he said. "It would be unwise."

"Then we must find a way to be married soon," Tatiana said. Then she blushed, glancing at Kouroush in embarrassment. "I am needed in the clinic, and I am anxious to practice medicine."

It was Gregor who finally came up with the solution. "I'm not sure if it's really possible," he said hesitantly. "But, do you remember, Tatiana, the Zoroastrian shrine hear Baku..., the place our father took us after the picnic years ago? If the old priest is still there, or if another has taken his place, you might be married there. That way the marriage would not have to be recorded in Rasht."

Philip Boustani considered the idea. "That's quite a distance to travel," he said skeptically. "So far away from family and friends."

"I know," Gregor said. "But we do have one family member in Baku. That is, if he is still alive."

Tatiana looked at him curiously. "Who is that?" she asked.

"Our Uncle Vladimir," Gregor said. "Our father's brother."

"I don't think I would want to visit him," Tatiana said, "After all I've heard about him."

Philip had been giving the idea considerable thought. "It might be a solution," he said. "If Kouroush could travel without being recognized. I will contact friends in Baku to see if arrangements can be made."

* * * * *

Before leaving the Valley of the Trees, Philip Boustani met with Mirza, who was interested in purchasing supplies of rice. Even if he had not begun to respect Mirza's cause, Philip would have been willing to do business with the revolutionaries. Because of his sympathies, he was willing to sell the grain at a special rate.

He could do this because he owned rice fields of his own, in addition to buying and selling the rice of others for export.

Arrangements were made for the first shipment to the *jangali* encampment within a week.

* * * * *

Tatiana began working at Dr. Heshmat's office in Rasht almost immediately, taking many of the less serious cases involving women and children at first. Even if she had been a man, she would have been required to go through a period of apprenticeship to another doctor before having a practice of her own. She was grateful to be using her medical knowledge, and looked forward to the time when she could work in the *jangali* clinic as well.

However, her travel to the Valley of the Trees could not be arranged. Dr. Heshmat was forced to take care of the patients there alone.

On those days when he was out, she had to take care of all the patients, and some of those proved to be Moslem men who were not happy about being treated by a woman. A few refused to see her, walking out of the office, saying that they would return on a day when Dr. Heshmat was in.

Within a few weeks, Philip Boustani received a letter from his friend in Baku. Arrangements had been made; the priest at the shrine of the eternal flame would be pleased to perform the marriage. He remembered the children of the Baranov family, and he would have no objection to uniting two lovers of mixed heritage. Tatiana's parentage was mixed, her father having been Parsee, and there were so few of their religion left.

He would not require that the couple be initiated into the religion, but he suggested they endeavor to learn something of the basic tenets and the requirements of the ceremony. Tatiana managed to obtain some old books about the religion, as well as a copy of the *Abesta*, the holy book of the Parsee, and they both read them with interest.

The end of March of 1915 would be an ideal time for the wedding party to travel unnoticed, because the Moslem population would be celebrating Noroose. Families everywere would be traveling together; the roads and the shops would be crowded.

The entire Boustani family would accompany Tatiana and Kouroush, and Gregor was invited to join them, so the wedding would be a festive occasion, even though it would be a simple ceremony.

They chose to sail from Enzeli on the seventh day of Noroose, when the government offices would be closed and the greatest number of people would be traveling, paying visits to friends and families. The authorities checking travelers between Persia and Russia would be most lax on that day because of the heavy number of travelers. If Kouroush could go unnoticed at any time, it would be that day.

From the time Kouroush had joined Mirza, he had begun to let his beard grow and to wear Moslem robes. He bore little resemblance to the dapper, mustachioed cossack the authorities were looking for. The only problem with his appearance was that he would seem out of place traveling with the rest of the group, unless he assumed at least a modified western suit of clothes, so that concession had to be made.

Since the marriage was to be recorded in Baku, he must travel with his own papers and take the chance they would not be checked too carefully.

As expected, on the day of their departure, there were crowds on the road to Enzeli and crowds at the docks. Moslem families were out in great numbers, the children were wearing their fine new clothes and making an effort to be on their best behavior but unable to subdue their excitement about the special occasion.

However, one thing was not as the wedding party had expected: as they lined up to board the Russian boat, the authorities were checking travelers' documents more carefully than usual. While Persia was officially neutral in the war, the Russians were concerned about Turks and Germans who might be enemy agents, especially since the fighting in Turkey had grown serious.

The boat's departure was being delayed. Russian soldiers were everywhere, keeping the crowds under control, while the officers stood at the boat's entrance, carefully checking papers and casting their eyes over the waiting people.

The eyes of a Russian major kept returning to their group, lingering on them with suspicion. Tatiana was the first to be aware of it, for she sensed the man's gray eyes boring through her with hostility. "They're going to stop us," she told Philip. "I think we should leave."

"No," Kouroush told her. "We must go through with it. If we were to get out of line now, we would arouse even more suspicion."

"He's right," Philip said. "It may be our own fear showing. He doesn't seem to be singling us out anymore than other people."

"I don't know," Gregor said. "I feel he's looking at me with more than ordinary curiosity."

"But if we chose to run," Kouroush argued, "there would be no chance of getting away in this crowd." He shook his head decisively. "No, we must try to remain calm and hope that we can bluff our way through. We must not show any fear."

They decided to keep Kouroush at the end of the line, just behind Gregor. Philip would go first, handling the papers for Judith, Nadia, and Tatiana, as well as his own. He was accustomed to traveling and felt confident he could take care of the situation.

When their turn finally came, Philip handed over the papers for his family confidently, almost casually. The lieutenant who took them studied them with a pensive frown, then handed them to the major who had been watching the group suspiciously. He gave only a quick glance at the documents, before turning to Tatiana and asking curtly, "What is your name?"

Trembling, Tatiana replied, "Tatiana Boustani."

"What is your connection to this family?" the officer demanded.

Before Tatiana could reply, Philip answered, "She is my daughter."

"She does not look like she could be your daughter," the Russian major said grimly.

"She is my adopted daughter," Philip explained with a smile.

"We shall see about that," the officer said, then gestured to two guards. "You will all have to come with me."

"Where are you taking them?" Gregor broke in rashly.

The officer turned to him. "Are you with this group?" he asked.

"Yes," Gregor replied.

The major smiled coldly. "Then you will come along as well."

Kouroush remained silent. But as the group was led away by the Russian soldiers, Tatiana glanced back anxiously, and Kouroush gave her a faint but encouraging smile.

Tatiana was more frightened for Kouroush than she was for herself. There was no reason the authorities should want her, and now Kouroush was left entirely on his own. If he were stopped, they would not be there to help him.

Their group was led to a small building on the docks and ushered into a military office, where another officer, a colonel, took over the interrogation.

After a brief, whispered conversation in Russian between the major and the colonel, the colonel surveyed the group coldly, then turned to Gregor and asked, "*Wie heis du?*"

"I'm sorry," Gregor replied. "I don't speak German."

The colonel smiled wickedly. "Then how did you know I was speaking German?"

Gregor blushed, shifted uncomfortably. "I speak several other languages," he replied. "And I've heard German spoken."

The Russian nodded, but he was clearly not satisfied. He turned and glowered at Tatiana. "*Sprechen zie deutsche?*" he asked.

Tatiana replied shakily, "I don't understand," she said. "What do you want?"

Philip Boustani stepped forward. "Excuse me, sir," he said, "but would you tell me why we are being questioned?"

The colonel scowled at him, as if trying to control his anger. "You claim to be this young woman's father?" he asked.

"Yes, sir," Philip replied respectfully. "Her adopted father." He gestured toward Gregor. "And this young man is her natural brother, adopted by another family."

"Their fair skin and hair?" the officer asked. "Were they German by birth?"

Finally, Philip began to understand why they were being questioned.

"No, sir," he replied. "They were born in Baku, of Russian ancestry."

"Why are you traveling to Baku?" the colonel asked. "Especially at this time?"

Philip hesitated, aware that he must not tell the truth or they might bring Kouroush into the interrogation. "The two young people have an uncle in Baku," he said. "Their only living natural relative. He is an old man, and they wish to see him again before it is too late."

"What is this uncle's name?" the Russian demanded.

"Vladimir Mehdovi," Philip said.

The officer looked surprised. "I am acquainted with the man," he said. "You are aware that we can check this matter with him?"

"Yes, sir," Philip replied. "But of course he is not aware that we are coming. He is not the sort of man who cares much for his family."

For the first time, there was a smile of genuine humor on the Russian's face. "From what I know of him," he said, "he is not the sort of man who cares much for the human race." He was pensive for a moment, studying Gregor and Tatiana carefully. "I can see there is a slight family resemblance. You may go."

They were all greatly relieved to find Kouroush safely and securely aboard ship, and he was relieved to see them. He had been passed through without question. His Moslem name had not seemed out of the ordinary on this day. His only worry had been that the ship might sail without his companions.

*   *   *   *   *

After their ordeal, the group was less anxious than they had been, and they managed to relax and enjoy the short sea voyage, watching the happy families traveling together and walking on deck that evening and the following morning. Nadia even took out her sketchbook and drew pictures of a group of little girls, no more than eight years old, playing in their veils and chadors, looking like miniature adults.

However, the experience with the Russian authorities had given them all a new concern. Would the Russian colonel check with Vladimir Mehdovi? To allay suspicions, should they, in fact, pay a call on the old man? Philip felt it would be advisable, but Gregor did not want to see Vladimir again, especially after the way he had left. He felt justified in stealing the information from his uncle, but he knew Vladimir would not see it in the same way.

Tatiana was not eager to meet her uncle, but she allowed Philip to persuade her to go with him to pay a visit. It would be only a courtesy call, to become acquainted and to inform her only living relative of her coming marriage. And, if the Russian should check, it would help prevent problems on their return to Persia.

Gregor would accompany them to Vladimir Mehdovi's home, but not to see his uncle. While Philip and Tatiana were with the old man, he would spend the time with Ali Jabbar, the servant who had been his only friend during the time he had lived there.

* * * * * *

As Gregor had expected, it was Ali Jabbar who opened the door of his uncle's house, and the elderly servent was delighted to see him. He was also pleased to meet Tatiana. However, when he learned why they were there, his face became concerned. "I must not tell your uncle that you have come," he told Gregor. "He would be furious. I'm not even sure he will see your sister. His health is very frail, and he can no longer get out of bed. Without friends, he is a very bitter man, and his money is no longer any comfort to him, for he cannot even have the joy of reading his financial books. His eyesight is almost completely gone."

"But you will ask him to see us, won't you?" Philip Boustani asked.

"Of course," Ali Jabbar replied politely. "But you must be prepared for him to refuse."

To Ali Jabbar's surprise, Vladimir Baranov agreed to see his niece.

The old man's bedroom was dark and airless and smelled of decay. When they first entered, Tatiana could barely see the frail, white-haired figure sitting up in bed against the far wall. She had an urge to go to the windows, part the heavy drapes, and open the windows to let some fresh air into the room, but knew she could not be so forward.

"So you're the girl Tatiana?" Vladimir barked gruffly, his eyes focussed somewhere in between Tatiana and Philip. "What do you want from me?"

"She wants simply to meet you," Philip said, before Tatiana could reply. "She has come back to Baku to be married and thought it might be the only opportunity to see you."

Vladimir grunted derisively. "Who are you?" he asked. "The intended husband?"

"No," Philip replied. "I'm her adopted father."

"Well, if you think coming here will convince me to leave my money to her," Vladimir said harshly, "you're wrong."

Tatiana could no longer bear her uncle's manner. "I have no need for your money," she said haughtily. "I've been well taken care of, and I now have a profession to earn my own way."

"A profession?" Vladimir spat derisively. "A woman?"

"Yes," Tatiana replied. "I'm a doctor. I received my medical degree in Moscow."

"A woman doctor!" the old man said incredulously. "Impossible!"

Tatiana moved toward him suddenly, studying his pale complexion. "What does your doctor say you're suffering from?" she asked, pausing at his bedside.

"I don't need a doctor to tell me I'm suffering from old age," Vladimir said defensively. "No need to pay a man to tell me that."

"You haven't seen a doctor?" Tatiana asked, surprised.

"It would be a waste of money," the old man told her.

"What else do you have to spend it on?" Tatiana asked.

Vladimir grunted. "Only fools spend money," he said.

Tatiana turned to Philip. "Papa, would you open the draperies?" she asked. "I'm going to check his condition."

"No, you're not," Vladimir protested. "I'm not going to pay your bill if you send it."

"There won't be a bill," Tatiana said. "Now, open your mouth and stick out your tongue."

While Philip watched in amused pride and the old man protested, Tatiana gave her uncle as complete a medical examination as she could without having her surgical bag with her. When she had finished, she said professionally, "Your condition isn't as bad as you think it is. You have a weak heart, but that's to be expected at your age and with as little nourishment as you seem to get. You're going to have to eat better, get a bit more exercise and fresh air, and stop lying in bed believing you're dying. You've got at least a few years left."

"Humph," Vladimir grunted. "Little you know. After all, you're only a woman."

Tatiana ignored him. "I'm going to give your servant a list of foods for you," she said, "as well as a prescription for some medication when you experience those chest pains. I expect you to follow my advice." She smiled. "And if you don't improve, see another doctor. It will be worth the money."

The old man was still protesting as they left him. The meeting had been a strain for Tatiana, but she felt pleased that she had met her uncle this once. She knew she would never have another opportunity.

* * * * *

The journey to the shrine of the eternal flame was a bittersweet one for Tatiana and Gregor. They delighted in recognizing certain landmarks, marveled at how much shorter the distance seemed now, and sadly commented on the increase in the number of oil wells dotting the landscape.

The shrine itself seemed even smaller and more crude than it had when they were children. It was incredible to them that Rama, the old priest, was still alive, thinner and more bent and wrinkled than before, but recognizing them with a clear mind, his dark eyes as bright as a child's.

Rama was truly excited by the prospect of performing the wedding ceremony, the only rite he had been called upon to conduct in many years.

"I regret that we have no comfortable room for the ceremony," he told the wedding party apologetically. "But the weather is beautiful and warm, so we may be comfortable in the open air."

He had cleared a space on the rocky ground in front of the shrine and had somehow managed to obtain a carpet to lay down upon it, as well as cushions for his guests to sit on.

They had all read about the ritual so that they would be prepared for the ceremony, but even so they found it unexpectedly moving. To Gregor, his sister had never seemed more beautiful, dressed entirely in green as the ceremony required, wearing the ancient Parsee dress for women, pants with a flowing robe over them. The green shawl for covering her head was of a gossamer fabric that gave her lovely face an ethereal quality.

Kouroush had never looked more handsome. He had trimmed his beard neatly, and he was dressed all in white, wearing a pure white robe and a white woolen cap.

They sat down, side by side, on the cushions Rama had provided, near the center of the carpet. The old priest sat facing them, then laid down a white cloth between him and the couple. Upon it, he neatly and carefully placed a series of items. First he laid out a portrait of Zarathustra, followed by two candles, a mirror, a bottle of rose water, and the holy book of *Abesta*. Next he placed a spool of green thread, with a needle, as a symbol that the husband and wife would be sewn together forever in a bond that could not be broken, then two small branches from a cypress tree, symbol of life because it can reproduce itself.

These were followed by seven kinds of nuts and dried fruits—almonds, pistachios, walnuts, hazel nuts, raisins, apricots, and figs—and by a few sweets, including baklava.

Once this had been done, Rama began to speak. His words wafted over Gregor like waves from the sea. He had never heard them before, but like the flame had done so many years before, they seemed to call forth knowledge he already possessed somewhere deep within his soul. Rama spoke of the commitment and responsibility between two people, of the sacred duties of family life, and of the obligation to serve humanity, through good thoughts, good words, and good deeds.

He told the couple that wisdom and goodness must come first, that they must use that before they used free choice. He advised them that their first objective in the marriage state was to make a good family, and then to work toward the betterment of the world, in unity and peace.

Following this, he read some of the poetry of Zarathustra.

Finally, he came to the ritual that would unite the couple. Rama gazed into Tatiana's eyes and asked, "Do you take this man Kouroush Jalili as your husband of your own free will?"

Tatiana answered, "Yes."

The old priest asked the question twice more, and Tatiana replied affirmatively each time.

Then Rama turned and asked Kouroush, "Do you take this woman Tatiana Boustani as your wife of your own free will?"

Kouroush replied, "Yes," each of the three times he was asked the question.

Rama picked up a handful of rice and oregano leaves and tossed the grain and the spice at the couple. Then he reached out with his bony, trembling hands, taking a hand of each of the partners, joining them together.

"You are now husband and wife," Rama said. "May the blessings of Ahura Mazda be with you all your lives."

The last part of the ceremony was for Kouroush and Tatiana each to take one of the sweets laid out before them to place in the mouth of the other.

After that, they rose, and Rama led the entire wedding party into the shrine. They passed around the flame three times, with Rama chanting prayers.

Gregor glanced at his sister as she passed near the flame. The light gave her face a timeless glow, made mystical by the green of her shawl. In the presence of the flame, Gregor was as moved as he had been that first time he had come here. But now, there seemed even greater meaning, for this place had joined his sister in marriage to his best friend. And in them, there was hope for the future, hope that their people could again be united against oppression.

Somehow Gregor felt this union was meant to be, proclaimed by fate, destined to have great meaning in the plans of the universe, a part of all things natural.

It was clear that Tatiana and Kouroush were in love, deeply in love. He prayed before the flame that they would always know happiness, though something within told him that sadness must be a part of the future, as essential as joy.

After the ceremony, Judith and Nadia set out the dinner they had brought with them, placing the dishes of food on the carpet that had been laid upon the ground outside the shrine. The old priest was asked to join them in partaking of the wedding meal, and he did so gratefully, though he ate only the fruit and the cheese, not sharing in the meat or the wine.

There was something magical about the rocky, barren mountainside. It was peaceful beneath the clear blue sky; life seemed somehow simple here, uncomplicated by the passions of mankind, as pure as nature itself. Once the meal was finished, Tatiana and Kouroush went for a walk alone.

Nadia and Gregor followed their example. Some distance away, they paused to sit beneath a tree and gaze off at the immense vista of mountains and valleys.

"I'm going to miss Tatiana," Nadia said. "We were always so close. We shared everything."

"But you'll still see her," Gregor said comfortingly.

"It won't be the same," Nadia told him. She leaned against his shoulder wistfully. "You know, we always thought that I would be the first to be married. It's strange how things turn out."

"Yes," Gregor replied softly. He felt an overwhelming desire to hold Nadia in his arms, to kiss her, to make love to her. But he knew he must restrain himself.

"I wonder if I will ever be married?" Nadia mused.

"Of course you will," Gregor said, and he could not resist bending over and kissing Nadia on the cheek.

Nadia turned her head, and her lips met his in a lingering kiss.

Chapter 26

Nadia was lonely without Tatiana at home. She missed having her sister to confide in, to share the events of the days, even if the days were merely ordinary. Most of Nadia's days, without Tatiana, were ordinary. She worked alone in her studio, painting. If she did not have a commission, she painted just for her own pleasure. She worked on the portrait of Mirza, adjusting it and changing it from time to time. There was no pressure to satisfy the subject's taste, for it could not be sold, or even exhibited.

She started a painting of the group of a little girls in chadors and veils, which she had sketched on the boat to Baku, but she didn't care for it, so she started over. The second time, she found herself reverting somewhat to her old native style and discovered that the painting worked, even though she wasn't happy about the shift she had made. However, she continued to work on it to see how it might develop.

In May, she was approached for a commissioned work, a portrait of a minor government official who had seen her work in the home of a merchant. His name was Isaac Mizrahi, and he was a middle-aged man who vaguely resembled a plump, self-satisfied owl. He told Nadia his position in the government with some pride, but she wasn't entirely clear on what it was. She understood it to be something connected with the collection of taxes.

In the beginning, he came three times a week for sittings for the portrait. Nadia had difficulty coming up with a composition that satisfied her; the man was just so odd-looking, she couldn't find an approach that would please her.

Again she felt the urge to return to her old style, but she resisted. She knew her subject would never accept it, but would expect the polished realism taught by Professor Nichola.

It bothered her that Mizrahi would linger after the sittings were over, wanting to talk to her, trying to persuade her to let him look at her other works. She wanted to be rid of him so she could concentrate on the problem she was having with his portrait. It annoyed her that he stayed on, although she was accustomed to this sort of thing from her subjects. She had very early learned that people of the merchant class, and sometimes even those of the lesser nobility, associated artists with a degree of romance they felt was missing from their own lives. To her, there was nothing particularly glamorous about painting; it was merely her work, and it had its problems, just as merchants, accountants, politicians, and—yes—tax collectors had their work problems. Yet she could never convey this fact to others.

Her cool, distracted manner did not succeed in driving Isaac Mizrahi away. If anything, it fascinated him, made him try even harder to get to know her.

He talked incessantly, his dark, heavy-lidded eyes staring at her unceasingly. Nadia was sure he had told her several times all of the details of his life. She knew that he was forty-six years old, had been married, and that his wife had died during childbirth very early in their marriage. The child had died as well. He had worked very hard to get where he had, and was very proud of the fact that he—as a Jew—had obtained such a high position in the government. He was a very powerful man in the tax department for the Rasht region, and was greatly respected by his superiors. He had managed to save his money through the years and was quite well to do now.

He had longed to be remarried after the death of his wife, but had not found a suitable woman. His wife had died thirteen years ago.

To be fair, Nadia had to admit that he was not entirely self-centered. He did try to get her to talk about herself, but she avoided answering his numerous personal questions when she could do so tactfully. She didn't mind telling him about her time in Moscow or about her studies with Professor Nichola. But she did not want to answer the questions he asked about her friends, family, and personal tastes.

Sometimes she suspected that his interest was romantic, but soon dismissed the idea. She certainly did not find him attractive, or even interesting. She wanted merely to complete his portrait, collect her fee, and move on to other things.

But that was not what fate had in store for her.

*   *   *   *   *

The political situation in Persia was growing very tense. The government had declared its neutrality in the European war, but other nations, stronger nations, did not respect a weak nation's declaration of neutrality. In January, Turkey had invaded the northwest territory, taking Tabriz, and Russian troops had crossed the borders to drive them out again. At about the same time, German agents had come into Persia, enlisting the aid of autonomous sheikhs, the leaders of the Gasgai and Bakhtiar tribes particularly, in the south and west against the British there.

In many places, German sympathies were growing. That was something the Russians—and therefore the Persian government—could not long permit.

In May, large shipments of arms from Russia began to be sent secretly to Tehran, Tabriz, and Rasht. More arms than the Russian Cossack Brigade could possible need.

*   *   *   *   *

In the Valley of the Trees, Tatiana was deliriously happy, no longer Tatiana Boustani but Tatiana Jalali—Dr. Jalali, the wife of Kouroush.

Marriage to Kouroush was everything she had hoped it would be; they were deeply, passionately in love, and it was a love that seemed to grow deeper every day. Their house was small and crude by comparison to what she had been accustomed to, but it suited their needs. It required very little housekeeping, which enabled her to spend as much time as possible at the clinic, doing what she enjoyed most—taking care of people who needed her.

The *jangali* encampment was growing into a large town, or at least a town with a large population. Over two thousand people had been drawn to join the revolutionary community, with others who came in periodically for military training, so that they would be ready to move with the rest when the fighting began.

The increase in the population of the camp inevitably meant more work for the small clinic. Very quickly the number of patients became more than Dr. Heshmat and Tatiana could handle alone. They desperately needed nursing assistants to take care of the routine cases. But the men were all needed for other duties, and most of the women were Moslem and prevented from doing such work by religion and custom.

Zahra came to her aid, enlisting the help of two Christian women as well. They would all do nursing work part time. Of course, for a while, this meant extra work for Tatiana, training them in their duties, but eventually it made things easier for her and Dr. Heshmat. There was also a greater need for medical supplies, and Tatiana was able to resolve that problem with the help of Philip, who managed to acquire most of the medications through his business, though the acquisition was difficult, even for him. Normal sources of medicines were now limited because of the war, but he managed to obtain them through an associate who traded with the United States.

Through their contact at the clinic, Tatiana and Zahra became good friends. To some degree, it made up for not having Nadia to confide in, though Tatiana never felt quite as close to Zahra as she had to her sister.

It was in June that Zahra told Tatiana confidentially that there would soon be a need for more beds in the clinic, more bandages, and morphine to treat wounds. Tatiana understood—the fighting was about to begin.

*   *   *   *   *

For Philip Boustani, the trouble began with the requisition of rice supplies by the Persian Cossack Brigade. It was a requisition he could not fill without cutting short other promises already made, including the order for Mirza's *jangali*.

Philip was not normally a suspicious man, but this demand from the cossacks made him suspicious. Had they somehow learned about Tatiana's marriage to Kouroush, who had become an outlaw in their eyes? Did they know that he was supplying Mirza's revolutionaries with grain and medicine? Was he now on the secret list of enemies of the state, to be hounded and punished until he was driven out of business?

Certainly they had singled him out among the merchants of Rasht. He was only one of three the cossacks had made large demands upon, and the amount required of him was greater than the other two combined. One of the other two was Rajik Sarkissian.

Philip decided that he could not accept the requisition, but must protest it. It was what he would have done if he had not had cause for suspicion.

When Philip went to cossack headquarters to lodge his protest, he was surprised to find that the officer in charge was Pasha Jalali. When he introduced himself, he was certain his fears were well-founded. But what was the specific reason? He wasn't sure.

Philip handed the requisition paper to Pasha. "I cannot fill this order," he said. "Not in the amount you require."

Pasha did not look at the requisition in his hand, but kept his dark cold eyes focused accusingly on Philip. "Why not?" he asked curtly.

"I simply don't have that much rice available," Philip said firmly. "I can give you only a little more than half that amount."

Finally, Pasha glanced down at the paper in his hands, frowning pensively. "According to our sources," he said, without looking up at Philip, "you have precisely this amount in only one of your warehouses."

Philip felt his anger rising. "I do," he said, "but much of it has been sold and is awaiting delivery."

Pasha looked up at him hotly, his eyes flashing. "You can cancel orders."

"Not when they've already been paid for," Philip retorted.

Pasha shrugged. "Delay an order or two. Let another merchant fill the orders."

Philip smiled. "That would be very poor business," he said. "I would be giving away my customers. You can't expect me to do that, can you?"

Pasha studied him for a moment before asking coldly, "Who are these important customers?"

So that was it after all—if he did not actually know that Philip was supplying Mirza with grain, he at least suspected it. Philip smiled calmly. "That, too, would be very poor business, revealing names of customers," he said. "A good merchant doesn't tell his private business matters."

Pasha scowled. "I'm not sure that's your reason," he said angrily. "It's very suspicious that your customers require so much rice—enough to feed a military brigade, an army."

Philip shrugged. "I sell wholesale," he said, "and I have a great many customers, all over this country and abroad. Some of my customers are very important."

"Certainly no more important than your own government," Pasha said intemperately.

Philip attempted to maintain his calm. "What is important to me is the payment," he said. "I'm in business for the profit. My own government pays me less than it costs me. How important should I consider that?"

Pasha could control his temper no longer. "You will find out how important your government is," he said loudly. "You have our requisition! You will fill it, or we will come and take it by force! Good day!"

*   *   *   *   *

Philip decided to make delivery of as much of the rice as he could that evening and the following day. The most critical shipment, he felt, would be that to the *jangalis*, for it was the single largest order. He scheduled it to go out first, using all of the wagons at his disposal.

It meant paying the lorrymen extra wages, but they would be taking the shipment only halfway to its destination. At the foothills of the mountains, Mirza's men would take over. By this means, no one would know precisely where the rice was going.

It was a hot, humid summer night. People were outdoors, but there was little movement. The usually noisy streets were quiet.

The surprise came only a short distance outside the city.

The cossacks attacked from three sides—from the rear, and the right and the left—quickly surrounding the caravan. The few armed guards had instructions only to protect the shipment from brigands; they were not prepared to fire upon Persian military troops.

The rice was taken with virtually no resistance.

In less than an hour, the guide in charge of the caravan reported the theft to Philip Boustani at his home in Rasht.

Philip realized instantly that he had no legal recourse. The government's requisition had been served to him. His protest had been denied.

This would be a big loss for the *jangali*. The large settlement was dependent on Philip's rice shipments for survival. It would be painful for Philip, but he must report immediately to Mirza what had taken place. Of course, he would repay the *jangali*, but some other arrangement must be made quickly. It represented a great embarrassment to Philip. He had no idea how Mirza would react.

*   *   *   *   *

Mirza took the news calmly, nodding in understanding as Philip explained everything, almost as if he had expected something of this sort.

"You did all that you could," Mirza assured him. "No one could have done more, even one of us. I am grateful you are willing to repay us the money advanced; unfortunately we must accept it, as our finances are limited."

"That is the least I can do," Philip told him. "I will try to find other merchants who can supply at least a part of your needs. Then, by the end of August, I may be able to provide the remainder from my fall harvest."

Mirza smiled at him gratefully. "We will appreciate any help you can give us," he said. "But of course you must leave Pasha Jalali and the cossacks to us."

"What do you mean?" Philip asked. "What do you intend to do?"

"As far as are you concerned, nothing," Mirza told him. "You must not be involved in any way."

* * * * *

Just over a week later, Philip understood. All of Rasht was humming with the news. A shipment of Russian arms and munitions, traveling under guard of the Persian Cossacks, had been attacked by over a thousand *jangali*. The cossacks, under the command of Pasha Jalali, had been defeated, and the arms taken. The *jangali* had been under the command of Mirza Kuchik Khan, as he was now called, since he was the leader of the *jangali* community.

Mirza had made his first move. The revolution was beginning.

But even more startling for Philip was the report that Pasha Jalali had been captured and was being held hostage by the *jangali*, who were demanding the payment of ransom for his release. Only Philip was able to realize the justice of the amount asked for his release—it was the exact price Mirza had paid for the shipment of rice from Philip.

* * * * *

Tatiana had dedicated her life to alleviating human suffering, but she knew all too well that there were different kinds of suffering. Some were the result of natural causes, the unavoidable illnessess and accidental injuries of human existence. Others were caused by poverty. But the kind that gave her the greatest pain were those inflicted by man himself, the wounds and injuries that resulted from war and conflict.

When the wounded were brought to the clinic from the raid on the munitions shipment, she had to squelch the natural anguish she felt at the suffering so that she could do the work of alleviating their pain.

Nevertheless, it was upsetting to her. The urgency of relieving the severe injuries of so many was a strain on her. She worked hard and she worked quickly, removing bullets, binding wounds, and—in two cases—severing limbs. By the time her work was finished, she was exhausted and emotionally drained.

But she did not have time to rest. As soon as she had sat down at the nursing station, she found Kouroush standing before her, a strange look on his face, a combination of sympathy, sadness, and anger.

"You have another patient to treat," he said softly. He extended a chador and veil toward her. "But for this one, you must change your clothes."

In her condition, the suggestion annoyed her. "Why should I have to wear this for a patient?" she asked, looking up at him almost angrily. "I am a doctor. Why should it matter that I am a woman at a time like this?"

Kouroush smiled sadly. "It has nothing to do with the fact that you are a woman," he said. "The patient you are to treat is an enemy. We do not want you to be recognized."

Reluctantly, Tatiana did as her husband instructed, still annoyed at having to wear the garments that were entirely foreign to her, the dress that was a symbol of woman's subjugation. She also resented the fact that Kouroush would not tell her who the prisoner was, but merely said it was best that she not know.

Kouroush escorted her to a small hut a short distance from the edge of the encampment, hidden in the forest. He carried her surgical bag for her, but paused and set it down a short distance from the hut, in order to tie a handkerchief over his face. Outside the hut were four *jangali* guards, whose faces were also covered by handkerchiefs. Again, Tatiana wondered about the reason for this secrecy, but this time she said nothing.

Once she was standing over the patient's cot, all natural curiosity was forgotten. Faced with human suffering, the instincts of the trained physician took over and her only concern was to treat the injuries to the best of her ability.

The man was middle aged, a Moslem, and wore the uniform of a cossack sergeant. His most serious injury was to his left eye, which would require very sensitive surgery. There was little chance of saving it, even in the best hospital in the world. It angered her that Kouroush should expect her to take care of this man in this dark and dirty hovel. It infuriated her even more that her husband lurked in the shadows, clearly fearful of being recognized.

"I can't do anything for this man here," she said irately. "We must take him to the clinic."

"We cannot do that," Kouroush whispered, his voice barely understandable muffled by the handkerchief. "We cannot risk having him see and recognize anything or anyone in the encampment."

This response angered Tatiana even further. "There isn't much chance I can save this man's eye," she said fiercely. "There's even a chance the other eye might be lost if I make the slightest mistake. In that event, he wouldn't be able to see or recognize anything, including your precious face!"

The look in Kouroush's eyes told Tatiana that she had hurt him deeply, but he said patiently, "It is Mirza's order that he be treated here."

Tatiana sighed with frustration. "Then come stand by my side," she said, "and hold the lantern so that I can see what I'm doing." She hesitated a moment, then said, "But first ask one of the guards to go to the clinic and get me a nursing assistant. I've got to have help.

Until Zahra arrived to assist her, Tatiana did what she could for the man's other wounds, which were relatively minor. She also determined, to her relief, that the eye injury was not the result of a gunshot wound, but from a severe blow to the head, possibly caused by hitting something in falling from his horse.

With what lucidity the patient had, passing in and out of consciousness, she managed to confirm this.

As soon as she started to work on the eye, Tatiana found that the chador and veil kept getting in her way. Angrily, she stopped work and ripped off the offending items. "I can't possibly work in these," she said.

Kouroush started to protest, but she was too quick for him. He relaxed and said, "I wish you hadn't done that."

"It's either secrecy," she said intemperately, "or this man's eyesight." Then she started back to work.

The surgery was a long and tedious operation, its delicacy a strain on Tatiana's already strained nerves. After hours of work, she wasn't sure whether she had saved any of the eyesight in the left eye or not, but she considered it highly unlikely. She was fairly sure, however, that the right eye would be unaffected, so long as the patient remained relaxed and undisturbed. For a few days, the chance of a blood clot forming and traveling to the other eye was possible if he became excited.

Once it was all over, Tatiana could think of nothing but going to her bed and sleeping. She was beyond exhaustion, her body limp and trembling, her mind incapable of focusing on rational thought. She permitted Kouroush to take her home and put her to bed as he would a child.

It was the next day, as she went to check on the condition of her imprisoned patient, that her natural curiosity returned. This time she flatly refused to wear the veil and chador. However, again Kouroush accompanied her, and again he paused before entering the hut to tie a handkerchif around his face.

This time the Cossack sergeant was fully conscious, awake and calm. As Tatiana approached his cot, he attempted to sit up to speak to her, but she quickly stopped him. "Please lie still," she instructed him firmly.

"Any sudden movement could cause harm to your unbandaged eye."

Lying back obediently, the man said, "So it was a woman who was treating me, after all. I was wondering if I had dreamed it."

"How do you feel?" Tatiana asked.

"There is pain," the man replied. "But it is bearable." He paused a moment. "Where am I?"

"I'm sorry," Tatiana smiled. "I can't tell you that." She turned to Kouroush, who was again lurking in the shadowy corner. "Would you come and hold the light for me again while I redress the bandage?"

Kouroush hesitated, started to protest, but finally complied.

As Tatiana began to work, she noticed the patient's right eye focused on Kouroush, as if studying him. It was only a moment before the ossack sergeant said breathlessly, "Kouroush, it is you, isn't it?" Then his body jerked, as if trying to rise.

"Lie still!" Tatiana snapped at him harshly, trying to shock him into obedience.

The patient did obey, but his excitment would not abate. "That man is my son," he said. "I know he is. I recognize his eyes."

Incredibly, only then did Tatiana realize that her patient was Pasha Jalali.

Chapter 27

The government refused to pay the ransom demanded for the release of Pasha Jalali, so weeks passed with him remaining a prisoner of the *jangalis*. For Tatiana, he was a difficult patient. He had been extremely upset after discovering that his son was one of his captors. Nothing they did would calm him that day; his anger had been uncontrollable.

Tatiana could not be sure if that had been responsible or not, but his left eye did not heal properly, and Pasha lost most of the sight in it. She was sure it had not helped. Luckily, however, the right eye had been unaffected. Pasha would see adequately, but he would have to wear a patch.

For a while, they refrained from telling Pasha that Tatiana was his son's wife, for that would surely have provoked another outburst of rage.

She had enough difficulty getting him to listen to her medical advice as it was.

After she was sure he had healed sufficiently, she decided it was time to tell him. And she determined that it would be best to do it when Kouroush was not there. She was astonished by her father-in-law's response.

Pasha listened to the announcement in silence, then simply stared at her for a long time. "You're a fool," he said finally. "The boy's not good enough for you."

"I don't agree," Tatiana told him. "Kouroush is a fine man, even if you don't realize it. He's just very different from you."

"He's failed at everything he's tried to do," Pasha said bitterly. "He'll never stick at anything long enough to succeed."

"That's because he's always tried to do things you've wanted him to do," she argued gently. "This is the first thing he's ever attempted that's been of his own choosing."

"This!" Pasha spat derisively. "This is doomed to failure! Even if you succeed in overthrowing the Shah, you *jangali* can never overcome the

Russians and the British."

"Perhaps," Tatiana said with a smile. "But we can never know, can we, unless we try?"

Pasha seemed for a moment to succumb to his daughter-in-law's charms, but then he braced himself and said staunchly, "That's just foolish idealism! You're as bad as he is!"

Numerous times after that, Tatiana attempted to persuade Pasha and Kouroush to sit down and talk to each other reasonably, but she could not succeed with either of them. Both refused to make the effort to try to understand the other.

In early August, Pasha's ransom was finally paid, but not by the government, which refused to deal with the *jangali*. The money had been raised by members of his family, a brother and the husbands of two of his sisters. In the middle of the night, the cossack sergeant was blindfolded and taken by a circuitous route to a spot a mile outside Rasht, where he was left shortly before dawn.

His captors were able to escape before he could reach the city. He had no idea where he had been kept prisoner. He thought it had been somewhere to the west of Rasht, toward Tabriz.

* * * * *

Once Pasha Jalali had been released, Philip Boustani knew that his difficulties would resume. Of course, there was no legal action that could be taken against him; there was only Pasha's suspicion and hatred, which had grown now that he knew his son was married to Philip's daughter. Whatever action Pasha took against him would be indirect.

The rice harvest that month was a good one. Philip had an abundant supply, not just from his own harvest, but from purchases he had made from other growers. His warehouses were filling rapidly, and he was bringing in orders that would soon be definite sales.

Again, one very large order—even larger than before—was from the *jangalis*.

In late August, on a Friday evening, just a few moments after Nadia had come into the house from her studio to join her parents in the parlor, there was a sudden loud knocking on their front door. It was one of Philip's employees, the watchman at the largest of his warehouses. He was extremely upset and out of breath from running.

It took a long time for Philip to understand that the warehouse was on fire, burning uncontrollably. There seemed to be no chance of saving any of the enormous amount of rice stored inside.

Quickly, Philip ordered his carriage, so that he could go to the warehouse to see if there was anything he could do. Nadia insisted on accompanying him. As they climbed into the carriage, Gregor was just approaching their house. Nadia called to him, and he hurriedly climbed into the carriage.

By the time they arrived, the fire had spread to an adjacent warehouse, that also belonged to Philip and was also filled with rice.

Philip organized a group of men, and they managed to save some of the rice from the second warehouse, but it was very little compared to all that had been lost.

Financially it represented a disaster for Philip. Added to the other difficulties he had faced so far, he knew his business was dangerously threatened. It would take virtually all of his capital to try to save it.

* * * * *

Other merchants were suffering as well. Not only was the government requisitioning supplies at their special low rate in enormous quantities, but taxes were being increased by large amounts every few months. That summer, many of the smaller merchants had gone out of business, not only in Rasht, but in Tabriz, and in Tehran.

Throughout the country there were complaints from the populace. Conditions were as bad as they had been under Muhammed Ali Shah, if not worse.

Philip's taxes were outrageously high, based on assets that had been taken by the cossacks or burned in the warehouse fires. He protested the assessment, but it did no good. He was forced to borrow money to pay what the government demanded.

But the government was not exempt from difficulties. The raid on the munitions shipment in which Pasha Jalali was taken hostage had been only the beginning of the *jangalis'* attacks on the cossacks and the foreign-dominated regime. There were numerous raids on shipments of government goods. And several minor government officials had been taken hostage and were being held for ransom.

In the south, the Arab sheikhs, aided by the Germans, were making trouble for the British.

As yet, however, there had been no major battle involving the *jangali*.

In November of 1915, the Russians invaded northern Persia, taking control of the government at Rasht, Tabriz, and Tehran, claiming they were doing so to protect their interests against German influences.

This was what Mirza had been waiting for. The enemy had stepped forward into the light, no longer hiding behind the screen working a puppet government. Mirza now had a strong, well-trained military force; all he had to do was rally the general population to his cause.

To do this, he would have to show himself in public—take the chance of appearing in town squares to speak. The best occasion for doing this would be during Moharram, the holiest of holidays for Moslems, commemorating the death of Muhammed's son. During this period, the Russians would exert great caution to keep from provoking trouble, for Moslem passions were at a religious peak.

* * * * *

In the course of his investigations to obtain information to publish in the newspaper *Jangal*, Gregor learned a great many things that ordinary people would not know, private things about some of the leading citizens of Rasht. One thing he had found out about Philip Boustani troubled him greatly. The town's leading merchant was having financial difficulties. He had been borrowing large sums of money.

Gregor did not know whether or not he should share this information with Nadia. He was fairly certain she was unaware of it, even though the reasons were there for anyone to see.

That fall, Gregor had been sitting for a portrait in Nadia's studio when he had spare time. There had been no commissions for a while, and she had suggested painting him just for something to do—and, perhaps, for the two of them to have something to do together. During those sittings, they had talked a great deal, growing even closer now that Tatiana was married and working hard at the *jangali* clinic.

Several times he had been tempted to mention her father's problems, but had held back.

One afternoon in November, as the sitting was nearing an end, Gregor decided finally to say something about it. Nadia was concentrating on a few last-minute brush strokes to Gregor's cheek, and she dismissed the matter, saying, "I'm sure it's not serious; otherwise Papa would have said something to Mama, if not to me. He should have everything all worked out in a few weeks."

Gregor walked over to stand beside her as she began to wash her brushes in turpentine. "From what I hear," he said cautiously, "this is only the beginning of his difficulties. There seems to be a deliberate effort under way to try to bankrupt him."

Nadia paused in her cleaning up, to stare at him. "Are you sure of this?" she asked. "Or is it merely rumor?"

"At the moment," Gregor replied, "it's only rumor. But from some very good sources."

Nadia smiled, as if to dismiss the subject. "I'll talk to Papa," she said. "But I'm sure he can handle it. He always has."

Gregor looked at the painting of himself. It was a good likeness, but the style could not be described as realistic. Quite the contrary. There was a flatness to it, and the work concentrated on the composition, which set the figure against Arabic words of all sorts. It was, Nadia had explained, the style a Paris art dealer had preferred to the realistic one and which she was beginning to find more and more interesting.

She had made him look very handsome, much better looking than he felt he truly was.

"Is that really the way you see me?" he asked, teasingly.

"Yes," Nadia replied. "Why?"

Gregor shrugged, somewhat embarrassed by the thoughts that were in his mind. "You make me look like someone who is very interesting," he said cautiously. "I see a lot of love going into this painting."

Nadia looked at him, startled, catching her breath momentarily. Then she smiled playfully. "What if I told you a lot of love has gone into it? What would you do?"

"This," Gregor said, reaching out and pulling her to him and kissing her tenderly.

Nadia did not protest, but seemed to melt into his arms, welcoming the embrace and the love from his lips. Throughout their friendship, they had expressed affection many times, hinted at how deeply they cared for each other, but both deliberately kept a distance. This was the first time they had given in to the passion they felt, and the kiss lingered in ebbs and flows like waves on a shore.

Suddenly and abruptly, it was ended by a knock on the studio door.

Nadia broke away, frowning in annoyance. "I can't imagine who that could be," she said, straightening her face and hair before moving toward the door. "I'm not expecting anyone."

When she opened the door, Gregor recognized the man standing there as someone whose portrait Nadia had painted. The last commissioned work she had done. But, to Gregor, he looked somehow ludicrous, for he was short and plump, and he had two large sleek Afghan hounds on leashes, standing obediently at his side.

"Mr. Mizrahi!" Nadia exlaimed in genuine surprise. Then to hide any annoyance that may have crept into her voice, she added, "How nice to see you."

"I am sorry to have come unannounced," he said, then glanced suspiciously at Gregor. "I hope I am not disturbing you."

"No," she said guardedly. "We've just finished a sitting. Please come in." She stepped aside to make room for the two dogs. "What lovely animals," she said. "They must be the ones you told me about—Major and Rajah?"

"Yes," Isaac acknowledged proudly. "That's why I've come. I've been so pleased with the portrait, I thought I would ask if you would consider doing a painting of them."

Somewhat nonplussed, Nadia studied the two dogs. "I don't know," she said. "I've only painted dogs as accessories in paintings, as a part of a portrait. I've never considered making them the center of interest."

"Of course I will pay," Isaac Mizrahi said, as if that were an important consideration. "Quite well."

"That's not what concerns me," Nadia told him, somewhat irritably. "It would be quite a challenge to do a portrait of two dogs. I'm not sure how I would approach it."

Gregor realized that Nadia was embarrassed. He decided it would be best for him to leave. "I believe we've finished for the day," he told Nadia, smiling to convey sympathy for her predicament. "I'll go and let you discuss business."

Oh his way home, he kept trying to recall how he knew the name Isaac Mizrahi. He was sure he had heard it quite recently.

* * * * *

When he received his November tax assessment, Philip Boustani was enraged. Clearly, the rumor that Gregor had heard and reported to Nadia was true. The only explanation for such a high assessment had to be that the government wanted to drive him to bankruptcy. The payment they demanded was more than the value of everything he owned.

He had already borrowed heavily to pay the last assessment; he didn't see how he could possibly borrow more.

He had to make a plea for a reassessment, though he felt sure it would do no good.

He did not even wait a day to go to the government tax offices to ask to speak to the deputy whose signature appeared cn his assessment. It was clearly a Jewish name—Isaac Mizrahi—and he hoped the man might be sympathetic to his plight.

The moment he stepped into the deputy's office, he recognized Mizrahi from the portrait Nadia had done. He had never known the man's name, only that it was one of those for which she had been commissioned. Almost immediately, Philip was filled with hope; there was a personal connection he could use to gain the deputy's sympathy. He might have an objective hearing after all.

Mizrahi's manner was very pleasant. He rose from his desk and extended his hand with a smile. "Mr. Boustani," he said, seeming genuinely delighted. "I'm very pleased to meet you. Have a seat and tell me what I can do for you."

Philip had been prepared for a tense situation—heated arguments, demands and counterdemands. This friendly reception made him relax, let down his guard. He sat down across the desk from the deputy, handing the assessment to him. "I have a problem with this evaluation of my holdings," he said pleasantly. "I believe there have been some errors."

Isaac Mizrahi smiled. "Our assessors don't make many mistakes," he said, "but I will have a look at it." He studied the document for a few moments, then looked up to say, "It all seems to be in order as far as I can see."

"There are goods listed that I do not own," Philip said, still in control. "The quantities of rice alone are five times what I actually have in storage. Two of the warehouses listed were burned to the ground several months ago."

The pleasant manner disappeared from Isaac Mizrahi. "Our assessors don't make that kind of error," he said. "Perhaps they found the rice in storage at some other location."

"I have no other storage areas," Philip challenged, his anger beginning to show. "If they can find other warehouses, let them prove it."

The deputy smiled coldly. "That's not the way we operate," he said. "I'm afraid you must pay the amount assessed."

Philip's hopes were dashed. Mizrahi's pleasant manner had meant nothing. "There is no way I can pay this huge amount," he said, attempting to maintain control. "I would have to sell my house, everything I own. I can't allow my family to be put out on the street, without a place to live."

"I can sympathize with your concern," Mizrahi said "As a matter of fact, I believe I know your daughter, Nadia. She painted a portrait of me; I've been very pleased with it. My friends have all admired it."

"Yes," Philip said distractedly, "Nadia is quite good."

"I also have a great admiration for Nadia herself," Isaac said clumsily. "This is perhaps not the best time to say this, but I have been wanting to speak to you for some time. However, it may be a solution to your problem."

Philip stared at the man curiously, as yet having no idea what he was trying to say.

"I might be able to assist you in paying your taxes," Mizrahi said bluntly, "if I were your son-in-law."

Still, it took a moment for the man's meaning to register. Philip stared at him blankly. "You mean . . . ?"

"I am very much in love with Nadia," Isaac said. "And I would like to marry her. I am prepared to pay a considerable settlement."

Philip was stunned. He could not envision this man with his daughter; he had to be twice her age. "How does Nadia feel about you?" Philip asked. "Does she love you as well?"

"I don't know," Mizrahi said. "I have not mentioned my love to her. I suppose I am somewhat old fashioned, but I believe in our tradition. I have spoken to you first, because a father will know better than the daughter what is best for her."

Philip was still having difficulty with the idea. "Yes, I understand," he stammered. "Well, I will want to take into consideration my daughter's feelings, and I must discuss it with my wife as well.

"I assure you I am quite wealthy," Mizrahi said. "I can provide you with a listing of my assets, as well as a family background, if you wish."

The man was beginning to annoy Philip with his talk of money. "First, I must speak to my daughter," he said. "That is my major concern."

"Of course," Mizrahi smiled confidently. "And if the marriage can be arranged quickly, I will be pleased to take care of your tax payment before the deadline."

Philip left the tax office, feeling somehow soiled by the confrontation. Arranged marriages had been a tradition for centuries, but he did not like to feel that he would be selling his daughter to save his own skin.

* * * * *

Against Philip's wishes, Judith Boustani spoke to Nadia before he had an opportunity to do so. "Normally I would not disobey him," Judith explained, "but this situation is truly desperate. He is about to lose everything he's worked for all his life, and I know he will not tell you about it. As always he will be concerned only about your wishes."

The thought of marrying Isaac Mizrahi horrified Nadia. Of course, she did not love him; she loved Gregor. But she knew that she could never marry a Christian; that would hurt her parents too much. It was that knowledge that had kept her from expressing her feelings to anyone except Tatiana. Yet, the thought of marrying someone she had no feelings for whatever was beyond imagining.

"I still have quite a bit of my inheritance from Professor Nichola," she told her mother. "Would that help Papa?"

"My dear, I don't think he would accept it," Judith told her. "And I'm sure it would be nowhere near enough. The assessment is incredibly high."

She felt a terrible sinking feeling in the pit of her stomach. She knew there was no other way. By offering her own money, she would be admitting to her father that she did not want to marry this man. She could not then follow the path that had been offered.

There seemed to be no other way of saving her father from financial ruin.

She would have to do it. Somehow, when Philip spoke to her, she would have to lie. She would have to tell him that she did, indeed, love Isaac Mizrahi.

She would have to marry the man. Perhaps it would all be for the best, since she could not marry the man she loved.

Chapter 28

For some time, Gregor had the impression he was being followed. In the beginning, he had no tangible reason for feeling this. Whenever he would be walking in the street, he would sense there was someone behind him, but when he turned around, he could not find anyone in particular who looked suspicious.

Yet, the sensation persisted.

One day, however, after turning around to look several times, he was able to pick out a young boy of about sixteen, dressed shabbily in dirty robes.

He decided he had to know the reason for it. After turning a corner, he stopped and waited for the boy to catch up to him, prepared to confront him.

When the boy turned the corner, he was startled to find Gregor there facing him. After a moment of confusion, he tried to dart out of the way, but Gregor grabbed him roughly by the collar.

"Why are you following me?" Gregor demanded.

"I'm not following you," the boy protested, frightened. "I don't even know who you are."

"You're lying! Someone is paying you," Gregor pressed, shoving the boy against the wall of a building. "That's it, isn't it."

"I mean no harm to you," the boy said, his voice shaking with fear. "I need the money."

"Who is it who's doing this?" Gregor demanded. "Who's paying you to follow me?"

"I don't know his name," the boy said, breaking. "He's just a rich man, who pays well."

Gregor relaxed, loosening his grip on the boy's collar. "Here, boy," he said more pleasantly. "I'll pay you even better." He took some money out of his pocket. "You tell me everything you can about the man. And you tell me what you've told him."

"Yes, sir," the boy said gratefully, taking the money. "I think he's Jewish," he told Gregor. "Older than you are, and fatter. Not too tall."

Gregor realized that could be any number of people. "He wasn't a Cossack?" he asked.

"Oh, no sir," the boy said definitely. "He wore a suit like a businessman." He paused. "And once when he came, he had two dogs with him."

That told Gregor the identity of the man. But why would Isaac Mizrahi want to know of his movements?

"And what have you told him?" Gregor asked.

"Where you go," the boy said, "and how long you stay there."

When he managed to get details out of the boy, Gregor was concerned, but not overly so. He had reported his movements to the building where he had the newspaper office, to the bazaar, and to the Sarkissian home, as well as to the Boustani home.

At least he had not managed to follow him to the Valley of the Trees.

Gregor gave the boy a little extra money, saying, "This is so you won't tell this man you've talked to me. And there'll be more for you if you come to me and tell me when he asks you any more questions."

Then, one morning when Gregor reported to his newspaper office, he had the impression someone had been there during the night. Nothing was missing, but a few items seemed not to be precisely where he had left them.

He was sure the boy would not have broken into his shop, and he could not imagine why Isaac Mizrahi should want to know what was in this room—unless he were working closely with the Cossacks. That was entirely possible, for Gregor had now learned enough about the government bureaucrat to know that he would do anything for his own profit or advancement.

Gregor had reason to be especially cautious about his newspaper work, since the Russians had taken complete control of the government, for the issues of *Jangal* had become blatantly seditious, demanding the Russians and the ruling government both be thrown out of the country, and insisting on the institution of a Persian government for the Persians, free of all outside influence.

Gregor decided it was time to find another location for printing and publishing the newspaper. He also had to notify Mirza of what had happened, to give him warning that they might expect trouble. On one of Tatiana's visits to the city, accompanied by Kouroush, he gave them the message to give to Mirza.

Kouroush was very concerned when he learned who was involved. "Isaac

Mizrahi has worked very closely with my father in the past," he explained. "Anything he knows, you can be sure the Cossacks will learn very quickly."

Gregor decided, to be safe, he would ask one of his government spies to find out if anyone in the government, particularly in the Cossack Brigade, had been asking questions about him.

The day before he was set to move the newspaper office to a new location, he received his report; the only person who had been inquiring about him was Sylvia Zinoviev.

Gregor was startled. "But she should be in Teheran," he exclaimed.

"Not any more," the spy told him. "Her father has been given a promotion and has been assigned to the Russian military government here in Rasht."

Sylvia. It had been a long time since Gregor had even thought about her. But he felt sure he would be in no danger from her. Even though they were no longer lovers, he was confident she would not betray him. And she had no idea where his newspaper office was in Rasht.

Even if she did, she would not slip into it secretly at night, when he was not there.

No, if there was someone in the government interested in his movements, it was someone other than Sylvia. It was probably, as Kouroush had suggested, Pasha Jalali.

The first week in December, he learned that his guess was correct.

He had already moved his newspaper office and was continuing to print. He was sure he had never been followed to its new location. As always, he spent much of his time working with Rajik in his shop in the bazaar. As far as the authorities knew, that was his sole occupation.

It was an ordinary day in the bazaar. Gregor was there with Rajik, and he was wearing his apron, in the process of scooping up some dates for a customer, when suddenly a group of Persian Cossacks burst into the shop, guns drawn, aiming them at him.

An instant later, Pasha Jalali strode in, lifted his arm, and pointed to Gregor. "That's the man," he said. "Seize him!"

Gregor was stunned. He did not move, but Rajik did. Swiftly, he stepped in front of the two Cossacks who were striding toward Gregor, intent upon taking him into custody, while two others kept their guns on him.

"What are you doing?" Rajik demanded. "No charges have been made against my son. He's done nothing wrong."

"Get out of the way, old man," Pasha sneered. "He will be charged at the proper time, before he is hanged as a traitor."

The two Cossacks tried to shove Rajik out of the way, but he struggled to prevent them from crossing the room to where Gregor stood.

Gregor could not bear to see his father injured, especially in trying to defend him. He rushed into the fray, crying, "No, Papa. You must let them take me."

The customer he had been helping, a woman, screamed.

As they scuffled, a gun was fired. A body fell to the floor. It was Rajik.

In the moment of shock, the scuffling stopped. Rajik's voice gasped hoarsely, "Run, Gregor! Run away! Don't let them take you!"

"No, Papa!" Gregor cried. "You're hurt!"

"I'm all right!" Rajik said more urgently. "They won't do anything to me! Go! Get away!"

Reluctantly, Gregor did as he was told. He dashed toward the door of the shop. Just as he leaped into the street of the bazaar, a gun was fired behind him, and almost immediately he felt a sharp burning pain in his right shoulder.

He stumbled momentarily from the impact of the bullet, but he managed to catch himself and keep running, shoving his way through the crowds of shoppers.

The Cossacks ran after him, but in the crowded bazaar street, they did not dare to fire their guns.

Despite the sharp pain in his shoulder, Gregor kept running. He had to try to elude his pursuers in the crowded bazaar. If they were still behind him when he was out in the open streets, they could easily shoot him.

His pursuers were close behind. Though Gregor was a good runner, the pain of his injury slowed him down. Glancing behind him, he saw they were gaining on him.

He turned a corner. Somehow he had to elude them, if not with speed, then with craft.

He was in the street of the rug merchants. Gregor did not like to be destructive toward other people's property, but he saw his chance ahead. A number of small rolled carpets were stacked precariously outside a shop.

Gregor knew from experience the one carpet that held all the others in place.

As he rushed by, he paused only long enough to dislodge the crucial carpet, setting the rugs to rolling behind him, right in the path of the pursuing Cossacks.

Quickly he turned a corner into another street, his mind racing, trying to think of a hiding place. Somehow he had to pause to rest. The pain in his shoulder was excruciating.

When he reached the street of the metalworkers, Gregor could see that the Cossacks were gaining on him again. As he passed a bin of copper pots, he overturned it as he had the rugs, hoping again to slow the pursuers.

This time he dodged into a narrow alley that connected with the street of the potters. On that street, he remembered, there was an empty shop, boarded up. If the door was unlocked, he might be able to slip into hiding.

It was! Glancing behind him, he saw that the soldiers had not yet reached the street. He dashed inside, closing the door behind him.

He did not want to remain there too long; he simply wanted to pause long enough to catch his breath and look to see how badly his shoulder was bleeding. He stood fearfully against the wall, just inside the door, breathing heavily, listening to the sounds outside. Yes, he heard the footsteps of the Cossacks running past. When he felt he had regained sufficient strength, he hurried through the empty shop and slipped into the back alley, which would take him outside to the city streets.

The Cossacks were nowhere to be seen. He hoped they had given up the pursuit. However, he would have to get away quickly and find someplace to hide until dark. He would also have to find some way to bind his wound to stop the bleeding.

He could not go home, for they would surely look there. The only other place Gregor could think of was the Boustani home, Nadia's studio, though they might also search for him there. But Nadia and Philip were the only people who might be able to help to get him to the Valley of the Trees.

Gregor wound his way through the back streets, hoping not to attract attention to his condition. When he finally reached the Boustani home, his spirits fell. Nadia was not alone in her studio. Gregor recognized the red automobile parked on the street; it belonged to Isaac Mizrahi.

What was he doing there again? Trying one more time to get Nadia to paint a portrait of his pampered dogs?

He would be the worst possible person for Gregor to run into at the moment.

Trying to avoid being seen from the house or the studio, Gregor slipped through the Boustani gardens to a small shed behind the studio. There he would rest until Nadia was alone.

While he waited, he began to wonder why the sly government official should be spending so much time at Nadia's studio. There had to be a reason other than his interest in her paintings. He wondered if he was up to something. The man was in the tax department, and he had considerable control over Philip Boustani's tax assessments.

When Gregor recovered, he would have to investigate this.

It seemed an eternity before Isaac Mizrahi left the studio, and then—for a moment—Gregor thought he might be discovered, for the dogs, sensing his presence, began barking at the shed.

"It's probably a cat," he heard Nadia tell her guest. Then the man and the dogs moved on.

Gregor waited until he heard the sound of the car engine starting and moving away before he left his hiding place and climbed the stairs to Nadia's studio.

When Nadia opened the door in response to his knock, she had to catch herself to keep from screaming. "What's happened?" she asked urgently, staring at the blood staining Gregor's shirt and coat. Swiftly, she helped him into the room and onto a small sofa.

Gregor explained as well as he could in his weakened condition.

"We must get you to a doctor," Nadia said anxiously.

"Not now," Gregor told her. "Just bind my wound to stop the bleeding. Then, after dark, get me to Dr. Heshmat. If he's not in, I have to find a way to get to the Valley of the Trees. To stay in the city would be to endanger anyone who helps me."

As it turned out, Dr. Heshmat was not in Rasht. It was left to Nadia and Philip to take Gregor to the *jangali* encampment. That would be difficult, because he could not ride horseback in his condition. They would have to find a wagon or a carriage.

Philip chose to use his own carriage, so they could close the shades over the windows to keep Gregor hidden. It would, however, have some difficulty making the last leg of the journey, because it was a lightweight cabriolet, meant only for city use.

By the time they reached the Valley of the Trees, Gregor was in an extremely weakened condition. Tatiana treated his wounds, and assured everyone he would survive, though he would need a long rest.

He was given a bed in the clinic and was very quickly asleep.

* * * * *

The next day, Gregor felt much better. Yet, for some reason, his friends all tareated him with far greater sympathy and concern than he felt his wound warranted. Nadia and Philip had stayed the night, and they visited him before making the trip back. Nadia could not even look at him without tears forming in her eyes. Then later, Kouroush, Tatiana, and Mirza called on him, and they, too, were extremely solemn.

Something was wrong, something much more than his injury.

Finally, Gregor could stand it no longer. He turned to Mirza and asked. "What is it? What's wrong? Why is everyone so concerned about me?"

He hesitated, glanced at Kouroush and at Tatiana. Then he heaved a sigh, smiled gently, and said, "We have heard some bad news, and we wanted to wait until you were stronger before telling you."

Gregor tried to sit up, but the pain in his shoulder was excruciating. "What is it?" he demanded. "What's happened?"

"Lie still," Tatiana ordered. "If you don't relax, we'll all leave."

"Don't treat me like a child!" Gregor snapped. He turned to Kouroush. "What is it?"

Kouroush did not reply, but looked questioningly at Mirza. "I think we're going to have to tell him," he said.

Mirza nodded. "You must try to remain calm," he told Gregor. "There was nothing you could do about it." He took a deep breath, and then said, "It's your father. Rajik is dead."

"No!" Gregor protested, sitting up painfully. "But he said he was all right!" His mind was racing. "The cossacks! They punished him because I escaped! That's it, isn't it?"

"No," Kouroush said. "He could not have survived the gunshot wound he received in the shop. He died only moments after you ran away."

Gregor fell back in the hospital bed, breaking into hopeless sobs, crying over and over again, "No! He should have stayed out of it! He should have let them take me!"

Tatiana placed a comforting hand on Gregor's shoulder. "He died very quickly," she said. "He couldn't have suffered long."

Kouroush added, "And you know how he felt about you. If you had been arrested and executed for treason, it would have killed him."

The pain Gregor felt inside was excruciating, far greater than the pain of his injury. Nothing anyone said or did could ease it. Rajik had given him everything, more than a natural father could have, and now he had given him his life.

And Gregor had never done anything to repay all his love and kindness.

His friends would not permit Gregor to go to his father's funeral. Not only was he not in good physical condition, but it would be too great a risk, for he was now a hunted man. The authorities had learned that he was "Baranov," the publisher of *Jangal*. His treason existed in black and white, and if he were caught, he was in greater danger than Kouroush or even Mirza, against whom no serious crime could be proven.

But Gregor could think of nothing but the need to comfort his mother. Dear, sweet, kind-hearted Jeanous. She would surely be heartbroken, for Rajik had been her very life. Rajik and now Gregor. If he could do nothing for his father now, he felt he had to do everything possible for his mother.

Gregor's friends understood this, and the day after the funeral, Mirza arranged to have Jeanous brought to the Valley of the Trees. Her reunion with her son was a tearful one, but she was much stronger than Gregor had given her credit for. "It was as he would have wanted to go," she told Gregor. "You don't know how much happiness you have given him . . . and me." She smiled at him and ran her fingers through his hair. "You must never blame yourself for anything."

Jeanous chose to stay at the Valley of the Trees, near her son, devoting herself to helping Tatiana in the clinic. Somehow it was less lonely and less painful for her to occupy herself with helping others.

* * * * *

But still, Gregor's friends treated him with a special deference. In the days that followed, Nadia and Philip did not return to the *jangali* encampment, but Tatiana, Kouroush, and Mirza were all subdued in his presence, as if watching and waiting for something.

They were especially guarded when he mentioned Nadia's name. Somehow, he sensed, there was some problem involving her. Finally he asked Tatiana.

She hesitated a moment, then sighed and told him what everyone else already knew. "Nadia is to be married," she said mournfully. "Her engagement is to be announced at a party this weekend."

Gregor was stunned. "Married?" he exclaimed. "To whom?"

"To a man named Isaac Mizrahi," Tatiana told him. "It was arranged through Papa."

The idea was incredible to Gregor. He laughed. "You must be joking," he said. "Nadia couldn't marry that man. She couldn't possibly be in love with him."

Tatiana smiled at him sadly. "She's not," she said. "She's doing it only to save Philip from financial ruin. But Philip doesn't know this. He must never know it."

"But Nadia can't marry a man she doesn't love," Gregor protested. "She would be throwing away her whole life."

"I'm not happy about it either," Tatiana confessed. "But it isn't our decision. It's hers. It's what she wants to do."

"But it's not her decision alone," Gregor insisted. "It affects others as well. It affects me. I love her."

"I know," Tatiana said softly. "And she knows. But she also knows she could never marry you."

"I have to see her," Gregor said suddenly. "I have to talk to her. I have to prevent her from doing this."

"Please don't, Gregor," Tatiana said. "Don't make it any more difficult for her than it is already."

*   *   *   *   *

After a lengthy argument, Gregor managed to persuade Kouroush to accompany him to Rasht on the evening of Nadia's engagement party. Tatiana had to have someone to escort her into the city so that she could attend, but she accepted their company reluctantly. They were both wanted by the authorities, and leaving the Valley of the Trees placed them in danger of discovery.

Neither of the two men could attend the party itself, for there were certain to be guests who might recognize them. Some of these might be guests of Isaac Mizrahi, representatives of the government.

Tatiana would try to slip them into the house and upstairs to the bedroom she had once shared with her sister, then arrange for Nadia to go there to speak to Gregor.

By the time they arrived, the sun was already down, and the house was ablaze with light. Carriages and automobiles were drawing up before the house, discharging passengers before moving on. Music from a phonograph drifted out the slightly open parlor windows.

"We'll take our horses to the back," Tatiana instructed. "Then go inside and up the back stairs, so I can wash and change clothes before joining the party."

Gregor and Kouroush had to wait while Tatiana checked to see if it would be safe to go inside and up the back stairs, then stealthily make their way to their hiding place.

After Tatiana went downstairs to join the party, they waited almost an hour before Nadia managed to get away and come upstairs to see Gregor. When she came into the room, she was clearly upset.

"You should not have come," she told Gregor, almost angrily. "The house is full of Russian and Russian Cossack officers. You must leave."

"No," Gregor told her firmly. "I won't go until we have a chance to talk."

"We can't possibly talk now," Nadia said. "If I'm gone too long, my absence will be noticed."

For a moment she softened; her voice became pleading. "I wish you would just go. You aren't going to do or say anything that will stop me."

"I just want to talk," Gregor said gently. "That's all."

"Then you must wait until the party is over," Nadia told him. "And you can't wait here. The only safe place is the studio. Wait for me there." She walked over to a lamp table and picked up a ring of keys. "Take the key and lock the door behind you. I will knock twice for you to let me in."

Gregor accepted the key, and he and Kouroush allowed Nadia to see them to the back stairs.

However, as they passed the front stair landing, Gregor heard a shocked voice cry out softly, "Gregor!"

Turning, he saw Sylvia Zinoviev ascending the stairs. She hurried up to greet him. "What are you doing here?" she asked.

Nadia looked shocked and rather worried.

"I can't explain, Sylvia," Gregor said hastily. "I'm just leaving." He hesitated a moment, then said. "I hope you won't tell anyone that you've seen me."

Sylvia smiled affectionately. "Of course I won't," she assured him. "It's good to see you again."

Kouroush and Gregor waited for hours in Nadia's studio; it seemed as if the party sounds from the house would never end. Even after it was quiet, they waited for the sound of a knock at the door.

Finally it came. Gregor opened the door and let Nadia and Tatiana inside. "I'm sorry it took so long," Nadia apologized, "but Isaac stayed long after everyone else had left."

Tatiana was tired, and it was decided that she and Kouroush would return to the Valley of the Trees, leaving Gregor there to return alone, after he had talked to Nadia.

As soon as they were gone, Nadia turned to Gregor and said, "Please don't tell me not to marry Isaac. My mind is made up. Nothing will make me change it."

"Not even if I tell you I love you?" Gregor asked.

Nadia hesitated; her manner softened. "Not even that," she said, "even though I love you, too."

"I want you to marry me," Gregor said. "You know that we belong together."

"Yes," Nadia admitted, "but I also know that it can never be. I can't do that to my parents."

"You aren't living your parents' lives," Gregor argued.

"Please," Nadia said. "I told you not to try to change my mind."

"You can't expect me to give you up without a fight," Gregor said, almost angrily.

Suddenly, Nadia threw her arms around him, hugging Gregor to her. "Hold me, Gregor," she said, beginning to weep. "Hold me tightly."

Gregor embraced her, held her as if he would never let her go. "Oh, Nadia," he said. "I want you so much. I've got to have you. You belong to me."

"Stay with me tonight," Nadia whispered to him. "Here in the studio. Stay with me and make love to me." She lifted her face to be kissed.

Gregor bent down to allow their lips to meet, at first gently, then gradually more and more passionately until each was consumed by the other's desire.

Nadia had changed her mind, Gregor was sure of it. She knew the mistake she was making; she knew that they must be together, that their love must be allowed to grow and to flower and to bear fruit.

They slept together that night on the small day bed in Nadia's studio, making love and sharing the intimacy of their bodies as a promise of eternal love, releasing the restraints of so many long months of trying not to express what each felt for the other. They were perfect together; if there had been any doubt of that, they disproved it that night.

As the morning glow slowly began to filter into the studio through the skylight, Nadia and Gregor gradually began to waken in each other's arms, content with their intimacy in sharing the hope of a new day.

When he saw her eyes looking at him, Gregor whispered to Nadia, "My dearest, My love, you make me very happy. Now that I have you, I will never let you go."

"But you must," Nadia whispered back. "This must not happen again, for soon I will be another man's wife."

"No," Gregor protested. "You can't mean that! Not after last night!"

Tears began to form in Nadia's eyes, flowing down her cheeks. "I'm sorry," she said, "but that's how it must be. You will always be the man I love, but you cannot be my husband."

Gregor felt angry, hurt, betrayed. But he could see pain as deep as his own in Nadia's eyes. "Please," she whispered. "Let's not talk about it anymore. Let's not spoil what we've had together. Just get dressed and go."

There was nothing more he could do or say. He realized that to fight now would be to destroy all chances he might have. But he could not allow himself to give up. He promised himself he would continue to try to change her mind.

As she had asked, he got out of bed and dressed. But before he left, he held her in his arms and kissed her passionately as a promise never to let her go.

Chapter 29

Mirza's plans for the demonstration during Moharram moved forward. It was scheduled for the eleventh day of the holiest of holidays, a Friday in late December. He was determined that it should pass as peacefully as possible, giving instructions to his followers that they should not carry guns, hoping to make it obvious to the authorities that they did not plan violence.

This was an edict, however, that disturbed many of his followers, who believed the Russians and the Persian Cossacks would provoke violence themselves, and the *jangali* would be left without defense.

As part of the plan, Gregor was to publish an issue of *Jangal* a few days before, calling the people of Rasht and surrounding areas to join in the demonstration. However, the authorities had taken possession of the newspaper office, along with all the copy and plates for that issue.

Hurriedly,he had to prepare a leaflet that would replace the issue for distribution before the important day. It was difficult to do in the short time, but the pressure had one benefical result—it prevented him from thinking too much about Nadia.

As the Friday approached, several of the *jangalis* went to Mirza to plead with him to reconsider the question of arming themselves. They did not like the idea of being completely defenseless in confronting the military. But Mirza remained firm in his decision.

He did not, however, rule out carrying other kinds of weapons. Some of the men hid knives in the folds of their clothing; others fashioned clubs from the wood used for the signs and banners they were to carry. The signs lettered in red and blue, contained revolutionary slogans, demanding that the Russians be thrown out of the country.

Mirza spent his time reviewing the plans with each of the cadre leaders— Kouroush, Kasmayi, and Dr. Heshmat—to make sure everthing went smoothly on the day. Each of the cadres would have smaller groups within them to enter Meydan Rasht, the main square of the city, at separate times, to make it all appear more spontaneous. Gregor would lead one of the smaller groups, under Kouroush's command. Mirza and Kouroush had advised him not to go at all, because the authorities were looking for him and, unlike Kouroush, whose appearance had changed, he would be very recognizeable, but Gregor insisted on being a part of the day.

The groups began to leave the Valley of the Trees early in the morning the day before the demonstration, allowing time between each group's departure, so as not to call attention to their secret location. Those who arrived early were to circle the city so as to enter from the north and west.

As the sun rose over the city on Friday morning, the sky was clear and blue; the city was peaceful, with only a little more activity than was normal for a Friday. Less than an hour later, people began to arrive, not just the *jangalis* from the forest, but also people from the surrounding villages and farms, answering the call printed in Gregor's leaflets.

As the morning progressed, the influx of people swelled enormously, and they were gravitating toward the square in the center of the city, Meydan Rasht.

Meydan Rasht was about fifty yards square, surrounded by a two-foot-deep drainage ditch, beyond which were brick buildings housing shops of all sorts. Wooden bridges crossed the ditch every few yards, affording access to the shops. At the center of the square was a fountain with a sculpture of a lion clutching a sword, the symbol of the Shah. Water streamed from the mouth of the lion. Most of the square was covered in cobblestones, with some areas of loose gravel.

To the south was Shabaz Avenue, Rasht's greatest street, where many official buildings were located, including the Russian Consulate, as well as the hospital and largest mosque.

Anticipating the throng, the police were out early, positioning themselves strategically around the square to be able to move swiftly in case of trouble at any point.

As the hour of the demonstration neared, the cossacks arrived, taking the positions established by the police, so that the police could move through the crowd, observing it at closer range. The crowd was relatively quiet and subdued, until it became aware that Mirza had arrived and was being escorted to the center of the square by a small group of followers that included Dr. Heshmat and Kasmayi. As they had been instructed, both Gregor and Kouroush remained in the middle of the crowd, some distance from the fountain, where they would be less noticeable.

The square was filled with people, in greater numbers than anyone had expected. Immediately surrounding the fountain and Mirza were the strongest of the *jangalis*, in case there should be an attempt by the authorities to take the leader. Others were positioned strategically throughout the square. Women and children took places at the outer fringes, the older children climbing up trees and walls to get a better view. Nadia and Tatiana, along with Philip, were on the sidewalk before the buildings on the south side, subdued and cautious. Those who feared direct contact with the crowd stood on nearby rooftops or watched from upper story windows and balconies. All anxiously awaiting Mirza's speech.

The first to address the assembly was Dr. Heshmat, followed by Kasmayi, who introduced Mirza. As Mirza stepped up on the small, makeshift platform before the fountain, the crowd waved their placards and banners, cheering. For years, the Persian people had longed for a leader to restore their pride and their liberty; here, they hoped, was the man they were seeking. If the articles they had read in *Jangal* were an indication, he was that man, for the ideas expressed there were their own.

As Mirza began to speak, the crowd fell silent. "My brothers and sisters," he said firmly, "we have long suffered the indignities of foreign intervention. The banner of Persia has been trampled in the dirt beneath the boots of Russians and British, who have treated us as conquered slaves without ever having conquered us. The time has come to put an end to their outrages and to restore Persia to the Persians!"

The crowd broke into cheers.

Mirza went on: "You know that I do not speak for the few. I do not speak for those who have scurried to their weekend *dachas* in fine coaches; I speak for a nation of hard-working, honest people who are angry! We are angry because our children—in the face of thousands of *toman* lavished on luxury, in the face of millions lavished on machines of war—go hungry. We are angry because our young men are kidnapped to fight against our neighbors the Turks in the name of Russian and British imperialism!"

A great roar of approval rose from the crowd.

Gregor's eyes scanned the people, observing their reactions. They were with Mirza completely. Near him an old man wept; a woman hugged her children to her, smiling with pride and hope.

Mirza's words vibrated in the clear crisp air, lodging securely in the hearts of his listeners. He spoke of Persia's past glory, of how it once ruled the world, and how others now sought to rule it because of its natural riches.

He called for the people to regain the courage and strength to restore its glory and its integrity.

By the time he had finished his speech, his passion had become the crowd's passion; they would follow him anywhere; he was their undisputed leader. People were weeping openly, men as well as women. Gregor could see that the cossacks and police were worried, almost fearful of what might develop. One policeman near him had even picked up the enthusiasm of the crowd, and was quickly ushered away by his associates, angry at his betrayal.

At the conclusion of the speech, the crowd began to chant vigorously, "Mir-za! Mir-za!" The chant became a powerful single voice of the will of the Persian people. Mirza was lifted onto the shoulders of a group of men who paraded him through the crowd. Banners waved, flowers were flung high into the air. People waved and cheered, adding to the rhythmic chant.

Finally Mirza was let down, and he and his aides passed among the crowd, receiving the adulation of the people more personally and directly. Throwing caution to the winds, Kouroush had left his post and joined the group of *jangali* leaders, accepting his rightful place at Mirza's side.

Gregor wanted to join the group as well, but he was torn between his personal desire and his responsibility for maintaining order in his area. Yet he could see that all of the organization so carefully planned was breaking down in the emotionalism of the moment. Other group leaders had left their posts.

It was only after Gregor noticed Nadia that he made his decision. She was standing against one of the buildings with Tatiana and Philip. Gregor's eyes met Nadia's for a brief painful moment; then Gregor noticed Isaac Mizrahi joining the group, claiming Nadia's attention.

In anguish, Gregor decided it no longer mattered if he were caught and arrested. His place was at Mirza's side. He left his post and moved through the crowd toward the *jangali* leaders.

As he joined his friends, Gregor noticed a trace of anger in Mirza's eyes and anxiety in Kouroush's, but it was only fleeting; they understood and accepted Gregor's decision, welcoming him into their midst. Whatever the consequences, he belonged.

Gradually the demonstration began to resemble a march, with Mirza's group moving toward Shabaz Avenue, and the people following, waving banners and flags, still chanting their support. There had been no order to move toward the Russian Consulate, but all knew the only conclusion to the demonstration had to be there, for the Russian power symbolized the Persian enemy.

*   *   *   *   *

The police, the cossacks, and the Russian military leaders had wanted to confine the demonstration to Meydan Rasht, but they had feared all along it would be impossible to keep them from Shabaz Avenue and the Russian Consulate. They wanted to avoid violence as much as Mirza did, and they were aware of how easily aroused passions could touch off extreme actions.

Major Zinoviev had posted his Russian troops outside the Consulate, surrounding the walls completely, while Pasha Jalali commanded a group of cossacks at the entrance to Shabaz Avenue. They had orders not to fire on the demonstrators, but simply to exert efforts to keep them controlled and contained within the public square.

Faced with over two thousand people attempting to enter Shabaz Avenue, and conscious of the need to avoid violence, Pasha Jalali was faced with a dilemma. There was truly no way to repel the onslaught without resorting to armed force. And, in the very forefront of the group, one of its leaders, was his own son. As much as he despised what his son was attempting to do, he did not want to cause him injury.

At Kouroush's side was Gregor Sarkissian, whom they had sought to arrest for blatant treason, but to attempt to take him now would surely provoke trouble from the crowd. However, the state faced an even greater threat from Mirza Kuchik Khan after this day; somehow he must be stopped, but any effort to do so today would be risky.

Pasha withstood the mob as long as he could do so without ordering his men to raise their guns. Finally he had to give the order to fall back and allow the people into Shabaz Avenue.

The crowd surged through, like water suddenly released from a dam.

*   *   *   *   *

The people resented the presence of the military, both the Russian troops and the cossacks; they were the only visible and tangible representatives of the hated oppressors. It was perhaps inevitable that they would be subjected to abuse, some of it extreme. The fragile thread of peace was dependent upon the ability of the soldiers to endure and take the abuse impersonally.

When the violence erupted, it began—as it so often does—for the most innocuous of reasons.

On the fringes of the group marched an elderly Moslem woman with her ten-year-old grandson. She had picked up a skewer from a pushcart food vendor and carried it for protection in case of trouble. She brandished it in the air under the noses of the soldiers posted along Shabaz Avenue, a tip of her long veil clasped in the same hand. As she did so, she yelled at the guards, "I hate these foreign devils! Look at them—police, soldiers— they think we are the enemy! But they have taken everything from us! They are the enemy!"

With each step, the old woman's fury increased, but her progress was made difficult by the jostling of the crowd. When she came face to face with a Russian soldier, standing in her way, she gave him a violent shove, sending him sprawling to the pavement, his handgun hanging loosely at his side.

Instinctively, the soldier grabbed for his gun and aimed it at the old woman, fear and rage in his eyes.

"Don't look at me like that!" the woman screamed at him, waving her skewer in his face. "I should jab out your eyeballs, you Russian pig!"

The woman's little grandson did not fully understand what was happening, only that the soldier on the ground was their enemy and that his grandmother was threatening him. Suddenly, without warning, the boy picked up a stone from the ground and hurled it at the soldier, striking him on the head.

Whether intentionally or unintentionally, the pistol fired its shot, hitting the old woman, who slumped silently to the pavement.

The crowd leaped on the soldier, bludgeoning him to death. In other areas of the street, the demonstrators knew nothing more than that a shot had been fired, and that it could only have come from a soldier, for none of them were armed with guns.

The attack with clubs and knives by the demonstrators came almost simultaneously with the firing of guns from other soldiers. Instantaneously, the demonstration became a riot. Men swung their placards at soldiers on horseback, trying to unseat them before they could fire at the crowd. Gunshots rang out, echoing loudly in the street. Officers, still trying to obey the order not to fire, swung rifle butts at attacking demonstrators to fend off blows.

Many of the demonstrators wanted only to escape the violence, and they pushed and shoved to try to get away, some trampling people in their paths.

There were screams and cries from children separated from their parents; there were cries of agony from the injured.

One aged blind couple struggled to pick their way through the melee with their canes, but they were swamped by people, thrown to the ground and trampled, unable to fully comprehend what was happening about them.

Major Zinoviev was extremely upset by what was happening, but now that violence had erupted, he had no choice but to order more troops into Shabaz Avenue, giving them the right to fire on the crowd when necessary. "Arrest as many of the troublemakers as you can," he commanded. "But most of all, I want the leaders—Mirza Kuchik Khan, the one they call Baranov, the Jalali boy, Dr. Heshmat, and Kasmayi. Arrest them at all costs—and I want them alive."

*   *   *   *   *

When the riot began, Dr. Heshmat and Kasmayi attempted to persuade Mirza to escape. At first, Mirza refused. "I am their leader," he said. "I have brought them to this, and I must not show cowardice."

But Dr. Heshmat told him, "You can do no good by staying. And if you are arrested—or killed— the people will have no leader. All we have worked for will be lost. We must get you to safety, so that we can fight another day."

Finally Mirza relented and allowed them to usher him away from the crowd. However, neither Kouroush nor Gregor accompanied the group. Their only thoughts were for the women they loved—Kouroush for Tatiana and Gregor for Nadia. They tried to push their way through the throng in search of the sisters, praying that they had not joined in the march into Shabaz Avenue, but had remained safely behind in the square.

But the situation in the square was no better than it was in the street. The violence had spread, and it was now beyond stopping. Bodies were falling everywhere, fired upon by the cossacks and Russian soldiers.

They had no difficulty in finding Tatiana. She was just inside the square, attempting to help the injured, treating those she could and mustering others to help get the more seriously wounded to the hospital.

"You must get away," Kouroush told her.

"No," Tatiana said. "I must stay and do what I can to help."

"Where is Nadia?" Gregor asked anxiously. "Is she all right?"

"She's safe," Tatiana told him. "Isaac Mizrahi has taken her home."

Gregor felt both relief and pain on hearing this, relief that his love was in no danger and pain that she did not need him for protection and that right now belonged to someone else. He and Kouroush set about helping Tatiana with the injured. The violence had been indiscriminate in selecting its victims. Not only were soldiers and strong men dead or injured, but women and small children, too. It was these innocents—little boys and girls—that were the saddest to see, for they did not understand what was happening.

Gregor and Kouroush made several trips to the hospital on Shabaz Avenue, carrying children for treatment, the battle raging about them.

They were returning from the hospital to make another trip when they suddenly saw a fresh troop of cossacks lining up in the square sabers raised, preparing to charge into the crowd still fighting in Shabaz Avenue. Between the soldiers and the street, Kouroush could see Tatiana still ministering to the wounded, oblivious to what was about to happen.

As the men on horseback started forward, Kouroush rushed toward Tatiana, screaming for her to get out of the way. Gregor started to run after him, but saw his sister running toward safety. Gregor called to Kouroush to do the same, but he ran heedlessly ahead, trying to reach his wife.

As Gregor himself leaped into a doorway to safety, he caught a brief glimpse of the cossacks passing his friend, one of them slashing downward at Kouroush's head with his saber. Once the phalanx of horsemen had passed him, Gregor rushed to his fallen friend, reaching him at the same time as Tatiana.

Kouroush was not dead, but he was badly wounded, with a large saber cut on the side of his face and neck. Immediately, Tatiana set about making a bandage from her undergarments to stop the bleeding. "This will work for a moment, she said. "But we must get him to the hospital quickly." She looked up at Gregor. "Do you think we can carry him?"

"Of course," Gregor smiled encouragingly. "We'll have to.

Supported by one on each side, Kouroush was able to walk. His progress was painful and slow through the devastated street toward the Rasht hospital, aware of even more injured all about them after the sweep of the cossacks.

It was Russian soldiers rather than cossacks who stopped them, only a short distance from their goal. "That's one of them," the sergeant said, pointing to Gregor. "The one they call Baranov." Then he commanded, "Take him!"

Swiftly two soldiers grabbed Gregor before he could even protest. "What about the other man?" one of the soldiers asked, nodding toward Kouroush.

"I don't recognize him," the sergeant said. "And from the looks of that wound, he's about done for anyway. Leave him."

Gregor had only a moment to look into his sister's pained eyes and at his friend, now slumped onto the pavement, before he was roughly led away by the Russians.

A short distance away, he was shoved into a jail wagon with other men taken prisoner. He recognized a few of them, but none were among the *jangali* leaders.

He was sure they had all gotten away to safety, all except him and Kouroush. And Kouroush's life now dangled by a thin thread.

Chapter 30

In the military prison barracks, the prisoners were divided into three groups. To Gregor, many of the arrests made no sense at all; they had just taken prisoners— indiscriminately—young and old, rich and poor. In his section, one of the prisoners was a deaf mute, middle-aged and poor, who walked among the others, frantically gesturing with his hands, trying to communicate his innocence to the guards and the other prisoners.

It was the same frustration that many of the men in the holding area felt; they had done nothing that warranted arrest and imprisonment. Gregor at least knew why he was there, and he had a good idea of what his fate would be, though a sentence of death could hardly be a comfort. He was calm, speaking very little to his fellow prisoners, but observing them with sympathy.

He also felt a degree of guilt, for the words he had written in *Jangal* had played a significant part in what had happened to these people. He had written nothing but the truth, and the ideals were important and still valid, but he could not help but wonder how many innocent people would die before they were achieved. And that made him sad.

They spent a long night without being charged, indeed without being told anything. Gregor spent the night sitting on the hard floor in a dark corner of the holding cell, unable to sleep. He did not know how many hours of life remained to him, and he did not want to waste them in dreams, though his mind and body ached for escape.

Throughout the night, his eyes were invariably drawn to the single barred window high up on the wall, the only portal to the outside world and freedom. The rising of the morning sun gave evidence through that opening, beginning with a dull pink glow, gradually becoming lighter until beams of sunlight filtered through, casting shadows from the window bars on the floor of the cell, and illuminating the frightened, desolate inmates.

Gregor wondered if it would be the last sunrise he would see. If not, how many more would there be? But did it really matter, living without the woman he loved? Could he stand to go on, seeing her with another man—and a man like Isaac Mizrahi, at that?

Perhaps it was for the best. Yet, something within him rebelled at the thought, insisted that he must go on living, that he must not give up.

A few hours after sunrise, the Russian guards began to take the prisoners from the cell, one at a time. They gave no explanation, but the prisoners assumed they were being taken for trial. None of those taken away were returned to the holding cell, but there were sounds of other cell doors opening and closing from time to time.

It was almost midday by the time the guards took Gregor. He was feeling weak and fatigued, having had nothing to eat or drink through the long wait.

He was taken to a simple, makeshift courtroom and placed before a military tribunal, comprised almost entirely of Russian officers. The only Persian present was Pasha Jalali. Presumably his presence was required so that prisoners could not complain that they were being tried by a foreign power with no legal jurisdiction. The presiding officer was Major Ivan Zinoviev.

But the real shock to Gregor was to see Sylvia Zinoviev seated at a small table to the right of the judges' bench, taking notes with pencil and paper.

Sylvia was equally shocked to see Gregor. He saw in her eyes a fleeting look of pain and terror before she looked away. From that point on, throughout the entire proceeding, she kept her eyes averted, looking only at the transcription she was taking for the court records.

Gregor was forced to remain standing before the long desk, facing the Russian officers, his hands manacled behind him, guards on each side of him. There was a long moment of silence as the military judges shuffled their papers.

Then Major Zinoviev looked up at Gregor coldly. "What is your name?" he snapped curtly.

"Gregor Sarkissian," Gregor replied simply but proudly.

"But you are also know by the name Baranov," Pasha Jalali broke in, "are you not?"

"That was my name at one time," Gregor acknowledged. "Sarkissian is the name of my adopted parents."

Zinoviev studied Gregor for a moment, then asked, "Have you written and published a newspaper using the name Baranov?"

"Sir," Gregor said, "with all due respect, I do not feel obligated to answer further questions unless I am told what crime I am being charged with."

Zinoviev scowled, his white brows furrowed, and his small mouth set grimly beneath his white mustache. "You are being charged with treason," he said almost angrily. "You are being accused of fostering revolution."

"But this is a Russian court, sir," Gregor said firmly. "And I am a Persian citizen. Am I being accused of being a traitor to Russia? If so, the charge is a foolish one."

Zinoviev started to speak, but Pasha Jalali broke in to say, "This is the man Baranov. We have witnesses who can link him to the offices of *Jangal*. You should pronounce sentence and get on with the others."

"In due time," the Major told Pasha, somewhat annoyed. "In due time." Then he turned back to Gregor. "You were born in Russian territory, were you not?"

Gregor glared at him defiantly. "I was born in Azerbaijan, a Persian territory occupied by Russians," he said.

Zinoviev looked down at a document before him, then asked, "And was your father Alexei Mehdovi, also known as Alexei Baranov, killed in the Baku riots in 1904?

"Yes, sir," Gregor replied proudly.

"And is your mother Maria Baranov being held in Siberia as a prisoner of Mother Russia?"

"Yes, sir," Gregor replied.

"And do you still deny that you are the publisher of the newspaper called *Jangal*?" Zinoviev snapped.

"I do not deny it," Gregor said. "Neither do I acknowledge it."

Zinoviev's gray eyes flashed angrily. "Gregor Sarkissian, also known as Gregor Baranov," he said loudly, "You are pronounced guilty of treason by this court. Furthermore, you are condemned to be taken from this prison at dawn, tomorrow, December 25, 1915, where you will be executed by firing squad."

He looked at the guards. "Take him away and bring in the next prisoner."

* * * * *

Sylvia Zinoviev had a great deal of difficulty keeping her emotions hidden. She had wanted to scream out to her father not to do this; she had wanted to tell him this was the man she loved, the man she would lay down her own life for; she had wanted to plead for his life to be spared. Yet she had remained silent, knowing her father would not compromise his duty for the sake of his daughter's feelings.

She would have to do something herself to save him. But what? Her mind raced in search of a solution.

As the next prisoner was brought in for trial, she was so concerned about Gregor she could hardly concentrate on her work. To make matters worse, this prisoner was a deaf mute, and she had to try to interpret and transcribe facial gestures and almost inaudible sounds as his responses to questions.

She realized she had to regain her control when she saw that she was getting two files mixed up—Gregor's and this deaf mute's, a man named Nosrat Yeganeh. She had to keep them straight.

It was then that the idea occurred to her. Could she possibly do such a thing? It would mean condemning an innocent man to death in order to save Gregor. Yet, someone such as this deaf mute could not possibly have a full and productive life. Would the world miss someone like him?

She handled all the files, all the orders for execution, all the release documents. It would be simple to make substitutions. Well, not exactly simple, but it could be done. It would take more than merely substituting files. Her father would remember Gregor Sarkissian, and he would recognize a release order as an error. But the only copies that would have to be correct were the file copies, the ones kept in her father's office.

The copies given to the guards to carry out orders were eventually destroyed.

Sylvia could alter those copies, and no one would ever realize it. Gregor could be set free, and another man executed in his place. Then, all Sylvia would have to do would be to get to Gregor to tell him what she had done so that he could assume another name. Officially, Gregor Sarkissian would have to be dead.

However unjust it might be, she decided this was the only solution.

The deaf mute was ordered returned to his cell. He would be released the following morning if an investigation revealed he had done nothing wrong.

Feeling fairly confident that Nosrat Yeganeh would be released, Sylvia began to make her preparations.

* * * * *

Gregor spent what was to be his last night on earth alone in a small individual cell, furnished with a single cot. Like the larger holding cell, it had a small barred window high on the outside wall.

This night, however, he slept. But it was a fitful sleep, interrupted by periods of nightmares and wakefulness. Gregor was not afraid of facing death; he knew it must come to all sometime, somehow. But he wanted more of living; he wanted more of sharing joy with those he loved—with Jeanous, Tatiana, Kouroush, and yes, with Nadia. Most of all with Nadia.

This morning he dreaded the pink light of dawn creeping in through the barred window, for it meant that—at any moment—the guards would be arriving to take him away, out into the prison yard to face the firing squad.

Gregor decided he would try to face death with dignity. He took his handkerchief and did his best to wash his face with spittle. Then, without benefit of a mirror, he tried to straighten his wrinkled clothes and his hair. He could do nothing about the fact that he was unshaven.

Very soon, as expected, there were sounds in the hallway of cell doors being opened and closed, followed by the footsteps of guards and prisoners moving along toward the outside. The footsteps approached his door, and Gregor felt his heart pounding fearfully. Then the footsteps passed, and the guards opened the door of the cell next to his.

Well, other guards perhaps would be coming for him.

But they did not. Within a short while the sounds stopped, and he could hear footsteps outside his window, followed by the sound of marching and military commands.

Gregor climbed upon his cot, straining to reach the window to look out. With effort, he managed to pull himself up into position to see what was happening. About sixteen prisoners had been lined up against the far wall, and a troop of Russian soldiers was being moved into position facing them.

Gregor noticed that the deaf mute was among the prisoners to be executed, and that puzzled him. Surely such a man could not have been capable of a serious crime.

Of all of the prisoners, Gregor knew that his crime was the most severe in the eyes of the Russians. Since he had not been taken with the others, he assumed that he would be executed alone.

To prepare himself for what he would have to face, he watched the others through the cell window, listening to the sharp commands of the lieutenant, and observing the lifting of the rifles, the preparation to fire, and the firing itself, followed by the sudden collapsing of the sixteen bodies.

It was not a pleasant sight. Feeling a queasiness in his stomach, he let himself down from the window and sat on the cot, breathing deeply to calm himself.

No, it was not how he would have chosen to die, if he had a choice.

Time passed as he sat on the cot, waiting and listening for the sounds of the guards coming for him. How much time he sat there Gregor could not be sure, but the sun was well above the horizon before his door was opened.

"Gregor Sarkissian," the guard said. "It's time to go. You're being set free."

"Free?" Gregor replied, uncomprehending. "I'm being set free?"

The guard waved a document in his hand. "That's what it says here," he said. "Come with me now, unless you want to stay here." He grinned.

Gregor got up from the cot and moved toward the door. Something was very strange.

* * * * *

Sylvia Zinoviev reported to work very early that morning. She wanted to make sure that everything went according to her plan; to make sure there was no mistake. She was there before dawn to hand the execution orders to Lieutenant Polokof personally.

She wished it had been some other officer chosen to take the orders, for she hated Polokof, a vain, arrogant man who was constantly making suggestive remarks to her, attempting to seduce her with what he considered to be his irresistible charms.

The lieutenant was surprised to find her there so early, but he accepted his orders with little comment, other than to say, "I'll get my job done quickly and come back for a visit."

Sylvia told him coldly, "I expect to have a very busy morning. Quite a lot of filing to be done."

He grinned suggestively. "I'm sure you can spare a few minutes for me," he said before closing the office door behind him.

For a while, Sylvia could not concentrate on her work. She sat at her desk listening for the shots that would tell her the deed had been done— that all of the prisoners scheduled for execution had been shot, including Nosrat Yeganeh.

When it came, it startled her, causing her to jump as if she herself had been shot. But then she sighed deeply and relaxed. However, she could not stop the tears that welled up in her eyes and began to flow silently down her cheeks. It was a cruel thing she had done, but she could not allow herself to dwell on it.

She took a moment to compose herself, then got up from her desk and went to the outer office to hand the order for Gregor Sarkissian's release to the sergeant, asking for it to be delivered immediately.

Still she could not concentrate on her filing. All of the file copies of the various orders were still lying on her desk when Lieutenant Polokof returned, his morning duty done.

He entered her office without knocking, his arrogant smile on his lips. "I told you I would be back," he said. "You can take a few minutes from your work now.

"I'm sorry," Sylvia said. "I'm really very busy."

The lieutenant surveyed her desk. "It looks like you've done hardly anything since I left," he said, picking up some of the file copies of the orders. "Here, I've just dispatched sixteen men to their rewards, and you haven't even put them in their files."

"I'll get to it," Sylvia said, grabbing the orders from his hands, "if you'll just leave me alone."

Polokof picked up a few others and began to glance through them. "I'll help you," he said. "I'm sure it will be much more enjoyable for you having my help."

"I'd rather do it alone," Sylvia said, trying again to retrieve the orders. But this time Polokof dodged away, studying one of them.

"Gregor Sarkissian," he said. "I don't remember which one he was." He frowned and looked at Sylvia in puzzlement. "In fact, I'm certain you didn't give me this order, but it states clearly he was to be executed."

"You've simply forgotten," Sylvia said anxiously, this time managing to retrieve the papers. "Now, please leave me alone and let me get my work done."

A sneer crept across Polokof's face. "No," he said. "I remember the name of every man I executed. This one was not among them. I don't know why, but you've done something you weren't supposed to do, and I think your father should know about it."

"No!" Sylvia protested too strongly, then caught herself.

"It would be foolish to bother him with this silly idea of yours."

Polokof moved toward her, putting his hand on her waist. "If you don't want me to talk to him about this," he said slyly, "you'll have to make it worth my while."

"Will you please leave me alone!" Sylvia demanded sharply. "If you don't want me to tell him about your advances, you'll forget this nonsense."

He pulled her to him suddenly, into a tight embrace, trying to kiss her.

But Sylvia managed to extricate herself forcefully, then slapped him across the face. "Get out of my office!" she cried.

He did as she asked, but a few minutes later she was called into her father's office.

Her heart was pounding fearfully as she entered, but she was relieved to find that her father was alone. Polokof was not with him; perhaps he had said nothing, after all.

But Major Zinoviev was scowling, and he did not greet his daughter with his usual fatherly banter. "What's this I hear from Polokof?" he demanded. "You did not give him the order to execute that Baranov?"

"He's lying," Sylvia protested.

"He wouldn't lie about a thing like this," her father said. "He swears that sixteen men were executed, but Baranov—or Gregor Sarkissian— was not among them. I insist upon an explanation."

"Papa," Sylvia said coyly, playing the affectionate daughter, "you mustn't believe what that man says. He's just angry because I refused his advances."

But Zinoviev remained grim. "He said you would say that," he told her. "Now, I want an explanation, and I want it immediately."

Her father had never spoken to her so harshly. Tears filled her eyes, threatening to flow uncontrollably, but she bit her lip angrily, attempting to hold them back. "All right," she said defiantly. "I'm in love with Gregor Sarkissian. I have been for years. I could not allow you to kill him."

Zinoviev stared at her for a long time in disbelief. "This is worse than I suspected," he said finally. "I thought perhaps you had been bribed. Who was executed in his place?"

By now, Sylvia was weeping, unable to keep back her pain and fear. "The deaf mute," she confessed.

"And where is Sarkissian?" her father snapped. "Has he been released?"

Sylvia nodded. "I sent the order down a short while ago."

The major stormed out of his office and commanded his orderly to go to the prison barracks to see if Gregor Sarkissian had been released. If not, he was to be returned to his cell immediately. If he had been released, a search must be instituted at once.

Then he returned to his daughter. "You have been a very foolish young woman," he told her. "Of course, I can no longer permit you to work in my office. As it is, my entire career may be ruined by this scandal."

His words gave Sylvia another idea. Until that moment, she had not realized the effect this might have on her father. She had always assumed he was invincible. She stopped her crying. "But, Papa," she said, "no one has to know that Gregor is alive. I've covered it in the files. Officially, he is dead, and the other one is alive. There doesn't have to be a scandal."

For a moment, he considered what she was suggesting. Then he dismissed it. "No," he said, "I couldn't possibly. It's a matter of honor. I must correct your mistake."

"Papa," Sylvia pleaded. "I love him. I love him with all my heart."

Zinoviev shook his head wearily. "All you can think of is love," he said. "You're just a foolish, spoiled young girl after all. I never would have believed it of you." He turned his back on her and walked to gaze out his window. "I will probably be stripped of my rank and be sent home in disgrace. And you are worried about love."

"But there is no need for anyone to even know," she said pleadingly. "Just let him go, and there'll be no trouble. He can change his name, give up his revolutionary activities."

Her father turned and looked at her. His face remained grim, but it was clear he had made a decision. "All right," he said. "I won't say anything, but I'm not going to set him free either. There is a group of prisoners being sent to Siberia. He will be among them."

"But, Papa . . .," Sylvia tried to protest.

"No," he cut her off. "My mind is made up. I couldn't possibly allow him to remain here in Persia, close to you. You must be insane to even consider falling in love with one of them—a Persian, and a revolutionary Persian, at that. He's going to Siberia." He paused, then added. "And you are going to stay home with your mother from now on, like a normal daughter. No more work for you."

* * * * *

Gregor did not understand any of the things that had been happening. First he was told he was being set free; then, at the last minute, the order had been halted, when he was only a few yards away form the prison gate. Finally, after being returned to his cell, he was informed that he was being sent to Siberia, to prison. None of it made sense.

He was still puzzling over the strange turn of events, weeks later, as he rode with the other prisoners in the railroad boxcar, traversing the vast snows of Russia, shivering from the cold and subsisting on stale bread and ice water.

He was alive, but was this kind of life better than death? That, he could not answer.

*   *   *   *   *

Sylvia was miserably unhappy. Not only had she lost Gregor, possibly forever, but she was now forced into the tedious idleness of her mother's daily routine. She felt as if she were imprisoned, just like the man she loved.

She could not bear for this to continue. She had to do something. She had to be with Gregor again, no matter what the cost.

She began to devise a plan to follow him to Siberia.

Chapter 31

Miraculously, Kouroush survived his injuries. It was as much Tatiana's deep love as it was her constant medical attention that helped to pull him through. The day of the demonstration, the Rasht hospital had so many emergency cases, they were able to give each patient no more than cursory treatment, releasing almost all of them immediately, for lack of beds and staff.

With Philip's help, Tatiana had obtained a wagon and transported Kouroush and several others to the clinic at the *jangali* encampment. For the next two days, the wagon was kept busy returning injured *jangalis*. The trips were slow, because of the necessity of avoiding being followed. But the cossacks and the authorities were also occupied with other matters, as a result of the violence.

On one of those trips on the second day they learned that Gregor had been executed by firing squad and that his body was to be buried in an unmarked grave without ceremony, as befitted a traitor.

Philip gave the news to Tatiana and Jeanous at the clinic, suggesting that Tatiana might want to break it to Kouroush after his condition was stable. Gregor's natural sister and adopted mother both attempted to endure the shock bravely, but it was a moment beyond control. They both wept, though Tatiana's were silent tears; embracing Jeanous, she knew that she must be strong, allowing the older woman to sob uncontrollably, having lost both husband and son in such a short time.

When the initial anguish had worn off, Tatiana turned to Philip to ask, "What about Nadia? Has she been told yet?"

"I don't know," Philip replied, looking somewhat puzzled. "I haven't had the opportunity to speak to her about it."

"If you can," Tatiana told him, "try to keep it from her. Let me break the news."

Philip smiled warmly. "I don't understand your reasons," he said, "but I'll try to keep anyone from telling her, and perhaps I can bring her out for a visit soon."

* * * * *

It was over a week before Philip was able to fulfill his promise. Once order had been returned to the city, there had been much to occupy him, for the military rule had become much more stringent, with reinforcements arriving from Russia to make sure there would not soon be a recurrence of the violence.

For some reason that Tatiana could not pinpoint, Nadia seemed radiantly beautiful, even more than normally so. It may have been the added luster to her dark hair, or a rosier glow to her cheeks, or perhaps a calm contentment that had settled over her. She seemed strangely happy.

When she saw this, Tatiana dreaded breaking the news to her, though it had to be done.

Tatiana was on duty at the clinic when Philip and Nadia arrived, but she arranged a break to have tea with her sister in her office. Philip excused himself to meet with Mirza on some business matters.

Over tea, they chatted casually about recent events. Tatiana told her sister about Kouroush's improved condition and about her work in the clinic, and Nadia talked about the plans for her wedding, which was to be in May, though she did not seem excited about the event. In fact, a distinct melancholy came over her as she talked about it.

Finally, there was a long pause, as Tatiana poured each another cup of tea. Nadia broke the silence by asking, "And how is Gregor?"

Tatiana set down the teapot, giving a deep sigh before saying, "There is something important I have to tell you . . . concerning Gregor."

Nadia knew instantly from her sister's tone that something serious had happened. "What is it?" she asked. "Has he been injured? Was it the demonstration?"

"Gregor is dead," Tatiana said softly. "He was arrested and executed."

"No!" Nadia screamed. "It can't be!" And she broke into hysterics.

Tatiana had expected a severe reaction, but such an extreme emotion was not typical of Nadia, whose sobs were interspersed with sounds almost like mocking laughter. Tatiana went to her and tried to comfort her, but it did no good. She could only wait until the grievous shock had run its course.

When it had finally done so, Nadia dried her eyes with a handkerchief and said, "I'm sorry to have lost control, but it's a very ridiculous situation." She paused, looking embarrassed. "You see, there's something nobody knows. Not even you."

"What is it?" Tatiana asked with concern.

Nadia tried to smile. "I think I'm expecting a child," she said. "I'm almost certain of it."

Tatiana was shocked. "And the child would be Gregor's?"

Nadia nodded. "By the time of my wedding," she said, "there will be no way of hiding it."

"Well," Tatiana said, "I will give you an examination so that we can be certain."

Nadia said weakly, "And if you confirm it, can you perform the operation to get rid of the child?"

"You can't mean that!" Tatiana gasped.

"No, I suppose I don't," Nadia said, tears beginning to flow again. "Under normal circumstances, nothing would give me greater pleasure than to bear Gregor's child, but this way . . . "

She broke into sobs, and again Tatiana tried to comfort her. "Perhaps you could arrange to have the wedding now," she suggested. "Isaac Mizrahi could be persuaded to accept the child as his own. It's been only a month."

"That may be my only choice," Nadia said sadly. "Until you told me about Gregor, I . . . I had hoped there might be some other alternative."

* * * * *

Tatiana's examination confirmed what Nadia had suspected. She was with child. Somehow she must persuade her father and Isaac Mizrahi to move the wedding date forward, to have it take place as soon as possible. Nadia was not quite sure how she would accomplish this, so she decided to speak to her mother, to tell her the truth about her condition, to enlist her aid in changing the plans.

Judith Boustani was not shocked by her daughter's confession. She was, on the contrary, very understanding. She knew her daughter's motives for marrying Mizrahi, and she had long suspected Nadia had been in love with Gregor. She was also sympathetic toward her daughter's desire to help, rather than to hurt, her father.

Judith suggested that she take responsiblity for altering the plans so that no suspicion would be attached to Nadia. She had a good excuse; an uncle in Tabriz was having a special birthday party in May, his ninetieth. Because of the wedding, she had assumed she could not go.

The plans were changed without difficulty. In fact, Isaac Mizrahi was so delighted, he suggested moving it up even further than the February date suggested by Philip. Two weeks did not give a great deal of time for completing the preparations and notifying the guests, but with extra effort it could be done.

* * * * *

It proved to be the largest, most elaborate wedding Rasht had seen in a long time. Most of the truly important people in town would attend, including Moslems and Christians, even though it would be a Jewish wedding. The ceremony was to be in the Boustani home, and the guest list included leaders from the government who were friends of Isaac Mizrahi, as well as friends and family of the Boustanis.

Despite his financial difficulties, Philip spared no expense on the wedding feast, nor on his daughter's gown. Not to be outdone, Mizrahi provided gifts, small mementos, for each of the guests. Officers of the Cossack Brigade, such as Pasha Jalali and Reza Khan, would be there, as well as Major Zinoviev and other Russian leaders. For that reason, Nadia could not invite either Mirza or Kouroush, but at least Tatiana could come, though they were not sure how she and Pasha would get along.

The weather in January was somewhat cold for a wedding, but the sky was clear and sunny on the day of the event, promising a pleasant evening.

The ceremony began at dusk with a candlelight procession through the town to the Boustani home, where the guests were welcomed warmly and ushered into the big double parlor, whose sliding doors had been opened to form a large hall where people could dance. The women set down their candles, and the men linked arms to dance the traditional *hora*.

When the dancing stopped, the bride came down the stairs on her father's arm, while a violinist played a haunting melody. The crowd was hushed, completely quiet except for a few whispered comments from the women about how beautiful Nadia looked in her wedding gown.

The groom waited at a canopied altar set up in the parlor, and he smiled proudly as his bride approached.

Nadia may have looked lovely, but she did not feel the joy she had always expected to feel on her wedding day. Instead, there was a sense of dread, of sad resignation. She wanted desperately to turn around and run away, to prevent the ceremony from occurring, yet she knew she could not do that. The decision had been made, and there was no turning back.

The vows were administered by a rabbi, and they were followed by the traditional drinking of the wine, with the empty glass then placed on the floor so that the groom could smash it with his heel, signifying the breaking of the hymen.

With this, the couple was offically married, and the guests cheered and applauded. It was now time to celebrate the union with toasts, dancing, and feasting.

After the bountiful dinner, the wine flowed freely, and the guests mingled and danced happily. Everyone made a point of speaking to the bride and groom to wish them a long and happy life together.

Tatiana was with Nadia when Major Ivan Zinoviev and his wife approached her to offer their felicitations. Although their words were warm and generous, there was a strangely sad look in their eyes, a wistfulness as they looked at each of the two young women.

"I am so sorry your daughter Sylvia was unable to attend," Nadia told them. "I understand she is away at the moment."

"Yes," Major Zinoviev said uncomfortably, his eyes averted. "She's in Russia visiting family."

*   *   *   *   *

At that moment, Sylvia Zinoviev was actually on a train traveling through the Ural Mountains, heading slowly and tediously toward Siberia, gazing out the frosty window at endless miles of snow, dotted occasionally with small log houses shut tightly against the weather, the only sign of life the wisps of smoke streaming from chimneys.

The reality of what she was doing had proved to be much more difficult than the way she had imagined it would be. She had never traveled alone before, and she wished she had company; it was very lonely, and very frightening at times. People were suspicious of an attractive young woman traveling alone. There was also the fact that she was riding in a lower-class coach, which she had never done before, having always had a compartment with her family or a chaperone. But she felt compelled to save her money.

To get the money for the trip, she had sold all her jewelry and furs, except for one sable coat, which she had been sure she would need in the Russian winter. She had no idea if the money would last her the entire trip, even with buying the cheapest train tickets and sparing on food.

She had left her father a note, waiting until after he had reported to the military garrison in the morning before slipping away, certain that her mother would not miss her. She traveled by coach to Enzeli, taking the boat from there to Baku, and then gradually moved north and east by one train after another.

After a week, she was beginning to have doubts about her action. What if she could not see or speak to Gregor? What if he was not happy to see her? After all, they had drifted apart when he had moved from Tehran to Rasht; perhaps he was no longer interested in her.

But somehow she did not believe that was true; she did not want to believe it. Once they were together again, she tried to tell herself, his feelings for her would return. She could be very charming and alluring when she wanted to.

And, in Siberia, Gregor would be very lonely. Even if they could not be together and make love as they had in the past, she would find some way to speak to him, to help him survive the rigorous life. And he would be grateful for that.

Yes, she had to keep believing that.

*   *   *   *   *

Traveling conditions for Gregor were far worse than they were for Sylvia. There was virtually no heat in the prison boxcar, only a small wood stove, with very little fuel provided to keep it going. Gregor quickly learned that coats, blankets, and shoes were the most treasured possessions for prisoners, and it was necessary to sleep lightly to protect what one had.

But the worst of it was the stench. They were unable to wash themselves, and they were lucky to be permitted to open the door even once a day to empty the slop jars that were their toilet facilities.

And when the door was opened, the light of day—especially bright against the snow—was painful to the eyes, for they had no light at all in the sealed boxcar. Invariably, a bitter cold wind blew in, chilling the prisoners to the bone.

At such times, Gregor was torn between a desire to look at the world outside and a need to protect himself against the cold. He had already perceived among his companions the inertia that takes over men imprisoned, the listlessness, the reduction of the world to their own confined situation. He did not want that to happen to him. He wanted to remember the world outside, he wanted not to forget what freedom was, how sunlight felt upon the face, and how clean crisp air could fill the lungs.

He wanted to remain aware of the people who had always been important to him, the people whose passion for freedom was his own passion.

* * * * *

More than the wedding ceremony, Nadia dreaded the wedding bed itself. Physically, she found Isaac Mizrahi repulsive, and she feared she could not pretend to feel otherwise. But because of her condition, the marriage must be consummated, and she must give him no reason to suspect that he was not the first man to make love to her.

Her mother had helped her with this problem, providing a small bladder of chicken's blood to break and spill on the bedsheets.

From her one experience with Gregor, she knew how she must feel and what sort of response would be expected. She could make a valiant effort at playing the part of a proper wife and lover. If necessary, she would close her eyes and pretend she was with Gregor.

Her plan, however, did not account for anything unpredictable from her husband.

It was not that Isaac was not a passionate lover; if anything he was too passionate. In his eagerness to possess Nadia, he was clumsy and inept, making it difficult for Nadia to maintain her pretense of pleasure. He did manage to succeed at penetration, which was a great relief to her, but it was accomplished with much sweat, exertion, and heavy breathing. She did not have to pretend pain at the breaking of the hymen, for his entry was truly painful.

The problem was that he was unable to complete the act, which meant that Nadia would have to encourage him to make love to her again, as soon as possible.

But the thing that frightened her was the possiblility that had not occurred to her until now: what if he was never able to achieve completion? Nadia had heard that was true of some men.

* * * * *

Philp Boustani had been saved from bankruptcy by the loan from Isaac Mizrahi, but that rescue was only temporary. The demands made by the Russian masters did not stop; instead they became increasingly greater with each passing month. The European war was costly for Mother Russia, and she was squeezing funds from any source she could find.

It was no comfort to Philip that the other merchants of Rasht were suffering as badly as he was.

In March, he was faced with another assessment equally as outrageous as the last. Philip did not feel that he could go to his son-in-law for more money; there was something about the man that did not encourage familial affection. But he did feel he could ask for advice.

One evening, when Isaac and Nadia were having dinner at the Boustani home, Philip called Isaac aside to talk to him about his problem. He had noticed a degree of coldness between the newly married couple, but he assumed it signified just one of the minor adjustments every husband and wife invariably passed through.

But when Philip asked for his advice in dealing with the Russian demands, Isaac was curt in his response.

"There's nothing I can do about it," his son-in-law snapped irritably. "I would get into trouble showing preference to my wife's family."

And he would not discuss the matter any further.

Chapter 32

Nadia tried to hide her pregnancy as long as she could. By the third month, it was obvious to anyone who looked closely, and after four months it was no longer possible to conceal at all.

She had no choice but to inform Isaac of her condition. It was difficult for her to do, because their relationship had not been good from the beginning. He sensed that she did not truly love him, and their lovemaking had been erratic, so much so that she doubted if it would have been possible for her to have conceived a child with him. Whether he was capable of perceiving this himself, she wasn't sure. Yet, she had to continue to attempt to bluff her way through this.

At first, Isaac was delighted with the news. "A child!" he exclaimed proudly. "That's wonderful! To be a father at last, at my age!"

For a while, he was extremely solicitous toward her, insisting that she not exert herself too much and even bringing her flowers and little treats. He did not even complain when she used her condition to avoid his lovemaking.

Whether it was the denial of the conjugal bed or perhaps a realization of his inadequacies as a lover, or even some other reason, after a few weeks, Isaac began to suspect that the child Nadia was carrying was not his. He did not say so outright, but Nadia could see that that was what lay behind his change of attitude.

Isaac became extremely jealous of his wife. He began to suggest that she give up painting in the studio behind her parents' home. He always wanted to know what she was working on and would slyly ask whom she had seen during the day. His concern about her leaving her home to go to her studio quickly became an obsession. He even began to appear at the studio unexpectedly at odd times during the day, always seeming to be disappointed to find her there alone, working on a painting.

He frequently made reference to the large loan he had made to Nadia's father, and he complained that Philip still had not managed to bring his business back to a profitable status. These complaints quickly turned to curt, disparaging remarks about her father, remarks that invariably angered Nadia so that she had to respond in kind.

Heated arguments became a regular occurrence at the Mizrahi household.

By the end of the fourth month of their marriage, Nadia had moved out of their bedroom into the guest room, where she locked the door before retiring at night.

With Tatiana far away at the *jangali* encampment and occupied with her medical work, the only comfort Nadia had was her mother. But in May, Judith Boustani left to visit family in Tabriz, and Nadia had to suffer her marital problems alone.

While Judith was away, the fights between Nadia and Isaac became worse. Several times, Isaac resorted to physical violence as an outlet for his anger and jealousy, striking Nadia, once giving her a black eye and at other times causing bruises to her arms and back. He began to call her a whore and charge that he had paid her father a high price for her.

But he stopped short of charging that the child she carried was not his.

* * * * *

The spring rice crop was almost ready for harvesting. If all went well, it would bring the amount Philip needed to pay the tax assessments demanded by the Russians, as well as those of the Persian government, with just enough left over to plant the fall crop.

If anything should happen to the rice, he again would face the prospect of bankruptcy.

That spring, the European war again infringed upon neutral Persia. The Turks had invaded the northwest several times, fighting the Russian troops there; each time the Russians had pushed them back behind their own borders. In the south, the British had increased their military presence, attempting to get rid of the German influence among the Arab tribes of the desert.

It worried Philip that Judith was in Tabriz, for several times the battles between Russians and Turks had come close to the city. There had also been an outbreak of influenza in the area, which some blamed on the war.

This became even more worrisome to Philip when he received a letter from his wife, informing him she was staying longer to help to nurse her uncle, who had come down with influenza. Judith's health had never been strong since she had suffered from cholera so many years before.

Philip should have been able to read behind the rumors and predict what was to happen. Under normal circumstances, he was an astute businessman and would have done so; however, he was so preoccupied with worries, he failed to realize the full implication of the stories of crop failures in the Ukraine, resulting from the war, along with reports of unrest and dissatisfaction among the Russian people.

But the actions of the Russian authorities in Rasht caught him by surprise. They took possession of his rice farms, along with those of others, before they informed him of the fact. The crop, ready for harvest, would be theirs, to be shipped to Russia.

Philip was outraged. The Russians had no legal right to do this; their presence in northern Persia was supposed to be merely to protect their "interests." The taxes that had been levied had been to repay the huge loans made to the Shah and to his predecessors of the Qajar dynasty. Taking possession of the property of Persian citizens was outright thievery.

He was so confident of his rectitude that he did not hesitate to approach his son-in-law about the matter, feeling Isaac would be as upset as he was.

But Isaac Mizrahi was not like other men of Philip's acquaintance. He was first and foremost a tax collector, a government bureaucrat; being a Persian and a Jew were secondary to him. His primary loyalty was to himself and his position within the power structure.

"I've told you there's nothing I can do," he informed his father-in-law after Philip had stormed into his office and told him the situation. "I'm concerned only with assessing and collecting the taxes of the Persian government. I have no influence whatsoever with the Russians."

"The Russians be hanged!" Philip raged. "Your office has the right—no, the duty—to preserve and protect the property you depend on for taxes! The property of Persian citizens! You certainly don't think you'll be able to tax the Russians for that land or that rice, do you?"

"Calm down, Philip," Isaac said nervously. "You seem to be mistaking my office for the police department. If you have a legal grievance, take it there. This is not my concern."

"Not your concern!" Philip retorted angrily. "This is land that your wife should inherit, land that should be passed on to the child she is carrying! You should care about keeping it in the family!"

"The child!" Isaac snapped. "I'm not even sure that child is mine!"

Philip was shocked. What do you mean?" he asked. "Of course it's yours. Who else's could it be?"

"That's what I would like to know," Isaac said with a sneer. "I just don't think it could be mine."

"You're insane," Philip said incredulously. "How dare you even suggest that my daughter, your wife, would...." He couldn't even bring himself to say the words. To him, this entire conversation had become absurd, and he saw no point in continuing it.

Suddenly, abruptly, he turned around and stormed out of Mizrahi's office, even angrier than he had entered it. He had decided, if his government would not help him protect what was his, there was someone who would. He would take his problem to Mirza.

*   *   *   *   *

Judith's uncle in Tabriz died of influenza. She stayed just long enough for the funeral, then returned home to her family, weak and exhausted from the strain of nursing the ninety-year-old man. The day after her arrival at home, she came down with the fever herself.

Philip did not want Nadia to visit her mother because of her pregnancy, but he wanted Judith to have the best care she could. He went to the *jangali* encampment and brought Tatiana home with him to look after her.

Tatiana knew there really wasn't much she could do for her except try to keep the fever down and make her as comfortable and free of pain as possible. She stayed by Judith's bedside day and night, as she had done once before so many years ago, resting on a small cot when she could, but most of the time sitting and applying cold compresses to her mother's face, neck, and chest.

Philip was there much of the time as well, going downstairs periodically for cold water and fresh towels that Tatiana would use for the compresses.

Most of the time, Judith was delirious from the fever, babbling almost incoherently about things from her past—her childhood, the childhood of Nadia and Tatiana, and the hopes and dreams she and Philip had shared.

On the morning of the third day, she awoke with a clear mind. The fever seemed to be down somewhat, and she was generally improved. However, Tatiana knew that this might be only illusory; often influenza patients seemed to improve, only to take a turn for the worse, from which they did not recover. She was guarded about her hopes.

Judith gazed up at Tatiana lovingly, reaching out a hand to caress her cheek. "My dear," she said sweetly, "you look very tired. You must get some rest. I'm much better now."

Tatiana reached up and took the hand that was caressing her cheek, squeezed it affectionately. "I'll get some rest later," she said. "After I've done everything I can."

Judith nodded weakly in understanding. "Where is Philip?" she asked.

"He's downstairs right now," Tatiana told her. "I'm sure he'll be up shortly."

"Good," Judith said. "There's something I must say to him, something he must know in case—in case I don't make it through."

Tatiana smiled encouragingly. "You must make it through, Mama," she said. "For the sake of all of us who love you."

"I'll try, child," Judith replied. "I'll try as hard as I can."

When Philip arrived, Tatiana allowed him to take her place at Judith's bedside. She went over to the cot and lay down to rest.

She was not eavesdropping, but she could not help hearing her parents' conversation.

"Philip, dearest," Judith said faintly, "I have done something very cruel to Nadia, and I will not have a clear conscience until it is set right. Promise me, if I should die, you will take care of it."

"Of course I will, my love," Philip said tenderly. "But I don't think you could ever do anything cruel, not to one of our daughters."

"It was done for the best of reasons," his wife said. "It was done for you. You know how much we all love you, don't you?"

Philip merely nodded.

"You must make Nadia come home again," Judith continued, her words now more urgent. "You must free her from that man Isaac Mizrahi. She does not love him, and he is a terrible husband, cruel and violent."

"But if she does not love him," Philip said, puzzled, "why did she agree to marry him?"

"She did it for you," Judith's voice was hoarse. "She did it to save your business. Now it seems that has been for naught, and we must not allow her to continue suffering."

"But she is expecting a child," Philip said. "Would you have her child grow up without his father?"

Judith hesitated, then spoke through tears. "Isaac Mizrahi is not the father," she confessed. "The father is Gregor Sarkissian. He is the one Nadia truly loves."

Suddenly full understanding came to Philip. "Oh, dear God, no," he gasped, then began to weep, bending down on the bed beside his wife to embrace her tenderly. "Of course I will bring her home, my dearest."

Later in the day, Judith Boustani's fever returned. By evening, she was no longer conscious, and she died that night.

* * * * *

The next morning, Philip went to the Mizrahi home and broke the news to Nadia. She was grief-stricken, unable to bear the thought that her mother was gone and that she could not have been with her at the end. Philip held his daughter in his arms and comforted her, while Isaac looked on dispassionately, emotionally unaffected by the death of his mother-in-law.

When Nadia's sobbing ceased, Philip said very quietly, "You must come home."

"Of course I will," Nadia said. "I'll come immediately."

"You don't understand," Philip told her. "You must come home to live. You must leave your husband. Your mother has told me everything." He hesitated, glancing across the room at Mizrahi. "She's told me why you agreed to marry him. I wish you had told me, because I wouldn't have permitted it."

Suddenly Isaac became interested. He got up from his chair and moved toward them. "What do you mean?" he demanded angrily. "You can't take her back now. She's mine. Bought and paid for."

"You'll be repaid!" Philip snapped at him. "I don't know how, but I'll do it! I can't let her remain with a brute like you!"

Suddenly Mizrahi grabbed Nadia's arm and tried to pull her away from her father. "You can't do it!" he said angrily. "I'll ruin you! And don't think I can't do it!" The two wolfhounds, which until now had been sleeping peacefully on the floor, suddenly got up and began barking, echoing the angry sounds.

"You've ruined him already!" Nadia screamed at Isaac. "I know about the bribes you take from the Russians! I know how you overtax people and keep a portion for yourself!" She spat in her husband's face. "Don't threaten him, or I'll tell all I know about you!"

"You can't do that," Isaac protested. "You are my wife! You belong to me!"

"Nadia," Philip broke in suddenly, "pack your things. We're going home now."

"What about our child?" Isaac protested, as Nadia left the room to obey her father.

Philip stared at him angrily for a moment. "You told me you didn't believe it was your child," Philip said grimly. "Whether it is yours or not is something you will never know. But I will make sure it will never grow up with you for a father."

Within a matter of minutes, Nadia returned to the parlor with a packed bag, all the possessions she wanted to take with her.

As they left, Isaac Mizrahi stood in his doorway screaming threats at them.

*   *   *   *   *

For Nadia, the past months had been a nightmare, and she was grateful now to be free of it. At first, she was hurt to learn that Judith had told Philip the truth about the baby she was carrying, but her father had been so understanding and accepting she realized it was for the best.

No one had ever had such a kind and generous and understanding father as Philip was. It hurt Nadia to see him suffering so much. It was, she believed, largely because of her. Isaac Mizrahi had manipulated Philip's tax assessments to place him in a desperate situation so that he could force her to marry him. Once Philip had been placed in difficulties, it was virtually impossible to get out again. And then the Russian demands had deepened his financial troubles.

Nadia wished there was something she could do. As she returned to work in her studio, after an absence of several weeks, she occupied her mind with thoughts of ways to raise a large amount of money.

Strangely, it took the entire day before the idea came to her, and it had been right in front of her the entire time—the paintings she had done in the style Roscow Molinar liked so much. The paintings he had told her he could get large amounts of money for.

Of course, that had been before the war. Now, she had no idea of what the art market might be like in Paris, for the French were at the very heart of the conflict. But it would be worth writing to him to ask.

No, even better, it would be worth sending him a telegram. If she could raise the money, she would have to act quickly. It would take weeks to ship crates of paintings all the way to Paris, with a war going on all over Europe.

The next morning, she asked Philip to take her to the telegraph office. There she sent a wire addressed to Roscow in Paris, stating simply:

IF STILL INTERESTED IN NADIA BOUSTANI ORIGINAL STYLE AM NOW READY TO CONSIDER OFFER STOP NEED LARGE AMOUNT OF MONEY DESPERATELY STOP

She signed it simply "Nadia."

Two days later, she received the cabled reply:

EAGER TO RECEIVE PAINTINGS STOP SHIP FASTEST ROUTE
AS MANY AS POSSIBLE STOP AM WILLING TO ADVANCE
LARGE AMOUNT OF MONEY STOP NOTIFY AMOUNT
NEEDED STOP

It was signed simply "Roscow."

In little more than two weeks, the funds were deposited in her father's bank in Rasht, arranged through a Swiss bank. It was enough to pay Philip's taxes, repay the loan to Isaac Mizrahi, and help to put his business back in operation.

Nadia shipped Roscow thirty paintings in the style he liked, including those she had done recently. She felt the money he had advanced was far more than they were worth, however, so she set to work doing more, hoping eventually to repay his generosity.

But in July, she received a letter from Roscow telling her that a dozen of the paintings had already been sold and she would be receiving a second payment soon. To her, the prices paid for her work seemed unbelievably high. She would have suspected Roscow of lying to her, except that he enclosed actual receipts as proof of the sales.

* * * * *

Philip was grateful for Nadia's help, but he refused to accept the money as anything but a loan. He was proud that his daughter could earn such large amounts for her work, but he considered it to be hers, to use for her own future.

He had already begun his plan to regain his own property by other means, discussing the idea with Mirza and several other merchants and growers who were suffering at the hands of the Russians. They had decided to raid Russian shipments of the appropriated goods and produce and to sell them secretly, with the payment going to the rightful owners. Philip and the other growers might not get their actual land back, but they would have the benefit of the crops grown upon it.

Philip now considered himself a member of the *jangalis*, no longer just a friend to them. Beginning with the raid to take back his own rice from the Russians, he participated fully in the revolutionary activities, committed to driving the Russians out of Persia and overthrowing the Qajar dynasty forever.

Most of the time he kept up his appearance as one of Rasht's leading and most respected merchants. But some of his absences from Rasht, on "business" trips, were spent with the *jangalis*. And many of those that were indeed business were spent in arranging the sale of goods obtained by the *jangali* raids.

* * * * *

In September, as time for Nadia's delivery drew near, Tatiana came to stay at the Boustani home in Rasht, so she could attend to her sister.

It was not a difficult birth. The child was a daughter, a beautiful little girl with the fair hair and eyes of her father. It was decided that her name should be Julia, in honor of Judith Boustani. By Jewish tradition, the newborn's name should begin with the same letter as the name of the last family member to die, but it should not be the same name itself.

From the beginning, Julia was adored by all. Philip swore that he would spoil his first grandchild even more than he had spoiled his daughters, though both Nadia and Tatiana protested that it was impossible to do so.

Two days after the birth, Isaac Mizrahi came to the Boustani home, asking to see his child. Philip did not want to permit it, but Nadia decided her husband deserved at least to see Julia, if only for a few minutes. After all, he had given her a name.

After Nadia had returned Julia to her cradle, Isaac spoke to her apologetically, begging her to return to him with the child. "Your home is with me," he said. "And so is the child's. I do love you, and I will try to be a good husband and father."

"I can't discuss it now," Nadia told him. "It is all too painful. Right now I don't see how you can change."

"I can," Isaac said. "If you will come and help me to change."

Nadia shook her head firmly. "No," she said. "You must change first. Then I will consider returning to you as your wife."

Isaac hesitated, his manner became almost shy, as he asked, "May I come to visit . . . my daughter?"

"Yes," Nadia told him. "An occasional short visit would be all right."

PART IV

FLAMES—1917 to 1921

Chapter 33

The year 1917 marked a turning point, not just for the European war, but for the Russian nation, and for Persia. It was a year of dramatic changes for countries and for the common people.

The first signs of the changes took place in March in Petrograd, with strikes and riots, which turned into a full-scale revolution within a week, toppling the Czar from his throne and establishing a democratic parliamentary government. But this regime did not itself have a firm hold on the huge nation, with its multitude of complex problems. In July, new leadership took power under Alexander Kerensky, who attempted to work with the more radical socialists and communists, whose leaders had returned from exile in Switzerland in April.

In September, Kerensky released more communist leaders from prison, along with a number of other political prisoners, sealing the fate of democracy in Russia.

By November, the communists, under Nikolai Lenin and Leon Trotsky, were ready for their own revolution, one that would have a vast impact far beyond the Russian borders.

The first months of the year were extremely difficult ones for Gregor. It was a bitterly cold winter in Siberia, adding to his problems of adjusting to prison life at Yakutsk. He felt as if he had been confined to a dark, damp, cold cave, where he would be unable ever to see the light of day again. There was virtually no heat in the prison, and none at all in the small cell he occupied alone. For that reason, its single window had been shuttered against the wind and snow outside, cutting out the light of day.

He saw the other prisoners only at mealtimes twice a day, when his shift was marched single file into the dining area. However, he was told by the others that, in the warmer months, they were permitted a brief period of exercise once a day in the central courtyard. That exercise consisted only of walking around in a circle, single file.

Most of the men he met were political prisoners, as he was, and so they were not permitted lengthy conversations together. To enforce this, they were allowed only fifteen minutes to sit and eat; if they had not fininshed by the end of the period, they had to leave what remained of their food. If they wanted to talk, they had to forsake nourishment.

Gregor was already sick with a cold when he arrived at Yakutsk, and he never seemed afterward to get rid of it. There was a doctor and a medical ward in the prison, but the guards informed him they were only for serious cases. A cold was insufficient cause for medical treatment.

By the end of February, however, his condition was much worse. He had developed a fever, with chills and a severe cough.

The guard would not believe his complaints, accusing him of exaggerating his condition.

Then, in the first week of March, he was notified that he had a visitor, and would be permitted fifteen minutes with her in the presence of a guard.

* * * * *

Sylvia had tried to get permission to see Gregor from the day of her arrival in Yakutsk in January, but she was told it would be impossible. Political prisoners could have no visitors. She found lodging in the home of a lower middle-class family, a couple with seven children. Mrs. Yakov provided room and board to supplement the small income her husband had from his work at the electrical company.

In February, Sylvia had still not found a way to see Gregor, and her money was beginning to run out, so she began to seek work. Because of the prison, the people of Yakutsk were suspicious of strangers, and with her assumed name of Zhukov, Sylvia could provide no references of previous work. There was also something in her manner that revealed to people that she was not really of working-class background.

Days passed with one refusal after another. She applied for all sorts of jobs—sales clerk, secretary, seamstress, even a position on an assembly line in a gun factory. But none would hire her, even though they had positions open.

Finally she heard of a job that was ideal for her—that of a governess tutoring the daughter of an official at the prison—the assistant to the director.

Sylvia had no experience as a governess, but she had an excellent education, and she did not think she would have much competition for the position in Yakutsk. Her first interview was with the mother of the little girl; Mrs. Shumiatsky was a typical middle-class matron with high aspirations, and she recognized an air of gentility in Sylvia. Her mind was made up. But before Sylvia could be hired to look after little Natasha, she would have to be interviewed by the head of the household, Shumiatsky himself.

The moment she met the man, Sylvia knew he would be more difficult to convince than his wife had been. He was a shrewd and intelligent man, and he began the interview by asking pointedly, "I understand that you cannot provide references; why? Is 'Sylvia Zhukov' not your real name?"

Sylvia realized that any lies she told must be plausible ones, and that she must stay as close to the truth as possible. "It is not my married name," she said. "I have come here to be near my husband, who is in prison—a political prisoner."

Shumiatsky smiled. "I see," he said, obviously relieved that she had told him what he took to be the truth. "And what is your husband's name?"

"Gregor Sarkissian," Sylvia told him. "But I have not been permitted to see him, and I must have employment to remain here."

"You would be better off to leave," Shumiatsky told her kindly. "Siberia can be a difficult place to live, and you can do little for your husband here."

"I know," Sylvia said, "but I would like to be near him."

"Have you ever worked as a governess?" the man asked.

"No," Sylvia said, "but I was brought up by governesses and tutors. "I'm sure I can do the job."

"I'm sure you can, too," Shumiatsky said. "If you wish to remain, you may have the position. However, I think it would be wise for you to speak to your husband—what was his name, Gregor Sarkissian?—first. I can arrange for you to see him. Then, if you wish to remain in Yakutsk, you will come to live and work here, a part of the family. However, you cannot expect any special privileges for your husband because of your connection to me. I hope you understand that."

Sylvia was elated. "Thank you, sir," she said. "I will expect no favors. I am grateful just to be permitted to see Gregor."

* * * * *

The Yakutsk prison was an oppressive place. Sylvia had felt its fearsome stone silence whenever she had come near it before; now, as she was permitted entry for the first time, an agonizing shudder chilled her to the bone.

Even more horrifying was seeing Gregor for the first time since the court-room in Rasht. He was virtually unrecognizable. His beard had grown and his hair was long and dirty. He was painfully thin and pale. There were dark circles under his dull eyes, and he coughed constantly.

A prison guard remained with them, so they were limited in what they could say. Sylvia was permitted to embrace Gregor, but then they were forced to sit on opposite sides of a table in the small barren room.

She could tell that Gregor was delighted to see her, but he did not quite understand how she had come to be in Yakutsk. "Has your father been reassigned here?" he asked.

"No," Sylvia told him. "I came to be near you, to do whatever I can to help you."

Gregor coughed. "There isn't much you can do," he said.

"You look and sound terrible," Sylvia commented. "Have you seen a doctor?

"No," Gregor told her. "They say my condition isn't serious enough."

"Then one thing I will do is make sure you get medical attention," she told him.

"How long do you plan to be in Yakutsk?" he asked her.

"As long as you are here," she replied.

Gregor looked amazed. "But why?" he asked. "It's a miserable place."

"Because I love you," she told him. "Because I want to be wherever you are. That is, as long as you want me. Do you still want me?"

Gregor smiled faintly. "Of course," he said. "But there isn't much chance for us . . . with me in here."

Those small words of encouragement were enough for Sylvia. She would stay in Yakutsk, even if she could see Gregor only occasionally, and only in this small confined room, seated across the table from him.

* * * * *

Sylvia accepted the position as governess to Natasha Shumiatsky, but she insisted on one favor before beginning; Gregor must be permitted to see a doctor. Her employer agreed, surprised that he had not been allowed to do so before, considering the seriousness of his condition.

It was clear that Gregor was suffering from pneumonia.

By the time he was admitted to the medical ward, he was so desperately ill, there seemed little chance that he would survive. His fever was very high, and he slipped in and out of consciousness.

Despite his protest that he would show Sylvia no special favors, Shumiatsky permitted her to go to see Gregor while he was ill. At first, her pass to the ward allowed her to be there only when the doctor or a nurse was present, but when it seemed that he was near death, she was allowed to stay by his side continually throughout the day and the night.

During that first long night, she was alone in the ward with Gregor and the other patients. A nurse was on duty just outside the door and would look in only occasionally. It was in the early morning hours before sunup that the old woman came in to mop the floors and clean the ward.

At first, Sylvia did not pay attention to her, so intent was she on watching Gregor for any sign of change in his breathing. But as the old woman's scrubbing came near the bed, she stopped and spoke to Sylvia. "Poor man," she said sadly. "There's not much chance for him, is there?"

"No," Sylvia said, startled by the sudden voice. "But I pray that he'll survive."

"Your husband, is he?" the woman asked.

"Yes," Sylvia replied. "I've come here from Persia to be near him."

The woman simply nodded sympathetically. "I've seen lots of them go this way," she commented. "This place is just too cold and damp in the winter. Not like Persia."

Sylvia was about to ask how she knew about Persia, but they were interrupted by the nurse stepping into the ward and calling out, "Mrs. Baranov! Will you come quickly? You're needed on the women's ward!"

It took a moment for the name "Baranov" to register with Sylvia, and by that time the old woman was toddling off in response to her call. Surely this could not be Gregor's mother; it was too great a coincidence. But then, Maria Baranov had been sent to prison in Siberia. Could it have been this very prison?

When the woman returned a short while later, she set to work again, not paying attention to Sylvia or Gregor. Sylvia got up and walked over to her. "Mrs. Baranov," she said. "Is that your name?"

The woman looked at her in surprise. "Yes," she said, surprised. Then her face lit up. "Oh, of course, you heard the nurse call me."

"Are you Maria Baranov, from Baku?" Sylvia asked.

This time the old woman was truly amazed. "Yes," she said, "but how did you know that?"

"Do you have a son named Gregor?" Sylvia continued.

With that question, Maria Baranov became cautious, guarded, almost frightened. "Why do you ask that?" she asked. "Why do you want to know about my son?"

Sylvia smiled reassuringly. "If you are Maria Baranov from Baku," she said gently, "and if your husband was Alexei Baranov, then the young man lying in that bed over there is your son Gregor."

Maria Baranov turned pale. Suddenly her eyes glazed over, and she seemed to focus far away. "No," she said tensely, "it's not possible."

Sylvia took her gently by the arm. "Come and look at him," she said. "And see if you do not recognize your son."

Standing at the bedside, Maria looked down silently for a long time. Then tears began to flow. "He looks like my Alexei," she whispered. "So much like my Alexei. But my Gregor is just a child . . . just a child."

"Not anymore," Sylvia said. "You have been here many years. Long enough for your Gregor to grow up."

Maria began to sob. "But here? Why is he here?" Suddenly she thrust herself down onto the bed, trying to embrace Gregor, sobbing painfully. "My child! Oh, my child! Just like Alexei!"

*   *   *   *   *

Miraculously, Gregor pulled through his fever, and slowly he began to regain his strength. Shumiatsky continued to allow Sylvia to visit him, as moved by the story of their reunion with Gregor's mother as they were. He recalled the visit, years before, from Maria Baranov's other child. He was truly a kind man, and Sylvia regretted the small deception she had played, claiming to be Gregor's wife.

But it was a deception she had played on Maria Baranov as well. To her relief, she had a chance to explain her deception and the reason for it to Gregor before he was able to speak to his mother at length. He understood: the only way she could be there to help him was to claim to be married to him.

His reunion with his mother was a tearful one. Like Tatiana had been, he was shocked by her appearance, by the way she had aged, well beyond her natural years. He also learned quickly that she had her good days and her bad days. Most of the time she recognized him and behaved rationally; but at other times she did not seem to know him at all, and at still others she called him "Alexei" and tried to talk about things that had happened years ago.

They did not hear about the revolution that had taken place in Petrograd until two weeks after it had occurred. And even then they could only conjecture about what the abdication of the Czar might mean for them. Still, whether they admitted it or not, all of the political prisoners began to hope for the first time since their imprisonment.

Yet, as weeks passed into months, there were no changes made in the prison at Yakutsk, and the changes in the government of the city and the province were only minor ones. The prisoners began to despair—the abdication of the Czar had changed nothing.

* * * * *

The Russian revolution caused much excitement in Persia, as well. As in Russia itself, there were all sorts of rumors about the differences there might be with the new parliamentary government, but there were no immediate changes.

For Mirza and the *jangali*, the most exciting news came late in April, when they learned that Lenin and other socialist and communist leaders had been permitted to return to Russia from exile in Switzerland. Mirza and two other revolutionary leaders who had joined with the *jangalis*, Elksanullah Khan and Haidar Khan, had been in touch with leaders of the Communist party in Russia, and had been given promises of help, once they had managed to gain power.

Elksanullah and Haidar were avowed communists themselves; Mirza was more moderate, but he was willing to support any change in Russia that would set Persia free of domination.

The Communists—or Bolsheviks, as they were known in Russia—had been promising their own revolution, a greater one than the democratic revolution of March.

They attempted a *coup d'etat* in July, but failed. Instead, the more moderate Alexander Kerensky became prime minister, attempting to work together with the socialists and communists for a coalition government.

To prove his willingness to work with all political viewpoints, Kerensky arranged to have Leon Trotsky and numerous other political prisoners released form the prisons of Russia and Siberia.

It was shortly after this that Mirza was invited to send a delegation of Persians to the Second All Russian Congress of the Soviets to be held in Petrograd in November. Delegations would be attending from the Ukraine, from Georgia, Armenia, Azerbaijan, and numerous other states now considered to be Russian. The promise was that they would discuss freedom and independence for peoples now under Russian domination—once the Bolshevik revolution took place.

It was imperative that Mirza and Haidar Khan should go. Mirza also wanted Kouroush and Tatiana to attend. However, only a few days before Mirza broached the subject with Kouroush, Tatiana had informed him that she was with child. He was worried about the strain of such a long journey on his wife.

"It will be no problem," Tatiana assured him. "I'm a very healthy woman. I'm also a doctor, and I know what's involved."

Still, Kouroush was reluctant. It was Mirza who finally persuaded him to allow her to come with them. "One of the men we will be meeting is Joseph Stalin," he said. "Tatiana has the advantage of having met him, of being known to him. In fact, she knows several of their leaders. And she has spent much time in Russia, and she speaks the language well. She can be very helpful to us."

It was decided. Kouroush and Tatiana would be part of the delegation to Petrograd.

*   *   *   *   *

Sylvia was aware that the Shumiatskys were pleased with her work. She adored little Natasha, and the child loved her governess. Sylvia had, indeed, become like a member of their family.

For that reason, she was surprised when Mr. Shumiatsky called her into the parlor for a conference, one evening during the second week of September. From the look on his face when he spoke to her, she sensed that something was wrong.

When they sat down facing each other in the parlor, however, he smiled at her, though it was a sad smile. "I have some good news for you," he said. "Today I received an order from the Kerensky government for the release of thirty prisoners. Your husband and his mother are among them."

Sylvia was elated. "That's wonderful!" she exclaimed. "When . . . ? When will he be set free?"

"Tomorrow," Shumiatsky said. "In the morning." He paused, looked down at his hands in his lap. "I suppose you will want to leave almost immediately for Persia?"

Only then did Sylvia recognize the full implications of what Gregor's release might mean. In Persia, Gregor was offically dead; for him to return would cause trouble for her father. For her to return with him would cause trouble for her. "I don't know," she told Shumiatsky. "Have travel arrangements been made?"

"Unfortunately, no," Shumiatsky said. "We have been instructed only to release the prisoners. Once they are out of the prison, they are on their own. If they have no money, they may have difficulties."

"I see," Sylvia said pensively. "It might take some time for us to save enough for the fare all the way to Persia."

Shumiatsky brightened. "Then you might not be wanting to leave your position immediately?"

"Not immediately," she told him with an understanding smile. "Of course, eventually we will have to go."

*   *   *   *   *

Grateful to have Sylvia remain even a few weeks, Shumiatsky provided rooms for Gregor and his mother in the carriage house behind his home. He even helped Gregor to find some menial work. The work paid little, but it helped toward their support and eventual departure.

Gregor was anxious to leave for home. His mother did not want to go at all. Strangely, she was afraid of freedom; the prison and its life had become all she knew; it was familiar and comfortable. The outside world was frightening after so many years.

After awhile, Gregor began to sense that Sylvia, too, was reluctant to return to Persia. Since his release, they had lived as husband and wife, as his mother and the Shumiatskys had expected them to do. He wondered if her reluctance was because they were not legally married, but it was a question he was not prepared to asked.

Certainly, he ought to marry her. She had given up everything to come to help him. He was grateful for all she had done, and he did care for her. Perhaps he did love her. Their lovemaking was truly exciting. Yet, somehow, even after almost a year in prison, he could not forget Nadia.

By October, Gregor decided they must find some way to leave Yakutsk with no further delay. He could not bear the thought of spending another winter in Siberia. One evening, after their meager supper in their rooms in the carriage house, he made his suggestion. "We could take the money we have and start home," he told her. "Then, as we need to, we can take work as we go along."

"But what if we can't find work wherever we happen to be?" Sylvia asked. "What will we do?"

"We mustn't think about that," Gregor told her. "We will simply have to find work. I'll do any kind of labor that's available. You must leave it to me. When I was younger, I had a great deal of ingenuity for such things."

Seeing that Gregor was determined to go home, Sylvia decided she must tell him the truth of what had happened in Rasht—of how she had saved him from execution, of the fact that he was officially dead, and of the problem both would face with her father.

At first, Gregor was horrified to learn that someone else had died in his place, and he was furious at Sylvia for doing such a thing, but eventually he forgave her, realizing that she had done it out of love.

But he still wanted to go home—even if he had to change his identity. He was Persian, not Russian; and if he had been chosen to go on living, the reason for the choice lay in his homeland.

Chapter 34

On their way to Petrograd, the Persian delegation stopped in Moscow. For Tatiana, this was a wonderful opportunity to visit with the Komineks and other old friends. Fyodor was not in Moscow, however, but was now a Bolshevik leader, occupied with the great changes taking place in Petrograd.

A joyful reunion for Tatiana was that with Vanitof. They had written to each other over the years, so she knew much of what had been happening for him, but correspondence could not convey the depth of the changes that had taken place with her dear friend.

Vanitof had continued to write, finally gaining the courage to show his work to others. In 1915, one of his plays, a work about a group of deformed people who attempt to set up a community of their own, was performed in Moscow, with great success. Virtually overnight, Vanitof had become one of the most celebrated of the new, young writers in Russia. Because all his plays and stories had revolutionary themes, his popularity was now increasing well beyond the intelligentsia.

While she was in Moscow, Tatiana and Kouroush were Vanitof's guests at the theater where his latest play was being performed. It was a work on the theme of the "Beauty and the Beast" fairy tale, and Tatiana suspected that much of it was based upon her own friendship with Vanitof.

From the look in his eyes when they were together, Tatiana knew that he was still very much in love with her, yet he was very cordial toward Kouroush, and he was delighted when he learned that Tatiana was expecting a child.

Tatiana wanted to stay longer in Moscow, but they had to be in Petrograd before the fifth of November, the day of their first meetings with the Bolshevik leaders.

Petrograd was very different from Moscow, in some ways even more beautiful, despite the fact that the cold of winter had already cast a gray pall over the grand palaces and churches. Known as St. Petersburg before 1914, Petrograd was a newer city than Moscow, and its architecture was more European in style, with classical style buildings, columned and domed. It was laid out in a planned gridwork of streets and parks, with fountains and statues everywhere. In the snow, it was bright and clean and crisp, almost untouchable in its grandeur and magnificence.

But in contrast, the mood of the people was as gray as the weather; almost everyone they met complained about the ineffectiveness of the new government and about the cost of the European war, both in money and in lives.

There was something in the atmosphere that suggested that change was imminent.

Tatiana had begun to notice while they were in Moscow that Mirza was very uncomfortable in his contacts with the Russian people. This was especially true of the Bolshevik leaders they met in Petrograd. She had met a number of them before, and felt she understood them as well as she did the *jangali* leader. She sensed that their mission was in danger of failure because of the distrust that was natural to both sides.

The only one of the Russian leaders that she distrusted was Fyodor Vachtangov, and that was because of the hostility she saw in his eyes when he met Kouroush.

Fyodor had arranged their first meeting with Vladimir Lenin, his wife, Leon Trotsky, and Joseph Stalin in the hotel where the Persian group was staying. The room occupied by Kouroush and Tatiana was chosen for the occasion because it was the largest available.

Tatiana liked Lenin and his wife very much. They were not quite so coldly intellectual as the other Bolsheviks were. There was a certain fatherly and motherly kindness and understanding about them. She found Trotsky somewhat fearsome, and still could not shake off her prejudice against Stalin for his betrayal of her father. She considered him a cold and devious man, and she could not make herself trust him.

They would not reveal when they planned their revolution; they would say only that it would be "soon," and this time they were sure of success. "However," Lenin told them, "we would like to be assured of friendly neighbors. Under the Czar and under the current regime, your country— and others—have been assured to us by the might of imperialism. We would like a stronger bond than that; we would like to know that there is an independent government that is of like mind. In short, we would like a socialist government in your country."

I have no objection to a socialist form of government in Persia," Mirza said cautiously. "What I want for my people is freedom and justice, with absolute autonomy from foreign intervention."

"That is what we want for all people," Stalin broke in coolly. "Not just the Russians and the Persians, but for Georgia, Azerbaijan, the Ukraine, Armenia, all parts of Europe and Asia. The only way this can be guaranteed is for people of our party to gain control in each of these areas."

"What he is trying to say," Trotsky interrupted, "is that we need your assurance that your government will be affiliated with the Communist Party Congress, and will abide by our international goals . . . if we are to help you achieve your independence."

Tatiana knew that this was the dangerous point. Mirza was not a member of the Communist party, though Elksanullah and Haidar were, and he had no desire to become a member. He also perceived that what they were offering was merely a ploy to keep control of Persia indirectly. "We do not ask for your help." Mirza said irritably. "We ask simply that you withdraw Russian support for the present government."

"But that is precisely the kind of assistance we are talking about," Stalin said. "We would certainly not be sending Russian troops to assist in your revolution."

"I hardly consider that assistance," Mirza said hotly. "That is merely noninterference."

Eventually, the meeting ended without the two sides reaching an agreement. Tatiana knew that the situation was a dangerous one; she wasn't sure if Mirza realized that. Unless Mirza himself joined the Communist party, the Bolsheviks might make other arrangements with Elksanullah and Haidar, arrangements that would eliminate Mirza, once the revolution was achieved, placing the power in the hands of one or the other of their party members.

There were several other meetings in the days that followed, but they were with subordinates of the Bolshevik leaders, and they were equally as inconclusive, in that Mirza remained determined to hold out for total independence for Persia.

The entire Persian delegation was not involved in each of the meetings, since some had meetings regarding economic matters, while others were discussing miltary concerns, and still others were concerned about rights of transit, both land and sea. (It had been a concern of Persia for many years that she could not sail on the Caspian, which Russia considered private property.)

For this reason, Tatiana was not involved in many of the conferences.

It gave her time for sightseeing and shopping, though Kouroush was concerned about her traveling alone in Petrograd.

It was while she was on one of these shopping trips that she happened across Fyodor, who was also alone. At first, she thought it was merely coincidence, but she quickly learned that Fyodor had planned the accidental meeting so they could talk alone. He met her coming out of a millinery shop and suggested that they walk a while so they could talk.

It was reminiscent of the old days; so much of their time together had been merely walking and talking. One of the first things he wanted to know was, "Are you happy?"

"Yes," she told him confidently, "very much so. I love my work in the *jangali* clinic, and Kouroush and I are perfectly suited to each other."

Fyodor smiled sadly. "Despite everything," he said, "you have ended up with a revolutionary."

Tatiana caught herself blushing. "Yes," she said, "I suppose that was inevitable."

"I . . .," Fyodor began shyly, much like the young Fyodor. "I . . . wish the inevitable had happened sooner."

"I could not have remained in Russia," she told him sympathetically. "I don't think I could be happy anywhere but in Persia."

Fyodor gave an understanding nod. "You love your country very much, don't you?" he asked.

"Yes," she said. "I could not understand your revolution. But I do understand ours; I believe in our cause with all my heart, because I care deeply for my people."

Fyodor stopped suddenly, his brow furrowed in a frown. She stopped and looked at him curiously. "I should probably not tell you this," he said. "I am breaking an oath by doing so. But you and your people should not have come to Petrograd. If you are wise, you will go home immediately."

"But why?" Tatiana asked. "I don't understand. There are still meetings scheduled. The party congress isn't until the day after tomorrow."

"I know," Fyodor said enigmatically. "But it would be far better for your people's cause if your leader Mirza were with his people on that day."

"What do you mean?" Tatiana asked.

"I can say no more," Fyodor told her. "I have said too much already."

* * * * *

When Tatiana told Mirza about her conversation with Fyodor, he understood. "That can mean only one thing," he said pensively. "The revolution is to take place while we and all the other leaders of revolutionary groups are here in Petrograd. It will give them time to consolidate their power before we can make moves of our own."

"Then we should go home now," Tatiana said. "Today."

"No," Mirza told her. "It is already too late." He smiled. "But I suggest you stay in your hotel room on the seventh of November."

*   *   *   *   *

Tatiana did as he recommended. She observed the Bolshevik revolution from the balcony of her hotel room, seeing the crowds surging through the streets, hearing the far-off gunfire and shouting, as the people attacked and took control of the Winter Palace.

When Kouroush arrived at the hotel from the party congress meeting, she learned that the revolution had been a success.

The next day, the Persians left for home, aware that it would be a long and complicated journey through territory that was still being fought over by Bolsheviks and troops still loyal to the parliamentary government, troops that would come to be known as the White forces, while the Bolsheviks would be referred to as the Red.

But the Persians left with an agreement with the Russian Bolsheviks that would permit the *jangalis* to take control of the government of northern Persia, so long as they would establish in that territory a socialist state.

*   *   *   *   *

Sylvia and Gregor were in Bratsk when they learned of the Bolshevik coup. It had taken them over two weeks to get that far, sometimes riding by train and occasionally persuading farmers to give them rides on their wagons. It was still less than one-third of the distance they would have to travel to reach Baku, and the cold winter was already beginning to take hold.

But one of the greatest difficulties for them was the fact that Maria was beginning to tire of the journey. Increasingly, as they progressed, she had more and more bad days, refusing to acknowledge what was happening to her, not understanding the urgency to keep moving across the vast Russian territory.

They could never be sure which side of the revolution was in control in a specific town—the Reds or the Whites. To them, the distinction between the revolutionary forces and the counter-revolutionary forces was immaterial. Under the circumstances, they were both the enemy to the travelers, for they were both the cause of delays. On several occasions, it required considerable ingenuity for them to get out of difficult situations with one side or the other.

*   *   *   *   *

It was late in November when Mirza, Kouroush, Tatiana, and the others arrived home at the *jangali* encampment. To their surprise, the Russian troops were already being removed from northern Persia, in gradual stages. Anticipating problems, the Persian government in Tehran had already begun increasing the number of Persian Cossacks stationed in the north, in Rasht, Tabriz, and Enzeli. However, Mirza was not greatly concerned about the cossacks; they would be no match for his own forces when the time came, especially with most of the populace sympathetic to him, at least in the province of Gilan.

He was more concerned that the British might make a move, now that the Russians were leaving.

This was confirmed to him by a communique sent from the Bolshevik leadership in Petrograd. Their spies had reported that a British force, led by General Lionel Dunsterville, would be moving toward Rasht from the south, to join with the troops of a White Russian leader, General Bicherakov, who was determined to remain in northern Persia and Azerbaijan.

The Bolsheviks promised to send a group of advisors to assist Mirza in defeating this force. The leader of the group would be a Comrade Chaliapin. Mirza was assured that Chaliapin would not attempt to do more than advise, except in cases involving Russian troops, for which he was to arrange an orderly evacuation. But Mirza still did not trust the Bolsheviks completely.

The first of the Russians to leave Rasht were the civilians—the diplomats, bureaucrats, and businessmen. Mirza decided, where possible, to move his followers into their positions as they left, to prevent the resumption of power by the Qajar government bureaucrats. When an office was vacated, he would place a *jangali* there and post *jangali* guards around the building. As Russians gave up appropriated farmlands and factories, Mirza would use his troops to retake them and return them to their orginal owners, if the owners were his own supporters. If they were not, they would be distributed among landless followers.

Philip Boustani was placed in charge of this program, and he was delighted not only to have his lands returned to him but also to see that others received justice as well. An honest and fair man, he performed his duties well, handling a responsibility fairly that other men might be tempted to abuse.

In establishing their authority at Rasht and other northern towns, the *jangali* faced occasional minor skirmishes with Persian Cossacks, but throughout the end of November and the beginning of December, there was little opposition. Emboldened by this, Mirza decided it was time to take over the entire rule of the north, overthrowing the Persian bureaucrats as well.

While the German von Passchen was to lead the overall attack, commanding the main thrust against the city offices, assisted by Kaouk, Kouroush and his troops were assigned the attack on the regional tax offices. He did not know if he would face resistance there, and if he did, what kind of resistance it would be.

On the day of the attack, he and his men approached the building of the tax office to find it surrounded by cossacks. Their leader was Pasha Jalali—his own father.

Kouroush hesitated only a moment before ordering the attack. The cossacks were fewer in number than the *jangalis*, but they had the decided advantage because they were on horseback and the attackers were on foot, though both were equipped with rifles. A few of the *jangalis* even had machine guns, obtained from the Germans and Turks, though they had not become extremely proficient in the use of them.

Kouroush could not bring himself to aim his rifle at his father in the attack; it was enough to lead men in battle against him. During the first volley, the *jangalis* suffered greatly; at least a dozen men in the front rank fell. But within moments, the *jangalis* with the machine guns had repaid the government troops double, felling both men and horses.

Among those hit was Pasha Jalali.

Kouroush felt a sharp sense of anguish at seeing his father fall bleeding to the pavement, but he could not allow himself to think about what had happened. Their objective was to take the tax office, and they must persevere.

In less than half an hour, they were in control, taking captive a number of cossacks and all of the bureaucrats inside the building. One of their captives was Isaac Mizrahi, who was loud in his outraged protests that they had no right to take him prisoner.

Once his duties had been executed, Kouroush returned to the scene of the battle to search for his father. As he feared, Pasha Jalali was dead. At the sight of the lifeless body, Kouroush did something he thought he would never do—he wept for his father. He lifted the body and held it tightly in his arms and grieved for the love that had never existed between them, for the love that now never could exist. He wept for the mistakes he had made, and for those of his father, who was—as death had proved—human, after all.

*   *   *   *   *

By the end of that day, the *jangalis* were in full control of the town of Rasht. By the next day, they possessed Enzeli, and within a few more Tabriz was theirs as well.

They took a great many prisoners. The Persians would be tried, and those guilty would be executed. The British and the Russians would be held hostage to use for eventual peace negotiations.

Mirza and his *jangali* committee declared all of northern Persia to be the Socialist State of Gilan. For that entire week, there were celebrations everywhere. It was a triumph for the people who had suffered so long at the hands of the Russians and the "ajar shahs.

One person sympathetic to the *jangali* cause was not happy, however. Nadia was extremely concerned about Isaac Mizrahi, a prisoner of the revolutionary government scheduled for execution. She knew that he was guilty of the charges of abuse for which he had been tried, and she felt no real love for him. But he was her husband, and he had given her child a name; she felt she owed him something, and she did not wish to see him die such a wretched death.

She felt compelled to go to Mirza to plead for mercy for Isaac, yet she feared doing it alone. Temporarily, he had his headquarters in Rasht, and during the week of celebrations and trials, Kouroush and Tatiana were staying at the Boustani home. Nadia decided to speak to them before approaching Mirza, hoping she could enlist their aid.

They understood her plight and agreed to go with her to see the new head of state, though Kouroush had some misgivings about sparing anyone guilty of crimes against the people. However, he was still grieving for his father, and he understood how Nadia felt. If his father had survived, he would now be in the same position as Nadia's husband, and Kouroush might have done just as Nadia was doing.

Still, Nadia had difficulty in making her request. "I know it is a lot to ask," she told Mirza in the beginning. "I realize that everyone who is awaiting execution has family and friends who want them spared. I know that Isaac is guilty of the charges against him; he is guilty of even more than he has been tried for. But I must beg that his life be spared; my child bears his name. His punishment will be hers as well. Imprison him for life if you must, but spare my child the lifetime disgrace of knowing her father was executed for crimes against the people."

When she had finished, Mirza smiled at her. "I understand your concern," he said. "We all hope for a better future for our children. If you had asked this for your sake or for your husband's, I might have refused. But, for the sake of your child, Isaac Mizrahi will be exiled. However, if he should ever return to Gilan, I will have no choice but to order his death."

"Thank you," Nadia said, feeling a great sense of relief. "I will forever be in your debt."

* * * * *

Nadia was satisfied with the life she had set forth for herself. She expected—and wanted—nothing more than to live in her father's house, looking after him, bringing up her child, and doing her paintings. But events have a way of altering the expected.

If Kouroush and Tatiana had not moved into the Boustani home with her and her father, she would never have even considered the offer that came to her in January of 1918. Roscow Molinar wanted her to come to Paris for an exhibition of her work. She had become a celebrity there, one of the most sought after of her generation of painters, and the art world of Paris wanted to meet her.

It was, as Roscow pointed out in his letter to Nadia, a great opportunity. He would sell as many of her paintings as she could provide.

The thought of going to Paris under these circumstances excited Nadia. As long as Tatiana was at home to look after Philip, there was now nothing to keep her in Rasht. She had committed herself to her native style of painting. She had no real reason to refuse what was truly the opportunity of a lifetime.

She discussed the matter with Tatiana before even mentioning the invitation to her father. She knew that Philip would insist that she go, that he could take care of himself. But, even though he was beginning to rebuild his business, and though he had an honored position in the new government, Nadia recognized that he was beginning to grow old, and she did not want him to be alone.

"It's wonderful," Tatiana acknowledged, "and I certainly think you should go. But what about Julia? Would you like me to take care of her?"

"Oh, no," Nadia said. "I would take her with me. She's a very contented child. She wouldn't be a problem traveling."

"But would it be safe?" Tatiana asked. "After all, France is at war."

"I've worked out a route to avoid the areas where there is fighting," Nadia told her. "And I'm sure it will be safe in Paris." She smiled. "It could be no worse than what we've gone through here in Rasht."

"How long would you stay?" Tatiana asked. "Would it be only a short visit?"

"I don't know," Nadia admitted. "I might like to spend some time there, seeimg museums and perhaps studying."

"I will miss you," Tatiana smiled. "But of course you must go and stay as long as you like. I do hope you can be back for the birth of my child in June."

So it was settled, everything but telling Philip. However, Nadia knew how he would respond. He would want what was best for his daughter, even if she would not see him for a long time."

Within a few weeks, Nadia had packed her paintings for shipment, notified Roscow of her expected date of arrival in Paris, and made her departure.

$$* \quad * \quad * \quad * \quad *$$

Tatiana had been concerned that Nadia would be traveling through battle lines in Europe. As it turned out, Nadia would see less of war in the coming weeks than Tatiana would, for all of the fighting that she had witnessed so far in Rasht was merely a prelude for what was soon to occur.

By the middle of March, the British forces under General Dunsterville, moving from Kermanshah, had reached Kasvin. Their stated objective was to join with White Russian forces at Baku to oppose the Bolsheviks now in control of the Caspian, but Mirza knew that this was only part of their intention. He and the Bolsheviks were allies. Mirza sent Dunsterville a warning that his troops would not be permitted to cross the territory of Gilan under any pretext.

The day after receiving Mirza's warning, Dunsterville began moving toward Rasht. But Mirza had plenty of time to make his plans, for the road from Kazvin to Rasht was long and difficult because of the mountains and desolate valleys between. It would take the British weeks, possibly months, to make it through the winter snows of the mountains.

Mirza consulted with von Passchen, and they chose an area known as the Menjil Defile to make their stand against the British.

* * * * *

For Gregor, Sylvia, and Maria, it was a long and difficult winter, traveling across the vast territory of eastern Russia. They had very quickly come to regret their decision to leave Yakutsk so quickly; for the hazards on their route were much greater than they had envisioned. Not only did they have to endure the snows and freezing temperatures, but they frequently passed through battle zones fearing for their very lives. Often, the languages spoken were so different from Russian that Gregor and Sylvia had difficulty communicating. They had thought they would be able to get menial work along the way to support themselves, but because of the winter and the war, this was almost never possible, and they were forced to depend upon charity. Some days they went without food or shelter completely.

It was spring before they reached the Caspian at Astrakhan, which meant that their destination was drawing near enough to hope. If they met no further difficulties, they might reach Baku or even Enzeli within two weeks. But by now they realized that difficulties must always be expected. From the very beginning, they had been aware that one of their greatest problems would be in entering their homeland without documents. However, since hearing that Mirza was now in control of northern Persia, having established his own state of Gilan, Gregor hoped he might find some way of contacting his old friend.

He was the one who kept his hope the highest. Maria alternated between hope and despair, depending upon whether she was having a good day or a bad one. It was Sylvia who grew more despondent as they drew nearer to their destination. Despite all the hardship, she had been happy because she had had Gregor and his love; she had had the joy of pretending they were husband and wife. Once they arrived back in Persia, she feared all that might end. She had no definable reason for that gnawing doubt, only a vague sensation that the barriers that had kept them apart would do so again.

For the last part of their journey south toward Baku, they managed to slip into an empty freight car, something they had done numerous times, but generally with other people. This time they had the entire boxcar to themselves. Believing there might not be another opportunity, Sylvia enticed Gregor into making love during one of their last nights of traveling. Maria slept soundly a good distance away in the darkened railway car.

That night Sylvia unleashed all of the love and passion she felt for Gregor, savoring the happiness she felt just being with him, treasuring every moment and gesture. When it was over, she lay by his side, weeping silently, so that he would not hear her.

But Gregor knew something was different. "What is it?" he whispered to her. "Is something wrong?"

"No," she told him. "You make me very happy. I love you so very much."

"And I love you," he told her. "You do know that, don't you?"

"Yes," she replied. But she wasn't sure.

It was the next morning that the train stopped at a mountain pass. Sylvia and Gregor slipped the freight car door open slightly to look out to see what was happening. They were nowhere near a city or a town. They saw soldiers moving swiftly down the line of the train, opening and inspecting the cars. They did not have a chance to escape before they had been discovered and taken prisoner. From the uniforms and the manner of the soldiers, Gregor and Sylvia knew instinctively they were Russians—White Russian counter-revolutionaries.

They and a few other people discovered in other freight cars were taken to a military encampment a short distance away to await interrogation by the soldiers' commanding officer. The interrogations were being conducted in a tent.

One group of men was taken in before them, then Gregor, Sylvia, and Maria were ushered in together.

"Oh, no!" Sylvia gasped when she saw the officer seated behind the campaign desk. Her heart sank. It was her father.

Major Zinoviev was equally as shocked, but he recovered his composure swiftly. He nodded coldly at Gregor and Sylvia, saying, "There is no need to ask your names." But then he turned to Maria and asked, "Who are you?"

Before Maria could reply, Sylvia said, "That is Maria Baranov, Gregor's mother." She hesitated only a moment before adding, "My mother-in-law."

Zinoviev glared at his daughter angrily for a moment, then his strong, massive body shuddered, and he began to weep.

Sylvia felt a deep surge of sympathy for her father. Impulsively, she rushed to him to embrace him, kneeling down beside his chair. Zinoviev welcomed the embrace, but he quickly regained control of himself and said, "My dear, it is good to see you; I am grateful that you are alive and well." He tried to joke, saying with a playful smile, "Though I can't imagine when you last had a bath."

"Oh, Papa," Sylvia said, "I'm so sorry to have left the way I did. But

I did have to leave, and I know you would have tried to stop me."

Zinoviev looked at her, then at Gregor. "You do love this young man, don't you?" he asked.

He looked slightly dismayed, but the smile he gave her and Gregor was not an unpleasant one. "I suppose the world is changing," he said, "and people must change with it." He shook his head sadly. "But I'm not sure I'll be able to go along with all that's happening; I'm afraid I'm too set in the old ways."

Zinoviev's face wrinkled into a pensive frown. "I don't suppose there would be much use in taking the three of you as prisoners," he said. "Where are you trying to go? To Rasht?"

"Yes, sir," Gregor replied. "My mother and I were freed from the prison in Yakutsk several months ago."

"Well," Zinoviev said with a sigh, "I might as well do what I can to help you get there. I will give you a pass that will help you with our army. It won't do you much good with our enemies, but then you should be able to deal with them, since they are your own people." He looked up at his daughter, who now stood back alongside Gregor. "And I'll give you some money. It won't be much, because I don't have much left, but it will buy you some food, and perhaps lodging."

He also arranged for them to be transported to the nearest village where they could book passage on a train to complete their journey to Baku. The parting between Sylvia and her father was a tearful one; neither was sure if they would see each other again.

The rest of the trip was uneventful, though there was a long wait for the boat from Baku to Enzeli. The Bolsheviks now had control of navigation on the Caspian, and they had not yet learned to adhere to timetables.

It was after they had reached Enzeli that Gregor began to worry about how he would notify his friends and family that he was still alive. He did not want to cause anyone a severe shock by suddenly appearing unannounced. In fact, now that they were no longer living in the Valley of the Trees, he wasn't sure where to find Tatiana, Kouroush, or even Mirza.

The logical place to go first was to the home of Philip Boustani. Philip could tell him where to find his sister.

* * * * *

In the last months of her pregnancy, Tatiana was no longer working in the clinic with Dr. Heshmat, but was spending most of her time at home,

Philip's home, supervising the servants and looking after the house.

It was a Saturday, when everyone was at home, not just Philip, but Kouroush as well. Tatiana was in the kitchen preparing a dinner menu with the cook and housekeeper, and she was not even aware that unexpected guests had come to the front door.

Philip came to the kitchen to speak to her, and she could tell from the expression on his face that he had disturbing news.

"My dear," he said gently, approaching her, "I want you to sit down. I have some very good news for you, but it may be a shock, and I want you to remain calm."

Tatiana did as she was told, but her heart began to race apprehensively. "What is it?" she asked. "Something to do with Nadia?"

"No," Philip told her. "It has to do with your mother, your natural mother, and with Gregor."

"Gregor?" Tatiana asked, confused. "But . . . "

"Your mother is here," Philip said. "She has been released from prison."

"Oh, but that's wonderful!" Tatiana exclaimed, rising to her feet excitedly. "Where is she? I must go to see her!"

"Just a moment," Philip cautioned. "Sit down. There is more."

Tatiana obeyed.

"Your brother Gregor," Philip began cautiously. "He is not dead. He is alive."

"Alive?" Tatiana asked, confused. "But how?"

"He has been in Siberia," Philip said gently. "He has returned with your mother."

For a moment, Tatiana felt faint, but she managed to compose herself.

"You must be calm," Philip said. "You mustn't get too excited in your condition. Your mother and your brother are in my study right now, with Sylvia Zinoviev and Kouroush. They are waiting to see you, but I want to be sure before you go in that it won't be too upsetting for you."

"I understand," Tatiana said, rising to her feet in full control of herself. "Please take me to them."

Despite her best efforts, Tatiana was overwhelmed by emotion seeing her mother again, and embracing the brother she thought was dead. It was a joyful, but tearful, reunion. To help calm her, Philip and Sylvia took her upstairs to rest.

After they left the study, Gregor turned to his friend Kouroush to say, "It's wonderful that you are soon to be a father, and I an uncle." He then said to his mother, "And you will be a grandmother. Tatiana will be giving you your first grandchild."

Maria looked at him mystified. "That is hard to realize," she said. "So much has happened so quickly. The last I knew my children, they were children."

"This has all been as difficult for you as for Tatiana," Gregor said kindly. "Perhaps you should rest as well." He turned to Kouroush. "Do you think one of the servants might take her up to a room where she could take a nap?"

"Of course," Kouroush said, promptly going to take care of the matter.

Once Gregor and his old friend were alone together, Kouroush said with some embarrassment, "You know, our child will not be the first grandchild for your mother." He hesitated. "You have a child as well, a little daughter."

"What do you mean?" Gregor frowned at him. "How?" Then, suddenly, he realized. "Nadia?"

Kouroush nodded. Gregor sat down and heard the entire story. Afterwards, he said sadly, "Poor Nadia. Poor, dear Nadia, to have endured all of this alone. I must do something to help her."

* * * * *

During the first week of June, Tatiana gave birth to a little boy, whom she and Kouroush named Jamshid, deliberately choosing a Persian name that was not aligned with any of the three modern religions. The baby was delivered at the Boustani home, in the room she had once shared with Nadia. She was attended by Dr. Heshmat, who told her she must get back on her feet soon, for she would be desperately needed at the hospital in the coming weeks.

* * * * *

During the month of June, the *jangalis* were carefully digging trenches and establishing a strong military position at the Menjil Defile to the west of Rasht, anticipating a move from the British troops under General Dunsterville and the Hussars under General Bicherakov.

Early in July, Dunsterville sent an emissary to Mirza to negotiate for unobstructed passage to Enzeli, but Mirza again refused. It was clear there would be a battle.

The Menjil Defile, which he had chosen for the defense of Rasht, was a long narrow gorge between mountains, hills, and cliffs, through which a river and a narrow road passed, with the road at one point crossing the river by a small bridge. Mirza and Colonel von Passchen chose to position the *jangalis* on top of the mountains and hills, above where the British and the Russians would attempt to pass. They would have the advantage of position, while the enemy would have the advantage of numbers and equipment.

Mirza had managed to acquire more machine guns, purchasing a number of them from the retreating Russian troops, but he had no artillery or armored vehicles as his enemy did. There was a strong chance that the British cannons could dislodge them from their entrenched positions.

The greatest number of the five thousand *jangali* troops were positioned on a small flat-topped hill directly above the bridge.

On July 12, Dunsterville's and Bicherakov's forces arrived at the position, setting up their artillery, preparing to fire at the *jangalis*. Kouroush and his men were among the smaller forces perched precariously in crags of the cliff opposite the larger *jangali* forces on the hill. They were the first to see the surprise the British had for them—airplanes.

The planes came suddenly, sweeping down over the hill from behind the *jangali* trenches, firing at them and distracting them from their main objective below. While the *jangalis* fired at the airplanes, the invaders managed to get their cannon and armored vehicles into position to begin the heavy fire.

The *jangalis* had never faced heavy artillery fire and were not prepared for the devastation wreaked by the terrible explosions all around them.

Within the first few minutes of battle, hundreds of *jangalis* were killed, and even more were wounded. Among the wounded was Kouroush, hit in the leg by shrapnel.

Colonel von Passchen quickly saw that the wisest course would be to retreat, preserving his forces to fight the British another day.

Unfortunately, it would give the British free and unobstructed passage to Rasht.

Chapter 35

The British occupation of Rasht was a tenuous one. Dunsterville and Bicherakov did not really have sufficient troops to station along the full route from Hamadan to Enzeli in order to maintain their hold on the conquered territory. Even the small number they did leave behind cut their army to dangerous levels for their assault on the Bolsheviks in the Caucasus and on the Caspian.

For Rasht, the largest city along the route, and the capital of Mirza's state of Gilan, they were able to station only 450 men and two armored tanks. The forces at other points were spread even thinner.

Mirza moved his headquarters to Kasma, twenty-five miles west of Rasht, and von Passchen took the main body of *jangali* troops back to the Valley of the Trees to prepare new plans to drive the foreigners from Gilan once and for all.

Gregor had hoped to arrive home to find a country at last at peace, striving toward the ideals he and Kouroush and Mirza had talked of so many years before. Peace now seemed an impossibility, and democratic ideals, while not forgotten by Mirza, had been set aside for pragmatism. Of a more personal concern was that his dearest friend, Kouroush, was seriously injured, hospitalized at Rasht, in danger of losing his leg. To care for him, and to look after the numerous other injured men from the battle at Menjil, Tatiana had been forced to place little Jamshid in the care of a hired housekeeper, with Maria offering help as she was able. The great strain she had endured for so long had had its effect; Tatiana was thin, and she, like their mother, was aging before her natural time.

Jeanous had been in frail health for some time, and Gregor was at her bedside when she died. She had meant as much to him as his own mother, and he felt a great loss.

But the greatest change Gregor perceived was in Mirza. Certainly, some changes were to be expected, because of the heavy responsibilities he now bore on his shoulders, and of course certain changes were inevitable with the passage of time. The *jangali* leader hardly seemed to be the same person Gregor had known for so many years. Mirza's boundless energy and the deep-felt faith in revolutionary ideas seemed to be waning, replaced by a kind a cynicism in which hopes and dreams had turned to fatalism.

It seemed as if Mirza had come to believe the adoration of the people and assume that he was invincible, closer to a god than an ordinary mortal.

There was no tangible evidence of this; it was merely a vague feeling conveyed to Gregor, something in Mirza's manner and attitude. Mirza did not treat Gregor any differently; indeed, he was overjoyed to find that his old friend was alive and well. He arranged for Gregor to rejoin the revolutionary committee.

But the defeat at Menjil had deeply upset Mirza; he had just begun to resolve some of the problems in Gilan, before his state was taken away from him again by foreigners. Now, driving them out, and keeping them out forever, became almost an obsession with him. The attacks of the British airplanes on his troops and headquarters particularly infuriated him.

He persuaded von Passchen and Kaouk to wage guerilla warfare on the British installations along the Menjil-Rasht road, attacking suddenly from the forests, causing damage, and then retreating just as quickly back into cover. His objective was to wear down the enemy before making a major assault to retake Rasht.

At the end of July, Mirza learned that Bicherakov had decided to forsake the White Russian cause and transfer his allegiance—and his troops—to the Bolsheviks, in an attempt to drive the Turks from Baku. This defection would weaken the British even further.

The *jangalis* made their move in the middle of August, attacking Rasht from the west and southwest, moving against the main body of the British defense camped on the southern outskirts of the town at the same time they attempted to take the British Consulate in the heart of Rasht, which was defended by only a small company of men.

The *jangalis* set fire to the consulate, but then they found themselves having to defend their flanks against the main body of British troops retreating toward the consulate from the outskirts of the city. Leading the retreat were the two armored tanks, which began to fire upon the trapped attackers.

It was a stand-off, but the *jangalis* had inflicted sufficient damage that the British again sent an emissary to treat for peace.

Gregor and Kouroush, who was now well enough to walk with a cane, were with Mirza and the committee when the peace emissary arrived. He was a civilian, a commercial adviser at the consulate, and Gregor recognized him immediately. It took Sidney Fleming a few moments, however, to recognize the young boy he had aided and befriended so many years before.

After realizing Gregor's identity, he smiled warmly and said with a degree of affection, "It appears you now have objectives other than locating your sister."

Gregor returned the smile and said, "I have been reunited with my sister, and this . . .," gesturing toward Kouroush, "is her husband."

Mirza perceived there might be an advantage in having Gregor serve as his representative in negotiating peace with the British. It was clear he had a rapport, if not actually influence with Fleming, who was Dunsterville's representative. It was agreed that Gregor and Kouroush would meet with Fleming and the British military officer, General Matthews, in Rasht to discuss terms for a peace.

The negotiations proved to be long and tedious, and Gregor wasn't sure that his friendship with Fleming gave him any advantage, for the British were determined to have the right to military passage through Gilan to maintain their defense of Baku against the Germans and Turks, who were Gilan's allies. In April, Azerbaijan, along with Georgia and Armenia, had declared independence from Russia, with the objective of forming the state of Transcaucasia, with its own autonomy, an objective that had Gregor's sympathy.

But in the end, pragmatism won over idealism. Gilan's independence was so recently won, it was necessary to protect its own autonomy at the expense of its neighbors, who had to fight their own battles. By the signed agreement, the British recognized the state of Gilan and acknowledged its borders, in return for the right to transport its troops through the territory without obstruction.

* * * * *

Tatiana was relieved to have peace restored. The weeks of fighting the British had placed a great strain on her and Dr. Heshmat. The medical facilities in Rasht were inadequate even for normal needs; it had been impossible to cope with the many injured suffering the wounds of modern warfare. More beds were needed, more medicine, and more trained medical staff. Even working twenty hours a day, with minimal sleep, they had been unable to give the wounded proper care.

In human terms, the damages of war lingered long after the battles had ceased. The inadequacy of the immediate care for her patients meant many weeks or months of trying to mend mistakes and oversights. Even as much attention as she had given Kouroush, her own husband, he might be hampered the rest of his life by a limp, needing a cane to walk.

The long hours at the hospital continued for Tatiana into September and October. Many nights, she had to walk home alone through dark and empty streets. She felt safe, however, for most people by now knew her as an angel of mercy, and even the thieves and brigands of the street respected her.

But one night, early in November, she was startled by a man slipping out of an alley to block her way. In the shadows, she could not see his face, but could determine only that he was short and heavy and threatening.

Tatiana attempted to cross the street to walk around him, but he moved after her, whispering urgently, "Tatiana! Wait! I must talk with you!"

Surprised that it was someone who knew her well enough to call her by her first name, she stopped and turned around. When he drew near, she recognized to her horror that the man was Isaac Mizrahi.

"What are you doing here?" she exclaimed. "Don't you realize how dangerous it is for you in Rasht?"

"Yes," he admitted. "That's why I have chosen to meet you in secrecy."

"Why should you want to talk to me?" Tatiana said.

"I want to see Nadia," he told her. "I must speak to her, but she doesn't seem to be at home. Where is she?"

Tatiana hesitated. "She's away right now," she said cautiously. "In Paris."

"I want her to come back to me and be my wife," Isaac said. "Please tell her I'm sorry for the way I've treated her. I want to make it up to her."

"You've risked your life to come here to say that?" Tatiana asked, amazed, wondering if she had misjudged the man.

"That's only part of the reason I'm here," he replied, somewhat embarrassed. "I have some business to attend to as well."

"Oh, I see," Tatiana said, realizing the man had not changed at all. "What sort of business could be so important?"

Isaac paused, determining just how he would present the matter. "I have funds in a bank here," he said guardedly. "I would like Philip to help me obtain them."

"Why should Philip want to help you?" she asked, with a trace of anger in her voice.

"I have some information to trade," he said confidently. "Information that could make you a very wealthy young woman."

Tatiana felt her anger rising. The idea that she would be susceptible to one of Isaac Mizrahi's contemptible schemes was unmitigated impudence "I doubt if either Philip or I would be interested in such an arrangement."

"But the money is there waiting for you," Isaac protested. "It's yours by right, millions."

"Where?" Tatiana asked skeptically.

"That's the information I will give in return for Philip's help in getting what is rightfully mine," Mizrahi told her guardedly. "It's only fair."

"I'm not interested," Tatiana told him.

"Then let me speak to Philip," Isaac pleaded. "I'm sure he would be."

"I don't think so," Tatiana said coldly. "You would be wise to leave Gilan before Mirza learns you are here. You know the circumstances under which he agreed to spare your life."

She started to move off, but Isaac hurried after her. "Please, Tatiana, don't be unreasonable," he begged. "I'll tell you where the money is. It's yours anyway. It's in Baku, your inheritance from your uncle."

Tatiana stopped. "Uncle Vladimir?" she asked. "How do you know my uncle?"

"Since my exile, I've been in Baku," he explained. "I was working for him until he died."

"He's dead?" she asked, a sympathy for the old man rising in her breast.

"Yes," Mizrahi acknowledged. "And his will left his entire fortune to you." He hesitated. "I can help you to claim what's yours, if you will help me to get what is rightfully mine."

Tatiana deliberated for a moment. "I really prefer to have nothing to do with you," she said disdainfully. "But money would be a big help right now for the hospital. I will arrange for you to meet with Philip, but I can't promise that he will agree to what you ask."

"That's fair enough," Mizrahi told her.

When Tatiana explained the situation to Philip, he agreed to meet with Isaac. It was unlikely that they needed his help for Tatiana to claim her inheritance, but there were numerous unclaimed bank funds in Rasht. Their disposal was a part of Philip's responsibility for the Gilan government, along with land ownership.

He could not, however, guarantee Isaac's safety while in Rasht. All transferrals of unclaimed funds or lands had to be reported to the central committee and to Mirza. When Mirza received Philip's report, Isaac's life would be in great danger.

Isaac was willing to take that risk. The transactions were completed; Tatiana's inheritance was transferred from the bank in Baku to the bank in Rasht, and Isaac Mizrahi recovered his funds.

However, he was taken prisoner at Enzeli, while trying to leave the country with his money. In less than a week, he was executed.

* * * * *

Suddenly, Tatiana had become a very wealthy woman. She did not feel that all of this money should be hers, however. Rightfully, at least half should belong to Gregor.

But when she offered it to him, Gregor replied, "No. It was willed to you, and it should all be yours."

"But you worked for Uncle Vladimir all that time without pay," she protested. "And if part of it was taken from our father, you should get something from it. After all, you are the only son."

Gregor shook his head firmly. "Your idea to build a new hospital with the money is a good one, a noble one," he said. "Considering how this fortune was built, with Vladimir's cheating and stealing and deception, I feel it should be spent on something good. I think I would feel soiled if I spent any of it on myself."

"But what about Sylvia?" Tatiana asked. "Shouldn't you consult her? What if you should have children?"

Gregor fidgeted nervously. That subject clearly embarrassed him. "I don't know what will happen between Sylvia and me," he said. "I have a responsibility to Nadia first, to the child that is mine. I cannot even think of marriage to Sylvia, if Nadia should still want me."

"I really would feel better if some of the inheritance went to you," Tatiana said ruefully. "Isn't there something you would like, if you suddenly found yourself with more than you need?"

"Well, there is one thing," Gregor said pensively. "I would like to see the Zoroastrian shrine at Baku restored and preserved. If you would like to devote some money toward doing that, it would please me very much."

"Then that's what it shall be," Tatiana said happily.

So Tatiana proceeded to make plans for a new hospital for Rasht, large and equipped with all of the most modern medical equipment available. There was more than enough left over to take care of Gregor's wish as well.

* * * * *

Sylvia knew that something was wrong between her and Gregor, but she did not know what it was. From the moment they had arrived Rasht, his manner had changed. They still lived together, they still talked, and they still made love, but there was a barrier she could see in his eyes when they were together that she did not understand. There was something he was not telling her.

Though they lived as husband and wife, there had been no talk of marriage. On the way home from Siberia, Gregor had talked of a real wedding ceremony once they were home in Rasht and life returned to normal.

Now that the fighting with the British was over and the state of Gilan was beginning to work, life had become as normal as it could possibly be. However, talk of marriage had stopped.

To make matters worse, that November, Sylvia began to suspect she was with child. It had not been confirmed, but she knew the symptoms. If she should speak to Gregor about it, she knew they would finally have to talk about marriage, but she could not bring herself to force the subject. If they were to be husband and wife, she wanted it to be because he wanted it as much as she did.

Because of her Russian background, Sylvia had few real friends in Rasht, certainly none that she could confide in. The only person she had become close to was Tatiana. She needed to see a doctor to confirm her condition, and decided that she might be able to talk to Tatiana without having Gregor learn of it.

The medical examination in Tatiana's office confirmed what Sylvia had suspected; she was pregnant. The child was expected in May.

Sitting behind her desk after giving Sylvia the news, Tatiana smiled and said, "Gregor will be so pleased when you tell him."

Sylvia shook her head. "Please don't say anything to him," she said. "I don't want him to know. Not just now."

"But why?" Tatiana asked. "He loves children."

Sylvia could not help herself; she began to weep.

Tatiana tried to comfort her. "What's wrong?" she asked. "You can tell me. I won't say anything to Gregor."

Taking the handkerchief that Tatiana offered her, Sylvia dried her eyes and, trying to maintain control, confessed, "I don't know what it is, but something has come between us. I don't think Gregor loves me anymore. There may be someone else. I don't want him to marry me just because of the child."

Tatiana rose to her feet and returned to her desk pensively. "I think I know what it is," she said, trying to decide how much she should reveal to Sylvia. "I don't know if there is someone else, but at one time there was. And there is a child that he feels responsible for, a child that is his. He did not know about it until you returned to Rasht."

"A child?" Sylvia asked. "Here in Rasht?"

Tatiana shook her head. "Not at the moment," she said. "The child and its mother are in Paris right now. Gregor has never seen the little girl."

"Tell me about it," Sylvia begged. "Please. I have to know. I think I have a right to know."

After a momentary deliberation, Tatiana decided to tell Sylvia everything, about Nadia, about her marriage to Isaac Mizrahi, about the one night Gregor and Nadia had spent together, and about little Julia.

Sylvia was surprisingly understanding. After knowing the entire story, she seemed much relieved, but she still made Tatiana promise to say nothing about her own pregnancy. Before leaving the office, she turned to Tatiana and asked, "When will Nadia be returning from Paris?"

"I don't know," Tatiana replied. "We haven't heard from her in some time. Her last letter told us not to expect her anytime soon. I suppose she has stayed there to study."

"I hope she doesn't wait too long," Sylvia said with a sad smile. "I would like Gregor to see her again and make his decision without knowing my condition. I want him, but I want him only if he loves me."

* * * * *

That November was a significant one in many ways. Not only was the independent state of Gilan on its way to full recognition in the world, but the war in Europe had finally ended, after much death and destruction. The victorious western allies were proclaiming that this would be the beginning of a new age, an age in which the people of the world had certain rights.

For the people of Gilan, as for people in many other parts of the world, one of the most significant of these rights was that of self-determination, the right to decide what sort of government would rule over them.

Beginning in January of 1919, now that the European war had ended, representatives from all over the world would meet in Paris to help ensure that these rights would be secured for all time.

It was an incredible promise, but an inspiring one. After all, there might be hope for humankind.

*   *   *   *   *

When Mirza asked Gregor to be a part of the Gilan delegation to the Paris Peace Conference, he was delighted. The new nation had not been officially invited to take part, because it had not been a belligerent in the European war. But, like many of the new and small countries seeking autonomy, Gilan wanted to ensure that its borders would be protected in the reshaping of Europe and Central Asia.

It was not only a wonderful opportunity to cover an important historical event for the newspaper and to do something for his country, it would also enable him to see and talk to Nadia again. He asked Tatiana to write to her and let her know that he was alive and that he would be in Paris.

Nadia wrote back that she would be delighted to see him, and gave him the new address where she was living.

Gregor had mixed feelings when it came to the decision he would have to make after arriving in Paris. He was torn between the love he felt for Nadia and that he had for Sylvia. Both meant very much to him. He felt a greater responsibility to Nadia, who had borne him a child. And now that Isaac Mizrahi was dead, it seemed inevitable that he should marry Nadia—if she would have him.

On the other hand, he owed Sylvia his very life; she had saved him from execution; then in Siberia she had nursed him back to health. On the long road home, they had pretended to be married; indeed, they still lived as husband and wife, and he had promised her a wedding.

Of the two, he considered the greater responsibility to be to Nadia, because of the child. Throughout it all, he did not even consider what he himself wanted, or which he loved more deeply.

Life with Sylvia had become rather difficult, and, though Gregor did not know specifically what was wrong, he was sure his attitude was at fault, for he had certainly changed toward her since learning about his child. He could not blame her for the cautious reserved manner she had developed as a defense against his distraction.

He felt guilt and shame for what he was doing to her, but he did not see how it could be avoided.

Their parting, as Gregor left for Paris, was a painful one, especially for Sylvia. She felt that she might never see him again, or if she did it would be only to say goodbye once more. It was as if her life were ending, for she had devoted it entirely to him; without him she had nothing except the deep love she felt for him. Within a few months, however, she might also have his child, and could transfer at least a part of that love to it.

When Gregor embraced her and kissed her goodbye, Sylvia held the moment as long as she could, forcing back her tears until he had walked out the door, and then she wept as if her heart were breaking.

*   *   *   *   *

With the close of the war, the city of Paris burst forth with life like new flowers in the spring. Even though the weather was cold and gray that January, there was about the city the sense and feeling of rebirth. Gregor had never seen such a city before; he was mesmerized by its size, its beauty, and the warmth of its people. He was awed by its grand and stately buildings, and by its wide boulevards and extensive parks. All other cities he had known paled by comparison.

He and the other members of the Gilan delegation stayed at a small hotel some distance from the Palace of Versailles, where most of the meetings of the peace conference were taking place. Paris was filled with dignitaries and government delegations from all over the world, and hotel space was at a premium. As a small, new nation, Gilan had found it difficult even to secure the tawdry rooms it had.

Gregor did not mind the accommodations, however, for the hotel was not far from the Left Bank area of the city, where Nadia was staying.

The Gilan delegation had numerous meetings and conferences scheduled, and Gregor had to spend additional time covering other meetings for the newspaper back in Rasht. However, a few days after their arrival, he managed to arrange a few hours free to pay a visit to Nadia.

He had some difficulty locating the building where her appartment was located because of the narrow jumble of streets in the Left Bank. He had heard something of the special nature of the artistic people who chose to live in the area, but he was still surprised at the appearance of these "bohemians" on the streets. There was a studied shabbiness about the men, and the women wore their hair cut short and their skirts above their ankles. Many of them also had painted lips and eyes and heavily rouged cheeks.

Still, seeing them did not prepare him for his reunion with Nadia. He did not recognize the woman who opened the door of the small apartment.

She threw her arms around Gregor to embrace him warmly, then kissed him on the cheek. It was only after she stepped back to look happily into Gregor's eyes that he realized this was Nadia, a very changed Nadia. Her hair was short, ringing her face in dark curls; her lips were a bright red, and there was rouge on her cheeks; her eyebrows were plucked and arched; and there was a blue shadow over her eyes. The dress she wore was short, loose, and flowing in brightly colored folds. The predominating color was red.

"It's so wonderful to see you!" she exclaimed happily to Gregor, ushering him into her apartment. Then she bit her lip and blushed. "But you're shocked at the way I look. I'm sorry; I didn't think. This is the new style for women here, but it must come as something of a shock to you."

She threw her arms around him and hugged him again. "Oh, my dear, old friend, you'll understand after you've been here a while," she said. "Paris is a very different place from Rasht. You'll love it."

She pulled him toward a sofa piled with cushions. "Here, sit down, and tell me everything about home. How is Tatiana? And Papa? And Kouroush?"

Gregor sat down, still mystified by this strange woman he was with, trying to convince himself that it was truly Nadia. Her surroundings—the apartment—were not what he could have ever envisioned. Of course, her paintings were all over the room, much the way they had been at her studio in Rasht, but there were also objects on the walls and tables from other countries, Chinese vases and Spanish shawls and bamboo shades.

Gregor gave her all of the news from home. She asked for details of Isaac Mizrahi's death, and Gregor told her as many of the circumstances as he knew.

As soon as he was able to start asking questions of her, Gregor inquired, "And where is . . . your daughter Julia? Isn't she here?"

Nadia looked at him suspiciously, obviously wondering how much he knew. "Oh, she's out with Roscow right now."

"Who?" Gregor asked.

Nadia smiled. "Roscow Molinar, my manager," she explained. "He's the art critic and gallery owner who has been responsible for the sale of my paintings. This is his apartment."

Gregor was surprised. "He lives here?" he asked.

"This is just his little apartment in the city," she told him. "He has a large house in the south of France. The apartment is just for use in the city."

"Will they be home soon?" Gregor asked. "I would like to meet the child."

"It shouldn't be long," Nadia said. She reached over to a case on the table and withdrew a cigarette, then lit it. Another change. "Would you like one?" she asked Gregor as an afterthought.

"No thank you," Gregor replied, embarrassed.

"What about some coffee?" she asked, unfolding herself from the sofa.

"Or some tea?"

"I'll have some tea," Gregor answered. "If it's no trouble." He had noticed that there seemed to be no servants about, as she would have had back home in Persia.

"None at all," she smiled, then walked into a small kitchen off the main room of the apartment.

Gregor looked around the apartment while Nadia brewed tea. He wondered how many oher rooms it had. He tried to look down the hallway to see how many bedrooms there were, but did not want his curiosity to seem obvious. There seemed to be only one bedroom, but he couldn't be sure.

Trying to make conversation, Gregor called out to her, "When do you plan to go home again?"

"I haven't made any plans," Nadia called back. "I really love Paris, and I'm making lots and lots of money here."

It seemed an evasive answer. Gregor couldn't help but wonder if she was trying to tell him she had no intention of ever going back to Rasht. But that was impossible to believe, even with all the changes that had taken place in her.

As she brought the tea in to set it down on the small table before the sofa, she said, "You must let me show you Paris when you have time. I can take you to wonderful places that visitors never see. I really feel that I belong here. Paris is my city."

As he accepted his cup of tea from her, Gregor said softly, "You know, Nadia, we all miss you in Rasht."

"I know," Nadia replied. "And I miss all of you." She hesitated. "But my life is very different now from what it was. I don't know if I can go back to the life I had before."

"I especially would like you back," Gregor said.

Nadia looked at him sadly. Gregor wondered if he saw a glisten of tears in her eyes. "But your life is different, too," she said. "When are you and Sylvia to be married?"

Gregor was stunned. It had not occurred to him that she would have heard about Sylvia. "I . . .," he stammered. "We don't have any plans for marriage." He looked down at his teacup, as if searching it for the words. Finally, finding them, he looked up at Nadia again. "I know about Julia," he said somberly. "I know she is my child."

Nadia smiled, then shook her head sadly. "No," she said gently. "She is my child; she has no father. As far as the world knows, her father was

Isaac Mizrahi, and he is dead."

"I would like to become her father," Gregor pursued. "I would like to marry you."

Again, Nadia shook her head with a smile. "It wouldn't work," she said. "We've both changed too much. And I'm very happy here in Paris, with my career. I couldn't give that up."

They were prevented from pursuing the conversation, because the door to the apartment opened suddenly, and a little girl burst into the room, running happily to her mother. She was followed by a middle-aged man, who was obviously Roscow Molinar. Gregor rose to greet him.

"Mommy, mommy," Julia shouted excitedly, waving a small clown doll. "Look what Papa bought me!"

Roscow walked over to Nadia, bent down and kissed her on the cheek. Nadia smiled. "I can see she had a good time as always, but you shouldn't buy her something every time you go out."

"I like to see her happy," Roscow said. He turned to nod to Gregor. "You must be Gregor Sarkissian," he said, extending his hand. "I'm very pleased to meet you."

Gregor responded pleasantly to Molinar, but from the moment he and Julia had entered the apartment, Gregor had felt out of place. Julia had referred to him as "Papa," and he had related to Nadia as a husband and lover would. It was clear that, married or unmarried, the three of them had become a family unit.

He felt foolish to have been so concerned about his responsibility to Nadia and the child she had borne him. Nadia had gone on with her life, making the best of her situation. Assuming Gregor had been dead, she had set herself on a different course, one that now excluded him completely.

After a few pleasantries, Gregor made up an excuse of an appointment, and left, promising to see them again soon. He did see Nadia several times while he was in Paris, but their relationship began to grow into one of brother and sister, friendly and affectionate, but not intimate.

* * * * *

For Gregor, the peace conferences in Paris were both exciting and frustrating. The ideas presented there for a League of Nations, proposed by President Woodrow Wilson of the United States, made lasting peace seem possible. The concept of self-determination for all people of the world made it seem that there was indeed hope for justice and freedom. Yet, in the actual meetings, no nation—not even the United States—seemed able to forsake petty grievances and self-interest.

For all their professions of justice, the five victorious powers—-the United States, Britain, France, Italy, and Japan—were primarily concerned with punishing the defeated nations. They were particulary wary of the new socialist states, making every effort to exclude them from the new League of Nations. Russia was not represented at the conference, so there was no strong voice to assist Gilan and others of their view.

Persia was given preferential treatment, supported strongly by the British, to the detriment of Gilan, whose territory Persia claimed. Persia was admitted to the League of Nations; Gilan was not.

To Gregor and the other Gilan delegates, it seemed clear that they were being ignored because the British sought domination of their territory and its rich store of oil. Its geographical position in the Middle East was also of strategic importance, especially now that the Allies looked upon Soviet Russia as a foe rather than a friend.

It was while they were in Paris that Gregor began to perceive a distinct division of views within his country's leadership, largely a result of their treatment by the British, French, and Americans. The Gilan delegation had gone to the conference unified in their belief that the democratic powers would support their desire for autonomy. All were disappointed, but some— including Gregor— continued to maintain hope that their goals would eventually be recognized; others, led by the Bolshevik contingent, espoused unequivacal alignment with Soviet Russia in opposition to the Allied powers.

Finally, their efforts frustrated at every turn, the Gilan delegation decided in late March to return home. They had achieved nothing.

* * * * *

Before leaving, Gregor decided to see Nadia one last time. He invited her and Julia to walk with him through the park alongside the Seine. It was now springtime, and nature was bursting forth with the hope that had accompanied the Gilan delegation to Paris in wintertime. With those hopes now dashed, Gregor felt a degree of melancholy in the fresh clear air and the brilliantly colored flowers beginning to bloom.

Was this, he wondered, the inevitable fate of hopes and dreams—to blossom vigorously but briefly, then fade and die with time? He was still a young man, but he had seen and experienced much in a short time, and he felt a growing cynicism. He did not want to give up, to compromise, to accept defeat for the ideals he and Kouroush and Mirza had espoused and had fought so desperately for. But did he really have any choice? Was his fate truly in his own hands? Or was he completely controlled by events surrounding him, the helpless puppet of powers stronger than himself?

As they walked along the Seine, with little Julia running ahead of them, Nadia sensed Gregor's despair. "You mustn't feel that your mission here has failed," she told him, "Whatever happens, it has had some effect. You may not know what that will be for months or even years. When I was in Russia, I never thought I would go to Paris; I never expected such public acclaim for my work. I didn't even want it. But it happened, and it has made me very happy."

Gregor nodded. "Yes, I'll admit you've been very lucky," he said. "I'm glad you're happy."

"I would like you to be as happy," Nadia said affectionately. "And I suspect that you can be." She hesitated a moment, then added, "When you get back to Rasht, you should marry Sylvia. I think she must love you very much."

Gregor felt an aching in his heart. "Yes," he said. "She does. And I guess I love her very much, too, even though I haven't made her secure in that love. I've been very unfair to her."

"Love makes a very big difference in life," Nadia told him softly. "Especially when it is shared and returned. It makes all the other trials and tribulations of life so much easier to face. I don't think I could have had the success I've had without Roscow's love."

And then Nadia confessed that she was expecting Roscow's child, and that they were making preparations to be married in a quiet, private ceremony.

They parted with an affectionate embrace. Gregor kissed Julia on the cheek the way an uncle would, accepting the fact that she must never know him as father. They promised to see each other again, but Gregor wasn't sure they would ever do so.

Chapter 36

Gregor sent Sylvia a telegram to notify her of the date of his return to Rasht, but she still seemed surprised to see him when he arrived at home. His mother, who had now begun to regain her health and had very few bad days, answered the door of their rented house, welcoming him warmly and telling him that Sylvia was upstairs in their bedroom.

It seemed strange to him that she would be there in the middle of the day, but he assumed she was merely doing household chores. He hurried up the stairs to see her.

Rushing into the room, he was startled to see her lying in bed, wearing her loose-fitting dressing gown. "What's wrong?" he asked. "Are you ill?"

"No," she said with a smile, rising with some effort. "I'm fine. Just resting my feet."

Only after she was in his arms to embrace him did he realize that there was a different shape to her body. She was pregnant, and obviously in the last weeks of her pregnancy.

"Why didn't you tell me?" he gasped. "How long have you known?"

Sylvia blushed, her eyes not meeting his. "Since before you left for Paris," she said nervously. "I didn't want you to worry when . . ., when you were away."

"But why should that . . . ?" he blurted out. Then he realized what she must have been going through, waiting for him to ask her to marry him, enduring the uncertainty in silence. He hugged her to him, exclaiming happily, "This is wonderful. It pleases me very much. Of course, we must be married immediately."

He hesitated, looking down at her belly. "When is it due?" he asked. "It must be very soon."

She blushed and grinned at his boyish behavior, delighted by his offhand proposal of marriage. "In about three weeks," she said. "Early May."

Gregor laughed. "I hope there's time to plan a wedding."

Tears welled up in Sylvia's eyes. "Oh, Gregor," she said, "do you really want to marry me?" Then she stammered. "I mean . . ., it's not just because of the baby, is it?"

Gregor smiled at her fondly. "No," he said, "it's because I love you very much. I haven't told you that lately, have I?"

Sylvia shook her head. "No," she said, "but it's enough that you're saying it now." He kissed her gently on the lips. "I intend to say it now, and every day for the rest of my life," he whispered lovingly. Then he kissed her passionately, holding her tightly. She clung to him gratefully, happily, not wanting to let the moment go.

* * * * *

Gregor and Sylvia were married a week later in a very private civil ceremony, with only Kouroush and Tatiana as witnesses. But the joy they shared could not have been greater if it had been a huge wedding with hundreds of guests. What was most important to them was that they would each love and cherish the other for the rest of their lives.

During the second week of May, Sylvia gave birth to a son, tended by Tatiana. They chose to name him Alexei, in honor of Gregor's father.

* * * * *

Gregor's report to Mirza on the Paris Peace Conference confirmed what Mirza had suspected for a long time—that the British intended to take control of Gilan as well as Persia, taking advantage of the Russian Bolshevik government's preoccupation with fighting off the counter-revolutionary forces and the troops of General Dunsterville in Baku. With the end of the European war, it was possible for the British effort to be concentrated on returning the northern provinces to the control of the Tehran puppet government, now under British domination. The *jangalis* would be no match for a concerted attack from the British.

It would mean not only the loss of the freedom and autonomy gained for the Persians of the north, but it would thwart Mirza's ultimate goal of achieving freedom and autonomy for all of Persia.

Mirza's revolutionary committee could not agree on a solution to the problem confronting them. As always, the Bolshevik faction wanted to turn to Soviet Russia for help. The conservative group was determined to fight it out to the death without assistance from anyone. And the moderates sought various compromises, the most promising of which was to ask the United States to intercede for them to influence the British to come to an agreement.

Gregor was among the moderates, and Mirza and Kouroush were inclined to that view as well, though Mirza also felt there was also some merit to the conservative approach. However, the Bolshevik contingent had greater support on the committee, and were constantly pressuring Mirza to align himself with them.

Haidar Khan led the group of Bolsheviks, and there were strong indications that he intended eventually to displace Mirza from power and take his place, linking Gilan with Russia in a planned Soviet Union.

"I don't trust the man," Kouroush told Gregor, after a particularly heated committee meeting. "He's working against Mirza behind his back."

Gregor nodded. "From what I've heard," he said, "that's typical of the way these Bolsheviks operate. They attempt to undermine the authority of moderate leaders, then step in when they're at their weakest."

"I wish we could make Mirza see what Haidar is doing," Kouroush said, shaking his head dismally. "But he refuses to think bad about men he feels have been loyal to him."

Gregor frowned. "I'm not sure it's quite that simple," he said. "As much as I love Mirza, I'm afraid administrating the government is beyond his capabilities, and I think he knows it. His strength was in leading the revolution, and now that it has been achieved, he's unsure of himself. He has to depend on others too much. He listens to the committee, and when the committee doesn't agree, he's confused and uncertain. He would be much more comfortable fighting from the jungle again."

"You may be right," Kouroush admitted, "but there isn't anyone else who could manage the government better. The only possibility would be Ehsanullah Khan, and that would be almost as bad as Haidar. Our freedom and autonomy would be gone. We would be trading Czarist Russia for Bolshevik Russia."

Their efforts, however, seemed to have the opposite effect on Mirza from what Gregor and Kouroush intended. Instead of becoming more wary of Haidar and Ehsanullah, he came to rely on them more and more for advice and guidance. As a result, by July, the factions of the revolutionary committee had become so divided they could not agree even on minor matters. The conservatives and moderates, among them Kouroush and Gregor, were on the verge of leaving the government entirely.

Only the memories of their years of affectionate friendship with Mirza kept Kouroush and Gregor on the committee.

The government was at its weakest and most divided when the Persian government at Tehran, aided by British troops, decided to make their move. That August, after a treaty signed between Persia and Britain, twenty thousand troops, cossacks and British regulars, began to march toward Rasht.

The *jangali* forces were more adept at guerilla attacks than they were at defending a city against an onslaught from the best-trained army in the world. Rasht fell very quickly. Mirza, the members of the committee, and other government leaders were forced to retreat from the city, returning to hiding in the forests.

There was a change in Mirza; miraculously, virtually overnight, he became the old leader again—strong, decisive, sure of himself. To the dismay of Kouroush and Gregor, however, his renewed assurance moved him toward the Bolshevik faction. Mirza agreed to go to Azerbaijan to meet with a Soviet emissary, Commissar Kolomyitsev, to discuss an alliance. During his absence, Ehanullah Khan would be in command of the *jangalis*.

* * * * *

Tatiana was growing weary of war. During the brief period of peace before the Persian and British forces took Rasht, she had managed to begin building her hospital. Now, work ceased and she wondered if it would ever be completed. Again, she and Dr. Heshmat had to divide their time between Rasht and the *jangali* encampment. And, to make matters worse, they were battling an influenza epidemic that had spread throughout the entire world after the end of the European war.

She saw little of Julia, who was cared for by Maria, and even less of Kouroush, who had escaped to the forests with Mirza. Tatiana began to despair that they would never achieve peace, never have anything resembling a normal family life. She knew that Kouroush and Gregor were both concerned about the direction Mirza was beginning to take, and that awareness increased her feeling that the difficulties would never end.

One morning, late in August, she had completed her rounds at the Rasht hospital and was on her way back to her office, when she was approached in the corridor by a Persian Cossack officer wearing the uniform of a colonel.

"Dr. Jalali," he said politely, "my name is Reza Khan. I wonder if you could spare me a few minutes. I would like to talk to you."

Tatiana knew who Reza Khan was. He had been Kouroush's sergeant when Kouroush had been in the cossacks. There was much talk of the man, for he had been the only native Persian to reach such a high rank in the Persian Cossack Brigade. For this reason, he was both respected and feared by the *jangalis*. Tatiana realized that she must be wary of him.

"Yes, of course," she said. "We can talk in my office."

Once they were seated across the desk from each other in Tatiana's office, Reza Khan came directly to the point. "I know that you and the members of your family look upon me as an enemy," he said. "At the moment, we are enemies, but I would like us to be friends."

Tatiana smiled at him. "That would be extremely difficult to achieve under the circumstances," she said.

Reza Khan returned her smile. "Not as difficult as you might think," he said. "I have a great deal of admiration for you and the work you are doing here. In fact, I would like to do whatever I can to help you see that work on your hospital continues. But that is something we can discuss later. Right now, I would like to do what I can to achieve peace between the *jangalis* and the rest of Persia."

"I'm afraid there's not much I can do to help you," Tatiana told him bluntly.

"I know that," Reza Khan replied. "But you can help me to meet with your husband and your brother, and perhaps even Mirza himself, so that we can discuss the matter."

Tatiana was cautious. Was this a trap? Was the commander of the Russian Cossack Brigade, now virtually the ruler of Rasht, simply trying to find a way to get his hands on the revolutionary leaders? "I'm not sure I can even do that," she told him.

"Our meeting can be held in absolute secrecy," he said, sensing the reason for her caution, "and I can assure their safety." He smiled. "I realize you have no reason to trust me, but my goals and Mirza's goals are ultimately the same. I would like to see all of Persia free and independent of foreign influence. It is the means to that end that we disagree on. And now I see Mirza taking a dangerous course, willing to deliver his people back to the Russians, merely to maintain the power he has achieved."

Tatiana frowned. "But aren't you doing the same with the British?" she asked.

"That may appear to be the case," he said. "For the moment, it suits my purpose to have that appearance." He smiled. "That is what I would like to discuss with Mirza. I would like to find some way we could work together rather than against each other."

"I can't promise anything," Tatiana told him. "But I will see what I can do."

* * * * *

Gregor was surprised at the message communicated by Tatiana from Reza Khan, but Kouroush was not.

"You have to know the man," Kouroush told him, "to understand. If he says he wants to work with Mirza, I would trust him. He is one of the most honorable men I've ever known."

"Then you think we should meet with him?" Gregor asked.

"Yes," Kouroush replied. "But, for the moment, I don't think Mirza should be involved, nor should any of the rest of the committee. Because of the split that's taken place, we must be sure of what is being proposed before they are involved."

The meeting was arranged to take place in a wooded area not far from the city, and only Gregor, Kouroush, and Reza Khan would be present. Both sides agreed to total secrecy.

Gregor had met Reza Khan before, but the circumstances of their meeting had hardly been sufficient to form an opinion of the man. However, from the moment they faced each other in the forest, he was impressed. Kouroush had been right in his estimation of the cossack colonel. Reza Khan, now in his forties, had that combination of commanding authority and gentle wisdom that few leaders acquire. He was tall, with graying hair and mustache, and dark intelligent eyes that seemed to take in and understand everthing.

Reza Khan was direct and frank about his motives for approaching the *jangalis*. "The only way Persia can hope to remain independent of the larger powers," he explained, "is to be united, north and south, under one government. I do not wish to see our people dominated by either Britain or Russia, and I think Mirza and I should talk before he commits Gilan to the Soviet Russians."

"But," Kouroush protested, "the Tehran government has committed itself to the British."

Reza Khan shook his head. "We have only an alliance with the British," he said. "Alliances can be broken. The British have no historical claim to our territory; the Russians do. Now is the time to break that claim, since there is a totally different form of government in Russia."

"Do you trust the British?" Gregor asked.

"No," Reza Khan acknowledged. "But they trust me, and I intend to use that trust to return Persia to an independent and democratic government, without the Qajar shahs."

"How do you intend to do that?" Kouroush asked.

"That I cannot tell you," Reza Kahn smiled.

"Do you intend to set yourself up as shah?" Gregor asked.

"No," Reza Kahn shook his head firmly. "Persia has had enough of shahs. It is time for an elected, representative form of government, with a powerful Majlis."

"What place would Mirza have in such a government?" Kouroush asked.

"That would depend upon the vote of the people," Reza Khan replied.

"In principle I like what you are saying," Kouroush told him. "But I'm not sure it can be achieved so easily. And I'm afraid Mirza would not accept what you propose. A few weeks ago, he still might have given you a fair hearing, but now he is completely under the control of the Bolshevik faction. He has committed himself to a course of action and is not be likely to turn from it."

"I understand," Reza Khan said. "But we must at least attempt to talk. Persia must be reunited, and if we are ever to regain our independence, it must be achieved now, before either the Russians or the British become entrenched in our homeland again. Right now, we would have considerable sympathy from the United States and the Wilson government."

"I agree with what you say," Gregor told him. "From what I observed at the Paris peace conference, pragmatism is as important as idealism, and we must be prepared to use the sympathy of other nations against those with imperialist objectives. I will do what I can to convince Mirza to meet with you."

Kouroush nodded, but he was frowning. "I will, too," he said. "But I don't think we will have much success."

* * * * *

Mirza returned from Azerbaijan without having achieved the agreement with Kolomyitsev. Indeed, after traveling so far, he had not even been able to meet with the emissary. Baku was in turmoil, with continual fighting between the Bolsheviks on one side and the British and White Russian forces on the other. Kolomyitsev had used this fact as an excuse to postpone one scheduled meeting after another, until Mirza had finally been forced to return home, completely frustrated.

The moderate and conservative members of the committee suspected there had been other motives, however, but they could not convince Mirza of this. Under the influence of Haidar and Ehsanullah, he trusted the

Bolsheviks and was unwilling to suspect ulterior motives.

Instead, he now distrusted Gregor and Kouroush. He was angry when they told him of their meeting with Reza Khan. "How could you do such a thing without consulting me?" he snapped.

"You weren't here," Kouroush replied hotly. "You were waiting for the beck and call of some Soviet commissar in Baku."

"Ehsanullah was in charge here," Mirza cut back. "You should have spoken to him."

"We don't trust Ehsanullah," Gregor replied. "He has his own interests to serve."

"His interests are my interests," Mirza said fiercely, his eyes blazing.

"No, they're not!" Kouroush snapped. "He's nothing more than a puppet of the Russian Bolsheviks! He's looking out only for himself!"

Gregor could see an almost irrational rage building in Mirza. Before a fight could erupt, Gregor tried to calm the discussion. "It would be worth a meeting between you and Reza Khan," he said, "just to see if there was some way of combining efforts. The Persian people, north and south, are getting weary of war. And, after all, they are what we've been fighting for."

"No," Mirza said firmly, his anger still high. "It will be my way or not at all."

* * * * *

In the weeks that followed, Mirza continued to refuse to meet Reza Khan. By mid-September, his emmissaries had connected with the Soviet emmissaries, and an agreement was worked out. Once the Bolshevik forces secured Baku, they would come to Mirza's aid. In return, Mirza would proclaim the "Soviet" Republic of Gilan, to be united with Russia and other Soviet states.

To be sure of the sympathy of the common people, Mirza began a program of appropriating rice from the large farmers and distributing it free to the poor of Gilan. He would, he announced, eventually appropriate the land itself and redistribute it as well.

The Bolshevik aid was expected in the spring. Meanwhile, the *jangalis* could carry on their guerilla warfare against the British and the cossacks in Rasht and Enzeli, to weaken their hold as much as possible.

* * * * *

In December, and in January of 1920, the fighting at Baku was especially intense. Gradually, the small and weakened White Russian forces were being defeated, despite the British aid. Late in January, Gregor received word that General Zinoviev, Sylvia's father, had been killed in battle.

It was sad news he had to report to his wife, but news they had known must eventually come.

* * * * *

In the spring of 1920, the Russian Bolsheviks came to Mirza's aid, as promised. In May, the Bolshevik fleet took control of Enzeli from the British, then their army and the *jangalis* swiftly captured Rasht. On May 18, Mirza proclaimed the Soviet Republic of Gilan. The central committee of the government would consist entirely of Bolsheviks; all the moderates and conservatives from the revolutionary committee were excluded, including Gregor and Kouroush.

Thus began the reign of terror.

Gregor and Kouroush were both angry and resentful about the changes that took place that spring, but neither would blame Mirza for them. They knew that Mirza was now nothing more than a puppet of the Bolsheviks, and that most of the outrages were ordered by Haidar and Ehsanullah. Mirza was a man of loyalty and conscience; if he had retained power, they were sure that none of the events would have taken place. It was the Soviet committee that had no conscience, that operated coldly, without ethics or compassion.

It began simply enough, without violence, according to Russian Soviet rules. Only Communist party members could hold positions of power within the government. Those officials who refused to join would have to be removed from office.

To his credit, Mirza did present this requirement directly to his friends and did not leave it to bureaucrats. "I would not ask you do anything I am not willing to do myself," he told Gregor and Kouroush. "I do not believe in the communist ideology, but I will join merely as a matter of pragmatism, a means to an end."

"I don't see that I can do that," Kouroush said. "My conscience would not permit it."

Gregor agreed. "I don't see that party membership should be necessary for a newspaperman," he said. "I write things as I see them. I could not adhere to a party line if I don't agree."

"Please don't be hasty in your decisions," Mirza asked. "If you do not join, I can do nothing to protect you or your positions, and I do want you at my side. We have been through much together, and I would be saddened to see this separate us."

"This was not the revolution we set out to achieve together," Kouroush said. "I cannot change, merely for expediency."

Because of their decisions, Kouroush was removed from his position in the foreign office and Gregor lost his post as editor of the paper, though he was permitted to continue as a writer, with all of his work subject to editing. Philip Boustani was removed form his office in the department of land and finance. Not long afterward, all his farmlands were seized by the government, along with those of other property owners, so as to be assigned to farm cooperatives. It was, Philip felt, no better than what the czarist Russians had done before.

Tatiana's unfinished hospital was seized as well, and turned over to the state for completion, and her medical work was subject to supervision by a nonmedical committee. Tatiana would not have minded losing her hospital as long as it proved beneficial to the people. However, as soon as it was seized, work on it ceased, because the medical committee could not agree on details.

If these had been the only kinds of changes, however, the people of Gilan might have been pleased with the new government, for these alterations affected only a few. But the central committee went even further. Those who spoke publicly against the government were arrested, tried, and executed. Many of those hanged or beheaded in the mass executions were former *jangali* leaders. Within a matter of weeks, the hundreds of "enemies" of the state became thousands dead. Almost every family in Gilan was affected in some way.

The abuses of power were even greater than they had been under the Qajar shahs when they were supported by the czarist Russians.

* * * * *

Kouroush knew that it was dangerous to speak out against the central committee, and especially against Haidar Khan, who was responsible for the arrest and execution of dissenters. But he was outraged by what had happened to the revolution he had worked for so hard and so long, and he refused to be silent.

He was a hero of the revolution; his lame leg was a visible sign of his service to his country. He had been a part of the *jangali* committee and had been an important member of the government before it had changed character. People would listen to him, and he was determined that they would hear the truth about the Bolsheviks—even if it meant martyrdom.

It was inevitable that he would be arrested.

The police came to his home one morning in July, after Tatiana had left for the hospital. He was taken to prison and confined to a solitary cell, where he was permitted no visitors.

* * * * *

The arrest of Kouroush was the last straw for Gregor. He had accepted the loss of his editorial position at the newspaper, and he had endured the censorship of the articles he had written as a lowly reporter. He expected no rewards for his service to his country on the revolutionary committee. But his personal ethics placed the loyalty of friends as high as loyalty to country, and he believed his friendship and Kouroush's had been betrayed by Mirza.

He went to the government offices in Rasht and demanded an audience with Mirza.

Gregor had never seen his old friend looking so pale and haggard. Mirza was thin, his shoulders slumped in defeat; his eyes had a lost and vacant stare within dark circles.

Gregor had intended to vent his rage in uncontrolled fury, but the sight of Mirza shocked him so that he spoke more reasonably. "These outrages have to stop," he told him firmly. "We all once fought together for freedom and justice, but apparently your pragmatism has made you forget all that, turning you into a greater tyrant than any Qajar shah."

"I have forgotten nothing," Mirza said wearily. "I do not want this, but I am helpless to prevent it."

"Helpless?" Gregor cut back hotly. "You are the head of state, the chairman of the committee. To ordinary people, you are absolute ruler, you are the one responsible for all of this!"

"But you, Gregor, know that's not true, don't you?" Mirza asked.

"I know that it is Haidar Khan who is issuing the orders," Gregor said coldly. "But I also know that you are doing nothing to prevent it, and that makes you equally responsible."

"But what can I do?" Mirza asked. "He has the majority vote of the committee."

Gregor exploded. "You can find the courage to speak out against this government just as you did against the shahs!" he shouted. "If necessary, you can resign from the government and lead another revolt! You are the man the people followed! They do not love and respect Haidar Khan as they do you!"

Mirza shook his head sadly. There were tears in his eyes. "I have already lost that love and respect," he said. "You don't have to tell me how I have failed. Zahra reminds me of it constantly. I remind myself of it every minute of every day."

Gregor felt a surge of sympathy for his old friend. "You have failed only because you have lost the courage to keep on fighting," he said firmly. "You think the revolution is over because one enemy had been defeated, but it isn't over until the objective of freedom and justice has been won. You must keep up the fight, even if the battle is with yourself!"

Mirza gazed at him with admiration and respect. "Of course, you are right," he said. "But it is not easy to restore courage once it has been lost."

"All it requires is a simple action," Gregor pressed. "You merely have to go to Haidar and demand that Kouroush and the other prisoners be released. And that there be no further arrests. If he refuses, call on the army to support you as they once did as *jangalis*."

"And if they do not follow me?" Mirza asked. "After all, Haidar Khan controls the army."

"Then you have done the best you can," Gregor replied. "And that will be better than doing nothing."

* * * * *

Kouroush was resigned to his fate. His trial had been a mockery of justice, and he had refused to even dignify the proceedings by pleading innocent. Instead, he had admitted making statements against the government and had insisted upon his right to do so, repeating all his criticisms and more.

There was one thing, however, that he felt bitter about—the fact that Mirza had not come to his defense, had not even appeared in the courtroom. The cruelest blow was that his dear friend had changed so greatly, had given up the dream they had shared and fought so bravely for together.

But he was determined to die with dignity.

On the day of his execution, he was led out into the public square before the prison at midday. The sun was bright and hot, high overhead, in a clear blue sky. With a guard on either side of him, Kouroush was taken by a phalanx of troops, many of them former *jangalis* he had led in battle, some he had considered his friends.

He was taken to the tall scaffolding, placed beneath it, and the rope tied around his neck and looped over the top beam. The hangmen stood behind him, grasping the end of the rope, preparing to pull at the signal from Haidar Khan. A few hundred silent spectators had come to watch the public execution; among them were many who loved and revered Kouroush.

Suddenly, into the square came a small contingent of the army, with rifles raised. They were led by Mirza Kuchik Khan, who called out in his most commanding voice, "In the name of the people of Gilan, I order these proceedings to cease!"

"Mirza Kuchik Khan," Haidar Khan shouted back, "you have no authority here! This prisoner has been tried and found guilty by the duly constituted judges of the Soviet Republic of Gilan! You are breaking the law and performing an act of treason! I warn you to lay down your arms or you will be arrested yourself!"

"It is you, Haidar Khan, who is the traitor," Mirza charged. "You are a traitor to the people! You have sold yourself to the Russian Bolsheviks! If you do not cease, the people will execute their own justice!" He turned to the troops that Haidar commanded. "And you, men of Gilan, former *jangalis*, I ask you to step over to our side now, forsaking this traitor, or be prepared to suffer the wrath of the people as well!"

There was a moment's hesitation, before over half the troops broke ranks and moved to join those behind Mirza. Haidar Khan looked worried.

"Fools!" Haidar screamed. "You are all fools! Gilan exists only because of the Soviet Russian troops at Enzeli! They will not stand behind Mirza against the forces of Tehran! They will support only me!"

At this, a few more troops abandoned the ranks to join Mirza.

Mirza turned to the hangmen. "Set this man free!" he commanded. "Remove the rope, or my men will fire at you!"

One by one, the hangmen let go of the rope. Then one of them removed a knife from his sash and cut the noose from Kouroush's neck.

Gratefully Kouroush walked across the square to stand beside Mirza. He felt as if his heart was bursting, not just with the joy of knowing that his life had been spared, but with the pride of having his friend returned to him and to the people he had led.

By this time, Haidar had realized that the forces he led were considerably weaker than Mirza's. "You have won the moment," he called to Mirza, "but you cannot win the fight! The next time we meet, I will have greater numbers!" Then he turned to his men and ordered a retreat.

Pleased that he had succceeded without his men firing a shot, Mirza addressed the spectators. "People of Gilan," he said forcefully and passionately, "I have promised you justice and freedom from the Czarist Russians, the British, and the Persian Cossacks, and you have stood behind me. I now promise you justice and freedom from the Bolshevik Russians. Will you stand behind me again?"

"Yes!" the cry rose from the crowd. "Persia for the Persians!"

* * * * *

The government of Gilan was split between the supporters of Haidar and those of Mirza. Most of the Central Committee stood with Haidar, the single exception being Ehsanullah Khan, who to Mirza's surprise, joined with him. The larger faction of the army supported Mirza, though there was a large number who returned to their homes, choosing to support neither. They were not the only ones who despaired of the new fighting; most of the ordinary people of Gilan had lost faith in both Mirza and Haidar, and believed each was equally untrustworthy.

Realizing that Mirza had greater armed forces on his side, Haider chose to retreat to Enzeli to enlist the aid of the Soviet Russians under Commissar Roskolnikov. Together they could defeat Mirza once and for all. With the army of Gilan weakened by half, it would be an easy prey to a large well-trained force such as those of the Russians.

* * * * *

But it was not Haidar and the Soviet Russians who made the next move. It was the Persian Cossacks, who moved north from Tehran in August, a large force under the command of the Russian Colonel Peter Storroselski. Within a matter of days, Mirza saw that it was hopeless to attempt to defend the city. Ultimately, they would lose to superior power, but more important, he did not want the people of Rasht to suffer even further than they had. The city was weary of war, of constantly being attacked by one group after another—taken and then retaken.

He and his forces returned to the forest, to their old encampment in the Valley of the Trees. When the *jangalis* had gained sufficient strength, they would return to guerilla raids against their foes, to wear them down as they had so many times before. Kouroush went with Mirza. This time Gregor did not. He had been reinstated as editor of the newspaper, and he would fight the battle with the best weapon he had—his words.

Chapter 37

Gregor's editorials in the newspaper had to be carefully worded. He was no longer subject to censorship, but he knew he must censor himself if he wished to continue publishing freely. With the Persian Cossacks now in control of the city, he was determined to voice his objections to their presence, yet had to keep his accusations veiled.

For his first editorial after Colonel Storroselski's cossacks were in power, he chose to attack the Russian influence "in all its forms," whether czarist or bolshevik or "even Russians as advisors or military leaders in powerful positions," hoping his readers would know that he meant Storroselski, who had remained in command of the Persian Cossacks through all of the changes on Russian power.

It quickly became clear to him that he had not veiled his words sufficiently.

The day after the editorial appeared, he was startled by the sudden unannounced arrival of Reza Khan in his office. Apprehensively, Gregor rose to his feet to greet him.

"May we close the door?" Reza Khan asked. "I would prefer that our conversation not be overheard."

"Of course," Gregor replied. "Please do."

Once they were assured of privacy, Reza Khan said, "I want you to know I appreciate your editorial in yesterday's paper, and I would greatly appreciate it if you would continue in a similar vein for a while."

Gregor was astonished. "You mean, you haven't come to try to silence me?" he asked.

Reza Khan smiled. "This is not an official visit of a Persian Cossack officer," he said. "This is a personal request, and not to be repeated."

"But why?" Gregor asked.

"I cannot answer that," Reza Kahn replied. "But you will know within a few days. As soon as our troops reach Enzeli." He paused, as if searching carefully for the right words. "You are a man of integrity," he said slowly, "and I wish to acquire your friendship. Again, I cannot explain why. But the most important thing I have come to ask is that you attempt once more to arrange a meeting between me and Mirza."

Gregor frowned and shook his head. "I'm afraid his answer will be the same," he said.

Reza Kahn nodded in understanding. He said, "Of course you realize, so long as he continues to hold out against all odds, without aid from any source, he will be doomed ultimately to fail."

"Yes," Gregor admitted. "But at least he will have made his greatest effort for his people. And you must admire that."

"I do," Reza Kahn replied. "I have much admiration for Mirza and what he has sought to achieve. It is his means that I have disagreed with. If I can convey that to him personally, perhaps we might be able to understand each other better."

"I will try to do what you ask," Gregor told him cautiously. "But I'm afraid the answer will be no."

"All I ask is that you try," Reza Kahn said with a smile. "And it might be most effective if you approach him after you receive word that I am in Enzeli."

* * * * *

Four days later, Gregor received the news from Enzeli, and he finally understood. After the Persian Cossack Brigade had successfully driven the Bolsheviks and Haidar Khan from the port city, Reza Khan had suddenly taken charge of the cossacks himself, dismissing Colonel Storroselski and all other Russian officers.

For the first time in history, a Persian officer was in complete control of the Persian Cossack Brigade. And that force was the strongest it had ever been—numbering over forty thousand troops.

Suddenly Colonel Reza Khan was a power to be reckoned with.

After the news spread through Rasht, Gregor walked in the streets and heard nothing but joy and excitement—and more hope than he had seen in the people since the early days of Mirza's revolution. He knew that, if Mirza could see and hear this for himself, he would surely agree to meet with Reza Khan. But Mirza was in the mountains, isolated from the people by the forests.

Reza Khan had said nothing to Gregor about his plans, but Gregor knew enough about the man to realize that this was only the beginning. Reza Kahn was not a man to act rashly; within time he intended to take control of the Tehran government, and then all of Persia.

Mirza would be wise to give up his own ambitions, and join forces with him, if not for his own sake, then for the sake of the country.

* * * * *

Gregor enlisted the aid of Kouroush before talking to Mirza, knowing that he would need all the help he could get.

Still, after hearing everything Gregor had to say, Mirza replied, "You may be right. Reza Khan may prove to be a great leader, but I cannot meet with him."

"But why not?" Gregor asked. "It can do no harm to talk."

Mirza shook his head. "I would be tempted strongly to join with him, and that would be a mistake. He is still supported by the British, and I must remain as a reminder that our country cannot permit *any* foreign nation to control it."

"Then you will oppose him?" Gregor asked, puzzled.

"Yes," Mirza said with a sigh. "I must fight my fight to the bitter end, even though I know what that end must be."

* * * * *

Early in February, with most of his forty thousand troops behind him, Reza Khan marched south to Tehran. On February 21, 1921, he took control of the Persian government, announcing he would assume the title of Minister of War and appointing Zia ed-Din as Prime Minister.

There were celebrations throughout Persia, even in the occupied territories of Gilan. The people admired Reza Khan as they had done no other revolutionary leader before, even Mirza. He had not preached revolution, talking endlessly of goals; he had acted, achieving the goals miraculously, virtually overnight.

Here indeed was a hero.

To achieve his *coup d'etat*, Reza Khan had made a secret agreement with the British, promising oil and trade concessions, making them believe the Russians would be cut out. Five days after he took power in Tehran, he achieved a similar secret agreement with the Russians. In both cases, he obtained promises to remove the foreign troops from Persian soil as soon as all of the dissenting revolutionaries had been defeated.

Reza Khan had performed another miracle; he had outwitted both Russia and Britain at their own game of secrecy, proving himself a master of diplomatic duplicity, using one against the other to achieve his own ends. Both countries would be allies of Persia, but neither would have dominance, or even "spheres of influence."

The one obstacle to his goals that remained was Mirza Kuchik Khan and his *jangali* forces.

*   *   *   *   *

The more Gregor learned about Reza Khan, the more he became convinced that he was the leader they had all been waiting for, the man who could make Persia free and independent. He desperately wanted to convince Mirza of this, and he believed it was only Mirza's vanity that prevented him from accepting the fact that someone else had given Persia what he had wanted to give it.

Kouroush rarely came into Rasht, and when he did, he had to be careful not to be seen and recognized. He was not a wanted man, but he was known to be a close associate of Mirza's, and he might be taken into custody for questioning. At least once a week, however, he came in to see Tatiana, who was now so busy with her work at the hospital and with the completion plans for the new hospital that she could not travel to the clinic at the jangali encampment. With the ouster of the Bolsheviks, the new hospital had been returned to her control.

One evening in April, while Kouroush was visiting, Sylvia invited Tatiana and Kouroush to dinner. It was inevitable that Gregor and Kouroush would discuss Mirza.

"I still wish he could be persuaded to give up and support Reza Khan," Gregor said sadly. "There is still time to save himself and his followers."

Kouroush shook his head wearily. "I'm afraid he's determined to become a martyr," he said. "Every day more and more of the *jangalis* are giving up and leaving him. I doubt if there are even two thousand left, but Mirza still talks about marching on Tehran to overthrow Reza Kahn."

"Perhaps if everyone left him," Gregor said, "he would finally be forced to see how foolish it is to hold out."

"I don't think so," Kouroush replied. "He has said he will continue his fight even if he has to stand entirely alone."

"Then you should leave him," Gregor said. "You know he's wrong."

"Yes," Kouroush nodded, "but you know I can't do that, and you know why."

Gregor did understand. He glanced at Tatiana and saw a pained expression in her eyes. He was sure that she had already tried to persuade her husband to forsake the fight, with no success. He looked back at Kouroush, who was gazing uncomfortably at his wife.

"He still has one chance left," Kouroush said, trying to be encouraging. "Now that the Russians have forsaken him, he has been in contact with the Georgians, asking for aid. So far, the response has been positive. They are not bound by the Russian pact with Reza Khan. If they supply enough troops, Mirza wants to march on Tehran."

Gregor was shocked. "That's incredible!" he exclaimed. "He will lose what little respect the people have for him by attempting to take the government with foreign troops!"

"I know," Kouroush said with a blush of embarrassment. "But that is his plan."

"I would not trust the Georgians," Tatiana said. "I know their leader, Joseph Stalin, only too well. And you have met him, Kouroush. He is not a man of his word."

"Your decision to stand by Mirza is foolish," Gregor said. "Under the circumstances, no one would blame you for forsaking him. And you have other friends who need your loyalty, not to mention a wife and son."

"I know," Kouroush said. "But you must realize, I owe Mirza my life. Even if I disagree with his course, I must stand by him to the end."

*   *   *   *   *

Events moved swiftly in the weeks that followed. In May, Reza Khan deposed Zia ed-Din as prime minister and took full power himself. About the same time, Mirza obtained the promise of the troops he had requested from Soviet Georgia, and he began to set forth his plan of attack to regain control of Gilan.

Mirza would begin by retaking Tabriz, where the Persian Cossack garrison was the weakest.

Before beginning the military offensive, Kouroush visited Tatiana, not knowing how long it would be before he saw her again, if indeed he did see her. He sensed that this might be their last parting, and he knew that she was with child again.

Tatiana did not want to let Kouroush go. She held him in her arms tightly, refusing to release her grip. "Please stay," she begged, tears in her eyes. "You have done all that you can for Mirza. Now, I need you, and little Jamshid needs you. Please don't give up your life for such a futile cause."

Kouroush tried to lie. "I will be back," he promised. "You will see. I will be here for the opening of your new hospital. I will see our second child born. I will be here to watch Jamshid become a man."

Tatiana shook her head fiercely. "You must not pretend with me," she said tearfully. "We have always been honest with each other."

"You're right," Kouroush admitted. "I don't know if I will return or not. If I do not, you must understand that it is something I had to do."

"But you don't have to do it," Tatiana said desperately. "This whole revolution has become nothing more than a means of satisfying Mirza's vanity."

Kouroush smiled sadly. "I hope it is not that," he said. "I hope it is as he believes—that he is satisfying his destiny."

* * * * *

Mirza's *jangali* troops did not even reach Tabriz. While his forces were crossing the bridge across the White River, the cossacks set off a charge of dynamite, destroying the bridge and leaving part of the *jangali* troops on one side and part on the other.

Upon hearing this, the Georgian forces, approaching Tabriz from the north, fell back to await the outcome, leaving Mirza's small army to face the onslaught alone.

Even fragmented as they were, the *jangalis* might have had a chance, but for the new Persian air force, obtained by Reza Khan from the British. The planes swept down upon the confused revolutionaries, firing into their midst, who were helpless to defend themselves.

Kouroush was standing by the remains of the bridge, calling to the men on the other side to swim across, urging them forward to Tabriz, when he was hit by fire from the air. He was killed instantly, his body toppling into the swirling water of the White River.

The troops that remained after the day was over fled back into the forest. Some returned to the Valley of the Trees with Mirza. Others forsook the cause and returned to their homes, accepting this as a final defeat. Kasmayi who had been loyal from the beginning, chose to surrender his entire regiment to the Persian Cossacks.

Fewer than eight hundred men remained loyal to Mirza after the battle, and those numbers continued to dwindle.

* * * * *

Gregor took the news to Tatiana that her husband was dead, and that his body had not been recovered from the river. Tatiana had expected to hear eventually that he was gone, but still she was overcome with grief. Held in her brother's arms, she wept uncontrollably. "Such a waste," she sobbed. "Such a foolish waste."

* * * * *

By September, Mirza was still attempting to negotiate aid from the Georgians, but finally they refused outright. The Russian troops, by agreement with Reza Khan's government, had to be out of Persia by the eighth of September. The order had come directly from Lenin that all Soviet states must abide by their treaty; none would be permitted to interfere in the internal politics of Persia.

It was not long after this that Mirza had a surprise vistor to his camp. Haidar Khan, with his few remaining followers, came to him to offer his aid in the struggle.

"You were right," Haidar told him, "not to trust the Russians. They have betrayed me just as they betrayed you. I ask your forgiveness and seek to serve with you once more."

Mirza, however, could no longer forgive. He ordered his men to seize Haidar and hang him from the nearest tree.

The execution was carried out, but Mirza's remaining followers were shocked by the action. They began to whisper among themselves that Mirza had, indeed, lost his reason. Within a matter of days, he had been abandoned by all but fifty of his followers. Even Ehsanullah Khan, who had promised to stay with him to the end, left with his regiment.

* * * * *

In the Elburz Mountains that October, the snows began early, and the cold was intense. The cossacks had been dispatched to the area in September with orders to capture Mirza Kuchik Khan. Since there were literally thousands of defectors from the *jangalis*, it had not been difficult for the cossacks to discover where their encampment had been. With the loss of his secret hiding place, Mirza and his few remaining followers had been forced to move from place to place, often being only a few steps ahead of their pursuers.

Gradually the remaining followers drifted away as well, until only Mirza and the Austrian Lieutenant Ernst Kaouk were left. They were wanted men, and even former friends would not take them into their homes for fear of reprisals, though some had enough pity to give them food. Each night they had to fashion a shelter for themselves from whatever was available in the forest or on the mountainside—rocks, twigs, evergreen branches. They would huddle together inside their makeshift shelters, wrapped in their cloaks, hoping to share what warmth their bodies had, just to sleep as much as they could, before getting up at dawn to move once more.

With each passing day, they became more aware that death was inevitable, but they refused to give themselves up, determined to make it as difficult as possible for the cossacks to do their duty.

In the end, they had a kind of victory, for it was not the military that sealed their fate; it was the weather, a particulary severe snowstorm in the mountains. In their flight, Mirza and Kaouk had climbed ever higher. When the thick and heavy snow came, buffeted by high winds and made more severe by below-zero temperatures, they were well above the forest area.

There was virtually no way they could devise shelter from the elements.

After the storm was over, their frozen bodies were found by a farmer, who was traveling alone. The farmer knew who the men were; he recognized Mirza, and he was aware of the search that had been halted only for the big storm. Mirza's face was powdered with snow, his beard caked in ice. There was an eerie, almost incandescent quality to his skin, and his eyes stared outward in defiance of some unseen enemy.

There was no way the farmer could transport the bodies without help, so he hurried down the icy, snow-packed mountainside to report the news to the nearest village, enlisting the assistance of a group of villagers to bring Mirza and Kaouk down.

By the time the group returned, hours later, the news had spread throughout the region, and a crowd gathered to witness the event. Before the cossacks could arrive, a local potentate name Salar took charge, ordering one of his followers, Reza Oskastani, to cut off the head of Mirza.

Seeking to become a public hero, Salar quickly ordered his men to follow him. Leaving the body behind, he took the head, placed it on a pike, and led a victorious procession to Tehran.

But the people of Persia did not respond as Salar had anticipated. Outraged by his cruel act, they gathered along the road from Rasht to Tehran to mourn and strew flowers in the path.

Nor did Reza Khan praise Salar. He severely reprimanded the man for lack of respect for the dead, then ordered the head to be returned and buried with the body.

* * * * *

In early December, Tatiana gave birth to her second child. It was a daughter she named her Touran. It grieved her deeply that her beloved Kouroush had not lived to see their child and that little Touran would never know her father.

In the spring of 1922, Tatiana's hospital in Rasht was completed. Reza Khan was invited the dedication ceremonies, and he accepted the invitation.

Although Sultan Ahmad was still shah and nominally the head of government, Reza Khan had become virtual dictator during what was to be a transitional period. He had announced that he did not want to move hastily toward any specific form of government until the special problems of Persia had been fully studied and taken into account. Now that he had successfully driven out the foreign powers that had long kept control of the shahs, he wanted to establish the country on the strongest possible footing, to keep them out.

The economy was the first priority in regaining strength, and for that he hired an American financial advisor, Dr. Authur C. Millspaugh, to come to Tehran to make sweeping reforms.

The people respected his efforts, but they watched him with a degree of caution. Many leaders had made promises, only to be corrupted after achieving power.

Gregor was one of those who had adopted a wait-and-see attitude, expressing in his editorials the need for patience to give Reza Khan the opportunity to solve the numerous and diverse problems of the country.

Upon his arrival in Rasht, Reza Khan did something he had done once before—he paid an unannounced call on Gregor at his newspaper office. Gregor was even more surprised this time than he had been before. On that other occasion, the cossack colonel had come asking for a favor; this time he truly did not need anything of Gregor.

"I've come to thank you for the help you have given me," Reza Khan told him.

Gregor was surprised. "But I've done nothing special," he protested.

"You have been willing to give me a chance to help Persia," Reza replied. "And you have asked your readers to do the same. In times like these, that is a great help."

Gregor nodded in understanding. "If our country has a hope for the future," he said, "I believe it rests in you. But if you betray the trust that people have placed in you, I will be among the first to protest."

"That's fair enough," Reza Kahn acknowledged.

"I am curious to know what you have planned for Persia," Gregor said. "What are your intentions?"

Reza Khan hesitated a moment, then said, "Not all of my plans have been formulated. It really is as I've stated publicly; I want the best possible form of government for the country, whatever that may be. My natural sympathy is for a republic, but I'm not sure our people are ready for self-government. A republic requires an educated, informed, knowledgeable citizenry; we do not yet have that.

"I can tell you this much, however. I intend to do everything I can to bring Persia into the modern era. If we are to remain strong and independent, our people must be educated. We must have schools and colleges; we must produce scientists and engineers, as good as any of the western nations."

Gregor nodded in agreement. "That will take many years to achieve, however," he said.

"It will," Reza Khan admitted. "And the real problem will be how to keep the country strong and independent while these goals are being achieved. I would prefer not to have a dictatorship for Persia, but if that is the only way, I will take that route."

"I pray that will not be necessary," Gregor told him with a frown.

"Persia has been accustomed to shahs," Reza Khan continued. "And ideally an enlightened despotism would achieve our goals. That was how the modern nations passed from kingdoms to democracies. However, the Qajar shahs could never compare to the kings of France or England or Germany. There is no way that Ahmad Shah could become sufficiently enlightened to lead Persia into the twentieth century. So there must be some other alternative."

Later, Gregor would reflect on that conversation and realize that Reza Khan had actually already made up his mind about the future course for Persia—or, as it would be called by that time, Iran. But, at the time, he had avoided revealing too much to Gregor, knowing his intentions at that early date would be misunderstood.

Reza Khan proved, indeed, to be a very wise man, far wiser than even Gregor had given him credit for.

* * * * *

The dedication ceremony for Tatiana's hospital was very well attended. Most of the citizens of Rasht had turned out, and quite a few came from Enzeli as well. It was acknowledged that a great many had come, not to see the new medical institution, but to see Reza Khan and to hear him speak.

It was a glorious spring day, with clear blue skies and a warm bright sun. There was a festive mood among the people who had known peace and the beginnings of renewed prosperity for the past year. The proceedings all went well.

A hush fell over the crowd when Reza Khan stood up to speak. Everyone listened carefully to his words. "I am very pleased to dedicate this hospital for Rasht, as fine a medical institution as can be found anywhere in the world," he said proudly. "Persia needs many more such facilities, throughout the land. We need hospitals and schools and universities and industries like those nations that now lead the world. Many leaders have made promises to you to restore the power and grandeur that was Persia; I cannot make that promise."

A murmur of surprise ran through the crowd.

"I cannot make you that promise," he continued more strongly, "because that kind of power and grandeur is a thing of the past. I promise you a new power that is much greater than anything Persia's past has witnessed, a power to equal that of the powerful nations of today.

"The grandeur of Persia's past was dependent upon military might, upon numbers of trained troops to conquer and control its neighbors. Today, that is not enough; that is why we have not regained our position in the world. Today's strength comes from knowledge, from science and technology, from the achievements of art and industry. We Persians must enter the modern scientific age and compete as equals with the most advanced of nations.

"Today, with the dedication of this hospital, we take a step toward that new Persia. It is the dream of one person, of Dr. Tatiana Jalali, a woman who should serve as an example to all of us. As a young woman, she set out to achieve what seemed an impossibility for a Persian woman—to become a doctor. She had to leave Persia, to go to Moscow to learn medicine. She had to fight against superstition and prejudice to reach her goal, but she did reach it and go far beyond it to bring good medical care to the people she loves.

"In the years ahead, I hope there will be many more women as well as men who will do what she has done. For a new, strong Persia must have such people to reach its goals."

There was applause from the crowd as he concluded, but there were also murmurs of astonishment. Many people did not fully understand what he had been saying. Those who did could not see how such changes could be accomplished, for they were contrary to all that was traditional in Persia. Some few understood and vigorously approved of what he had said, excited by the prospect of growing and changing and learning new ways.

Among those who understood and approved were Tatiana and Gregor and Sylvia. They looked forward eagerly to a future filled with hope, not just for themselves but for the country, at last united, free, and independent.

Of the older generation, only Maria Baranov and Philip Boustani were present to witness the proud moment for the child they had loved and cared for, and to experience the joy of the new promise for their country.

Epilogue—1926

Gregor had grown accustomed to the fact that all things changed with time, some things radically, others imperceptibly. People were responsible for some of the changes, both good and bad; nature was responsible for others.

Sometimes, nature could repair the damages caused by people, and that knowledge was gratifying to Gregor. Such was the case in the mountain region above Baku, along the road that led to the Zoroastrian shrine. There were still great scars in the landscape where new oil wells were being drilled, but other areas Gregor had remembered from earlier trips had given up all their riches and the wells had been abandoned. In these places, nature had begun making repairs, covering the scars with wildflowers and young trees and grass.

This trip to Azerbaijan and the shrine, in the spring of 1926, was a special one for Gregor. Its object was to see the completed restoration, the wish granted him by Tatiana from her inheritance.

They decided to make it a family holiday. Not only were Gregor and Sylvia making the long journey, but Tatiana and Philip as well. They also brought Jamshid, Touran, and Alexei, and the daughter born to him and Sylvia two years ago, little Farideh. Maria was too old and infirm to travel, so she stayed home in Rasht, but Philip accompanied them; despite his infirmities, he would not miss this occasion.

After years of struggle, sorrow, and tragedy, they had reached a plateau of contentment, in which the simple joys of family outings and home life were sufficient. Their homeland still had far to go to achieve the dreams of years before, but at least, under Reza Khan, it was moving slowly toward them.

Only a few months before, in December of 1925, Reza Khan had been proclaimed shah, with all of the powers he needed to make the sweeping changes he desired for Persia. Already, he had begun to build highways and railroads and airfields, to make it possible for his people to communicate with the outside world more easily. He had made plans for schools and universities and begun to carry them out. And he had made phenomenal efforts to attract industries from the west to build plants within his country.

And this was only the beginning. Each day seemed to bring new prospects for changes that could only improve the lives of the people. There was even talk that he intended to outlaw the chador and permit young women to be educated with young men in the schools and universities. Many objected to this.

The one regret for Gregor was that Reza Kahn had chosen a kingdom as his form of government, rather than a republic. However, he understood the reasons. Perhaps one day Persia would be ready for a more enlightened form of government.

For this trip to the shrine, Gregor had chosen to drive his newly acquired automobile on Reza Khan's new highway to the north, rather than to take the traditional route by sea. In some ways, travel was more strenuous by auto, but it was a marvellous experience, seeing parts of Persia none of them had seen before, and being able to stop and look at the scenery whenever they chose.

Once they were in the Caucasus Mountains, the roads were old and rutted and often too steep for the auto to make it without everyone climbing out and walking, while Gregor slowly drove to the peak. But that was no different than traveling by horse-drawn wagon.

Finally, after many days, they reached their destination. Because of the reconstruction of the shrine, a small road had been built, permitting them to take the auto right up to its location.

The rocky, almost barren mountainside was unchanged, left for nature to care for it. But the area immediately around the shrine had been leveled to create a flagstone courtyard, and around it a low wall had been built, in traditional Persian style, plain except for a small decorative motif at the top.

That motif had been repeated in reconstructing the shrine, which remained small, but now had an open dome for a roof, with a small spire at each of the four corners.

Just inside the gate of the walls, they had built a small cottage for the caretaker priest, so that he could live more comfortably. Rama, the old caretaker did not come out to greet them as he had done on the previous occasions, but they understood the reasons. His condition was now extremely weak, and he did not have too many days of life left to him. Instead, the visitors went into the cottage to see him, lying on his simple cot, looked after by the new priest who would replace him as the guardian of the sacred flame.

Rama greeted them as warmly as his frail body would permit. It was clear that there was recognition of Tatiana and Gregor in his dark eyes; his mind seemed to be as alert and powerful as always; it was simply his body that was failing him.

"Thank you for what you have done," he said, his voice quavering. "I can move on with the knowledge that there will always be someone to guard over the flame."

Then Rama's eyes fell upon the three children, and they flickered with a special brightness, as if he were inwardly smiling. "Are these your children?" he asked.

"The older boy, Jamshid, is Tatiana's," Gregor replied. "And this little girl, Touran, as well. The other two are mine—Alexei and Farideh."

"It pleases me," the old man said, "that I have lived long enough to see another generation of your family. I pray that they will see in the eternal flame what you have seen and will remain faithful to its call."

The Parsee wished to introduce the children to the mystery of the flame himself, asking Gregor and the young caretaker to help him to his feet to walk the short distance to the shrine. It required great effort for the dying man, depleting what little strength he had left, but Gregor understood that it was important to him.

Inside the shrine, the guardian spoke to the children of the significance of the flame, much as he had to Gregor more than thirty years before. Farideh and Touran were too young to understand, but the two boys listened in fascination, staring entranced at the leaping, flickering tongues of fire. Gregor sensed that Jamshid and Alexei did understand, that they were affected by the experience just as he had been.

The words that were spoken echoed in his memory, as clearly as if he had heard them only yesterday—"It is the light against darkness, the warmth against cold, the truth against deceit, the good against evil. The fire is the reminder to God's chosen people, the Persians, to serve goodness and truth."

Spoken by the dying guardian of a dying faith, the words were a revelation to him all over again. The faith truly would not die so long as there were only a few who understood and believed. The goodness in humanity would survive, just as the flame would burn, eternally.